# 子連れ狼

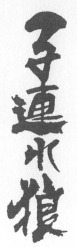

# LONE WOLF AND CUB

子連れ狼

story
**KAZUO KOIKE**

art
**GOSEKI KOJIMA**

**DARK HORSE COMICS**

translation
**DANA LEWIS**

lettering & retouch
**DIGITAL CHAMELEON**

cover illustration
**MATT WAGNER**

publisher
**MIKE RICHARDSON**

editor
**TIM ERVIN-GORE**

assistant editor
**JEREMY BARLOW**

consulting editor
**TOREN SMITH** for **STUDIO PROTEUS**

book design
**DARIN FABRICK**

art director
**MARK COX**

Published by Dark Horse Comics, Inc., in association
with MegaHouse and Koike Shoin Publishing Company.

Dark Horse Comics, Inc.
10956 SE Main Street, Milwaukie, OR 97222
www.darkhorse.com

First edition: August 2002
ISBN: 1-56971-596-3

1 3 5 7 9 10 8 6 4 2

Printed in Canada

To find a comics shop in your area, call the
Comic Shop Locator Service toll-free at 1-888-266-4226.

# IN THESE SMALL HANDS

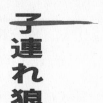

By KAZUO KOIKE
& GOSEKI KOJIMA

# VOLUME

## 24

# A NOTE TO READERS

*Lone Wolf and Cub* is famous for its carefully researched re-creation of Edo-Period Japan. To preserve the flavor of the work, we have chosen to retain many Edo-Period terms that have no direct equivalents in English. Japanese is written in a mix of Chinese ideograms and a syllabic writing system, resulting in numerous synonyms. In the glossary, you may encounter words with multiple meanings. These are words written with Chinese ideograms that are pronounced the same but carry different meanings. A Japanese reader seeing the different ideograms would know instantly which meaning it is, but these synonyms can cause confusion when Japanese is spelled out in our alphabet. *O-yurushi o* (please forgive us)!

# LONE WOLF AND CUB

子連れ狼

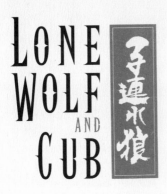

# TABLE OF CONTENTS

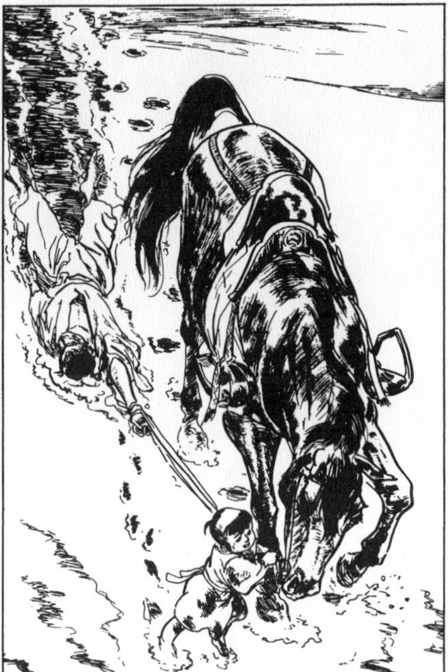

the hundred
and seventeenth

# Child of the Fields

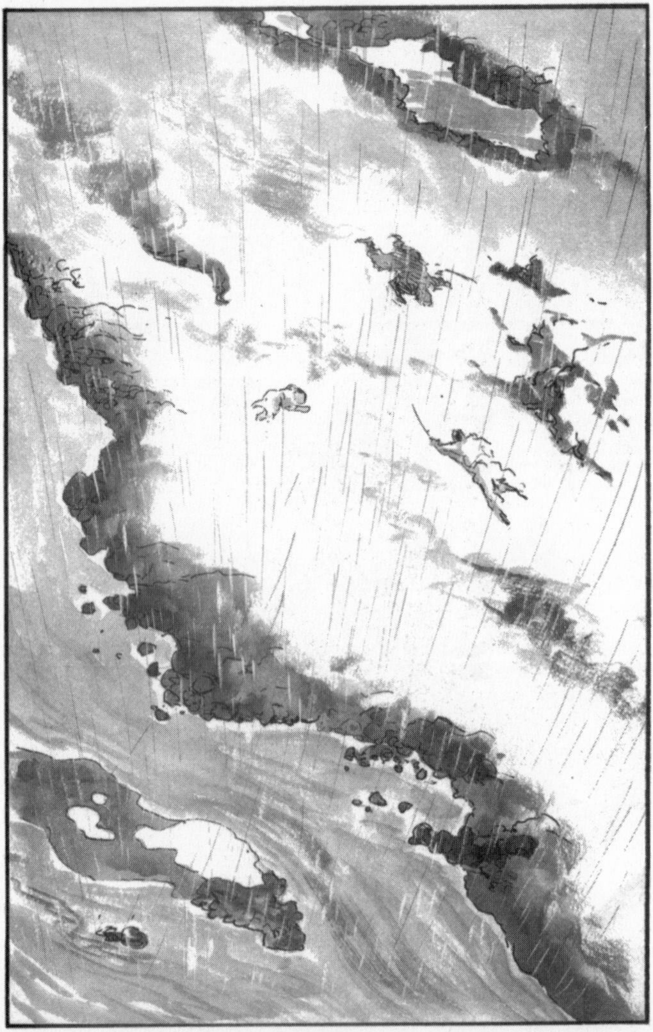

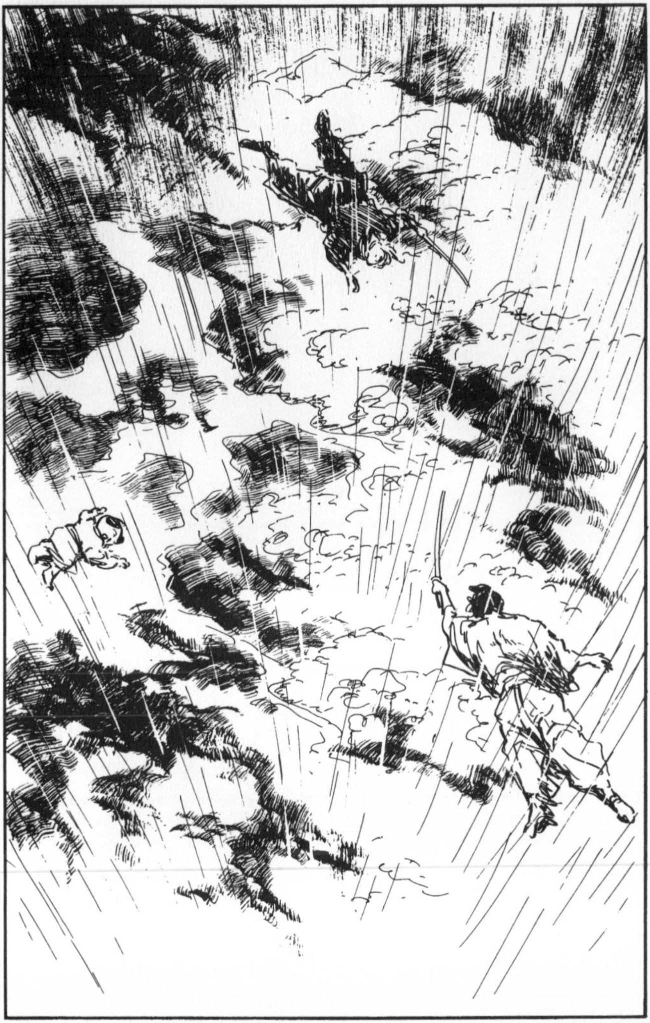

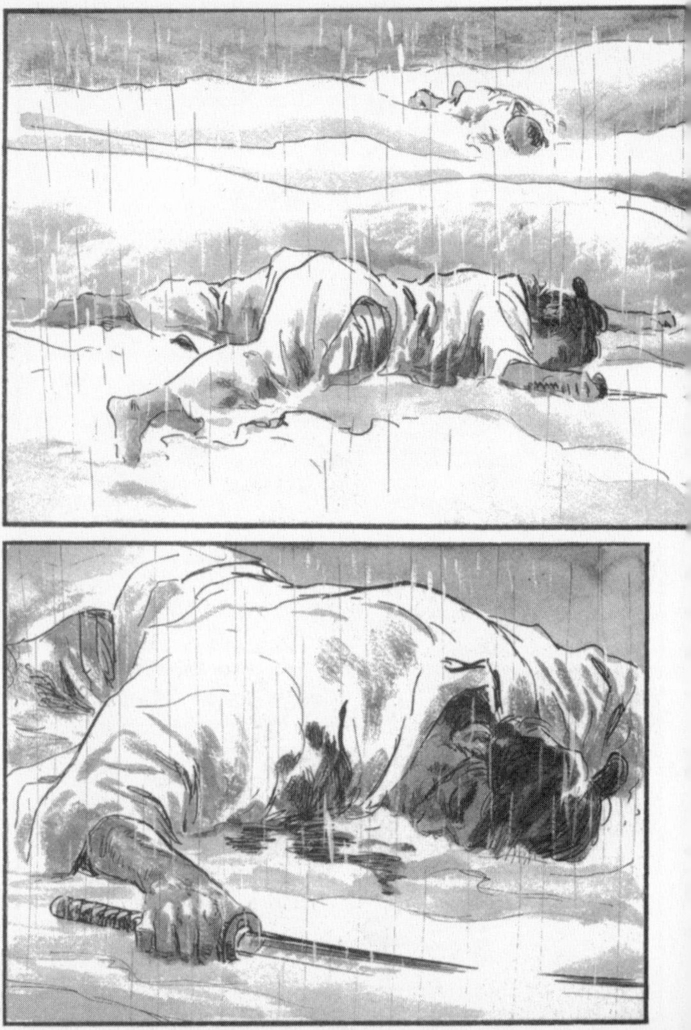

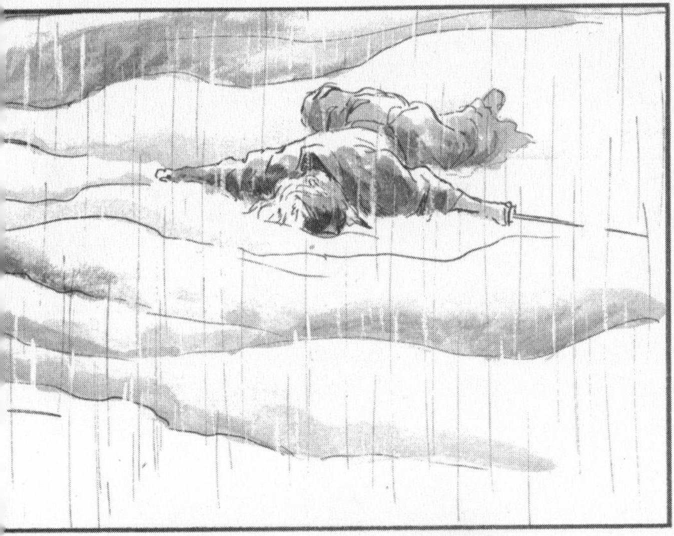
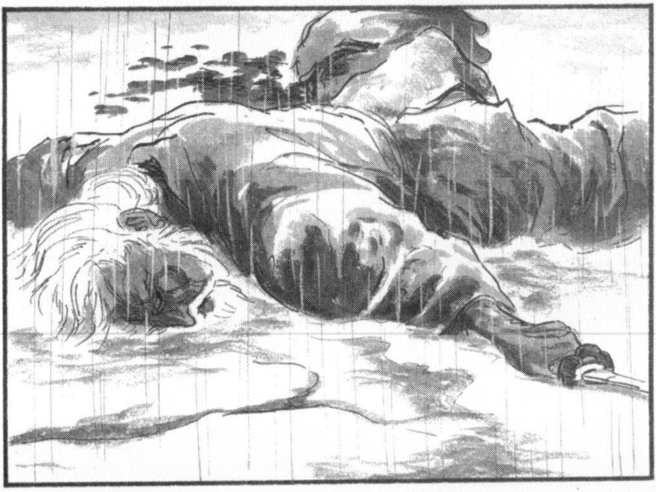

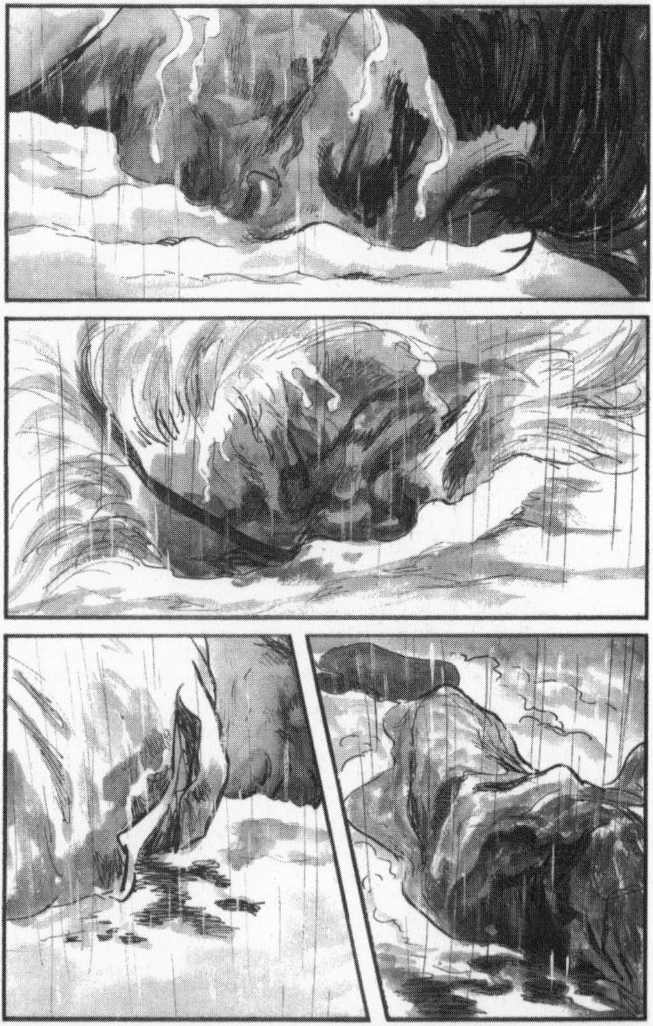

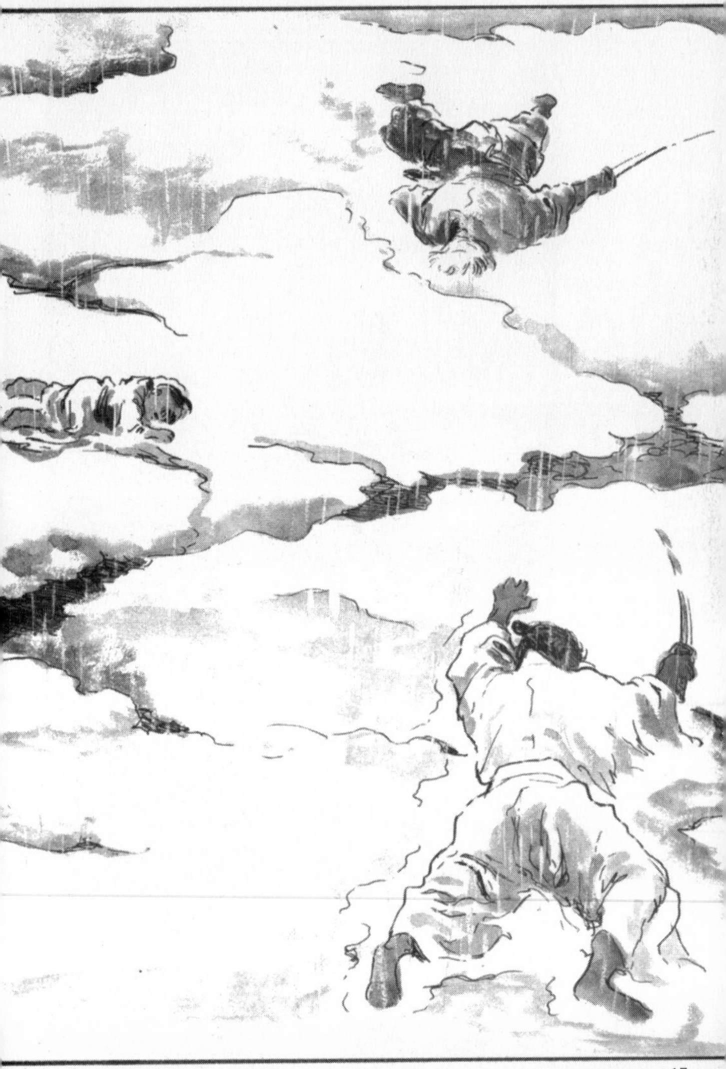

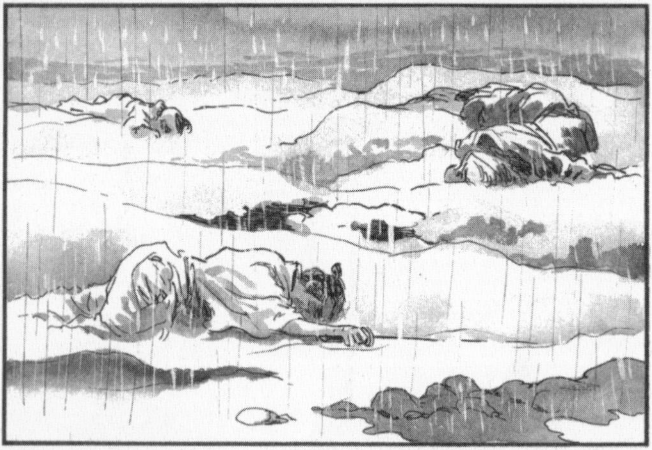
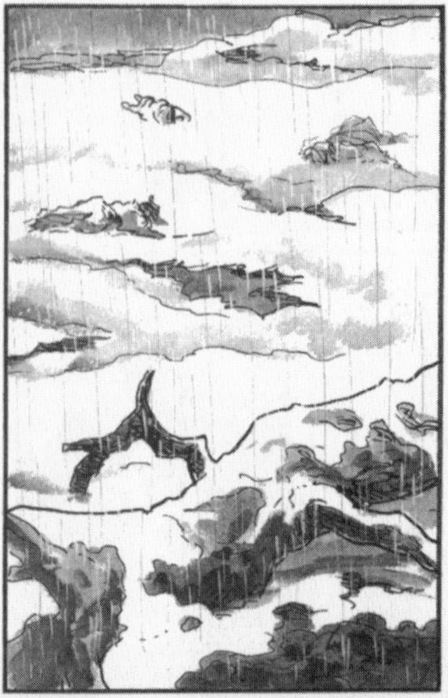
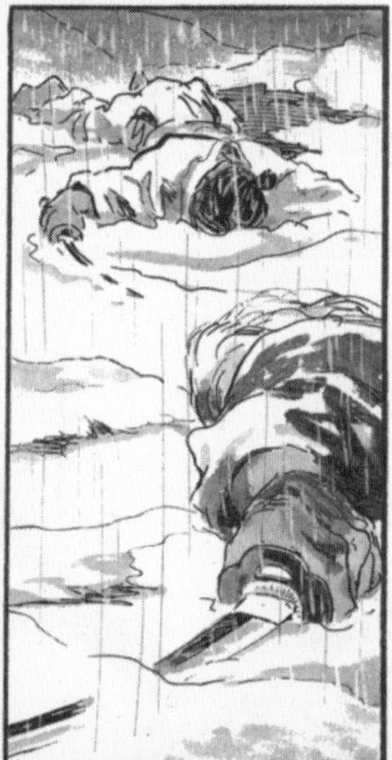

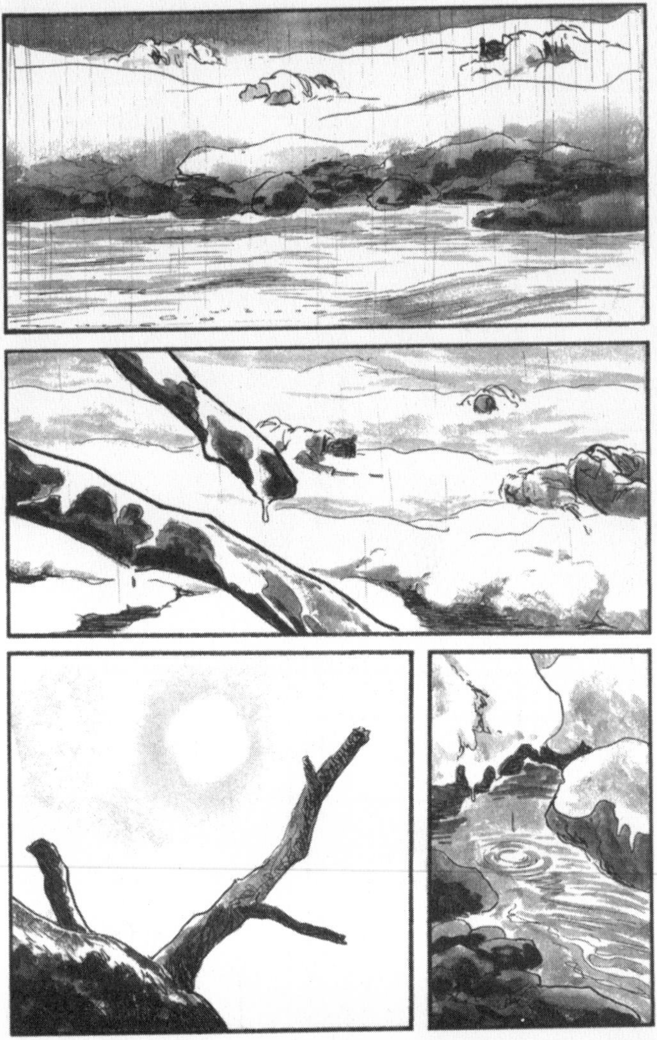

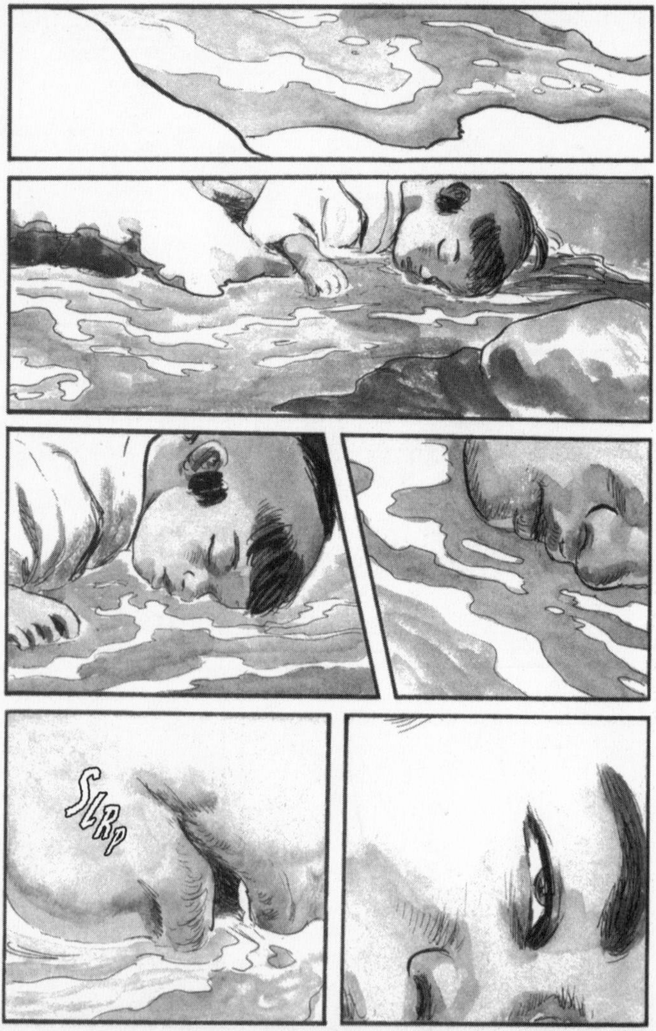
SLRp

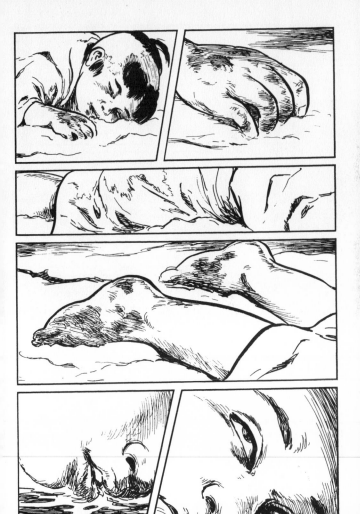

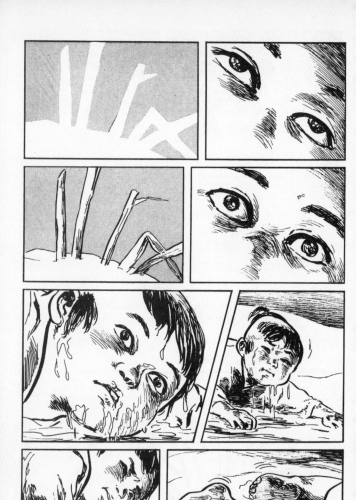

20

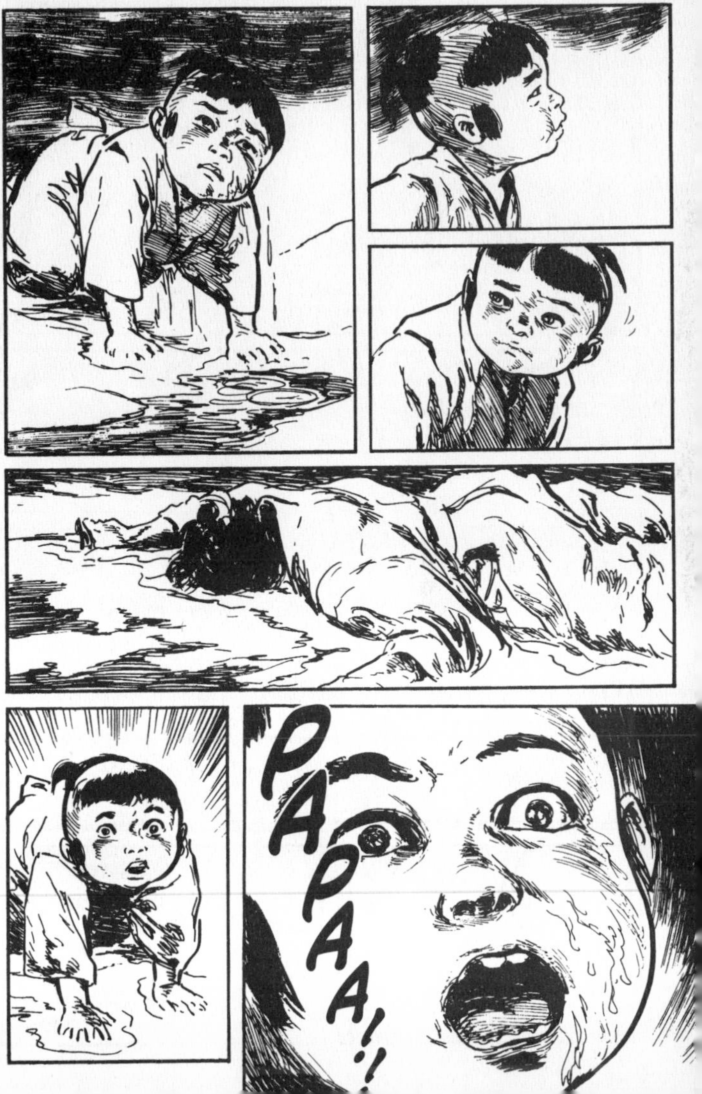
PAPAA!!

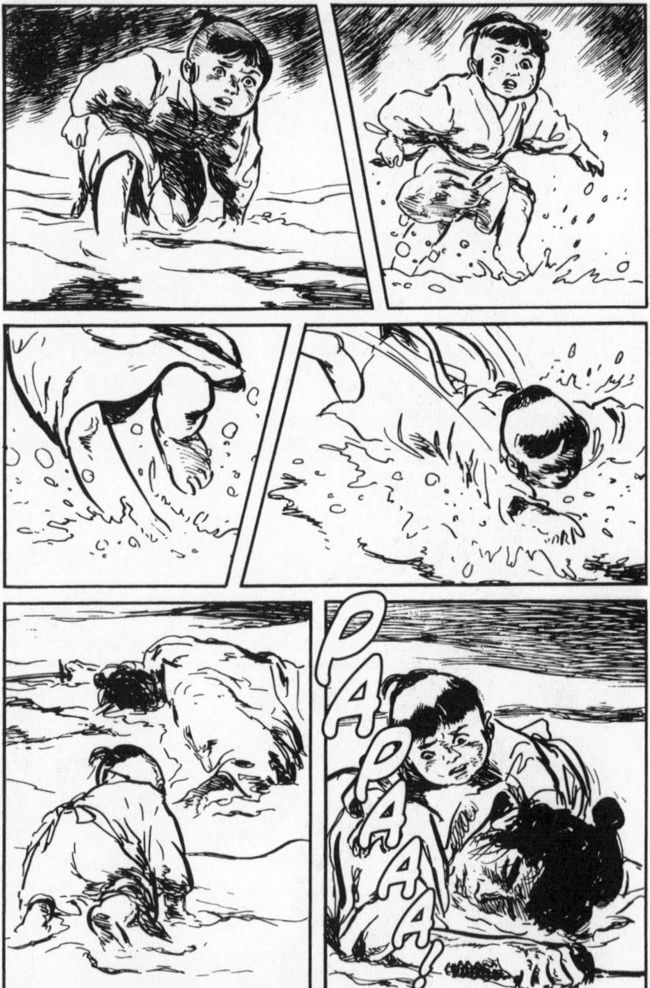
PAPAAAA!

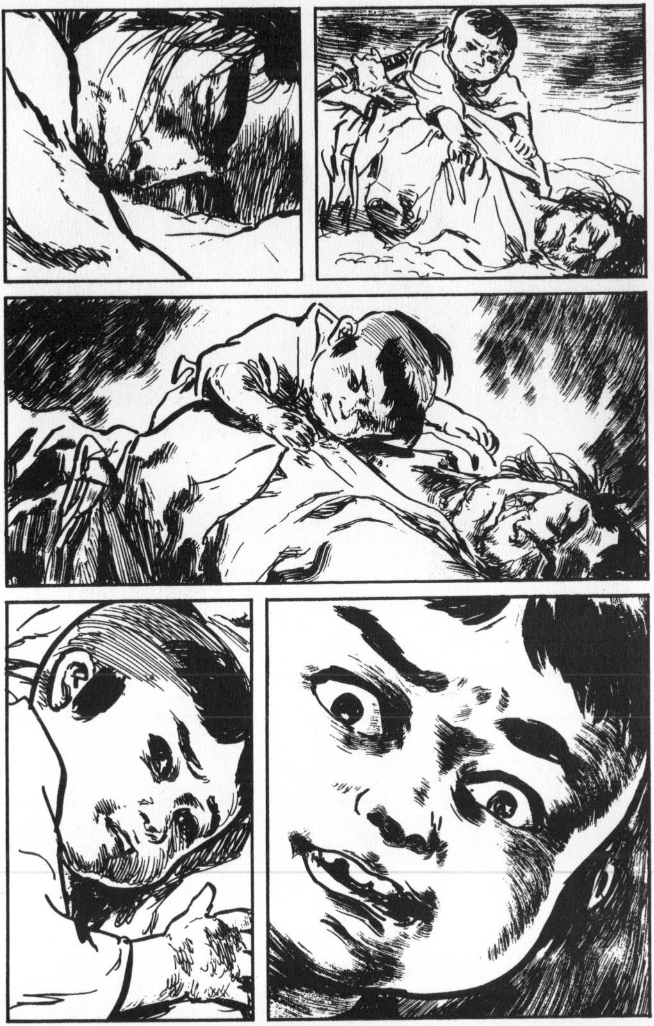

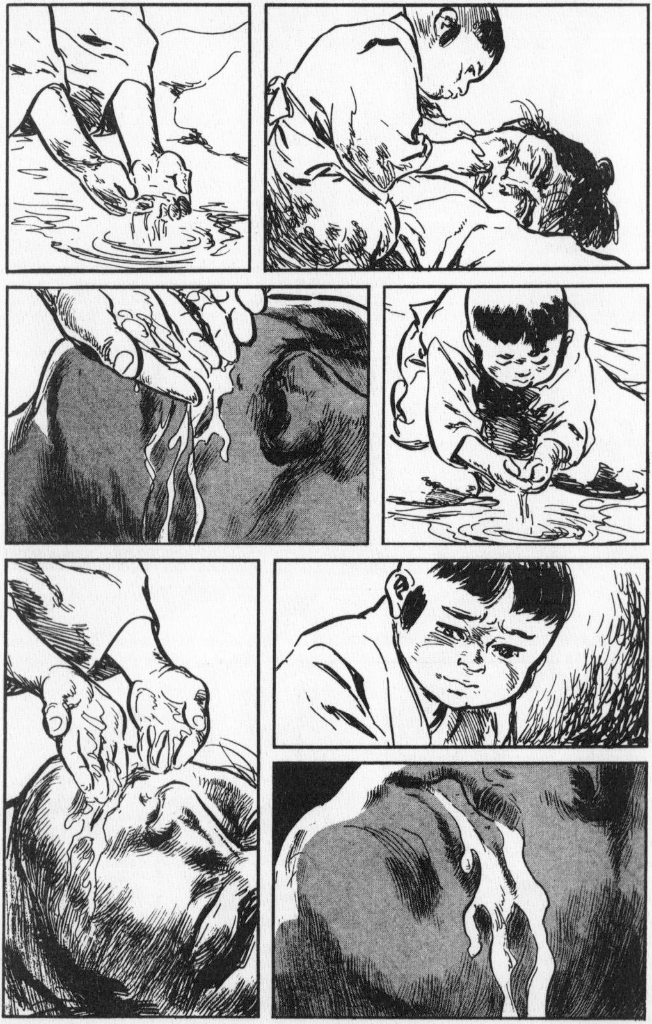

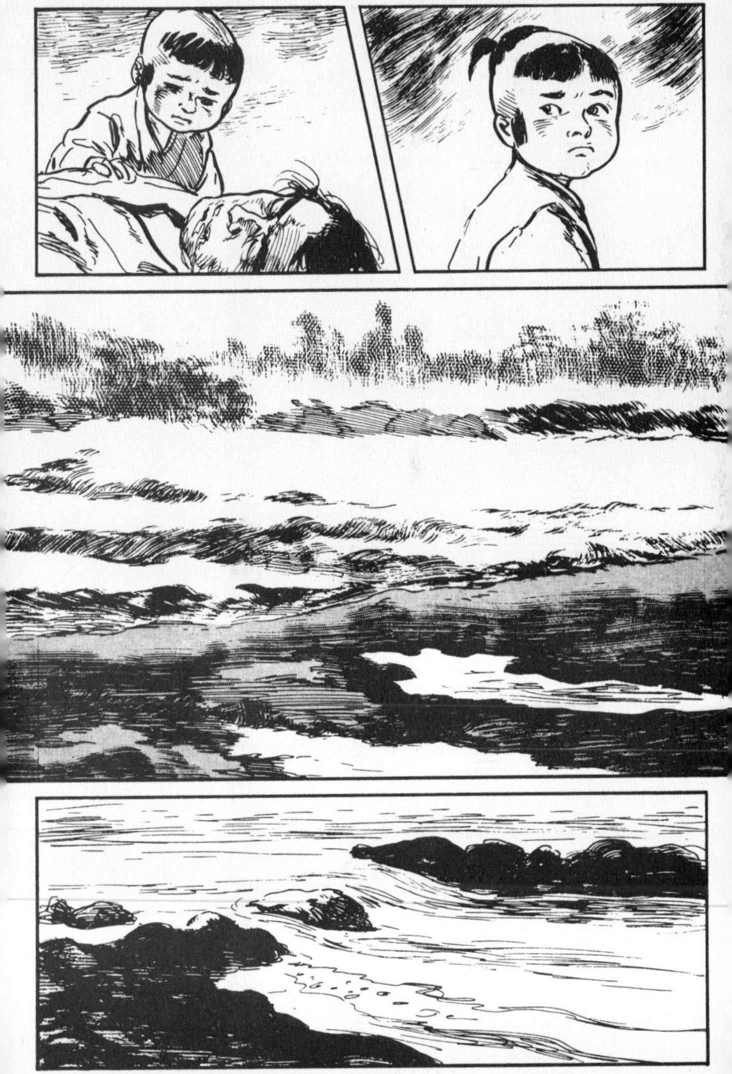

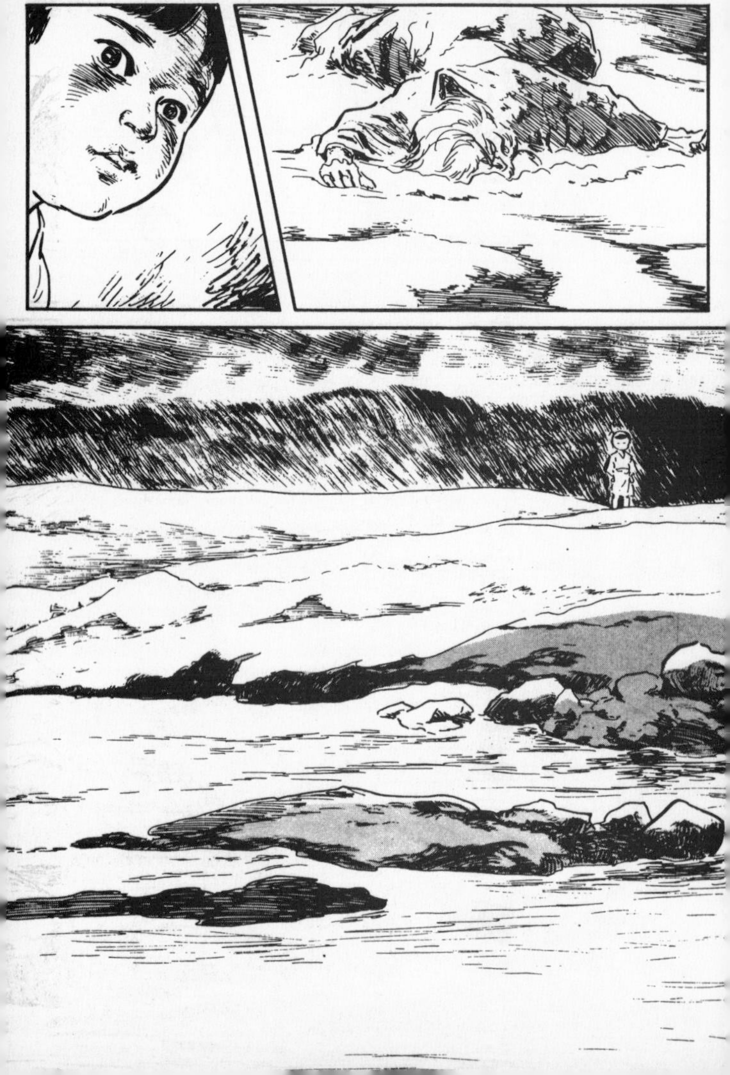

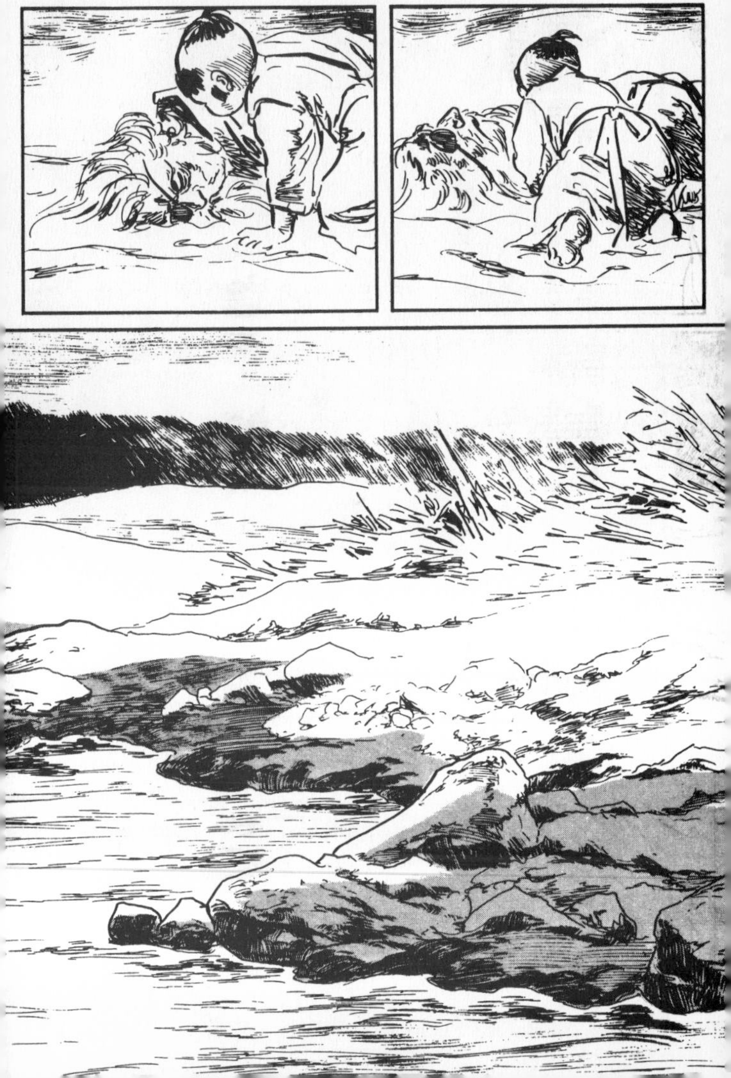

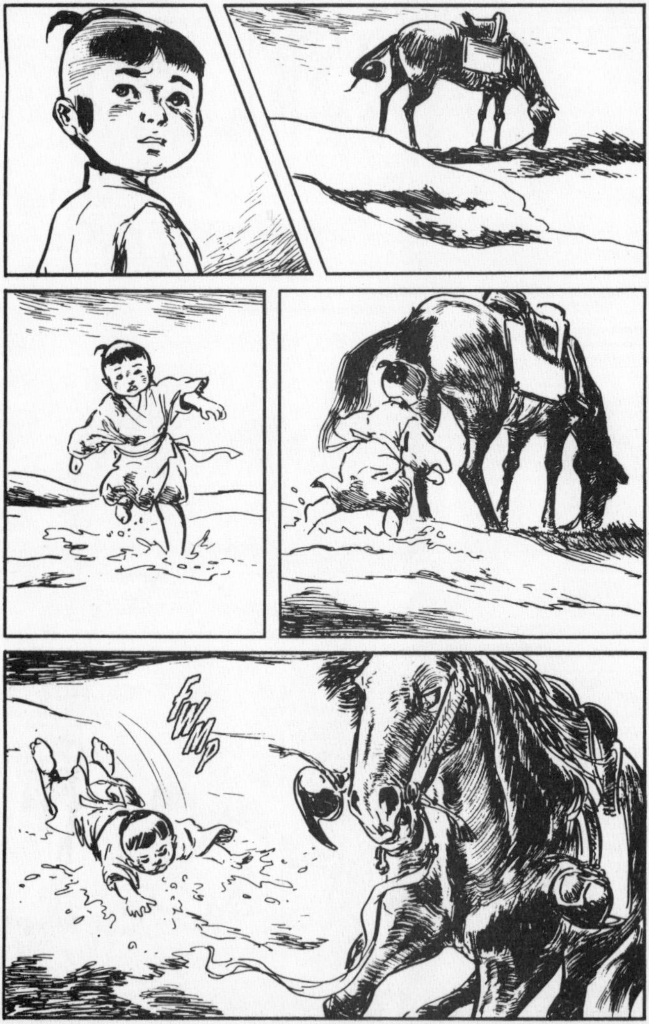
FWMP

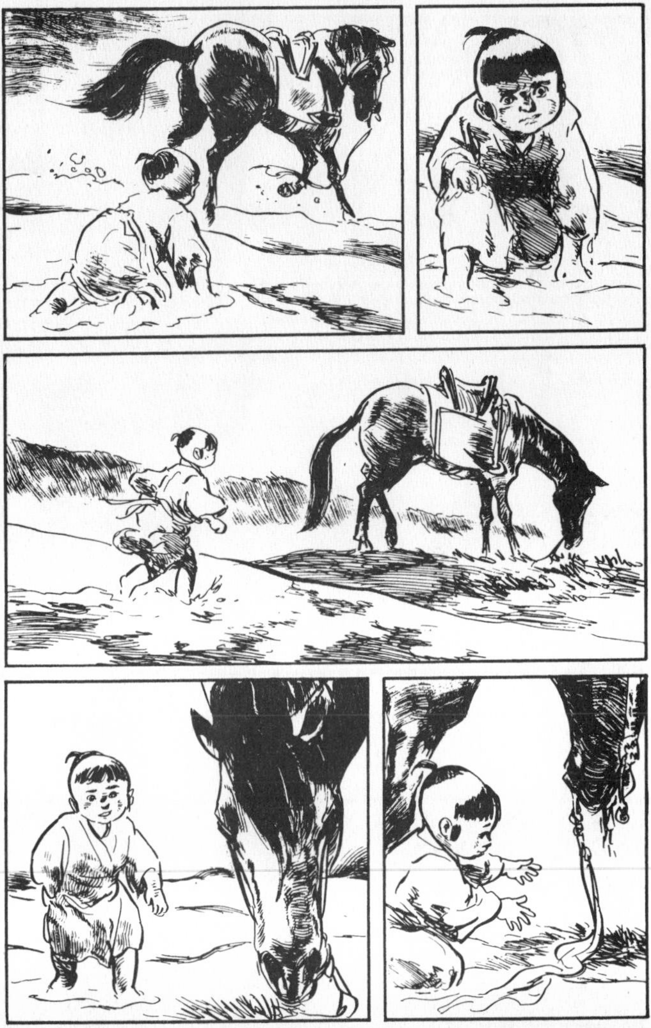

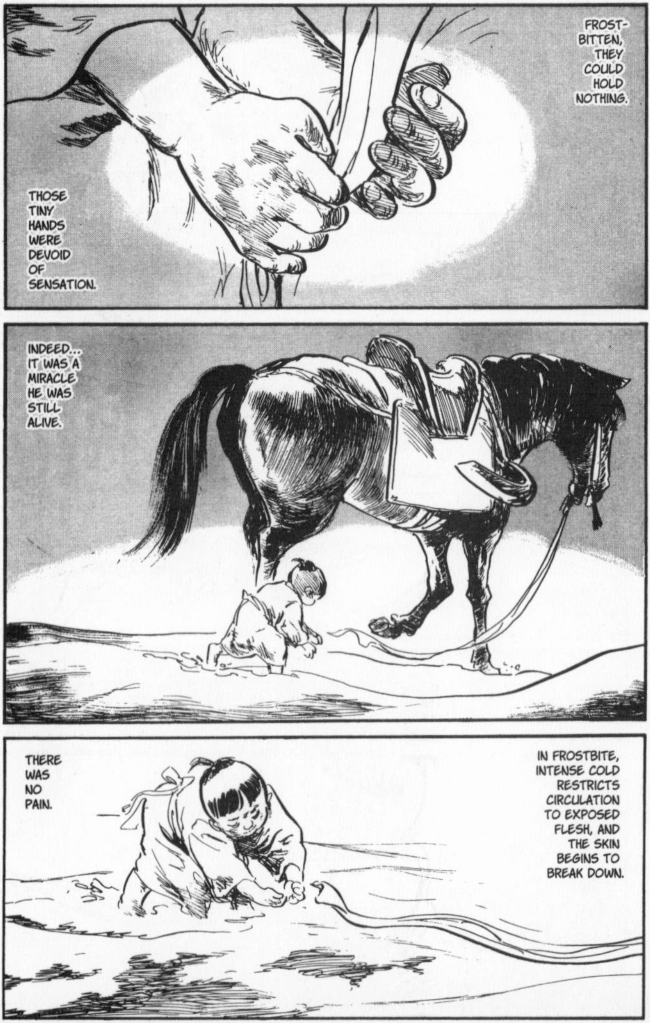
FROST-BITTEN, THEY COULD HOLD NOTHING.
THOSE TINY HANDS WERE DEVOID OF SENSATION.
INDEED... IT WAS A MIRACLE HE WAS STILL ALIVE.
THERE WAS NO PAIN.
IN FROSTBITE, INTENSE COLD RESTRICTS CIRCULATION TO EXPOSED FLESH, AND THE SKIN BEGINS TO BREAK DOWN.

AT FIRST,
BITTER COLD.
NEXT,
SEARING PAIN.
AND FINALLY...
NOTHING.

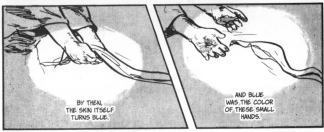

BY THEN,
THE SKIN ITSELF
TURNS BLUE.

AND BLUE
WAS THE COLOR
OF THESE SMALL
HANDS.

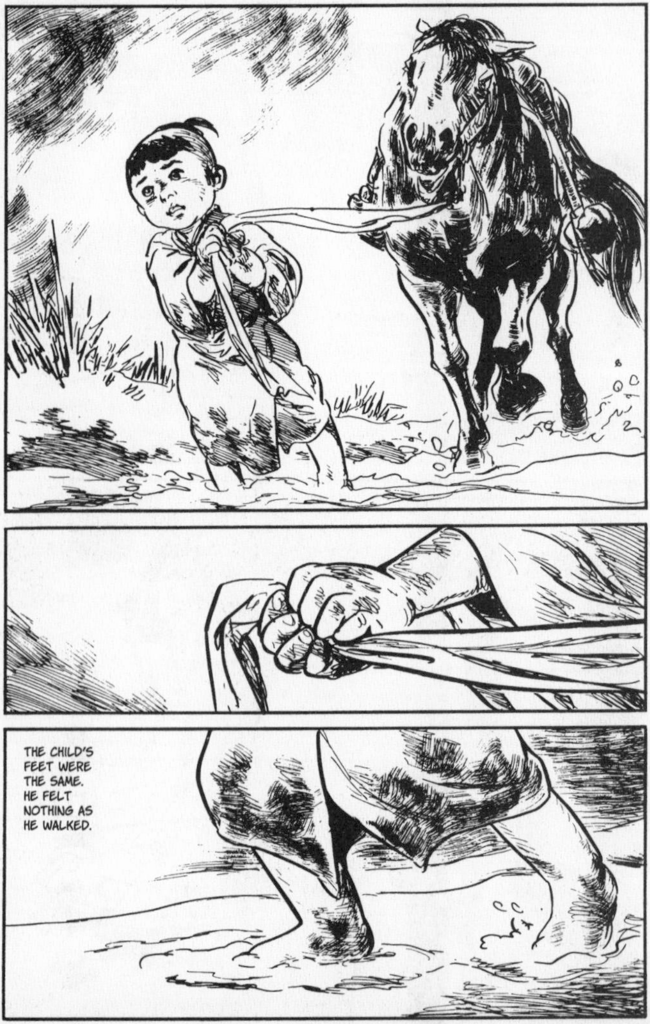
THE CHILD'S FEET WERE THE SAME. HE FELT NOTHING AS HE WALKED.

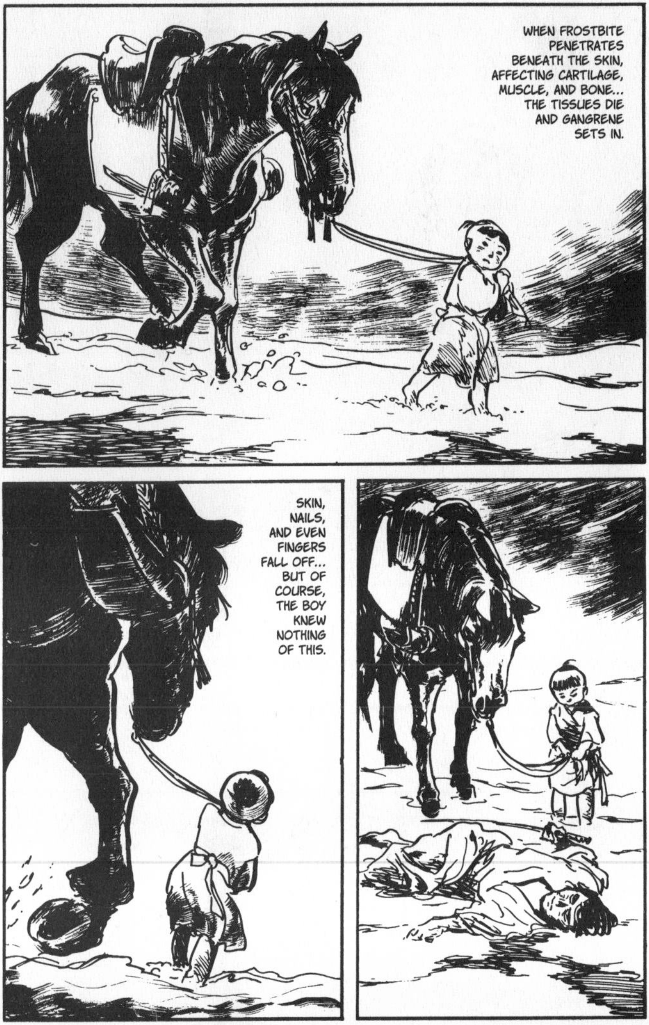
WHEN FROSTBITE PENETRATES BENEATH THE SKIN, AFFECTING CARTILAGE, MUSCLE, AND BONE... THE TISSUES DIE AND GANGRENE SETS IN.
SKIN, NAILS, AND EVEN FINGERS FALL OFF... BUT OF COURSE, THE BOY KNEW NOTHING OF THIS.

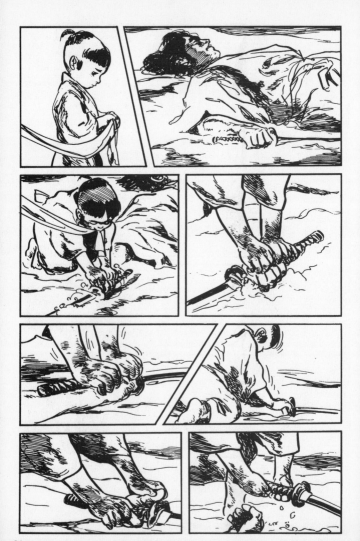

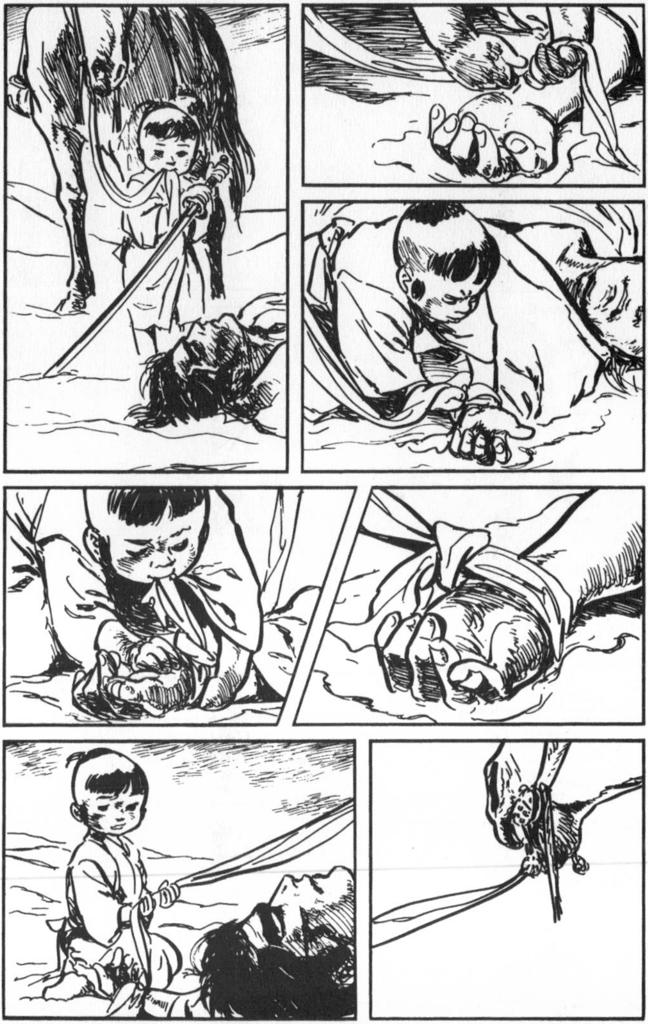

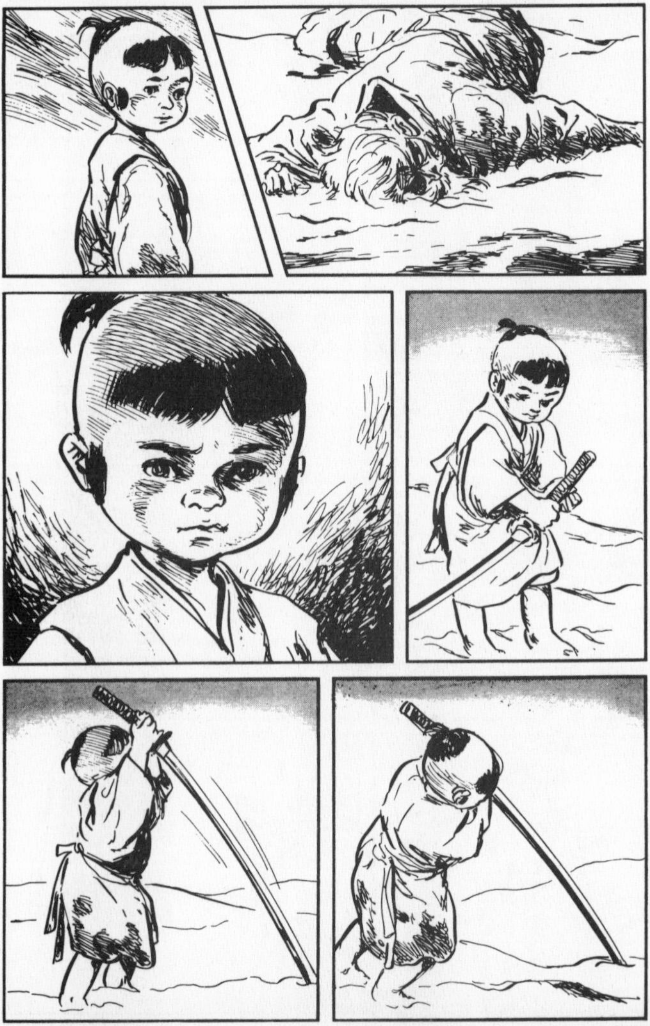

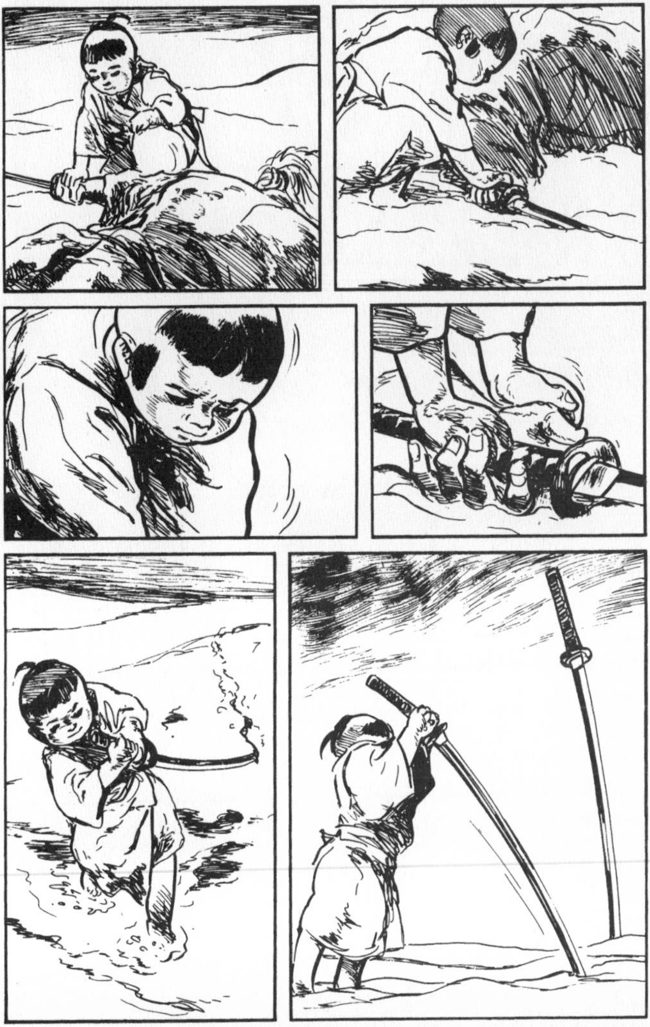

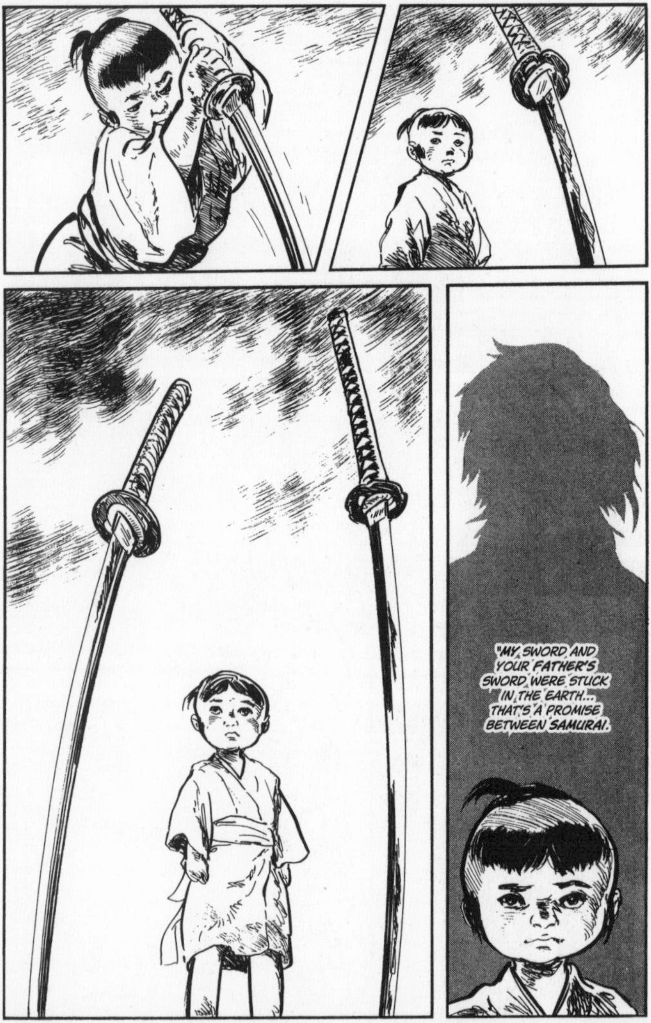
"MY SWORD AND YOUR FATHER'S SWORD WERE STUCK IN THE EARTH... THAT'S A PROMISE BETWEEN SAMURAI.

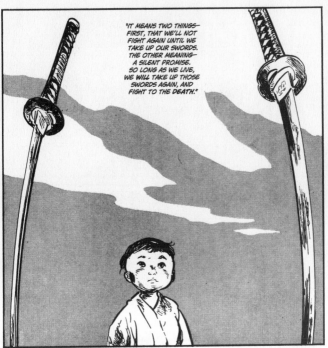

"IT MEANS TWO THINGS—
FIRST, THAT WE'LL NOT
FIGHT AGAIN UNTIL WE
TAKE UP OUR SWORDS.
THE OTHER MEANING—
A SILENT PROMISE.
SO LONG AS WE LIVE,
WE WILL TAKE UP THOSE
SWORDS AGAIN, AND
FIGHT TO THE DEATH."

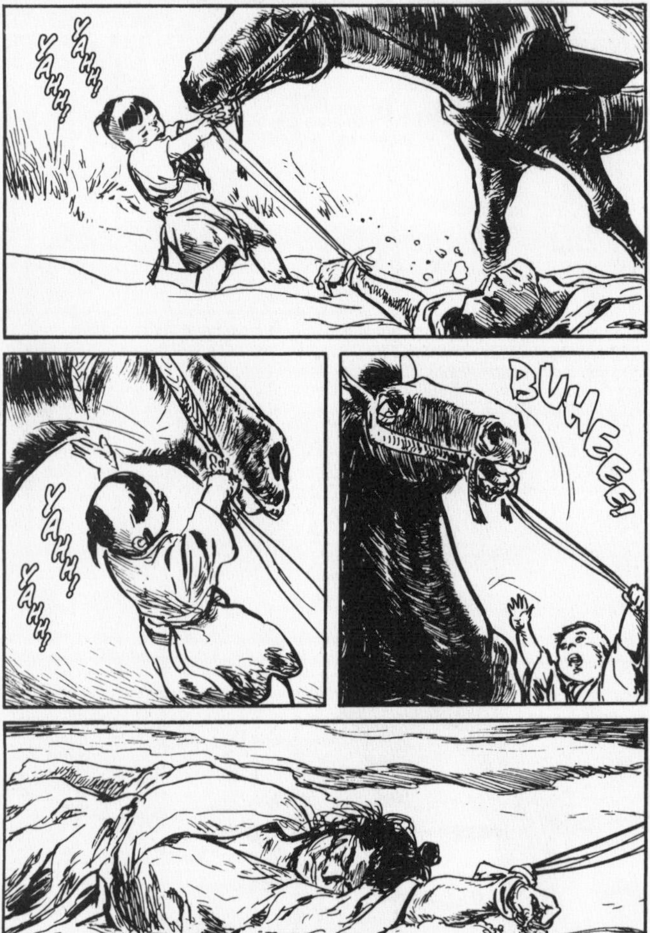
YAHH!
YAHH!
YAHH!
YAHH!
BUHEEE!
SKSSH

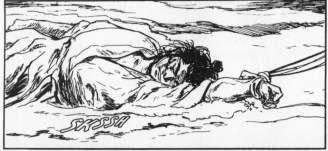

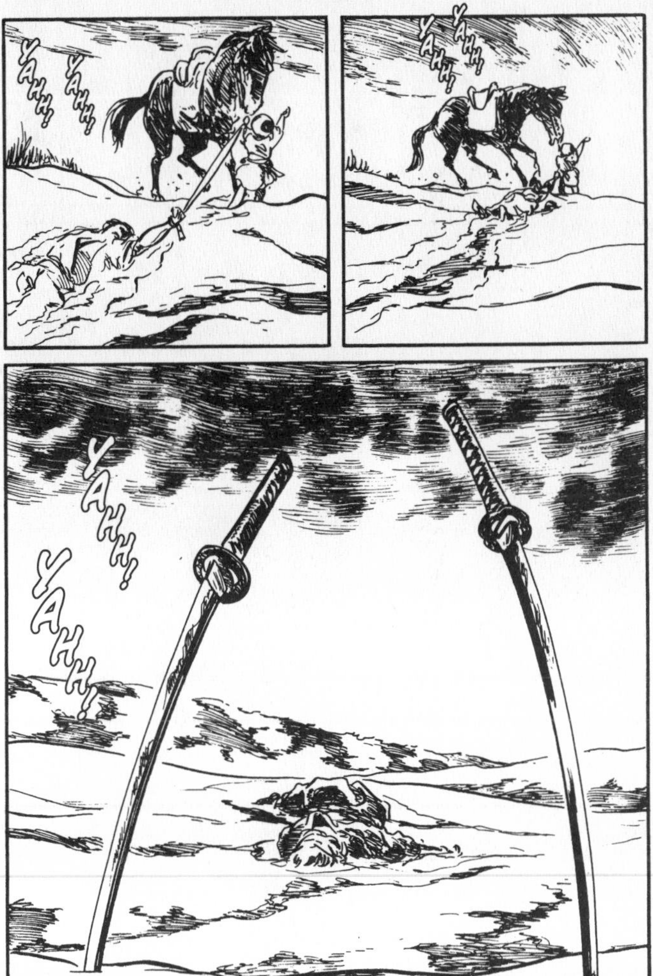
YAHH!
YAHH!
YAHH!
YAHH!
YAHH!
YAHH!

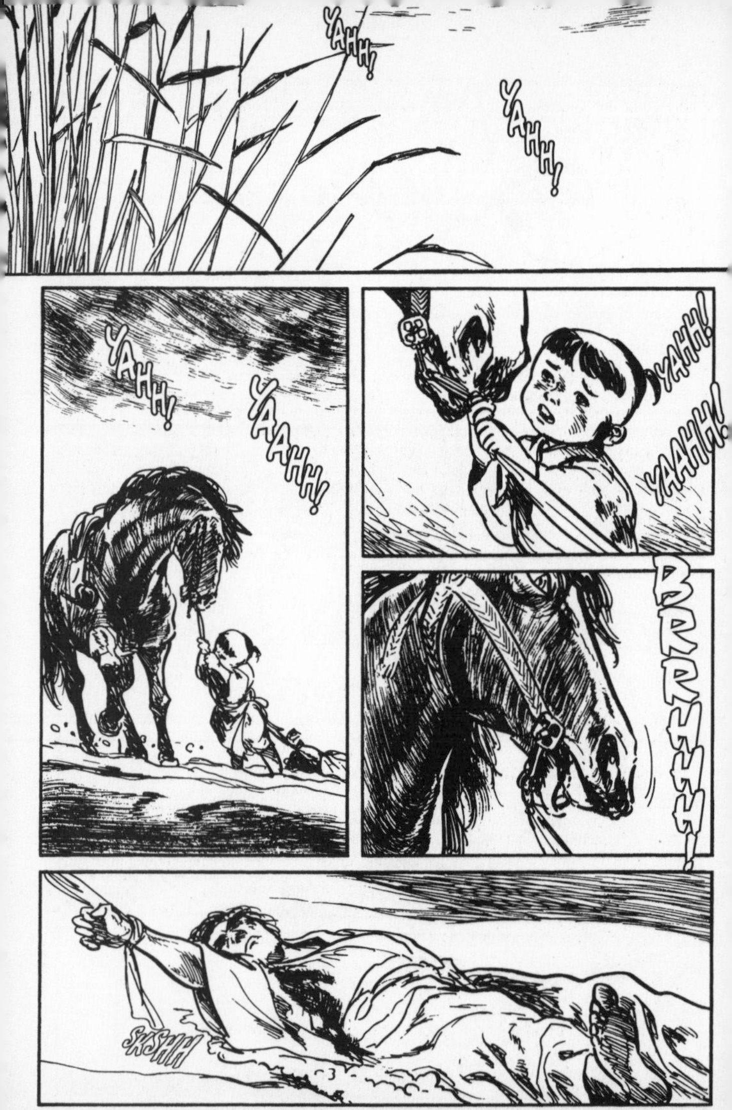
YAHH!
YAHH!
YAHH!
YAAHH!
YAHH!
YAAHH!
BRRUHHH!
SKSHH

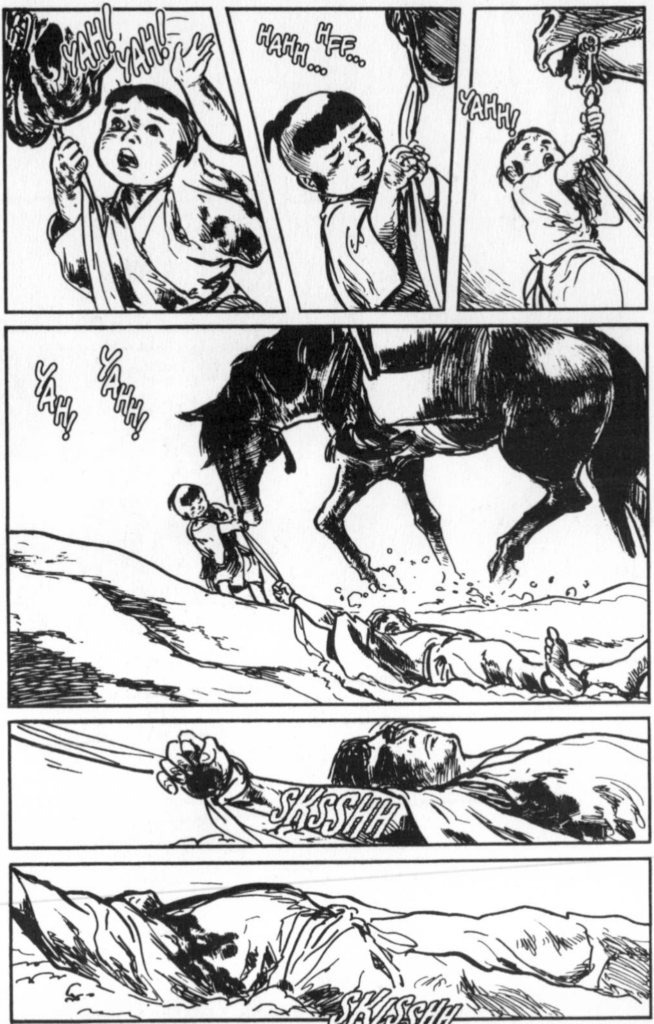
YAH! YAH!
HAHH... HFF...
YAHH!
YAH!
YAHH!
SKSSHH
SKSSHH

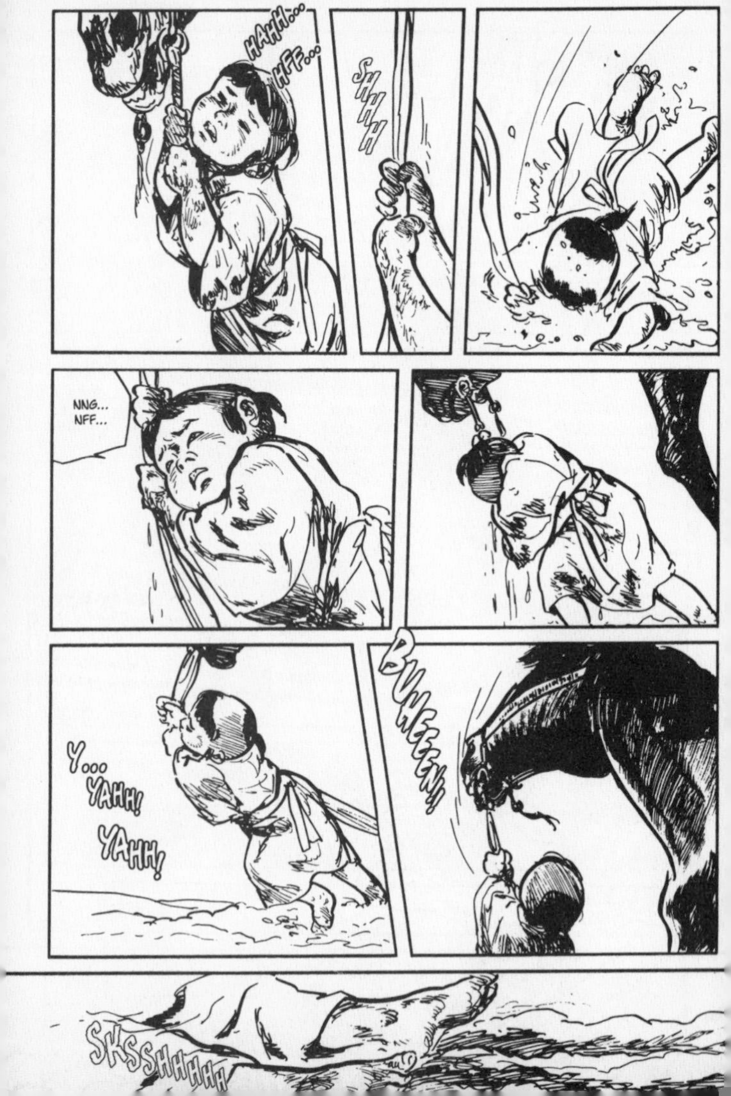
HAHH...
HFF...
SHHH
NNG...
NFF...
Y...
YAHH!
YAHH!
BUHEEEN!!
SKSSHHHHH

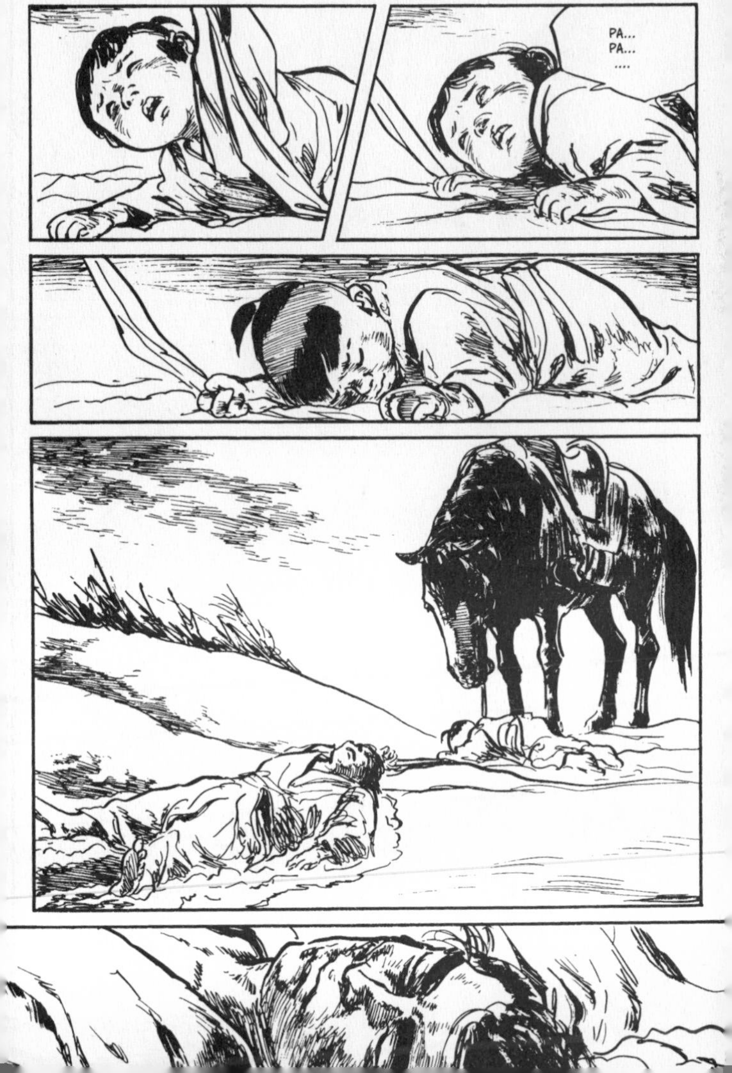
PA...
PA...
....

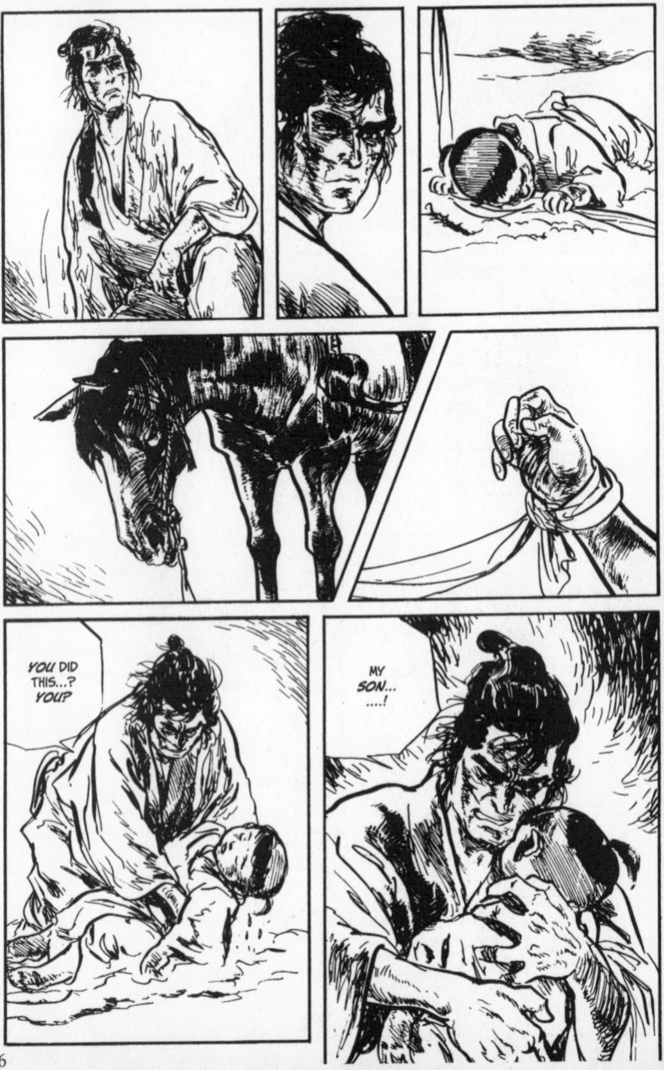
YOU DID THIS...? YOU?
MY SON... ....!

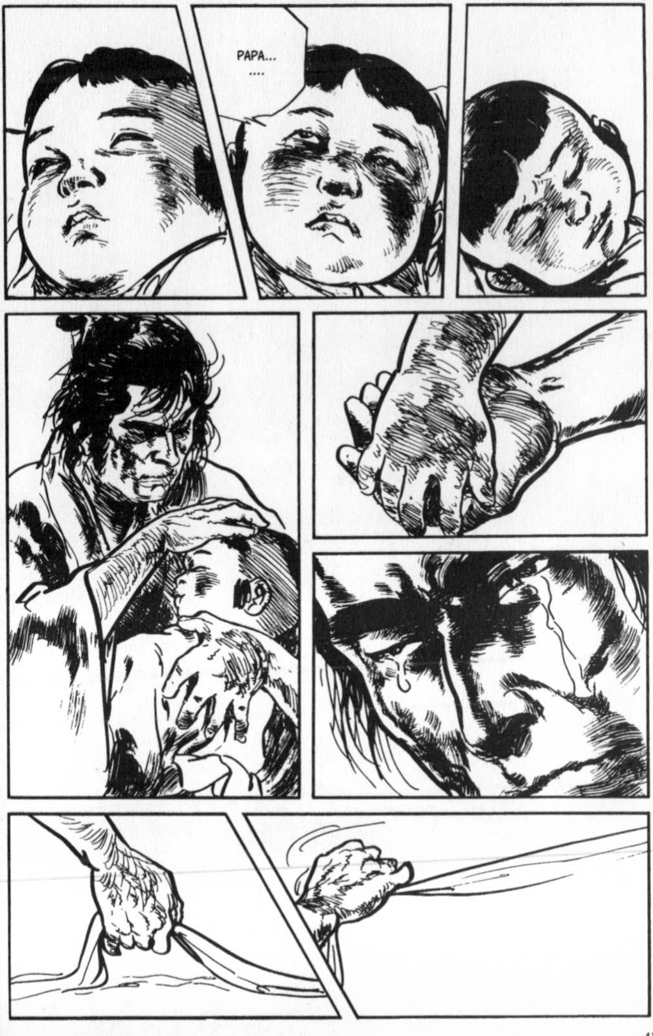
PAPA...
....

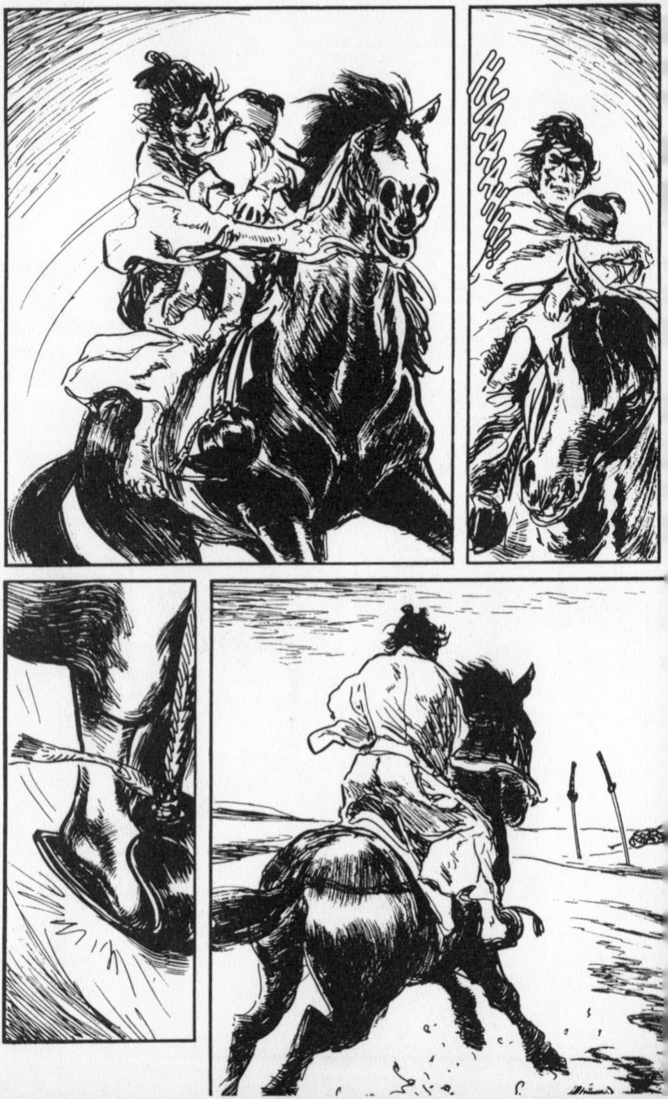
HYAAAAHH!!

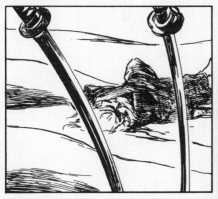

HRGFFH!

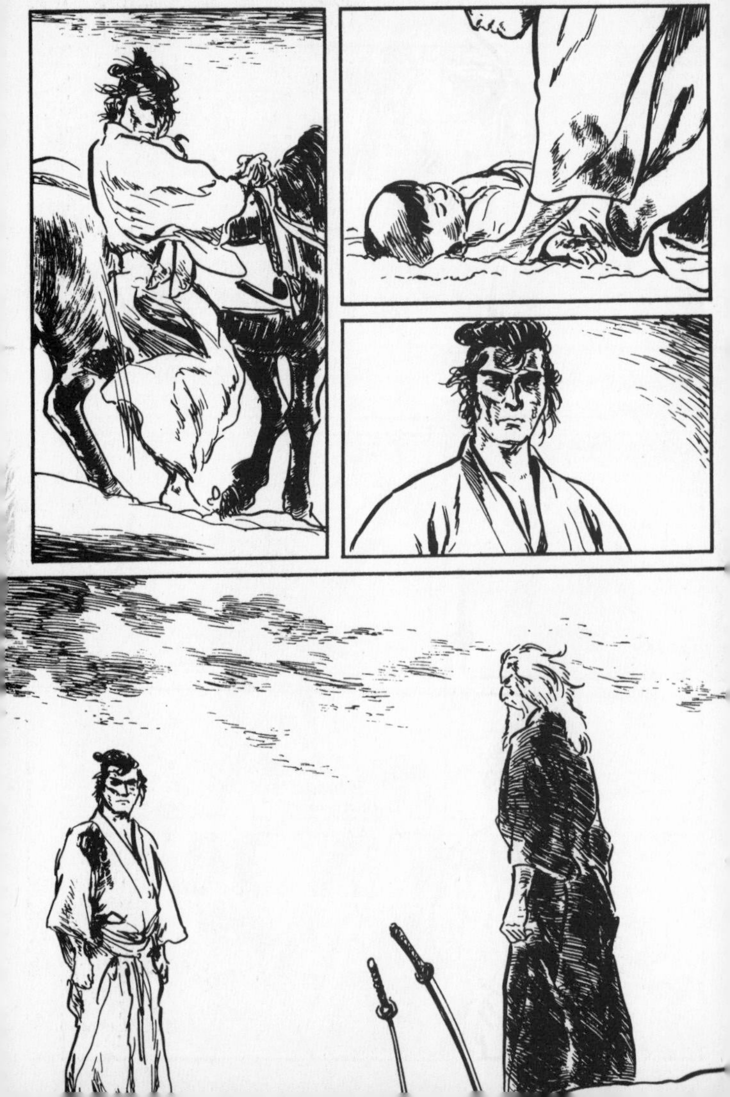

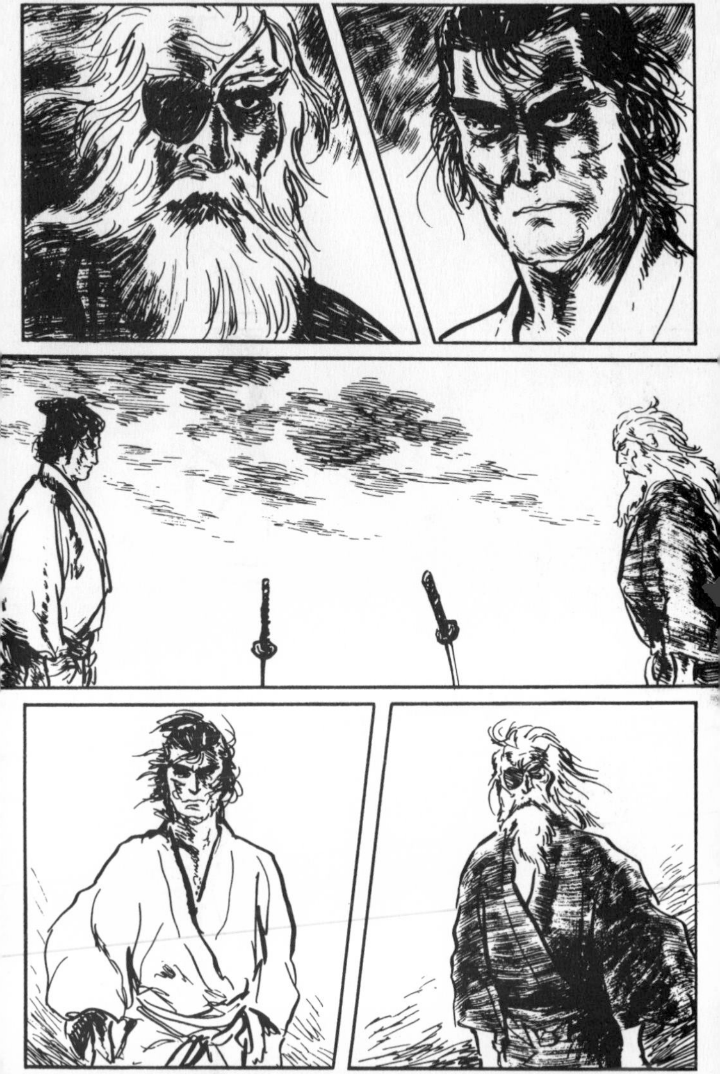

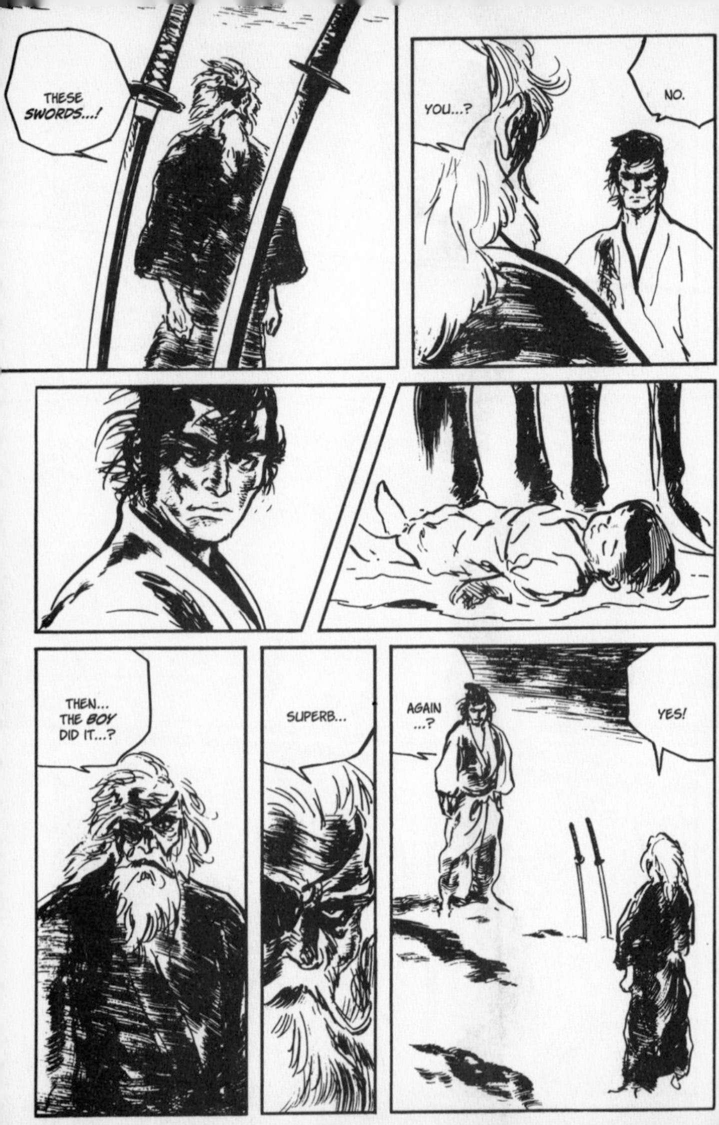
THESE *SWORDS*...!
YOU...?
NO.
THEN... THE *BOY* DID IT...?
SUPERB...
AGAIN ...?
YES!

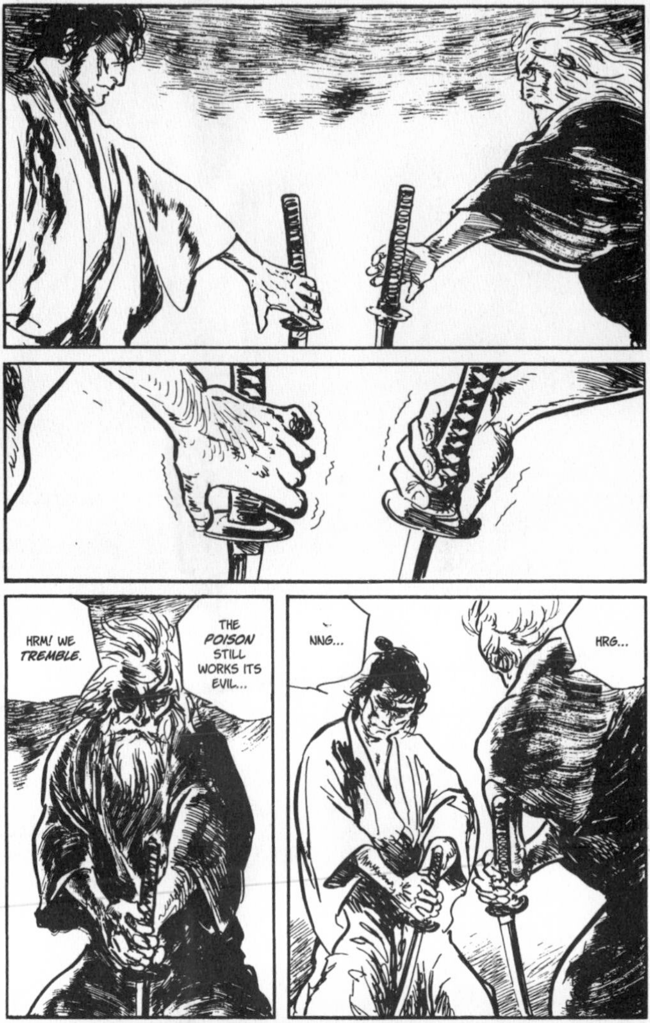
HRM! WE *TREMBLE.*
THE *POISON* STILL WORKS ITS EVIL...
NNG...
HRG...

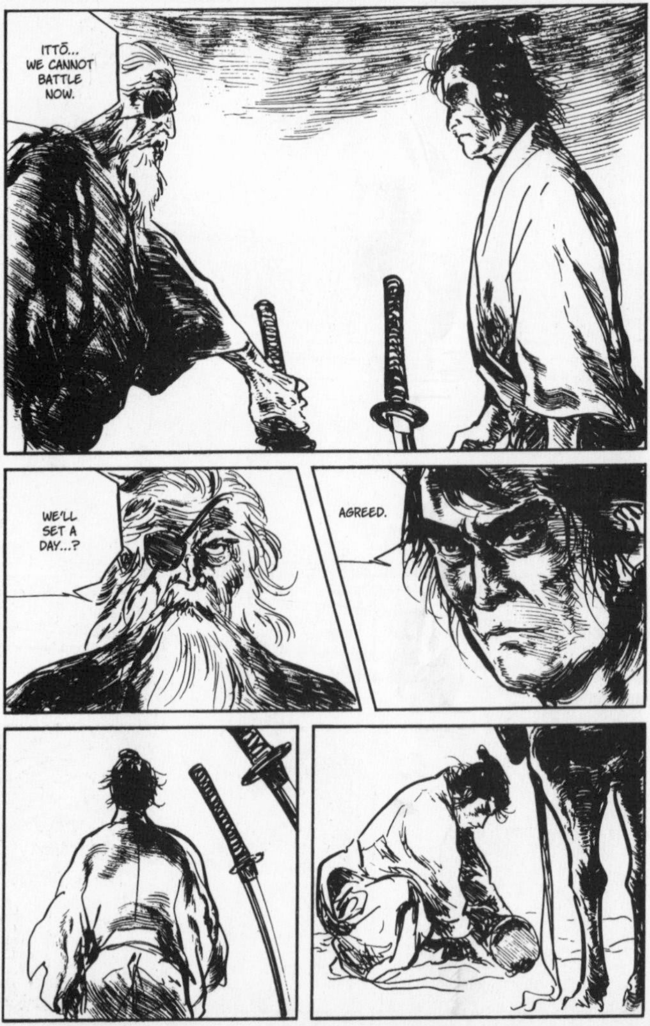
ITTŌ...
WE CANNOT BATTLE NOW.
WE'LL SET A DAY...?
AGREED.

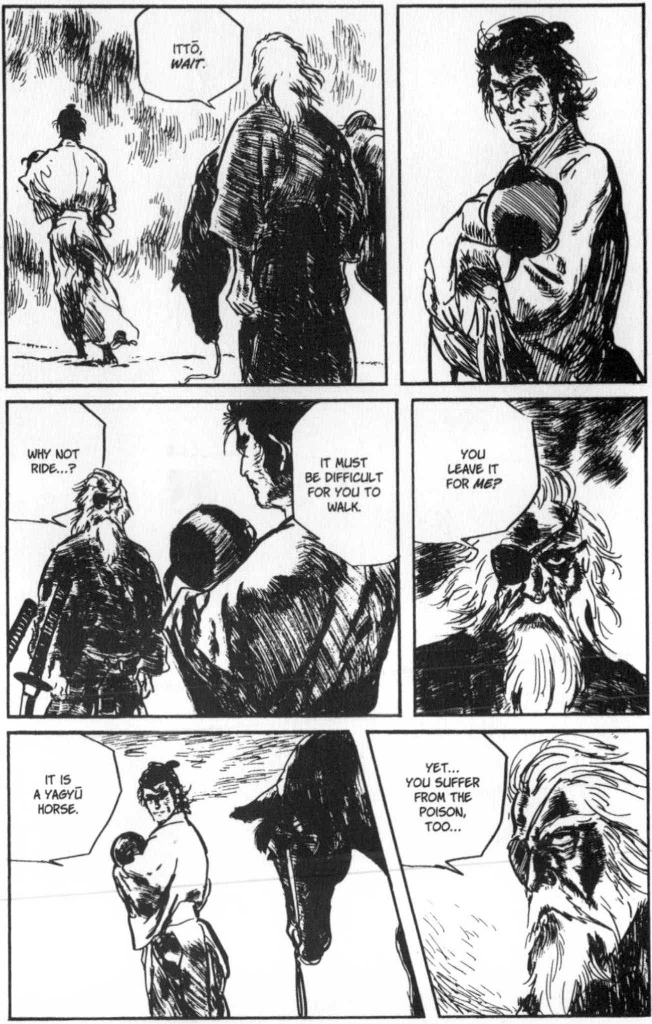

ITTŌ, *WAIT.*
WHY NOT RIDE...?
IT MUST BE DIFFICULT FOR YOU TO WALK.
YOU LEAVE IT FOR *ME?*
IT IS A YAGYŪ HORSE.
YET... YOU SUFFER FROM THE POISON, TOO...

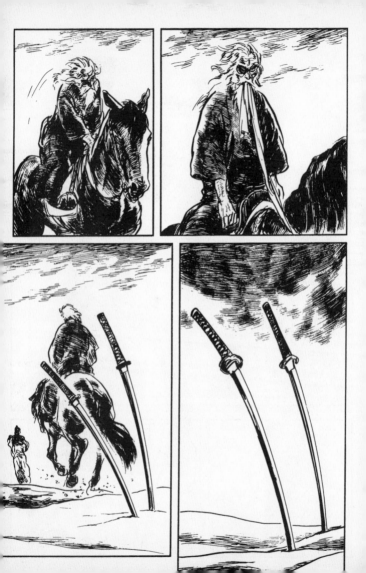

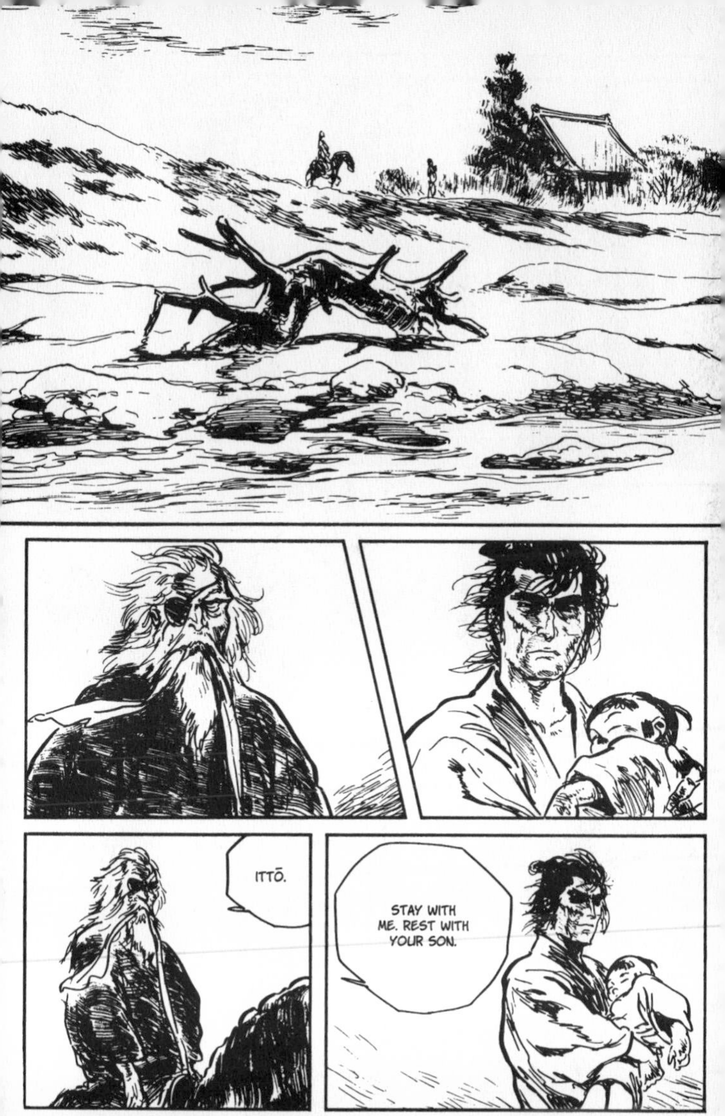
ITTŌ.
STAY WITH ME. REST WITH YOUR SON.

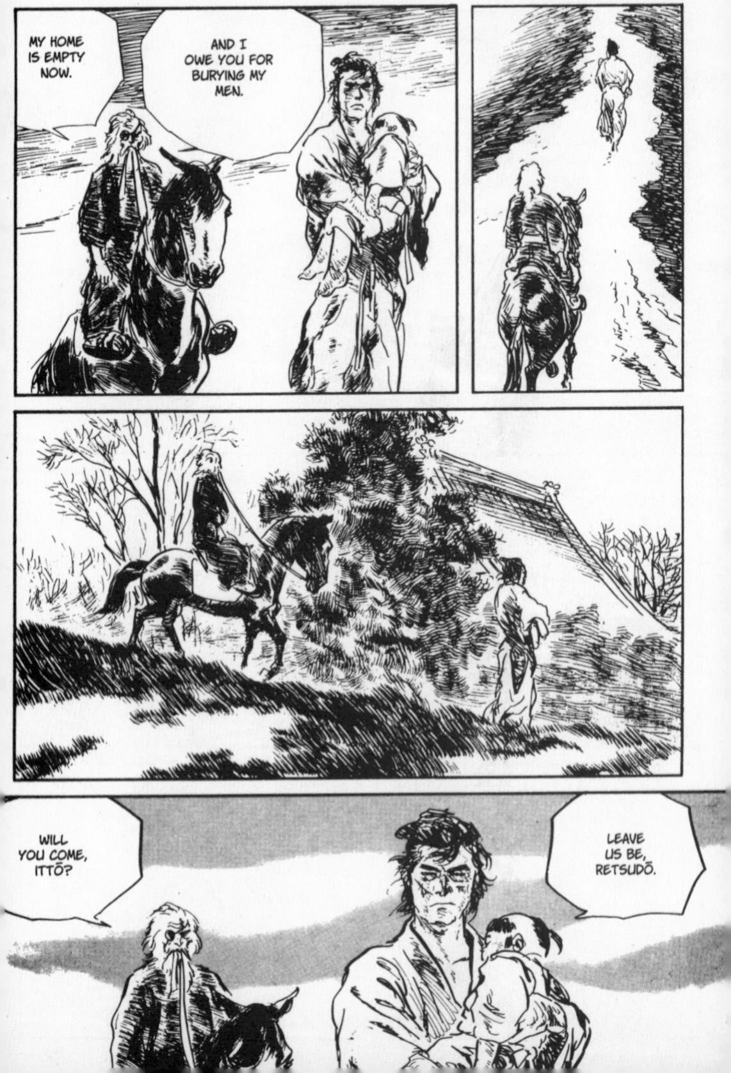
MY HOME IS EMPTY NOW.
AND I OWE YOU FOR BURYING MY MEN.
WILL YOU COME, ITTŌ?
LEAVE US BE, RETSUDŌ.

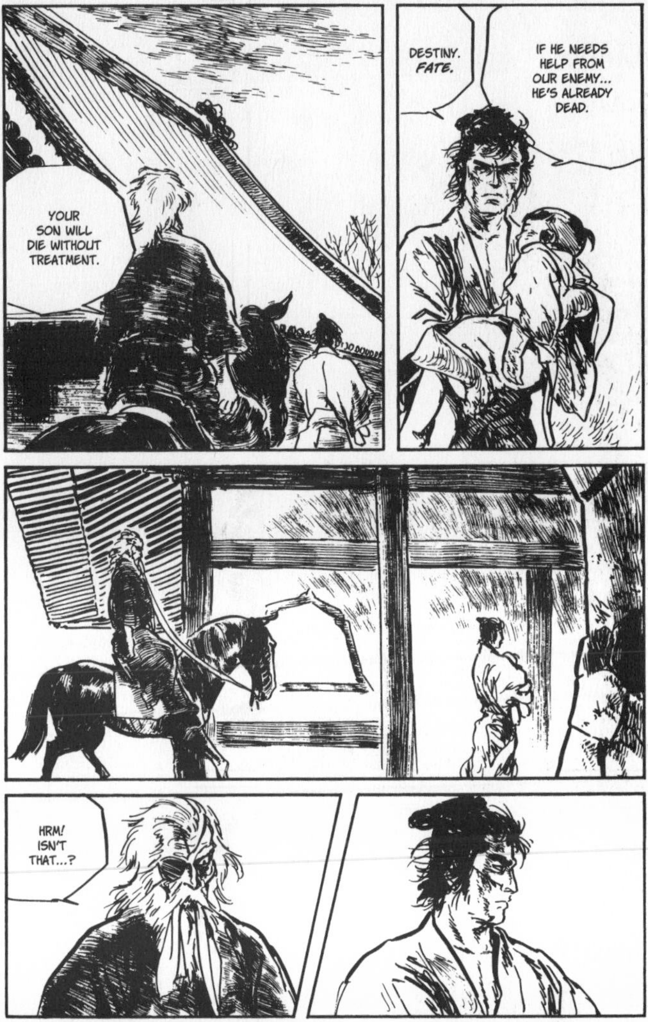
YOUR SON WILL DIE WITHOUT TREATMENT.
DESTINY. *FATE.*
IF HE NEEDS HELP FROM OUR ENEMY... HE'S ALREADY DEAD.
HRM! ISN'T THAT...?

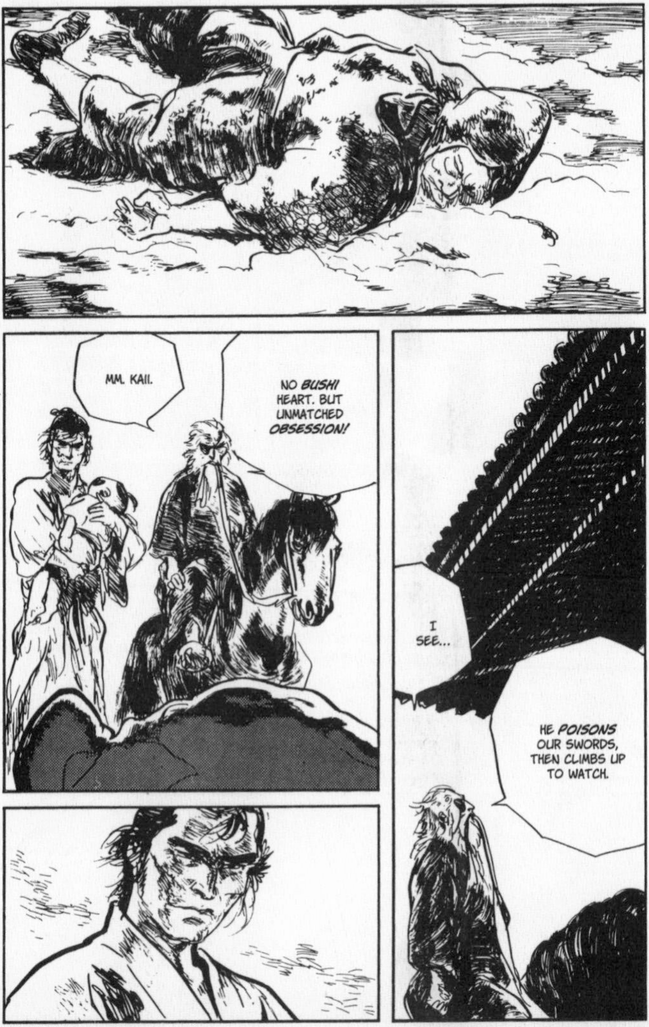
MM. KAII.
NO *BUSHI* HEART. BUT UNMATCHED *OBSESSION!*
I SEE...
HE *POISONS* OUR SWORDS, THEN CLIMBS UP TO WATCH.

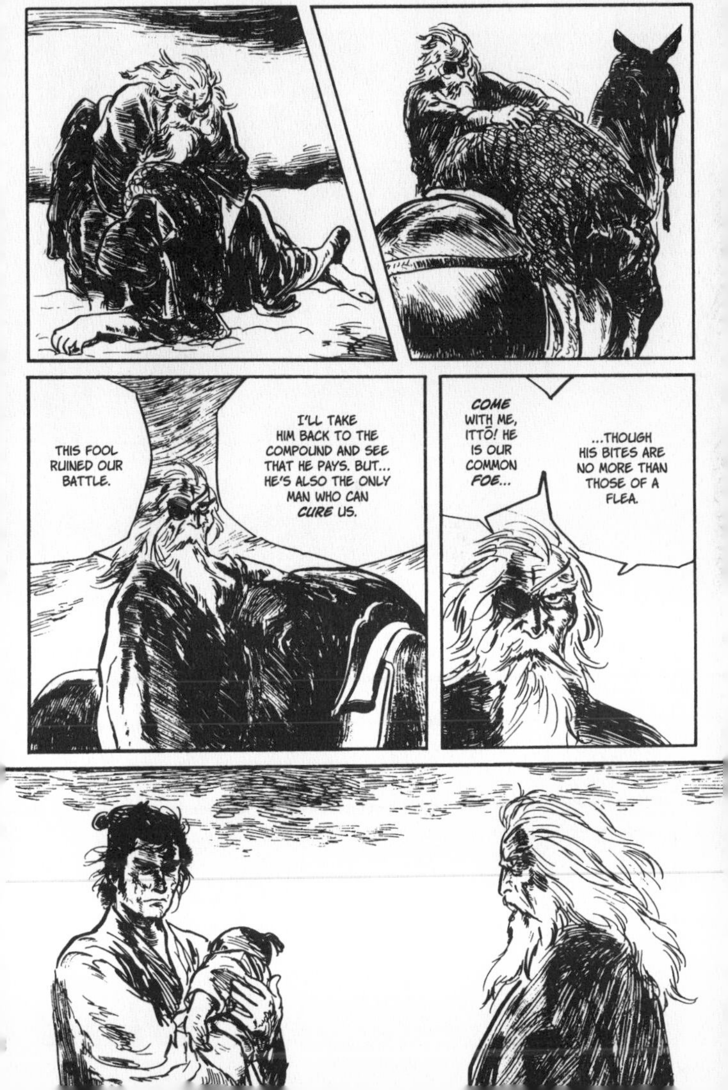
THIS FOOL RUINED OUR BATTLE.
I'LL TAKE HIM BACK TO THE COMPOUND AND SEE THAT HE PAYS. BUT... HE'S ALSO THE ONLY MAN WHO CAN *CURE* US.
*COME* WITH ME, ITTŌ! HE IS OUR COMMON *FOE*...
...THOUGH HIS BITES ARE NO MORE THAN THOSE OF A FLEA.

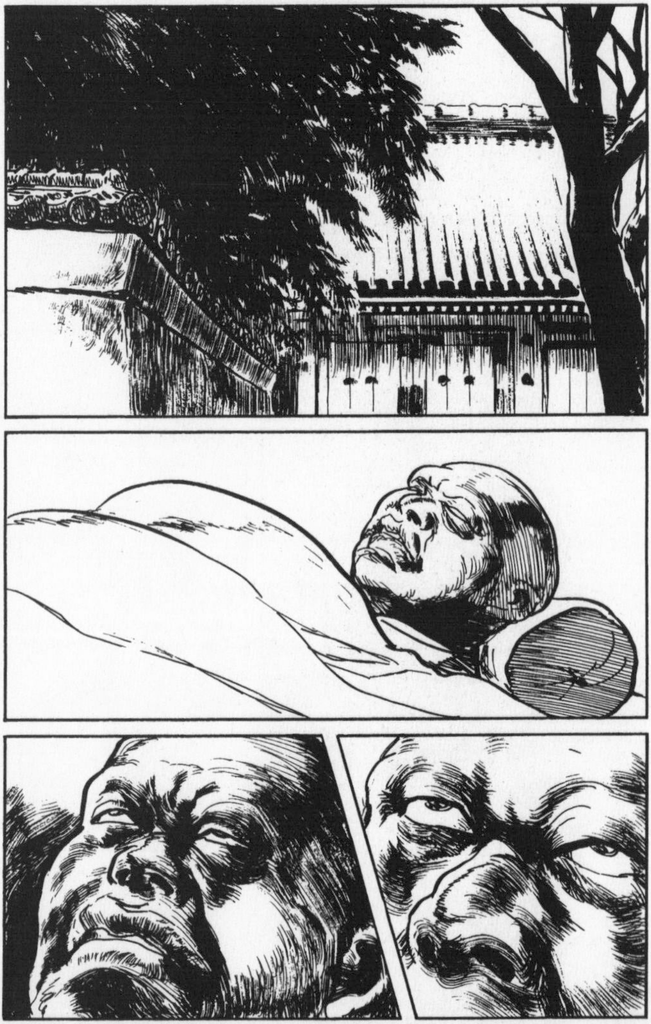

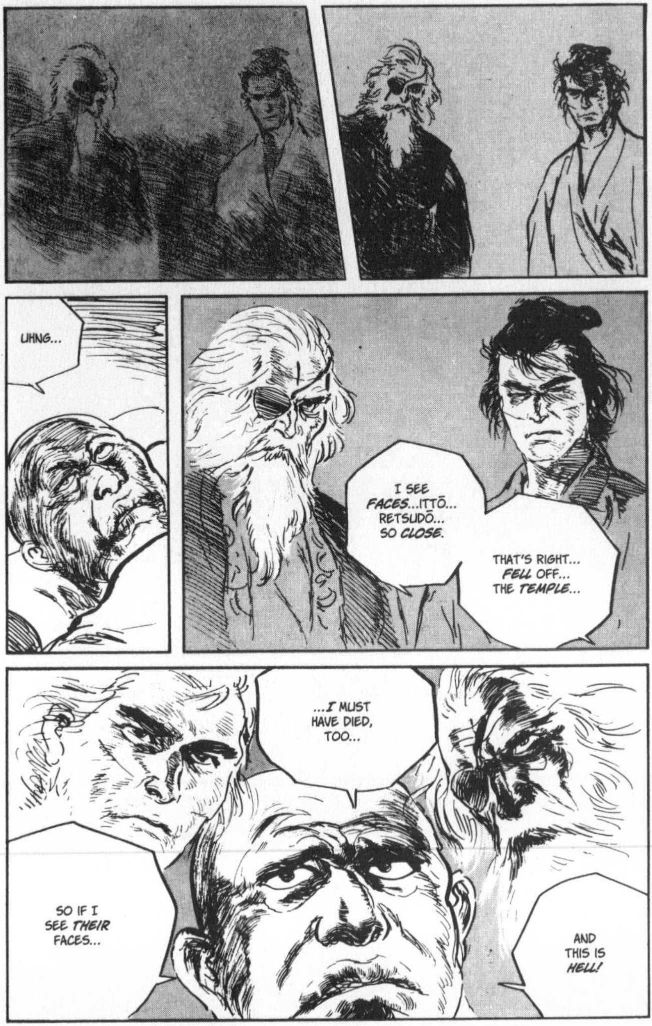

UHNG...
I SEE FACES...ITTŌ... RETSUDŌ... SO CLOSE.
THAT'S RIGHT... FELL OFF... THE TEMPLE...
...I MUST HAVE DIED, TOO...
SO IF I SEE THEIR FACES...
AND THIS IS HELL!

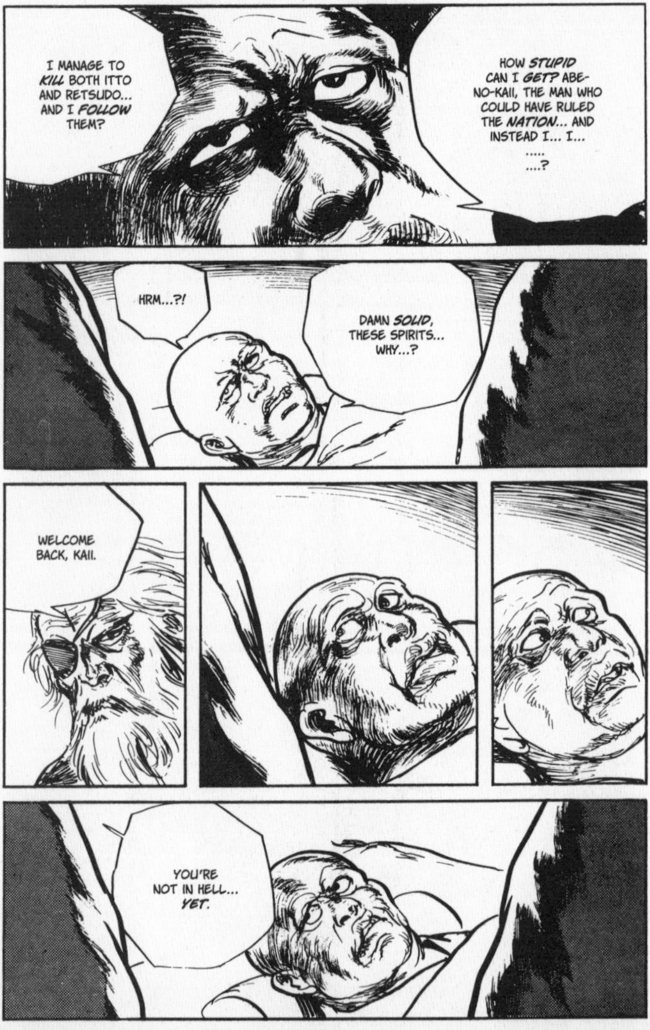
I MANAGE TO KILL BOTH ITTO AND RETSUDO... AND I FOLLOW THEM?
HOW STUPID CAN I GET? ABE-NO-KAII, THE MAN WHO COULD HAVE RULED THE NATION... AND INSTEAD I... I...
.....
....?
HRM...?!
DAMN SOLID, THESE SPIRITS... WHY...?
WELCOME BACK, KAII.
YOU'RE NOT IN HELL... YET.

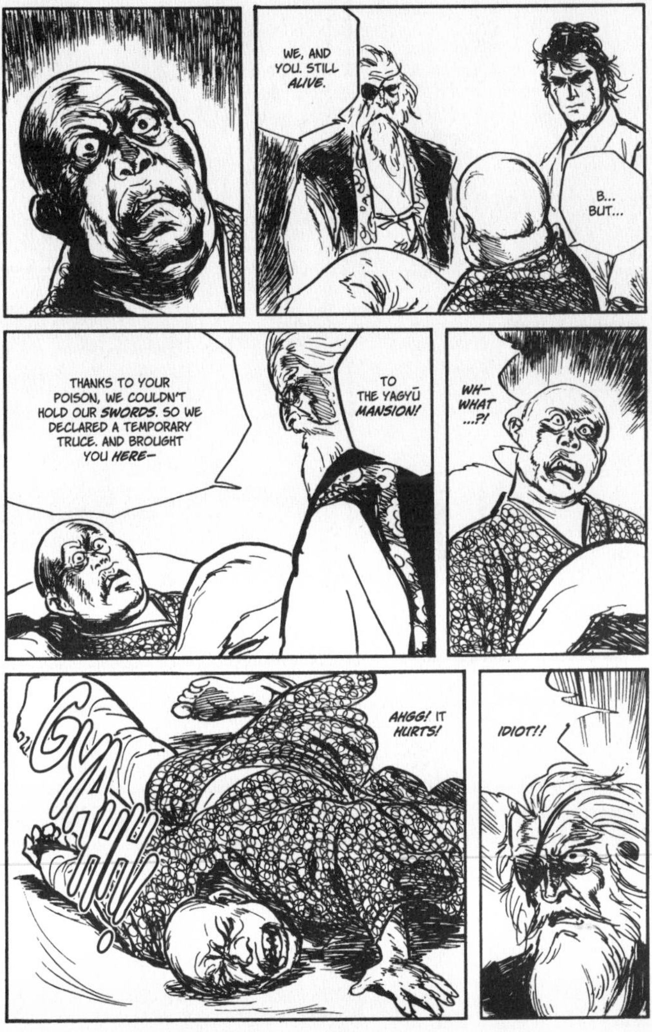
WE, AND YOU. STILL *ALIVE*.
B... BUT...
THANKS TO YOUR POISON, WE COULDN'T HOLD OUR *SWORDS*. SO WE DECLARED A TEMPORARY TRUCE. AND BROUGHT YOU *HERE*—
TO THE YAGYŪ *MANSION!*
*WH— WHAT ...?!*
GYAHH!
*AHGG!* IT *HURTS!*
*IDIOT!!*

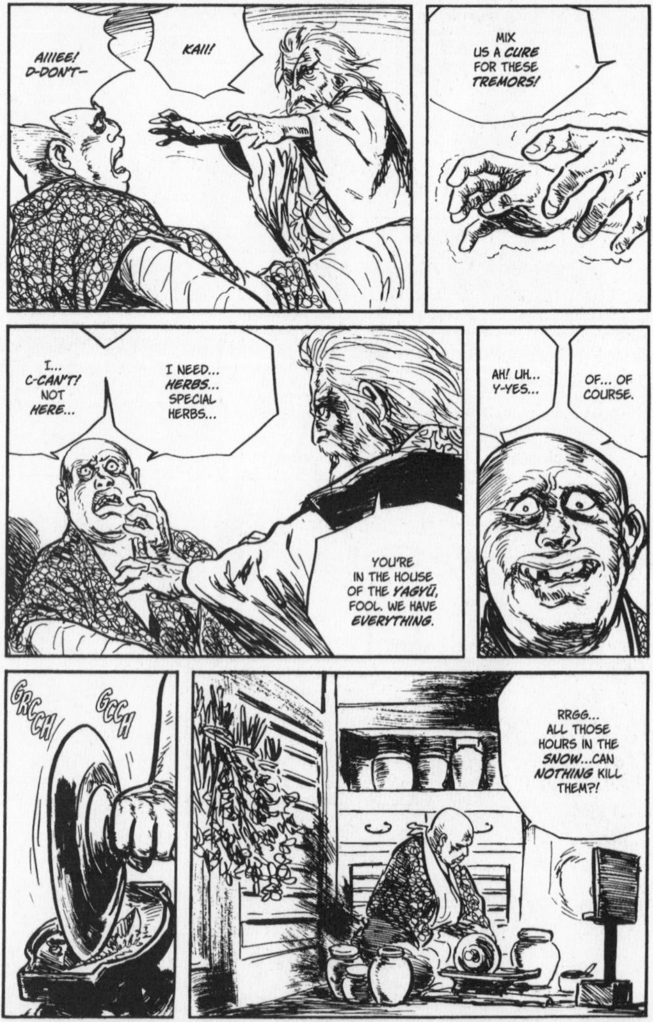
AIIIEE! D-DON'T—
KAII!
MIX US A CURE FOR THESE TREMORS!
I... C-CAN'T! NOT HERE...
I NEED... HERBS... SPECIAL HERBS...
YOU'RE IN THE HOUSE OF THE YAGYŪ, FOOL. WE HAVE EVERYTHING.
AH! UH... Y-YES...
OF... OF COURSE.
GRCCH
GCCH
RRGG... ALL THOSE HOURS IN THE SNOW...CAN NOTHING KILL THEM?!

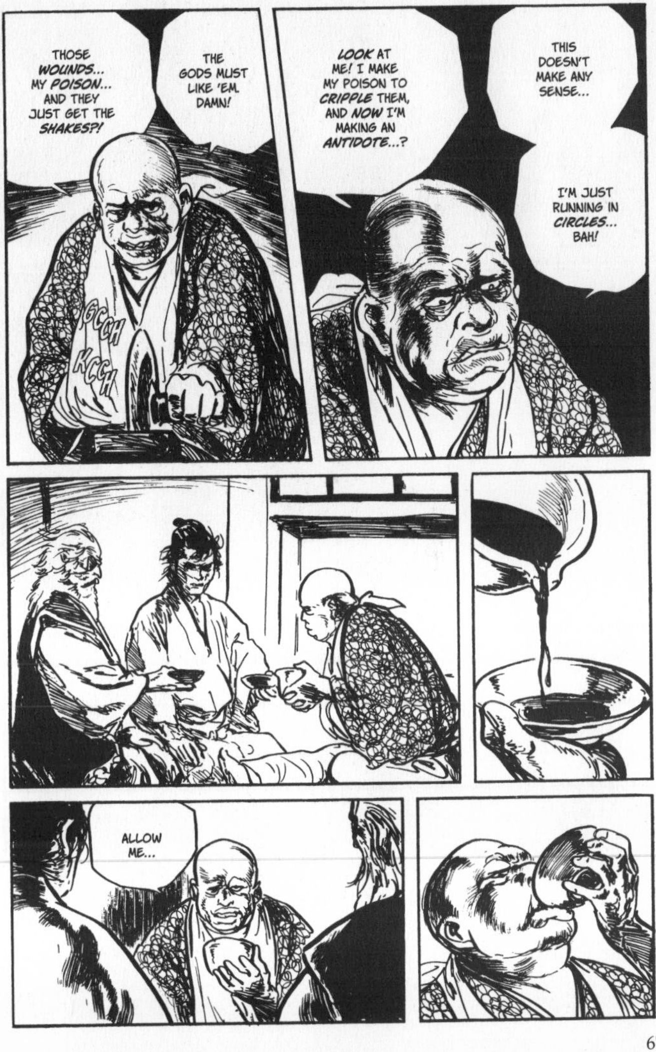
THOSE WOUNDS... MY POISON... AND THEY JUST GET THE SHAKES?!
THE GODS MUST LIKE 'EM. DAMN!
GCCH
KCCH
LOOK AT ME! I MAKE MY POISON TO CRIPPLE THEM, AND NOW I'M MAKING AN ANTIDOTE...?
THIS DOESN'T MAKE ANY SENSE...
I'M JUST RUNNING IN CIRCLES... BAH!
ALLOW ME...

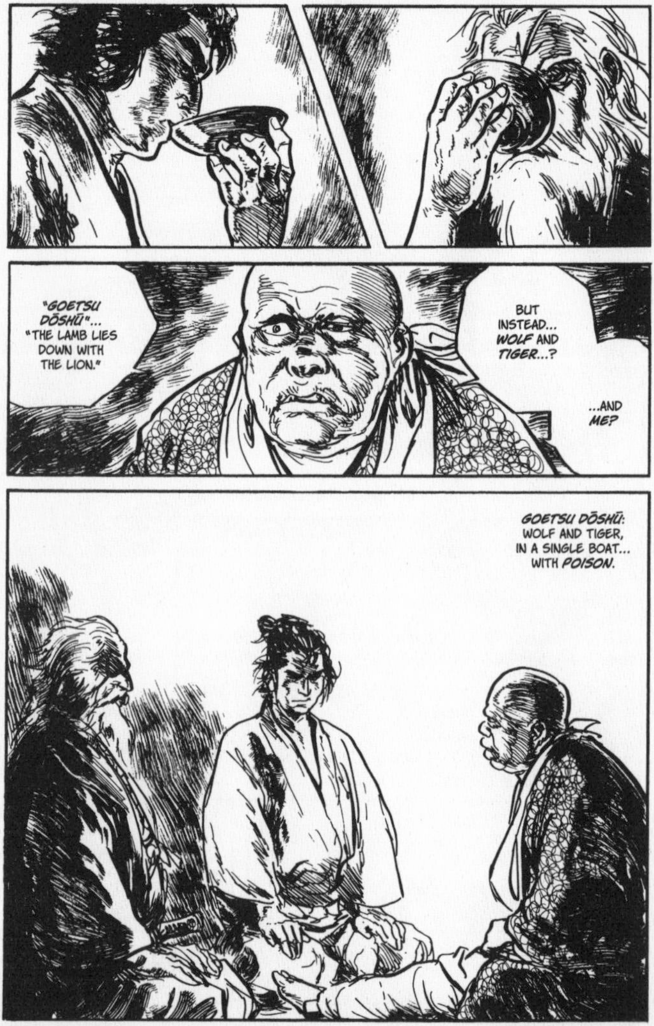
"GOETSU DŌSHŪ"... "THE LAMB LIES DOWN WITH THE LION."
BUT INSTEAD... WOLF AND TIGER...?
...AND ME?
GOETSU DŌSHŪ: WOLF AND TIGER, IN A SINGLE BOAT... WITH POISON.

the hundred and
eighteenth

# In These

# Small

# Hands

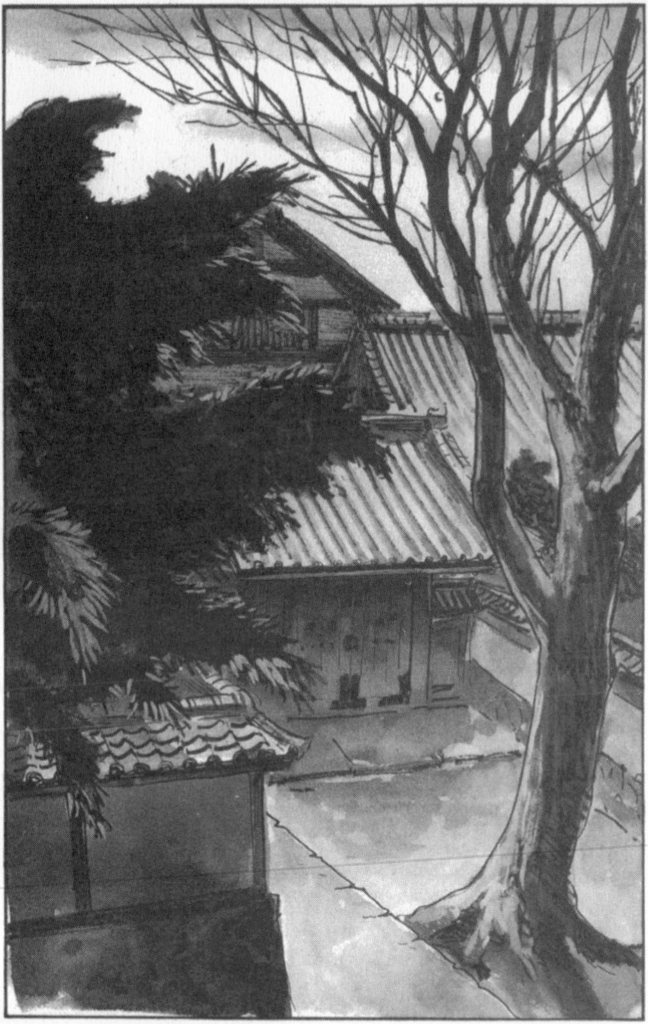

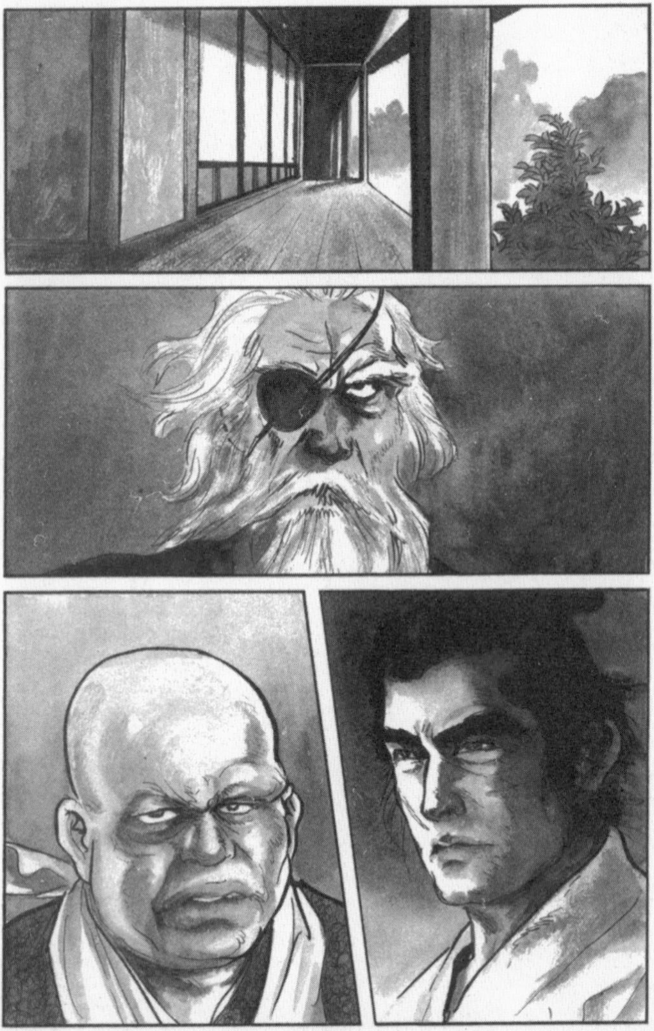

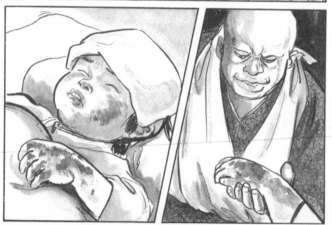

73

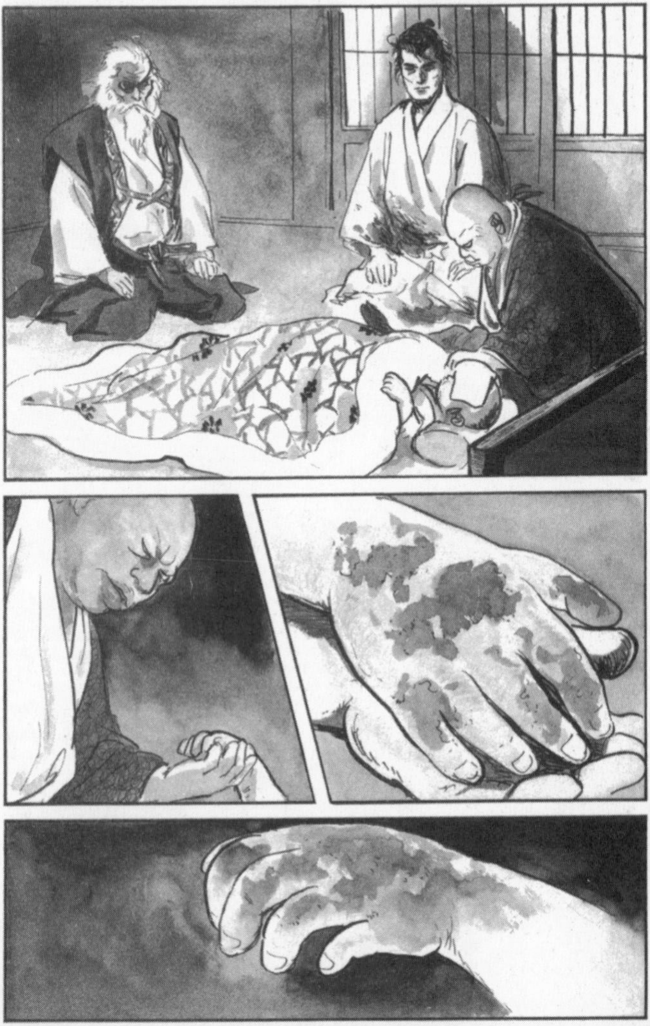

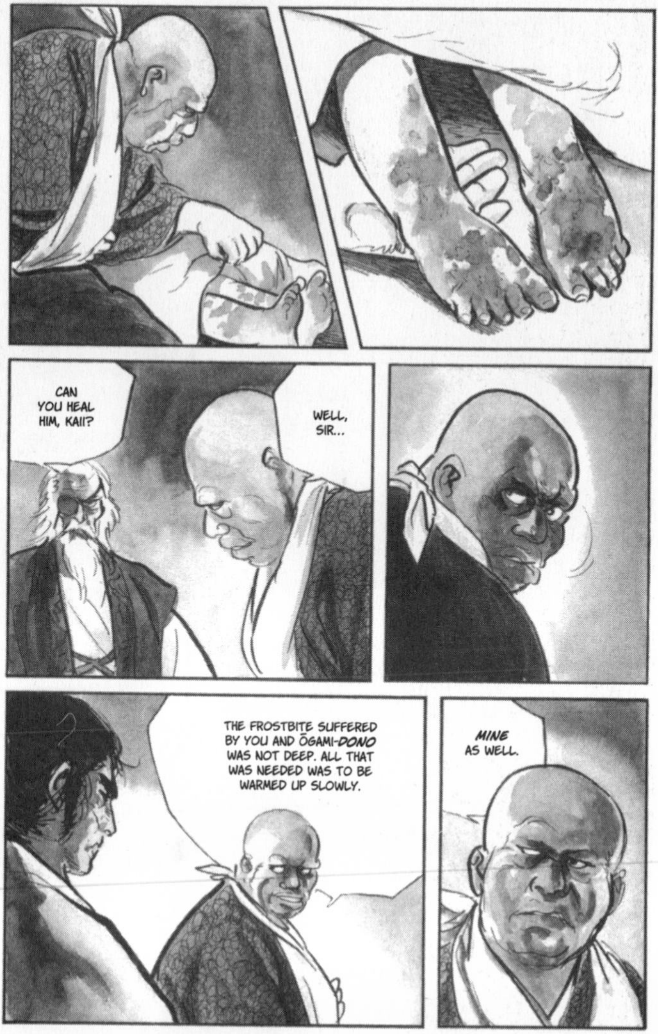
CAN YOU HEAL HIM, KAII?
WELL, SIR...
THE FROSTBITE SUFFERED BY YOU AND ŌGAMI-*DONO* WAS NOT DEEP. ALL THAT WAS NEEDED WAS TO BE WARMED UP SLOWLY.
*MINE* AS WELL.

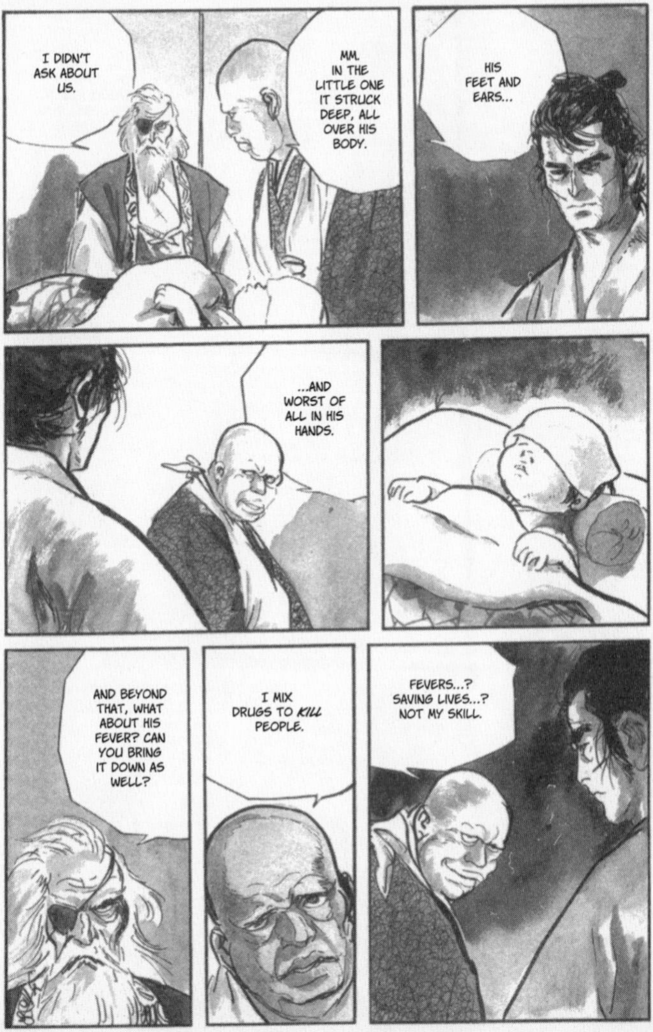
I DIDN'T ASK ABOUT US.
MM. IN THE LITTLE ONE IT STRUCK DEEP, ALL OVER HIS BODY.
HIS FEET AND EARS...
...AND WORST OF ALL IN HIS HANDS.
AND BEYOND THAT, WHAT ABOUT HIS FEVER? CAN YOU BRING IT DOWN AS WELL?
I MIX DRUGS TO *KILL* PEOPLE.
FEVERS...? SAVING LIVES...? NOT MY SKILL.

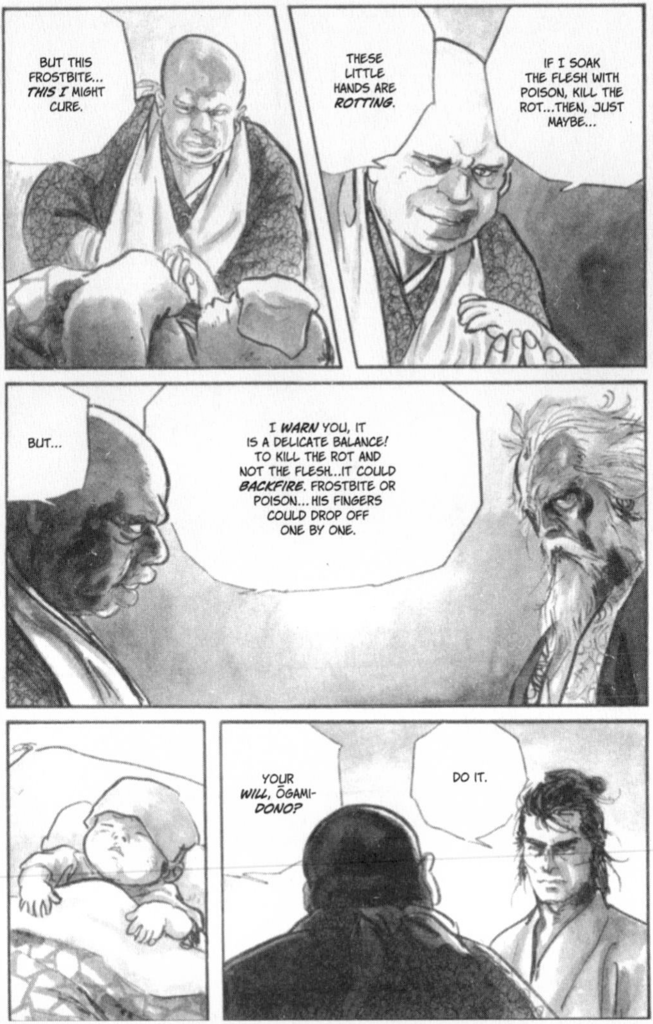
BUT THIS FROSTBITE... THIS I MIGHT CURE.
THESE LITTLE HANDS ARE ROTTING.
IF I SOAK THE FLESH WITH POISON, KILL THE ROT...THEN, JUST MAYBE...
BUT...
I WARN YOU, IT IS A DELICATE BALANCE! TO KILL THE ROT AND NOT THE FLESH...IT COULD BACKFIRE. FROSTBITE OR POISON... HIS FINGERS COULD DROP OFF ONE BY ONE.
YOUR WILL, ŌGAMI-DONO?
DO IT.

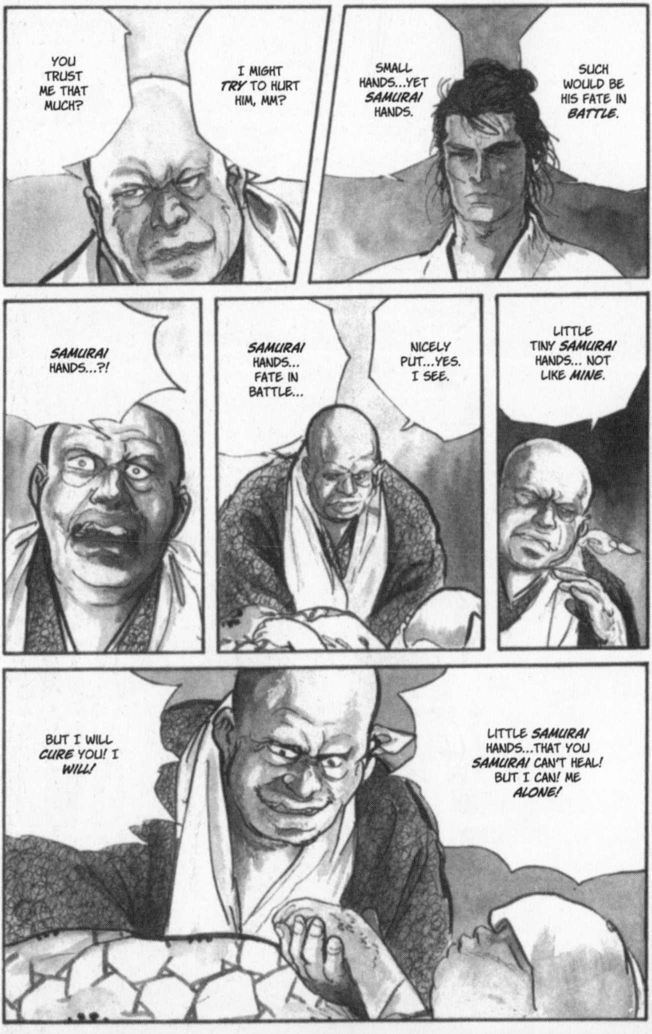

YOU TRUST ME THAT MUCH?
I MIGHT *TRY* TO HURT HIM, MM?
SMALL HANDS...YET *SAMURAI* HANDS.
SUCH WOULD BE HIS FATE IN *BATTLE.*
*SAMURAI* HANDS...?!
*SAMURAI* HANDS... FATE IN BATTLE...
NICELY PUT...YES. I SEE.
LITTLE TINY *SAMURAI* HANDS... NOT LIKE *MINE.*
BUT I WILL *CURE* YOU! I *WILL!*
LITTLE *SAMURAI* HANDS...THAT YOU *SAMURAI* CAN'T HEAL! BUT I CAN! ME *ALONE!*

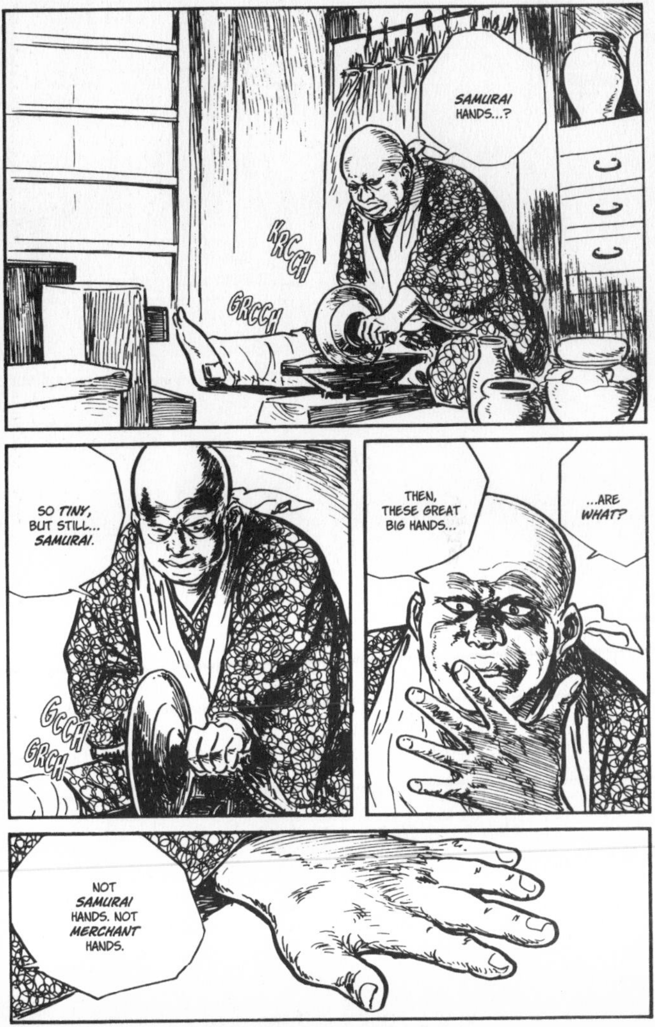
SAMURAI HANDS...?
KRCCH
GRCCH
SO TINY, BUT STILL... SAMURAI.
GCCH
GRCH
THEN, THESE GREAT BIG HANDS...
...ARE WHAT?
NOT SAMURAI HANDS. NOT MERCHANT HANDS.

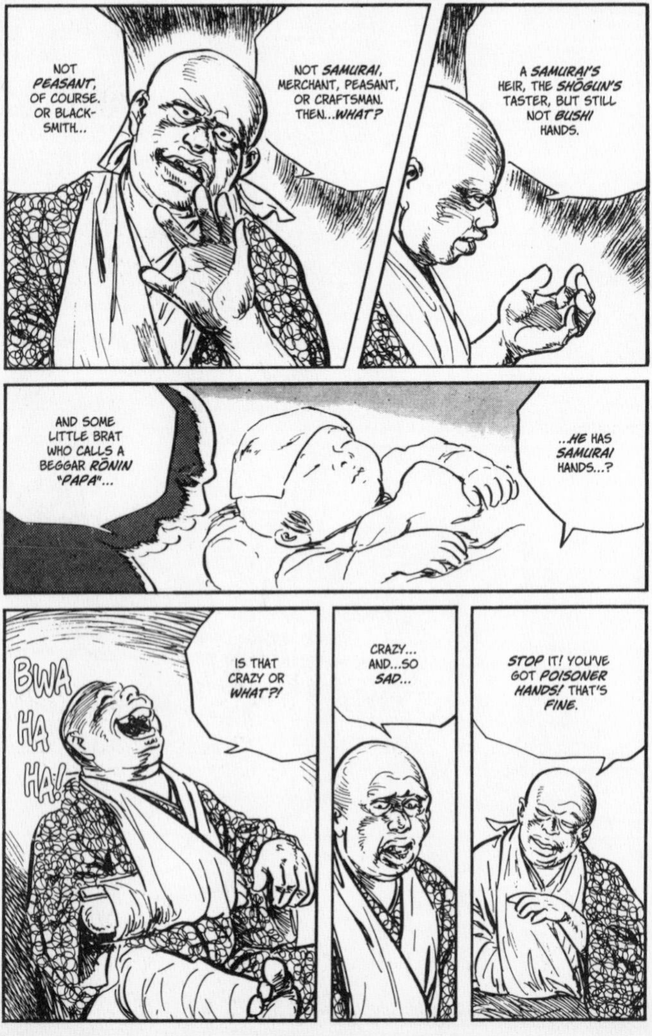
NOT PEASANT, OF COURSE. OR BLACK-SMITH...
NOT SAMURAI, MERCHANT, PEASANT, OR CRAFTSMAN. THEN...WHAT?
A SAMURAI'S HEIR, THE SHŌGUN'S TASTER, BUT STILL NOT BUSHI HANDS.
AND SOME LITTLE BRAT WHO CALLS A BEGGAR RŌNIN "PAPA"...
...HE HAS SAMURAI HANDS...?
BWA HA HA!
IS THAT CRAZY OR WHAT?!
CRAZY... AND...SO SAD...
STOP IT! YOU'VE GOT POISONER HANDS! THAT'S FINE.

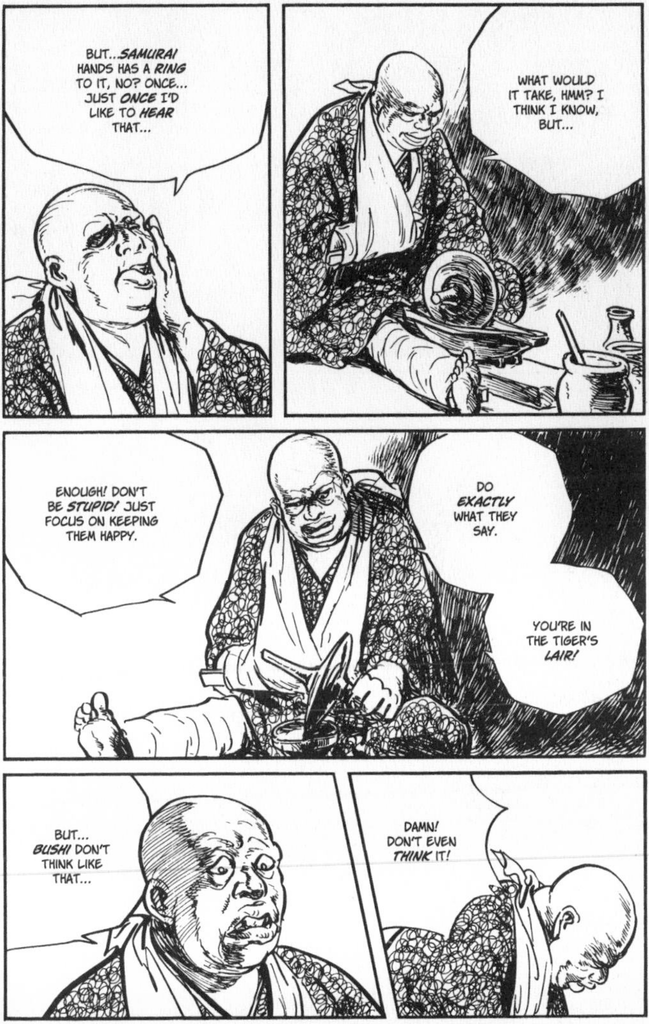
BUT...SAMURAI HANDS HAS A RING TO IT, NO? ONCE... JUST ONCE I'D LIKE TO HEAR THAT...
WHAT WOULD IT TAKE, HMM? I THINK I KNOW, BUT...
ENOUGH! DON'T BE STUPID! JUST FOCUS ON KEEPING THEM HAPPY.
DO EXACTLY WHAT THEY SAY.
YOU'RE IN THE TIGER'S LAIR!
BUT... BUSHI DON'T THINK LIKE THAT...
DAMN! DON'T EVEN THINK IT!

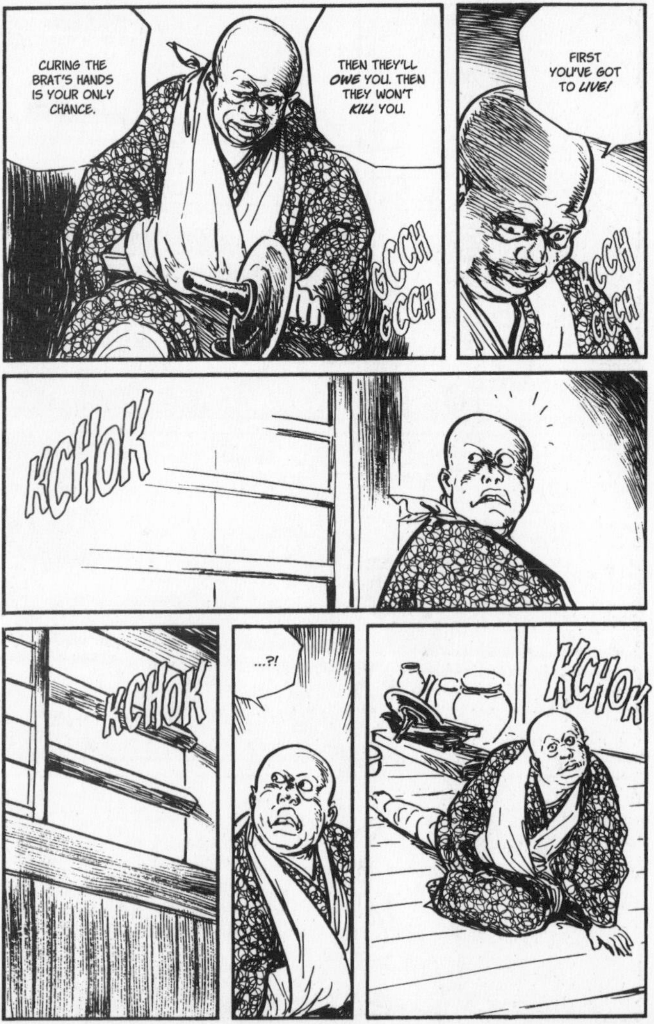

CURING THE BRAT'S HANDS IS YOUR ONLY CHANCE.
THEN THEY'LL *OWE* YOU. THEN THEY WON'T *KILL* YOU.
GCCH GCCH
FIRST YOU'VE GOT TO *LIVE!*
KCCH GCCH
KCHOK
KCHOK
...?!
KCHOK

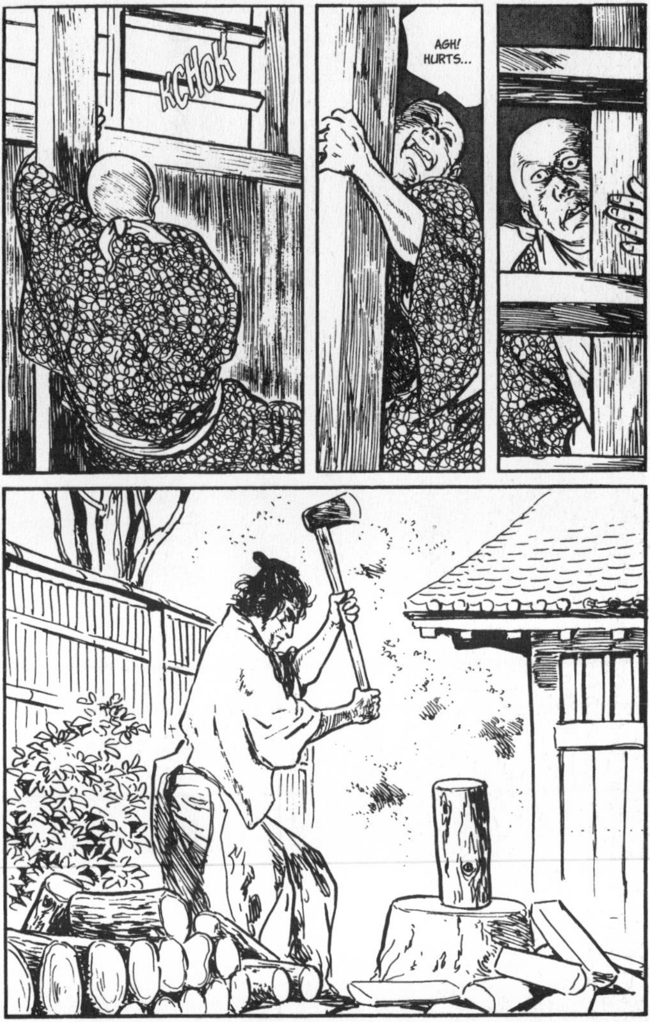
KCHOK
AGH! HURTS...

NOW *THAT'S* AN EXECUTIONER... EVERY *CHOP!* EVEN *WOOD!*

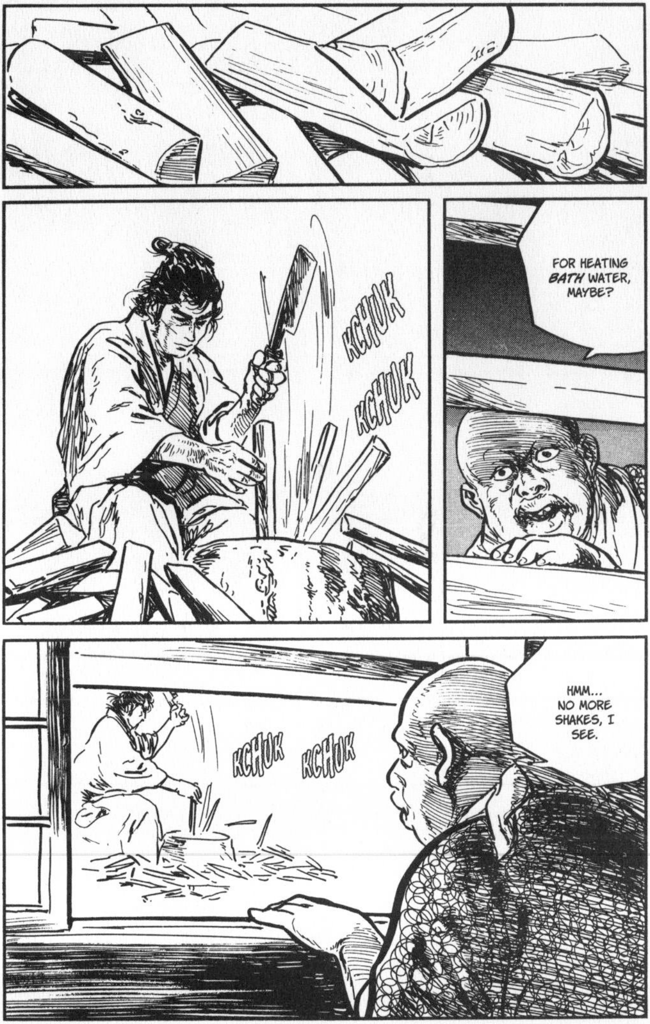
KCHUK
KCHUK
FOR HEATING BATH WATER, MAYBE?
KCHUK
KCHUK
HMM... NO MORE SHAKES, I SEE.

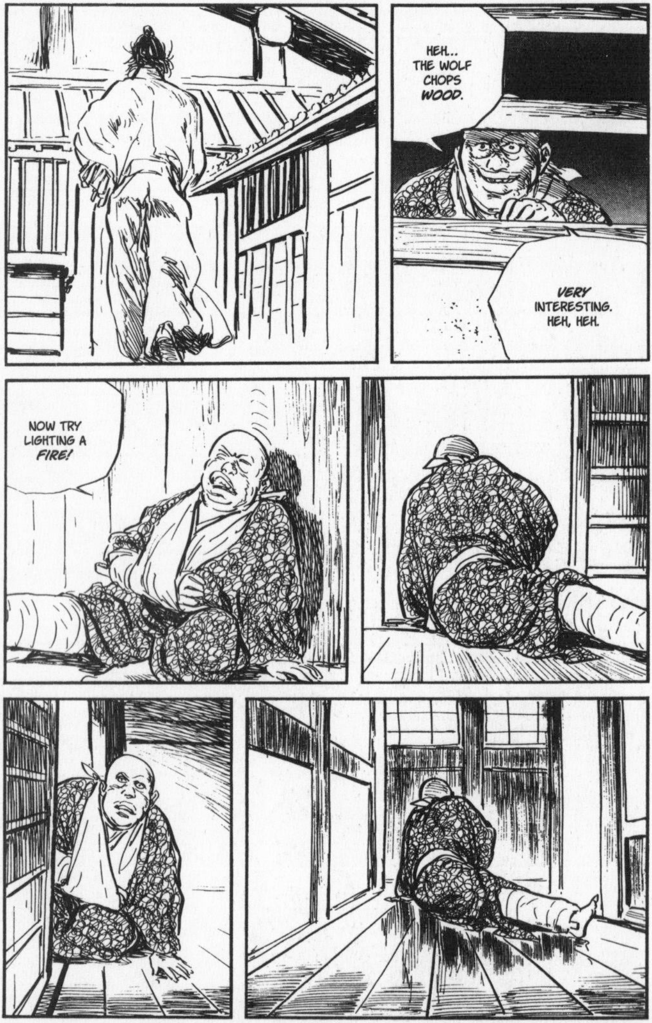
HEH.. THE WOLF CHOPS WOOD.
VERY INTERESTING. HEH, HEH.
NOW TRY LIGHTING A FIRE!

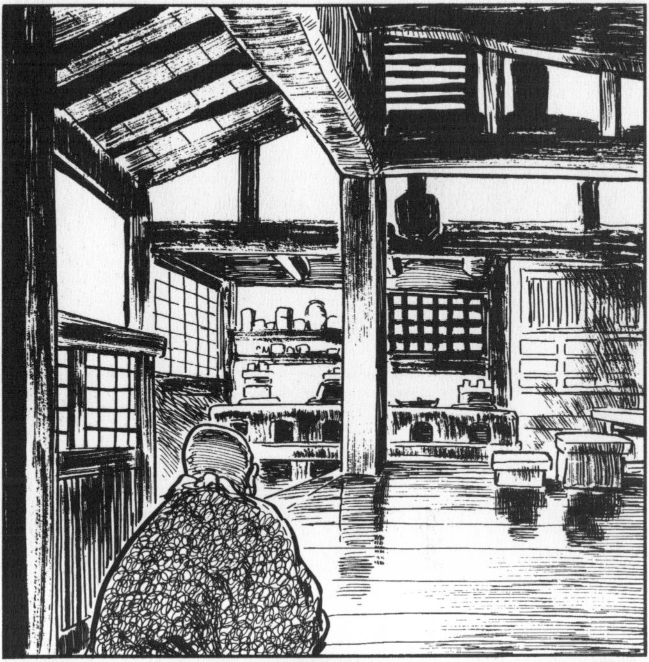

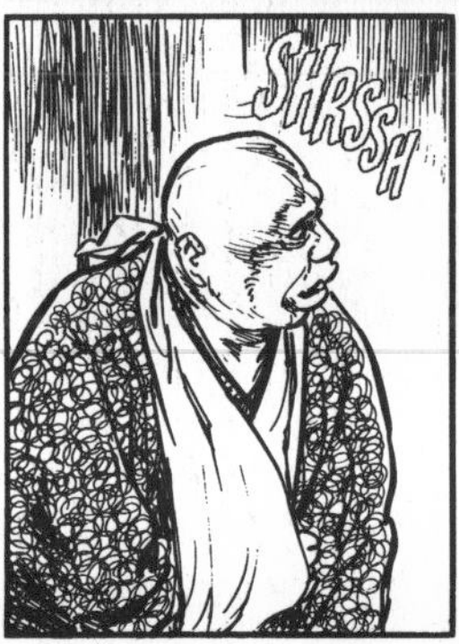
SHRSSH

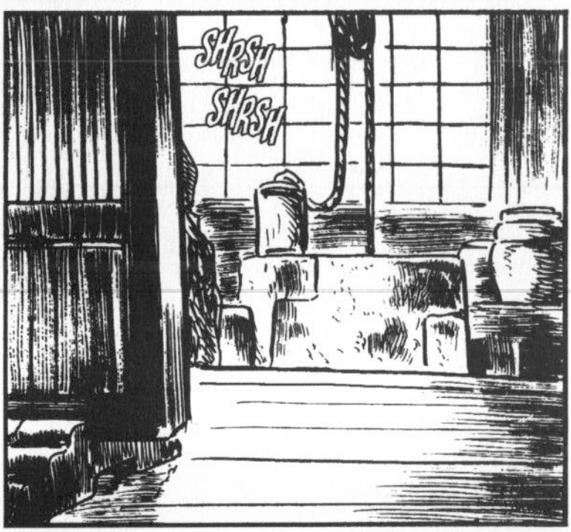
SHRSH
SHRSH

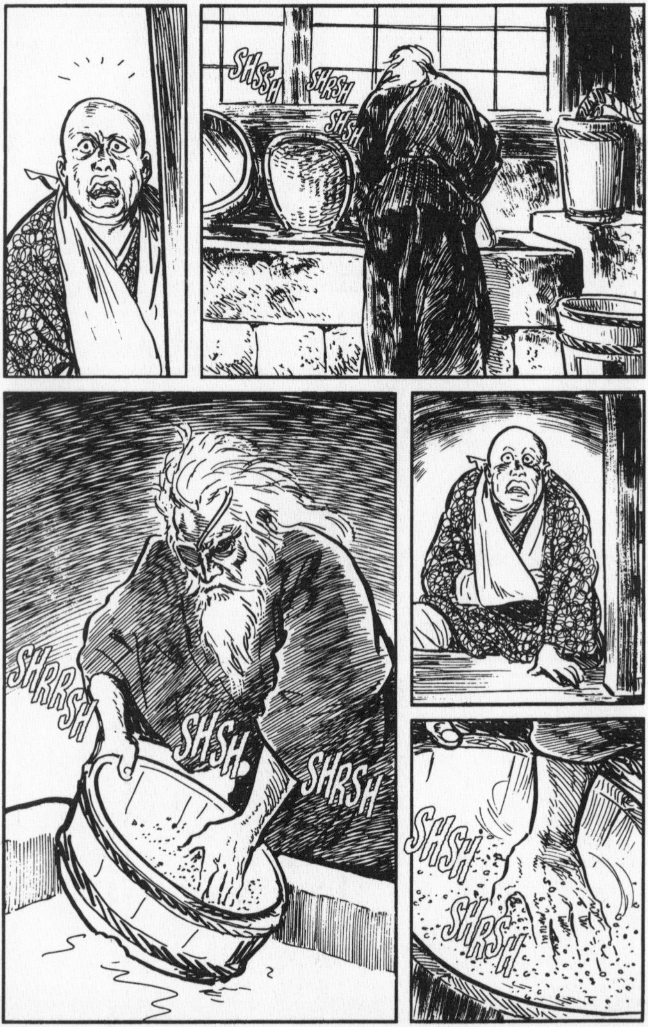
SHSSH
SHRSH
SHSH
SHRRSH
SHSH
SHRSH
SHSH
SHRSH

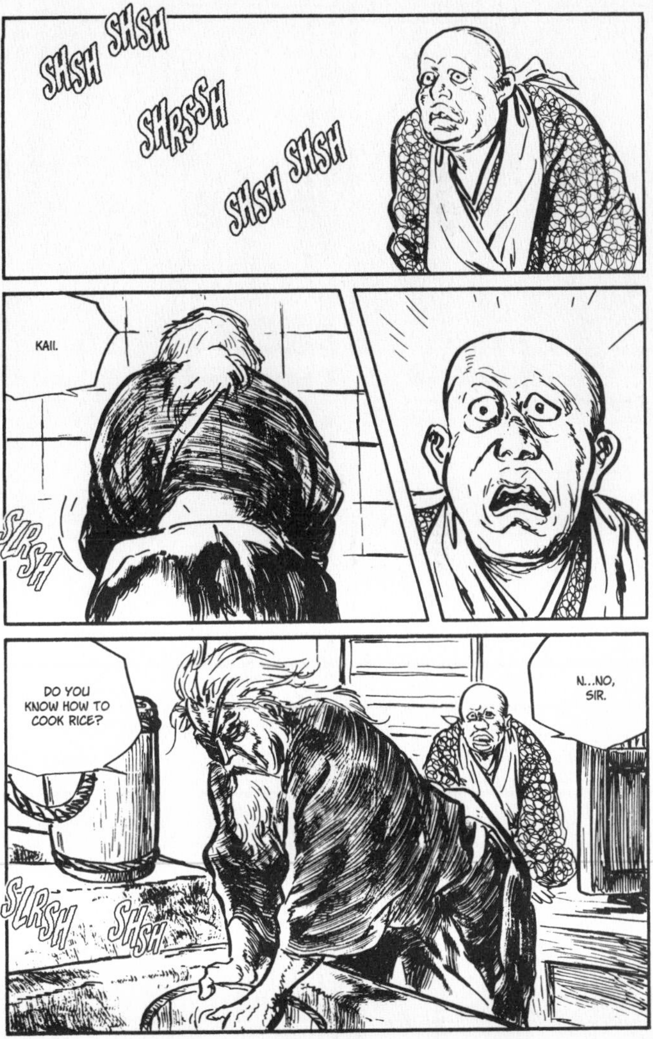
SHSH SHSH
SHRSSH
SHSH SHSH
KAII.
SLRSH
DO YOU KNOW HOW TO COOK RICE?
N...NO, SIR.
SLRSH SHSH

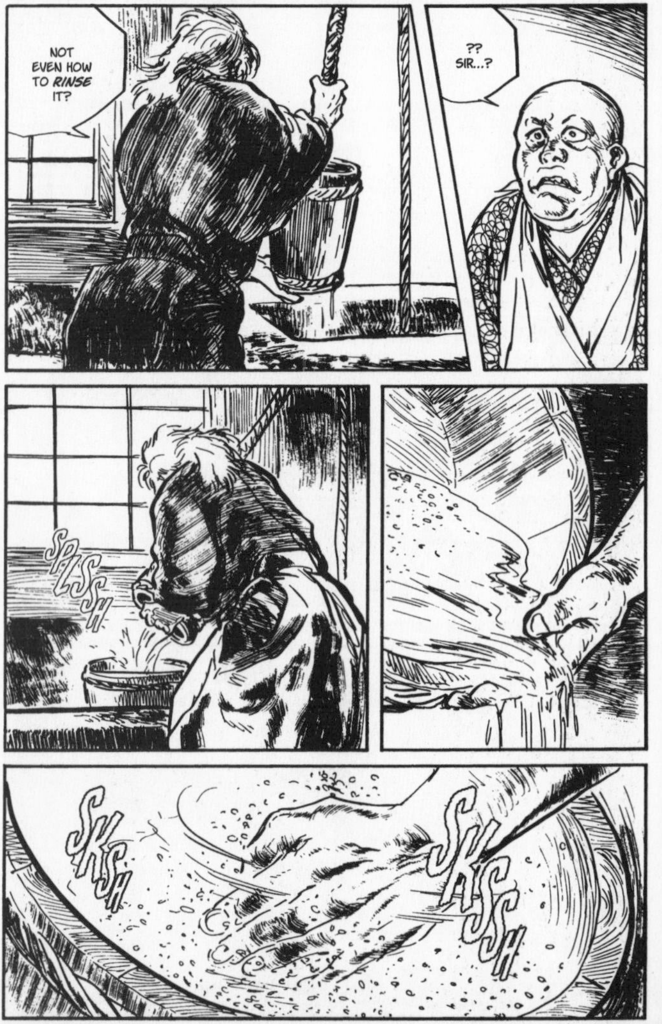
NOT EVEN HOW TO *RINSE* IT?
?? SIR...?
SPLSSH
SKSH
SKSSH

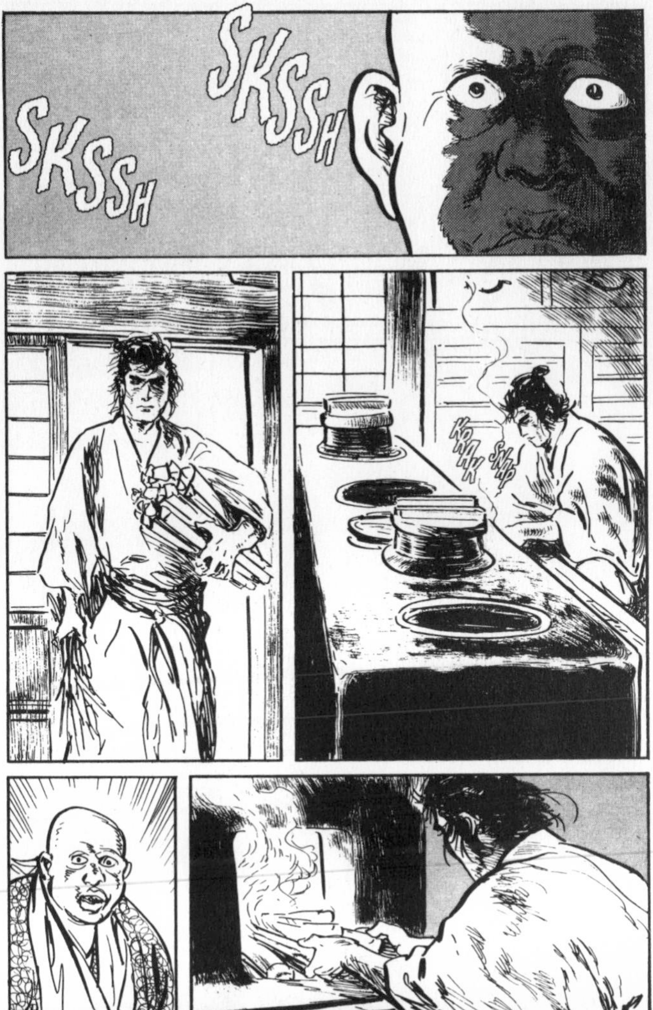
SKSSH
SKSSH
KRAK
SNAP

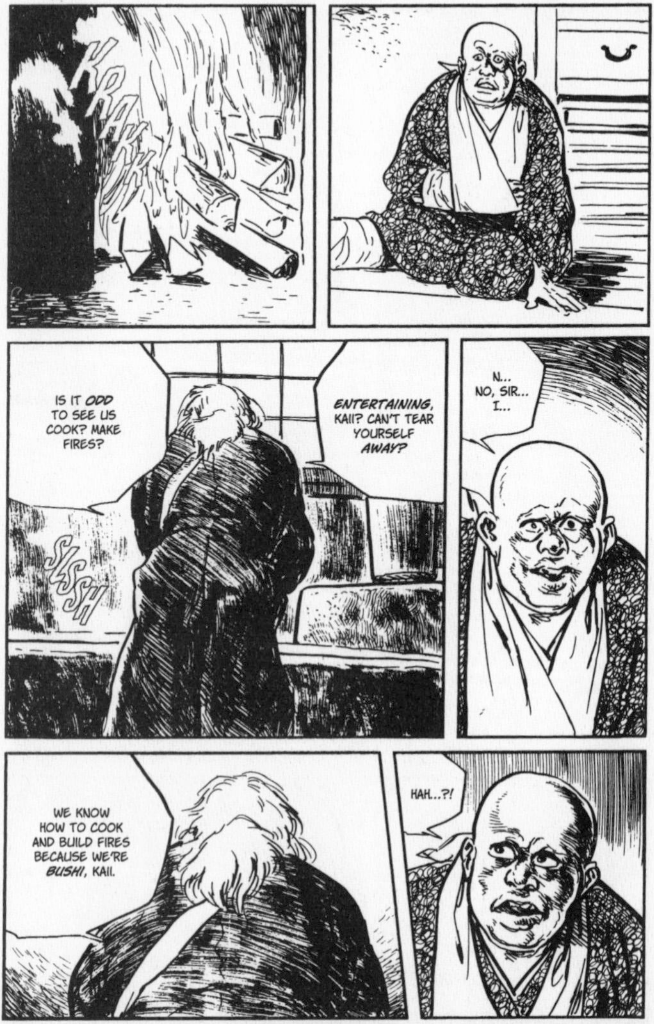
KRAKK
IS IT ODD TO SEE US COOK? MAKE FIRES?
ENTERTAINING, KAII? CAN'T TEAR YOURSELF AWAY?
SISSH
N... NO, SIR... I...
WE KNOW HOW TO COOK AND BUILD FIRES BECAUSE WE'RE BUSHI, KAII.
HAH...?!

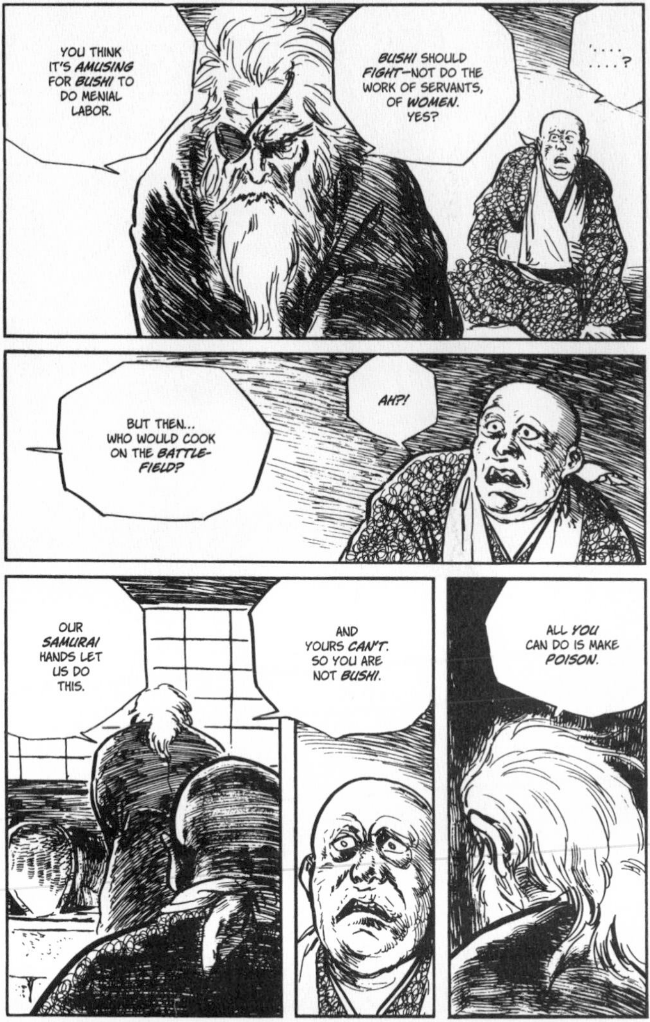
YOU THINK IT'S AMUSING FOR BUSHI TO DO MENIAL LABOR.
BUSHI SHOULD FIGHT—NOT DO THE WORK OF SERVANTS, OF WOMEN. YES?
'. . . . . . . . ?
BUT THEN... WHO WOULD COOK ON THE BATTLE-FIELD?
AH?!
OUR SAMURAI HANDS LET US DO THIS.
AND YOURS CAN'T. SO YOU ARE NOT BUSHI.
ALL YOU CAN DO IS MAKE POISON.

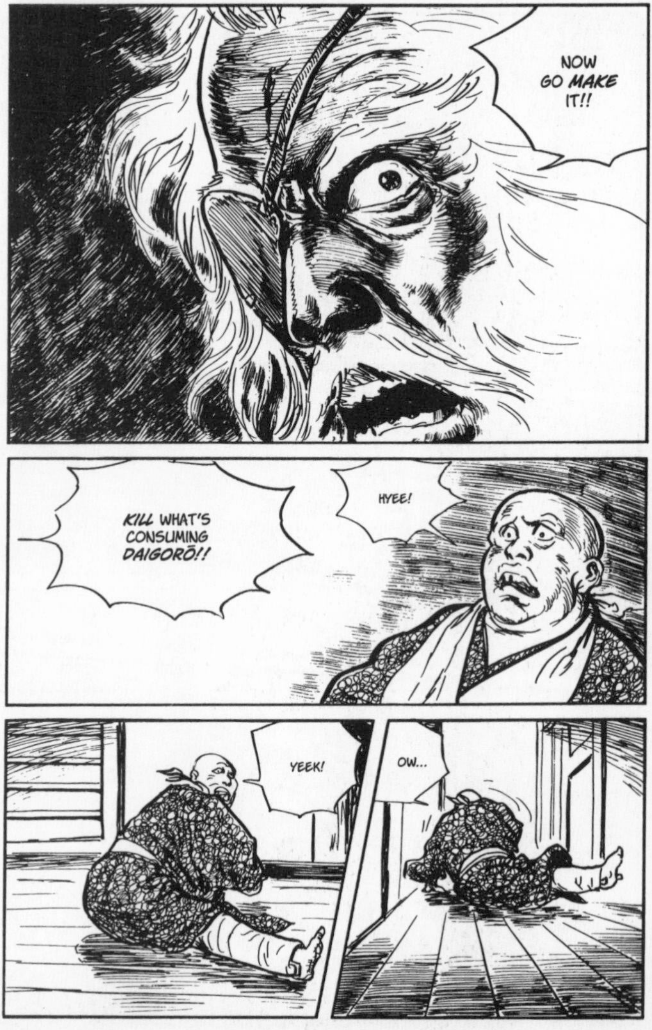
NOW GO MAKE IT!!
KILL WHAT'S CONSUMING DAIGORŌ!!
HYEE!
YEEK!
OW...

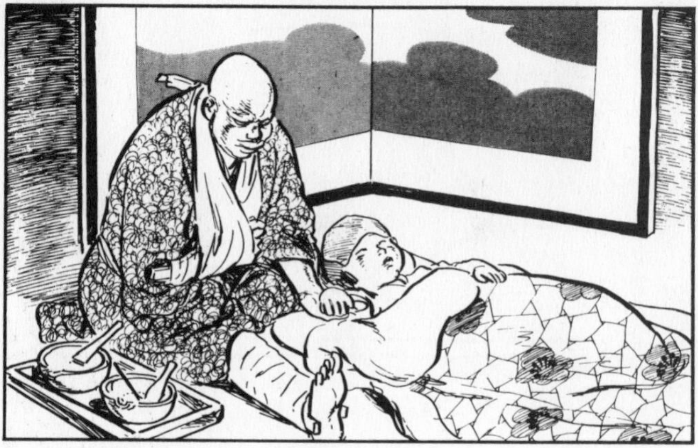

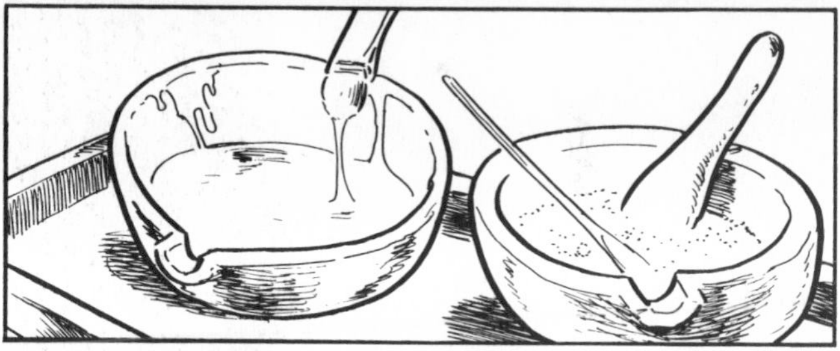

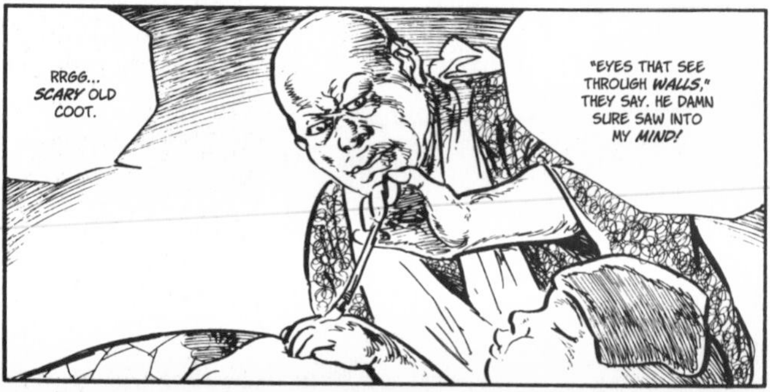
RRGG... SCARY OLD COOT.
"EYES THAT SEE THROUGH WALLS," THEY SAY. HE DAMN SURE SAW INTO MY MIND!

 IT'S *TRUE*. I *CAN'T* BUILD A DECENT FIRE.

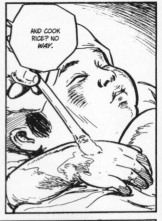 AND COOK RICE? NO *WAY*.

 *WAIT* A MINUTE! THEN...THEN THE *SHŌGUN* AND *DAIMYŌ* AREN'T TRUE *BUSHI*, EITHER!

*THEY* CAN'T COOK!

THE *SHŌGUN* AND *DAIMYŌ* COOK RICE...? *NONSENSE!*

I'VE *GOT* IT! RETSUDŌ AND ITTŌ ARE *BUSHI* WHO *SERVE!* NOT *RULE!*

THEY'VE GOT A *RETAINER* MIND. SERVANTS!

I JUST HAVE TO BE... A *RULING BUSHI!*

IN WHICH CASE...

...I'M JUST NOT *THEIR* KIND OF *BUSHI.*

97

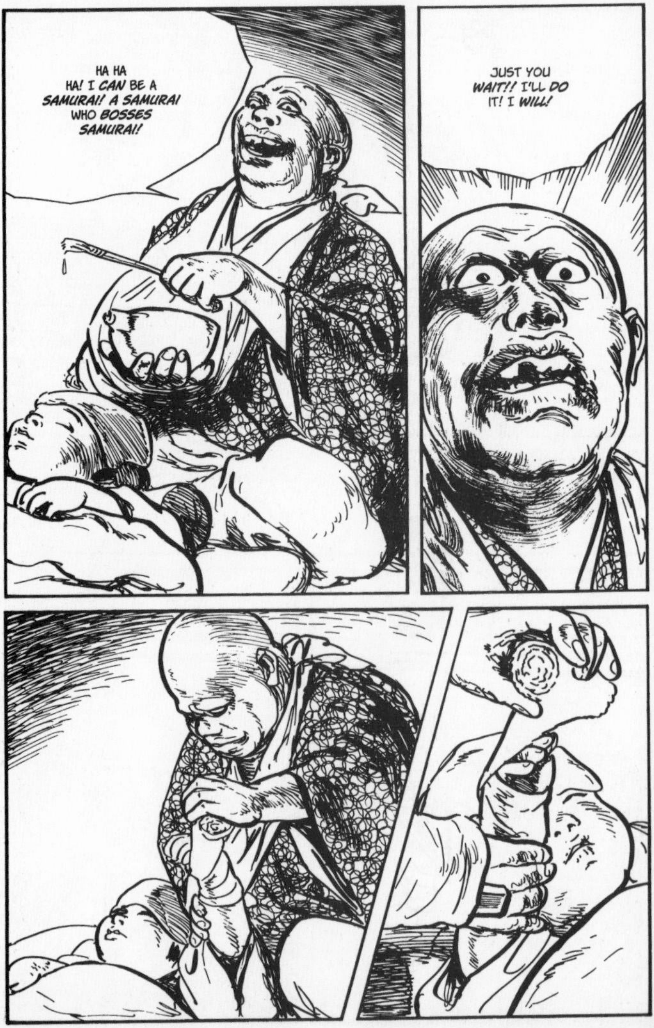

HA HA
HA! I CAN BE A
SAMURAI! A SAMURAI
WHO BOSSES
SAMURAI!
JUST YOU
WAIT!! I'LL DO
IT! I WILL!

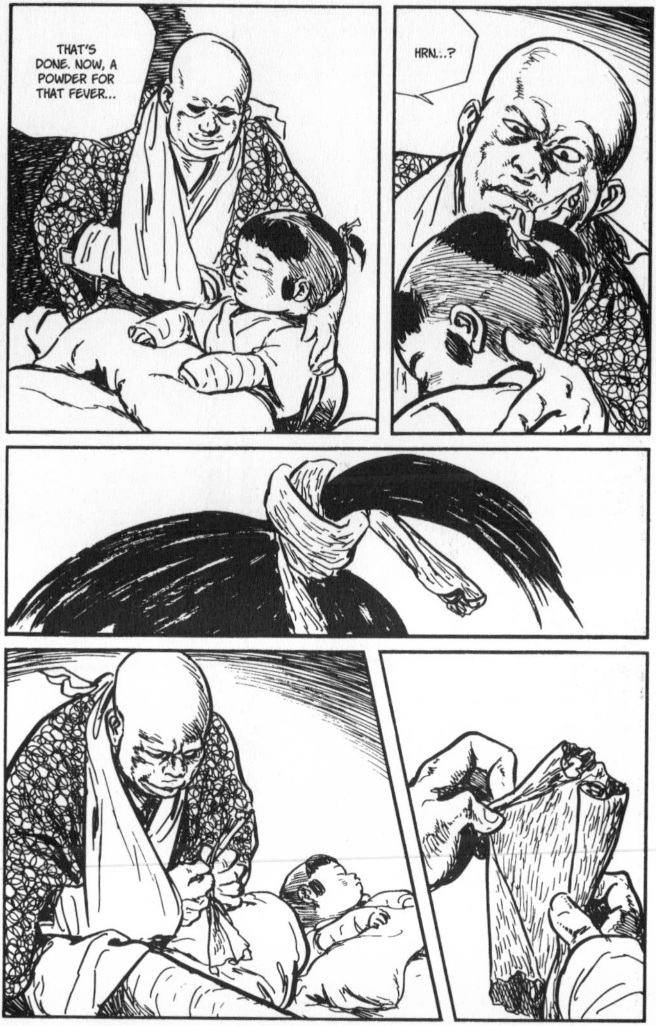
THAT'S DONE. NOW, A POWDER FOR THAT FEVER...
HRN...?

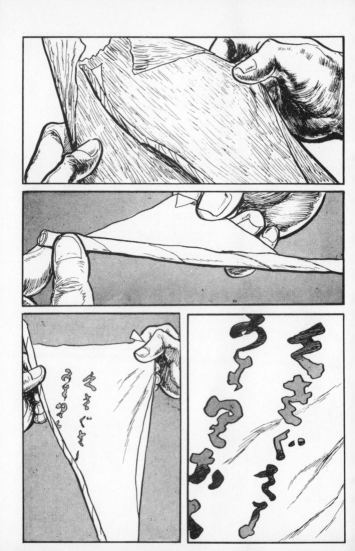

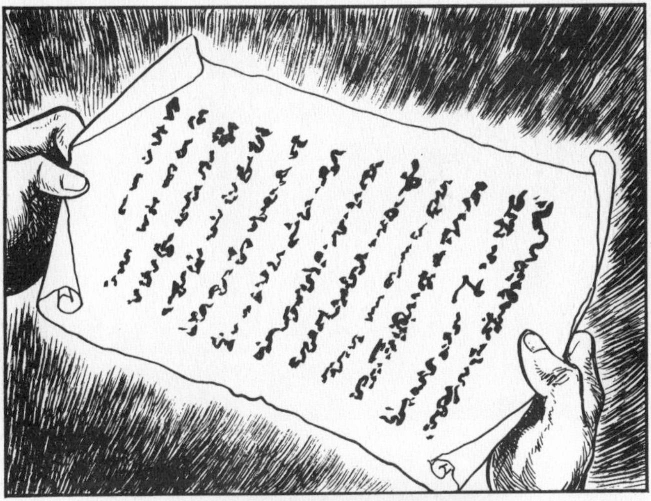

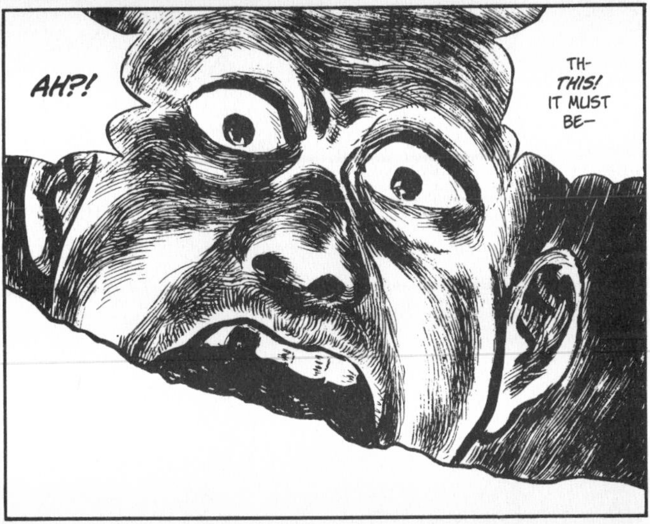
AH?!
TH- THIS! IT MUST BE—

—THE *YAGYŪ* LETTER!

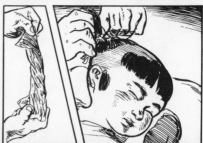

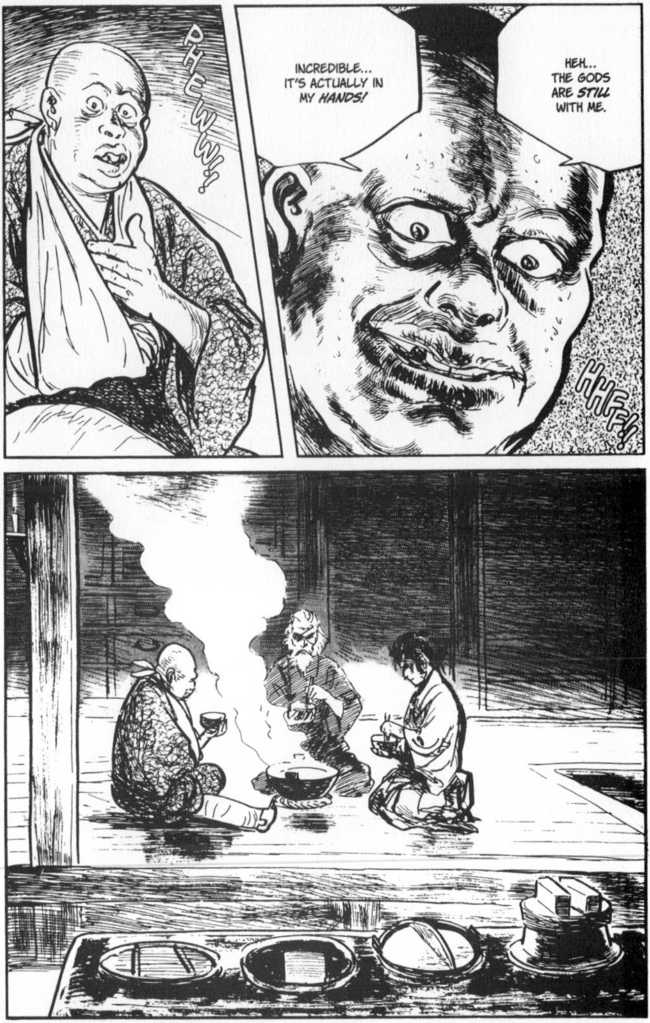
PHEWW!!
INCREDIBLE... IT'S ACTUALLY IN MY HANDS!
HEH... THE GODS ARE STILL WITH ME.
HHFF!!

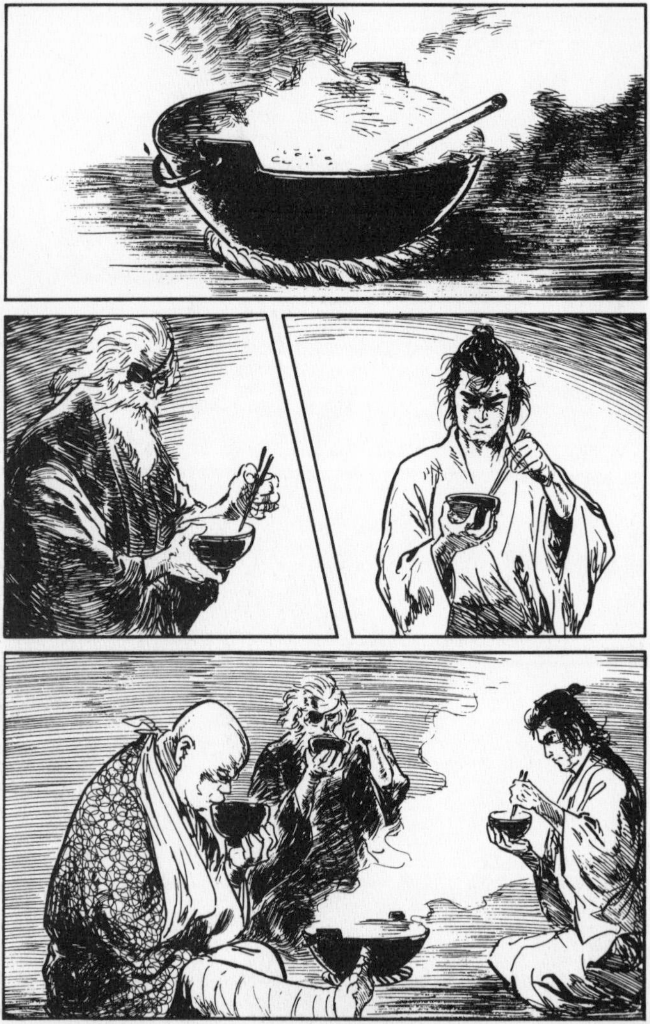

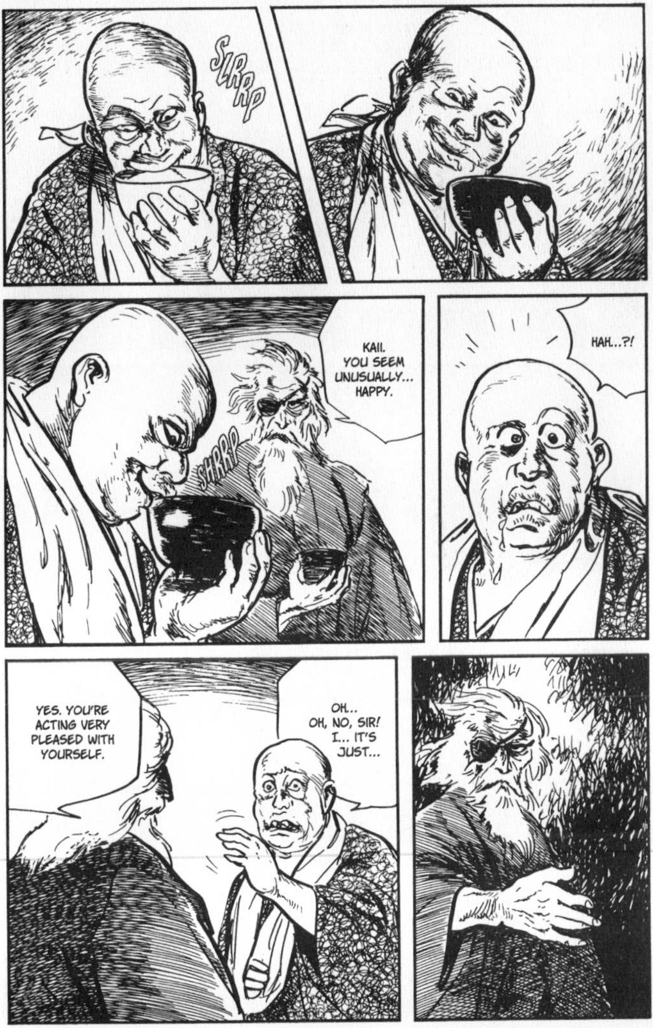
SLRRP
KAII.
YOU SEEM
UNUSUALLY...
HAPPY.
SHRRP
HAH...?!
YES. YOU'RE
ACTING VERY
PLEASED WITH
YOURSELF.
OH...
OH, NO, SIR!
I... IT'S
JUST...

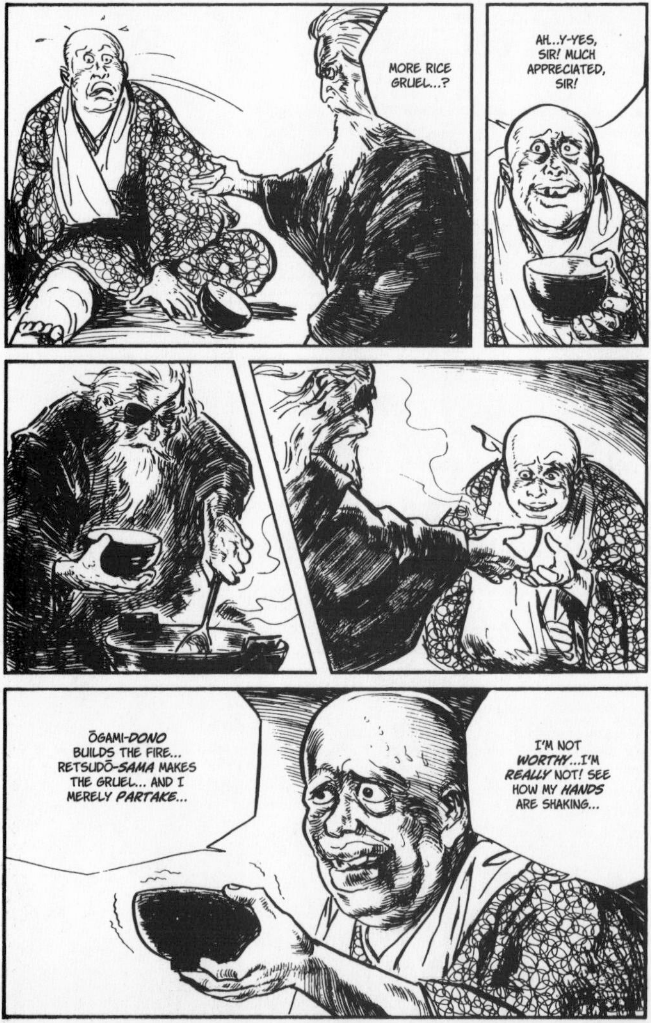
MORE RICE GRUEL...?
AH...Y-YES, SIR! MUCH APPRECIATED, SIR!
ŌGAMI-*DONO* BUILDS THE FIRE... RETSUDŌ-*SAMA* MAKES THE GRUEL... AND I MERELY *PARTAKE*...
I'M NOT *WORTHY*...I'M *REALLY* NOT! SEE HOW MY *HANDS* ARE SHAKING...

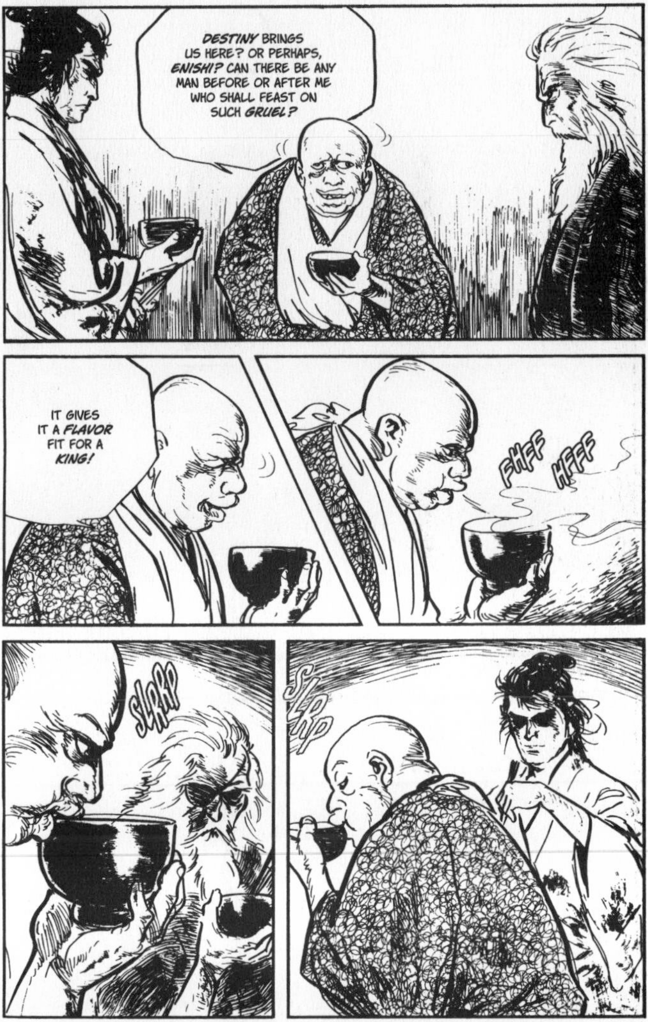
DESTINY BRINGS US HERE? OR PERHAPS, ENISHI? CAN THERE BE ANY MAN BEFORE OR AFTER ME WHO SHALL FEAST ON SUCH GRUEL?
IT GIVES IT A FLAVOR FIT FOR A KING!
FHFF
HFFF
SLRRP
SLRRP

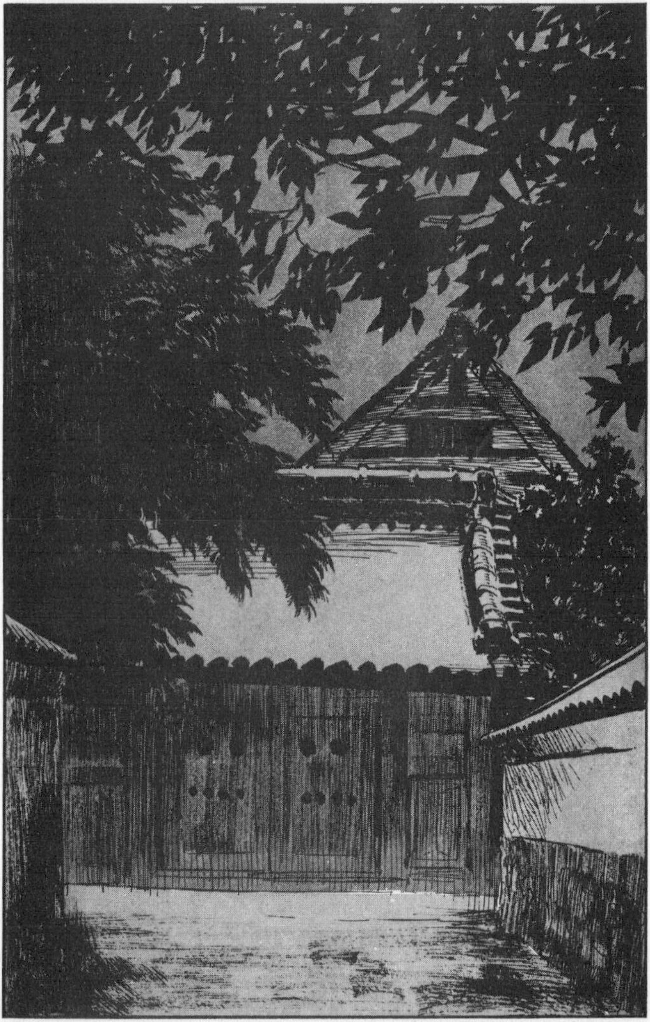

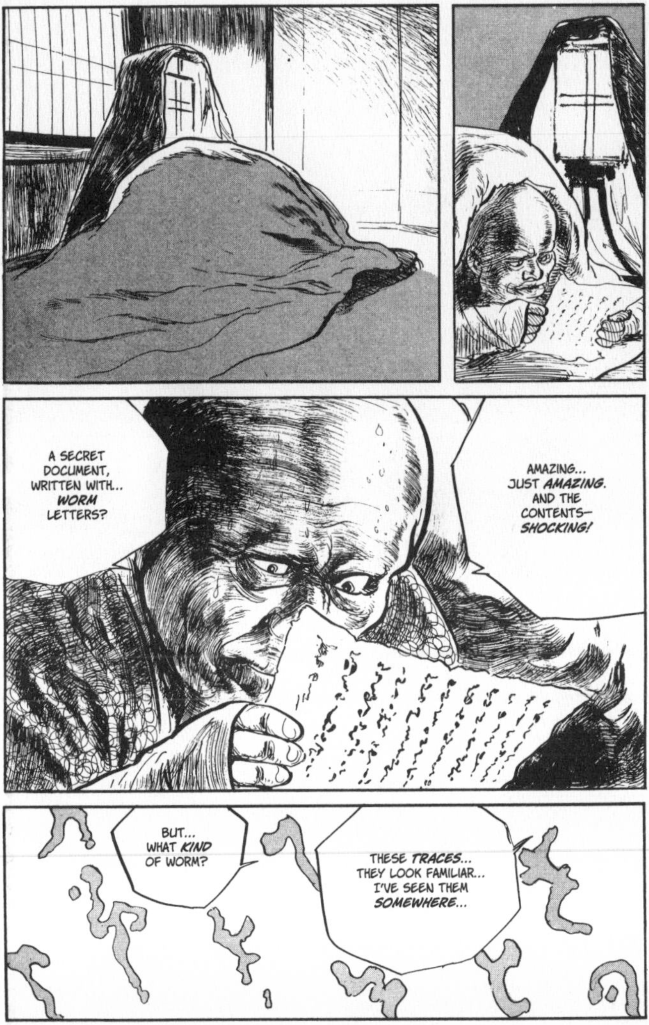
A SECRET DOCUMENT, WRITTEN WITH... WORM LETTERS?
AMAZING... JUST AMAZING. AND THE CONTENTS— SHOCKING!
BUT... WHAT KIND OF WORM?
THESE TRACES... THEY LOOK FAMILIAR... I'VE SEEN THEM SOMEWHERE...

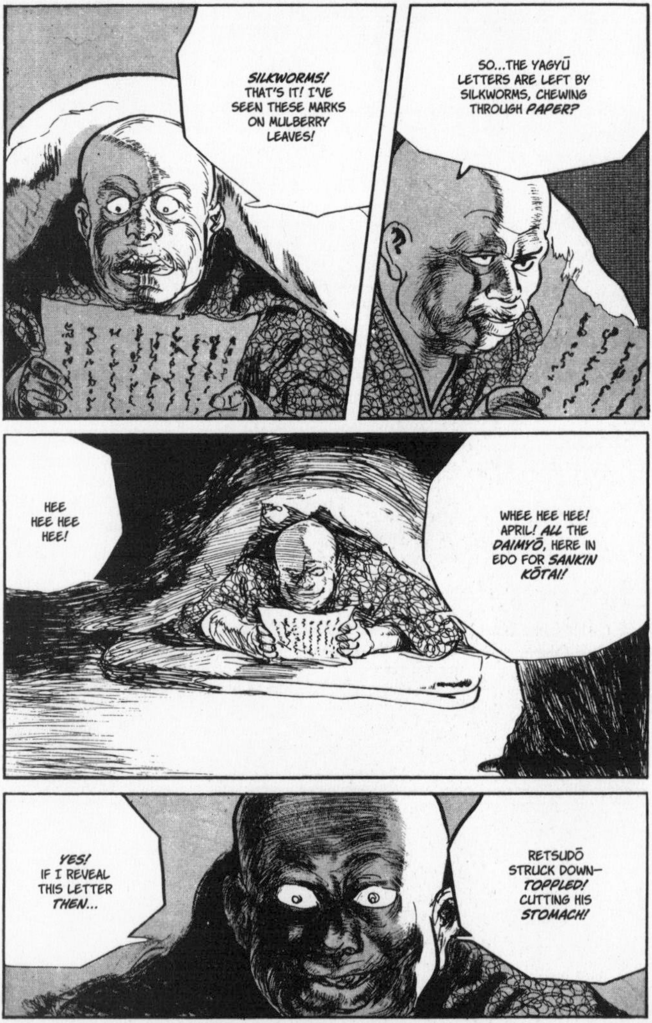
SILKWORMS! THAT'S IT! I'VE SEEN THESE MARKS ON MULBERRY LEAVES!
SO...THE YAGYŪ LETTERS ARE LEFT BY SILKWORMS, CHEWING THROUGH PAPER?
HEE HEE HEE HEE!
WHEE HEE HEE! APRIL! ALL THE DAIMYŌ, HERE IN EDO FOR SANKIN KŌTAI!
YES! IF I REVEAL THIS LETTER THEN...
RETSUDŌ STRUCK DOWN—TOPPLED! CUTTING HIS STOMACH!

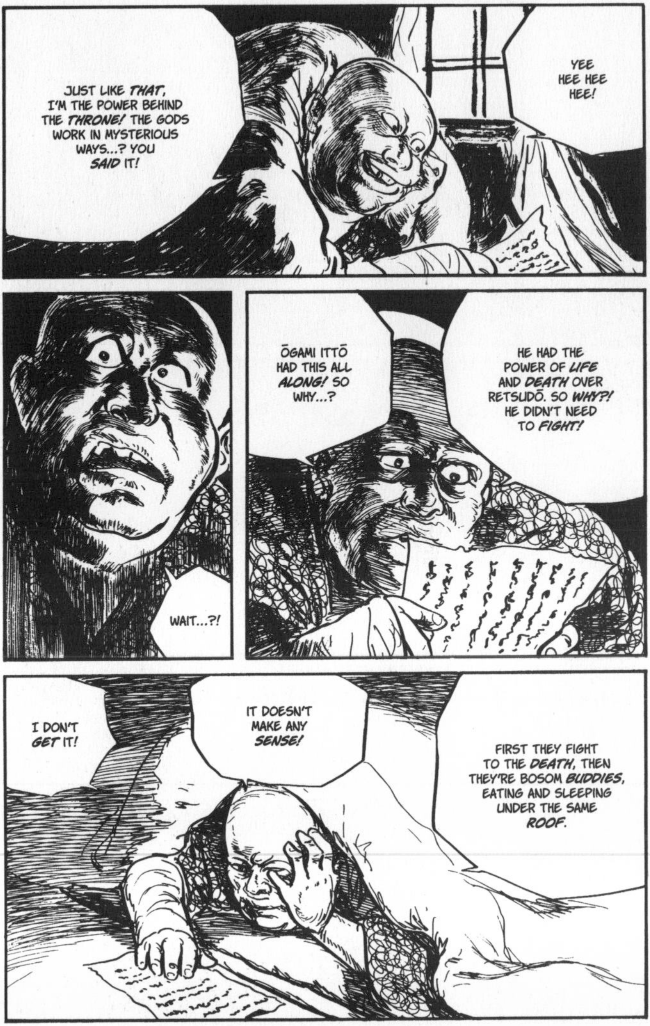
JUST LIKE THAT, I'M THE POWER BEHIND THE THRONE! THE GODS WORK IN MYSTERIOUS WAYS...? YOU SAID IT!
YEE HEE HEE HEE!
WAIT...?!
ŌGAMI ITTŌ HAD THIS ALL ALONG! SO WHY...?
HE HAD THE POWER OF LIFE AND DEATH OVER RETSUDŌ. SO WHY?! HE DIDN'T NEED TO FIGHT!
I DON'T GET IT!
IT DOESN'T MAKE ANY SENSE!
FIRST THEY FIGHT TO THE DEATH, THEN THEY'RE BOSOM BUDDIES, EATING AND SLEEPING UNDER THE SAME ROOF.

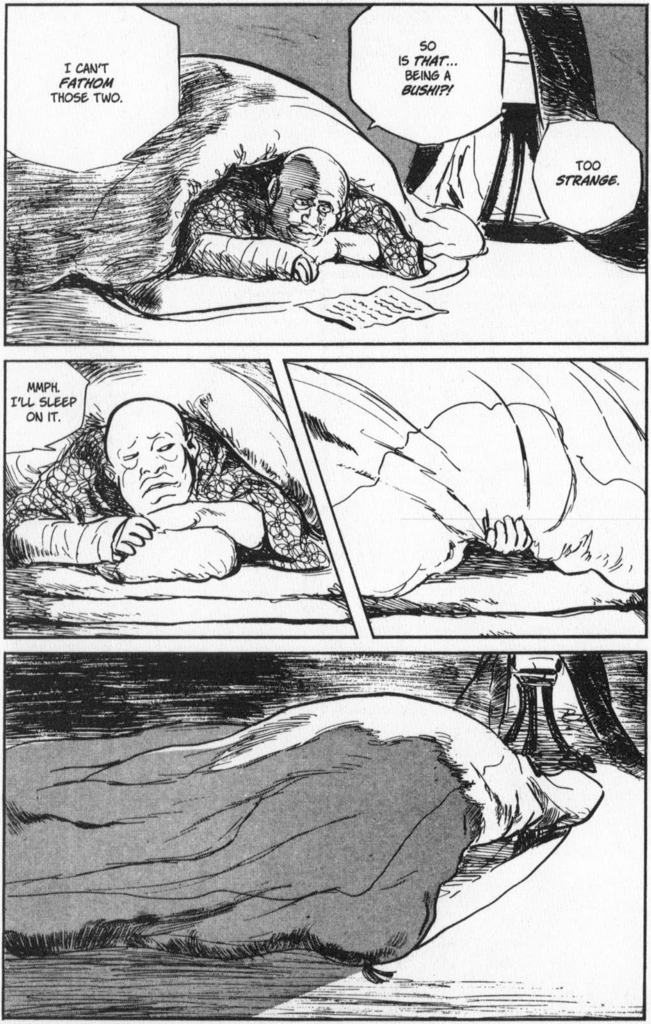
I CAN'T *FATHOM* THOSE TWO.
SO IS *THAT*... BEING A *BUSHI?!*
TOO *STRANGE.*
MMPH. I'LL SLEEP ON IT.

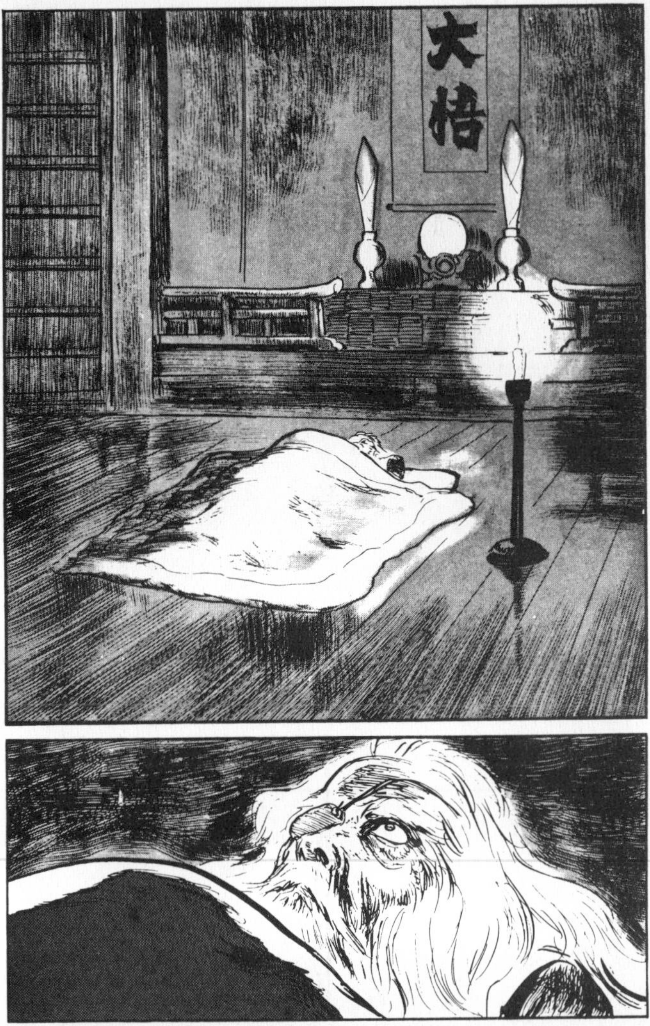
大悟

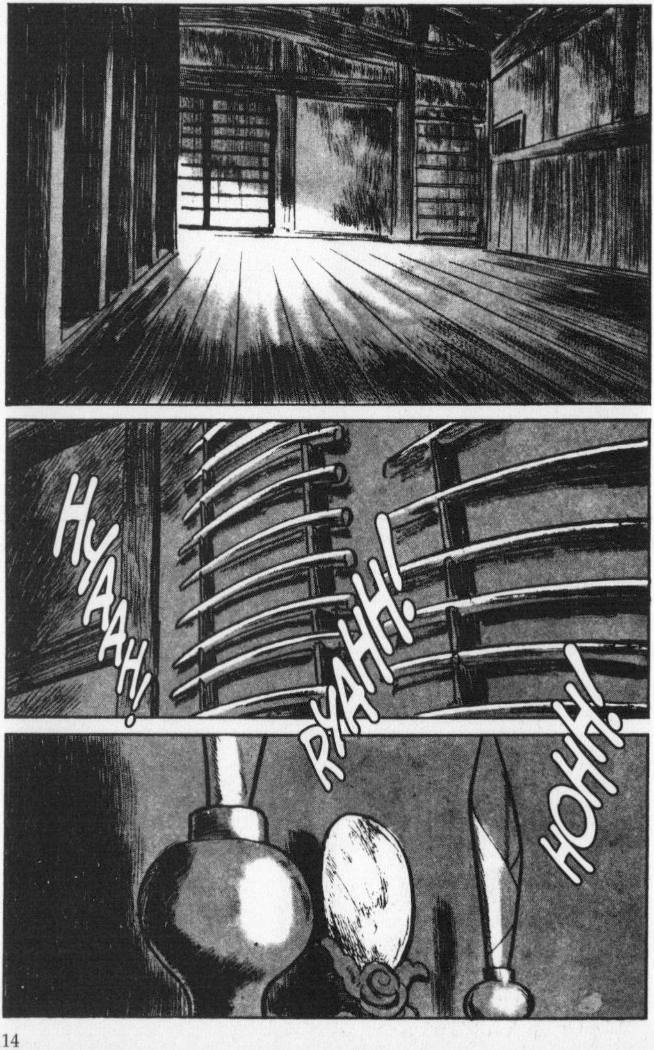
HYAAH!
RYAHH!
HOHH!

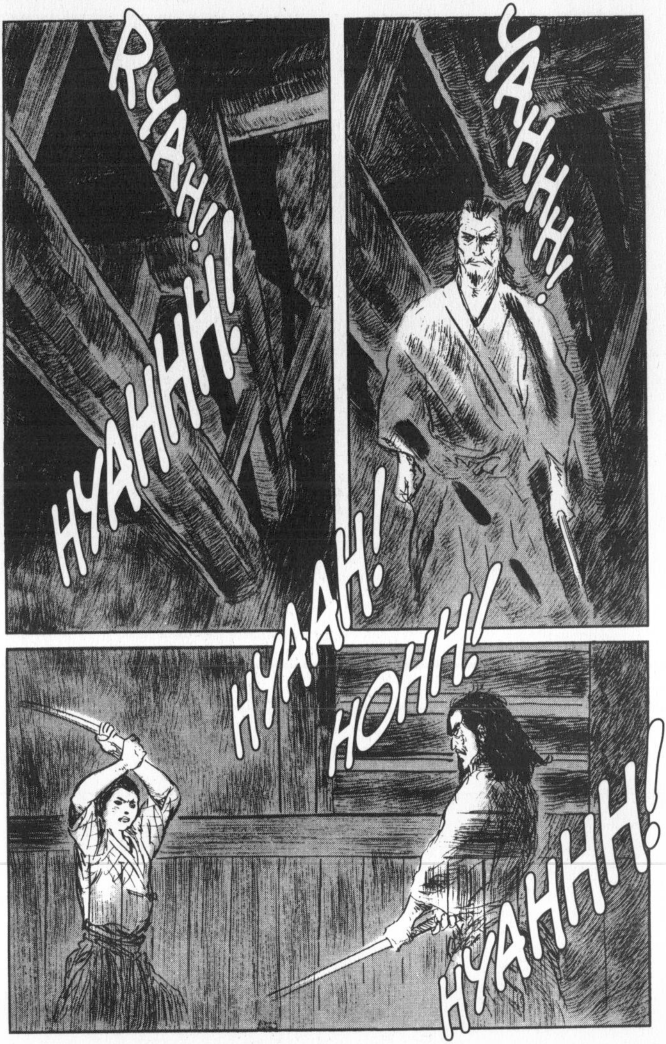
RYAH!!
HYAHHH!
YAHHH!
HYAAH!
HOHH!
HYAHHH!

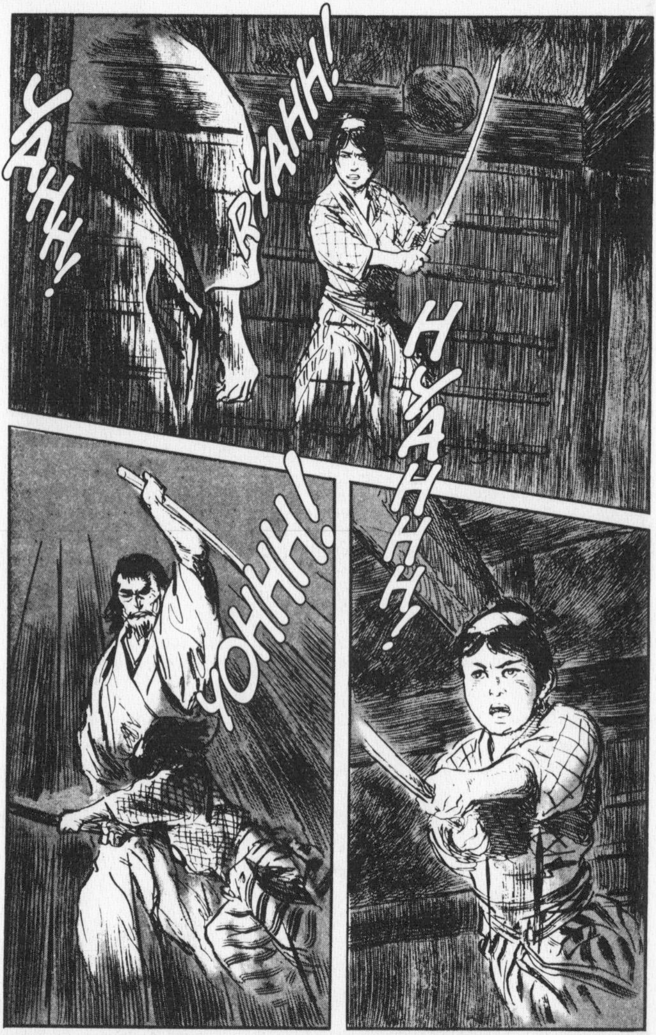
YAHH!
RYAHH!
HYAHHHH!
YOHHH!

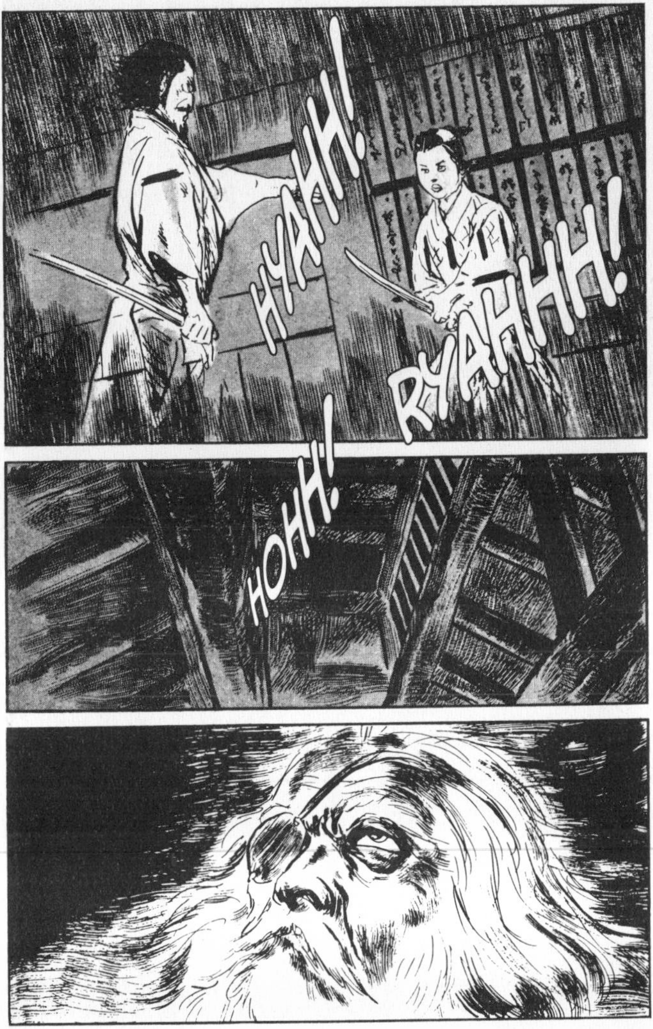
HYAHH!
RYAHHH!
HOHH!

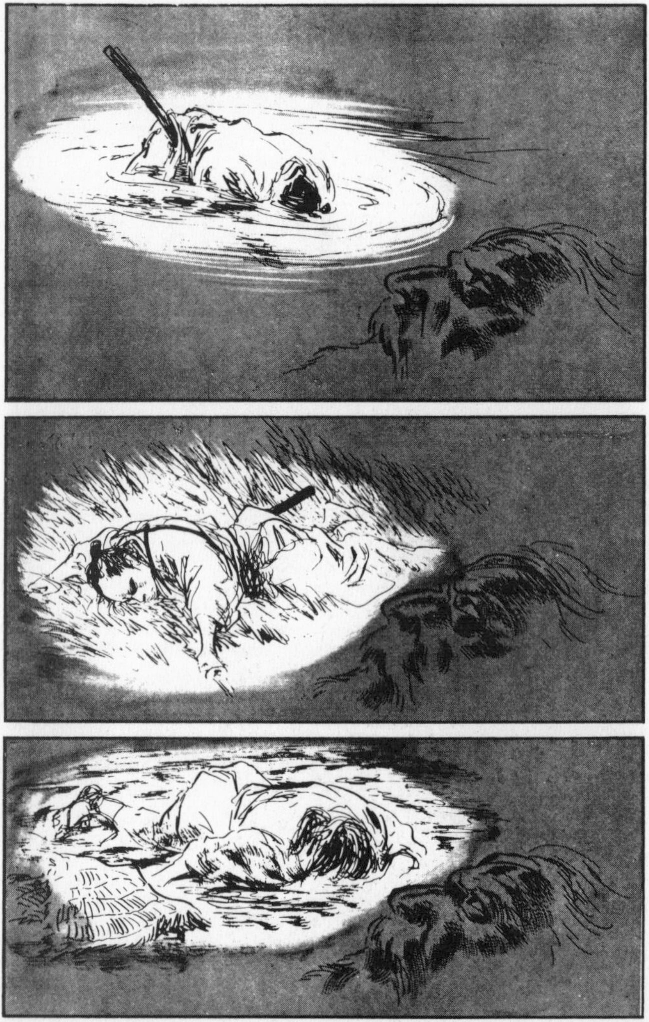

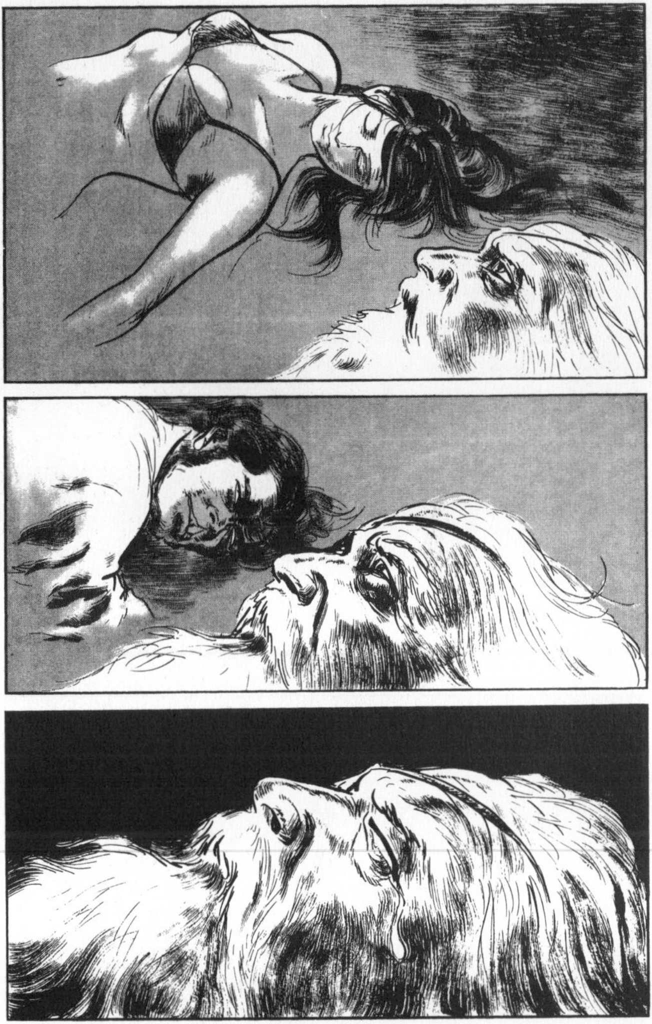

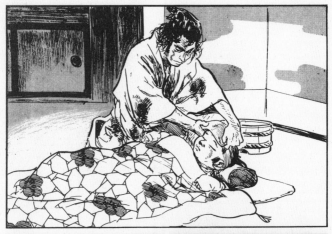

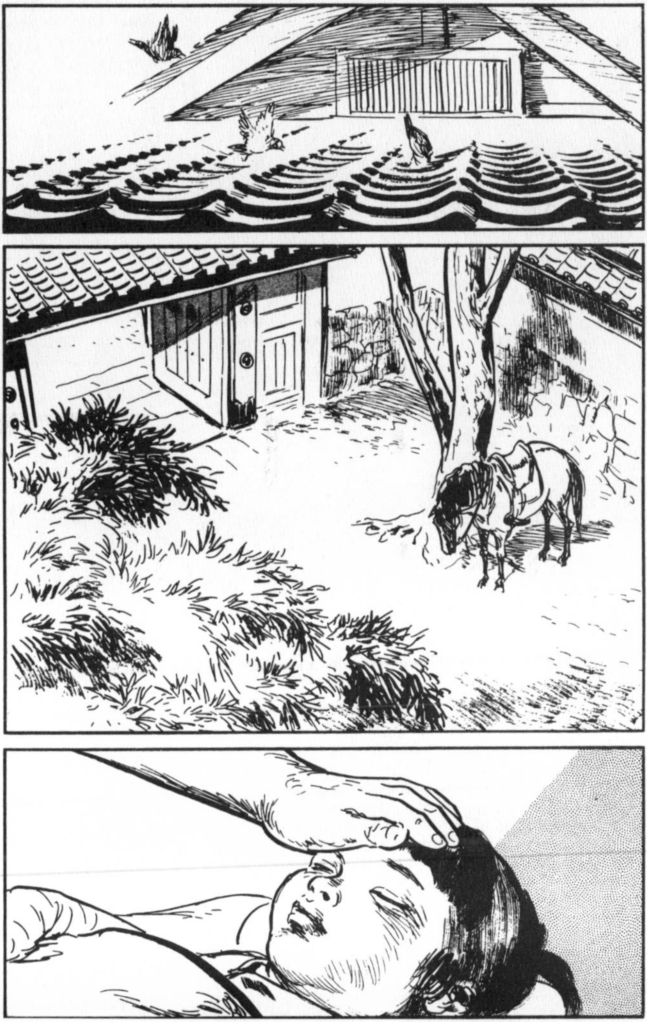

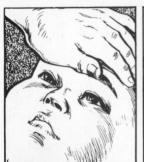

KRNCH

GYAHH!

OWW!
THAT
HURT!

DAIGORŌ...

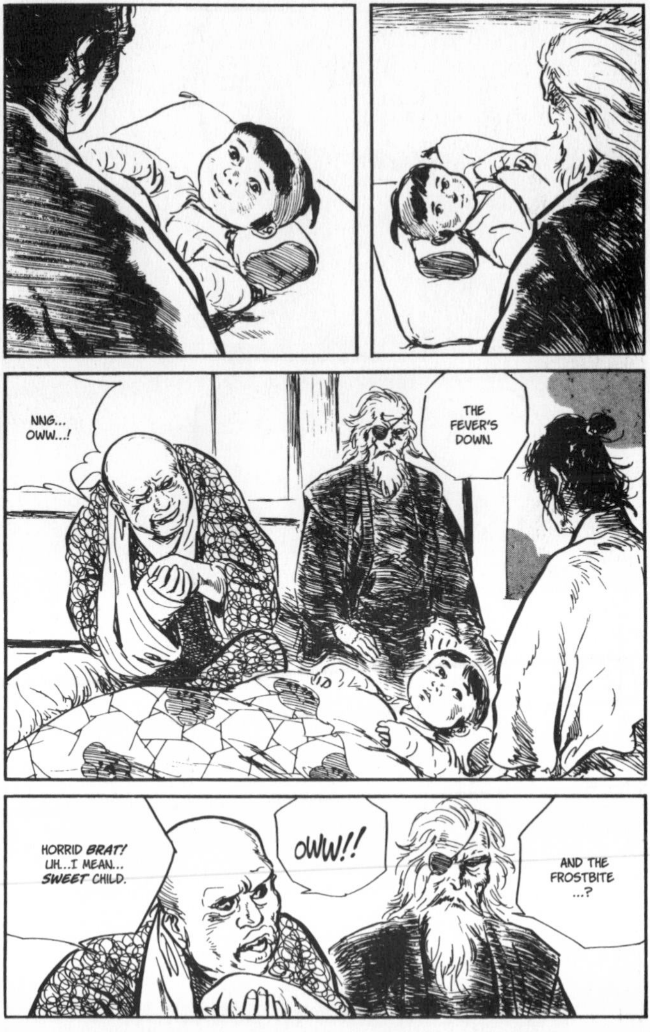
NNG... OWW...!
THE FEVER'S DOWN.
HORRID BRAT! UH...I MEAN... SWEET CHILD.
OWW!!
AND THE FROSTBITE ...?

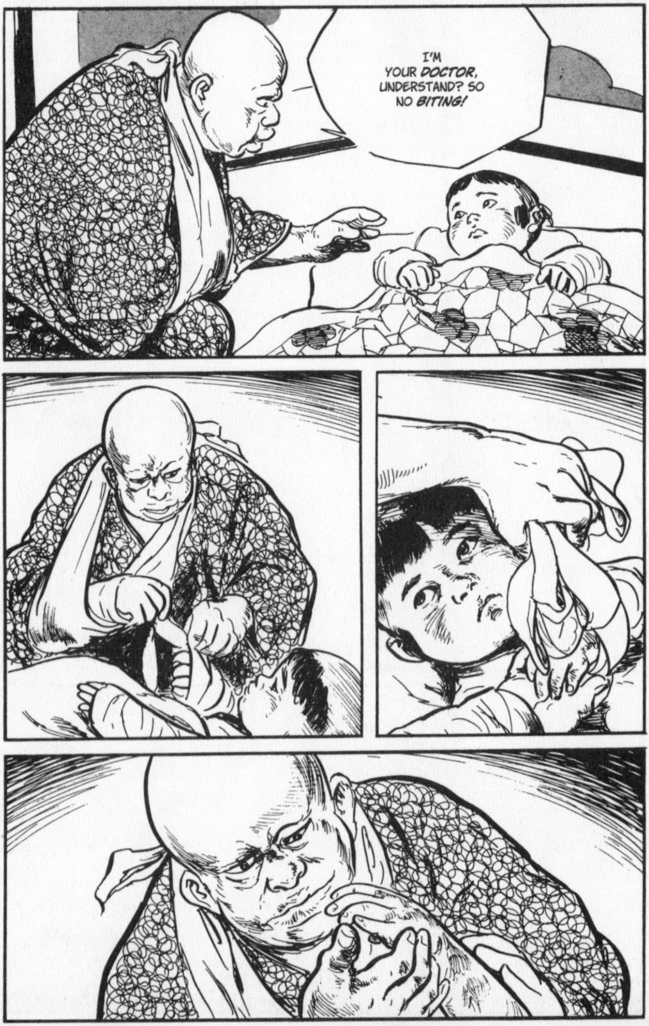
I'M YOUR *DOCTOR*, UNDERSTAND? SO NO *BITING!*

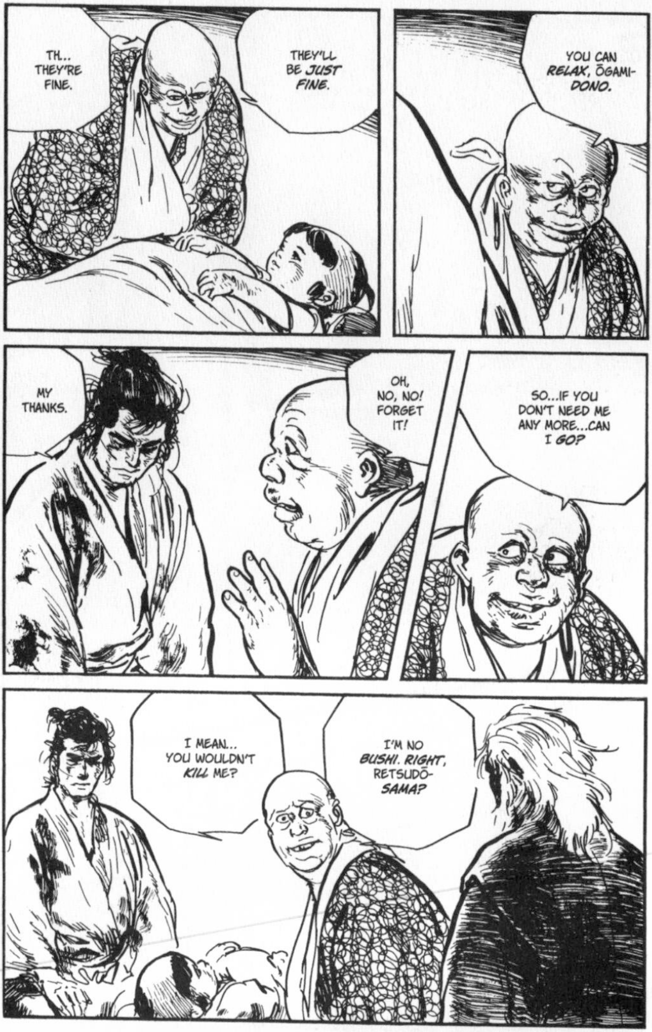
TH... THEY'RE FINE.
THEY'LL BE JUST FINE.
YOU CAN RELAX, ŌGAMI-DONO.
MY THANKS.
OH, NO, NO! FORGET IT!
SO...IF YOU DON'T NEED ME ANY MORE...CAN I GO?
I MEAN... YOU WOULDN'T KILL ME?
I'M NO BUSHI. RIGHT, RETSUDŌ-SAMA?

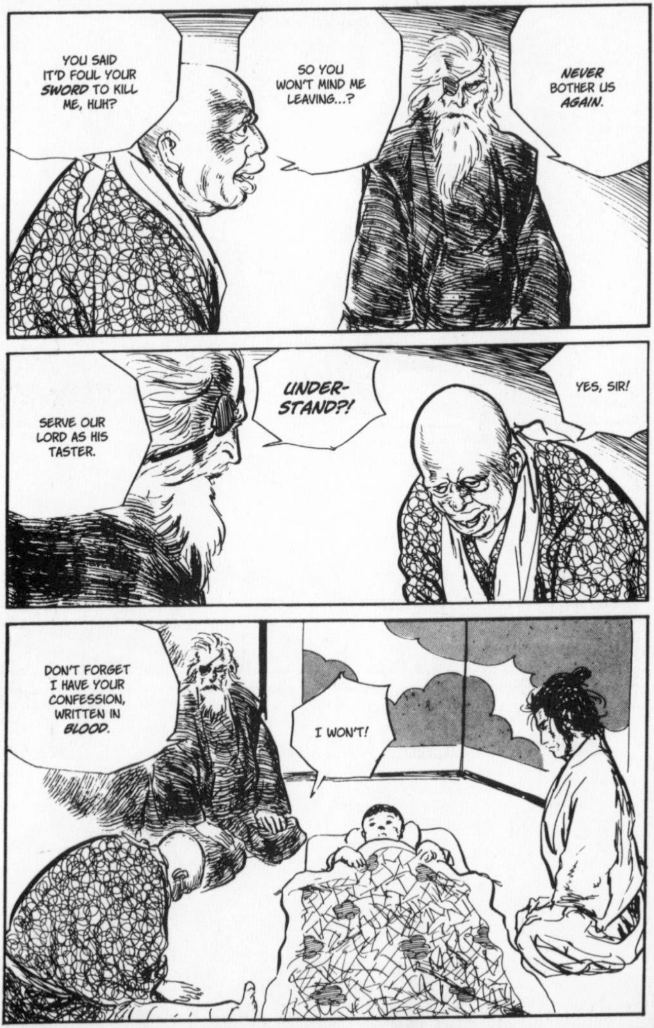
YOU SAID IT'D FOUL YOUR SWORD TO KILL ME, HUH?
SO YOU WON'T MIND ME LEAVING...?
NEVER BOTHER US AGAIN.
SERVE OUR LORD AS HIS TASTER.
UNDER-STAND?!
YES, SIR!
DON'T FORGET I HAVE YOUR CONFESSION, WRITTEN IN BLOOD.
I WON'T!

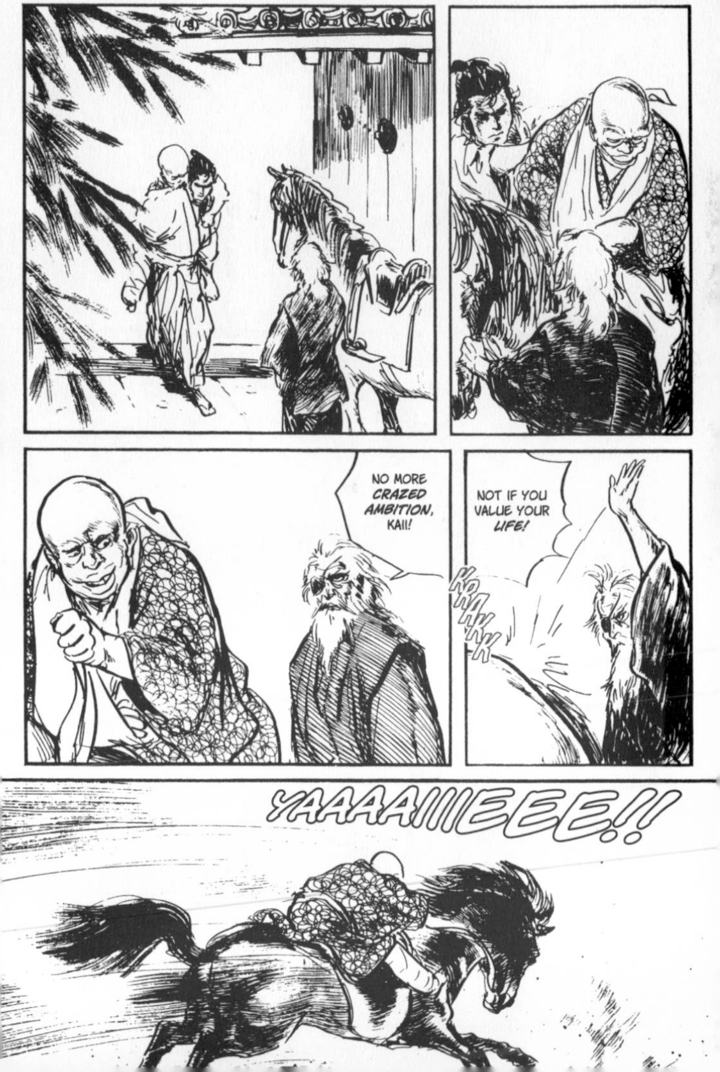
NO MORE CRAZED AMBITION, KAI!!
NOT IF YOU VALUE YOUR LIFE!
KRAKK
YAAAAIIIEEE!!

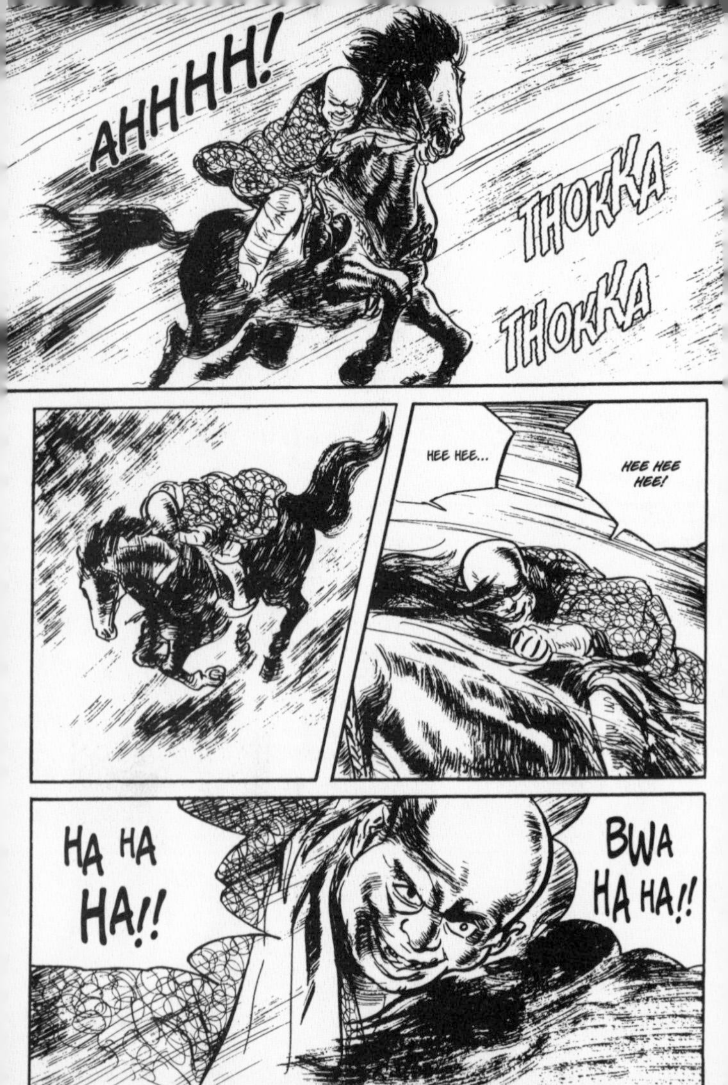
AHHHH!
THOKKA
THOKKA
HEE HEE...
HEE HEE HEE!
HA HA HA!!
BWA HA HA!!

the hundred and
nineteenth

Kaii

Triumphant

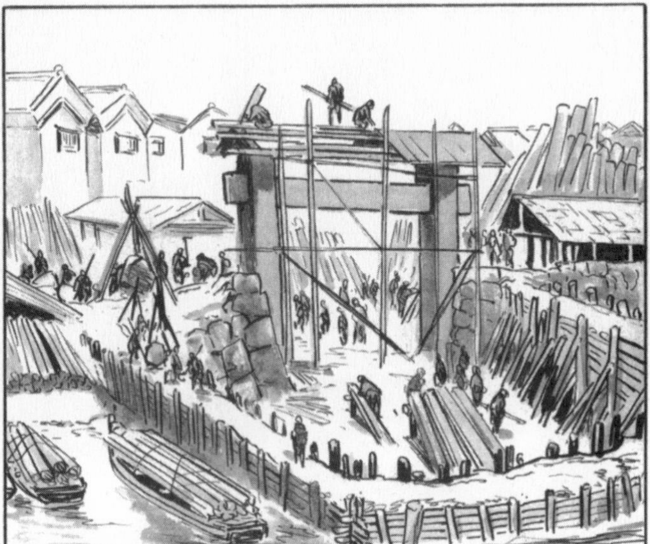

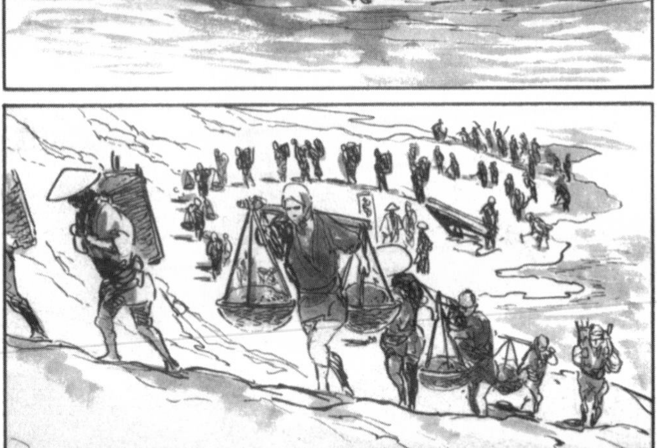

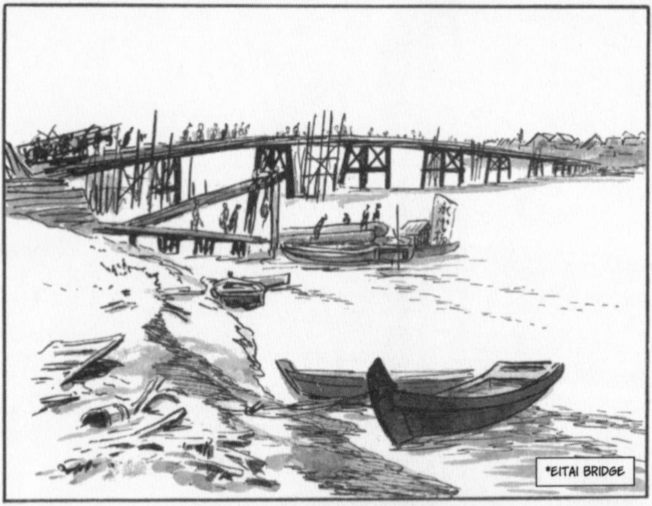
*EITAI BRIDGE

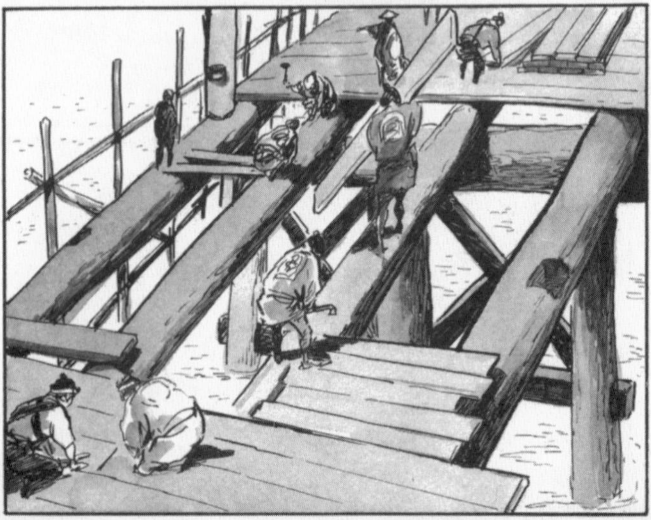

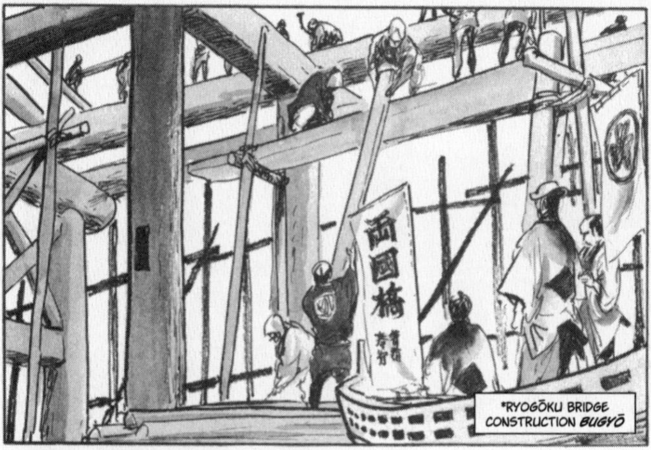
*RYOGŌKU BRIDGE
CONSTRUCTION *BUGYŌ*

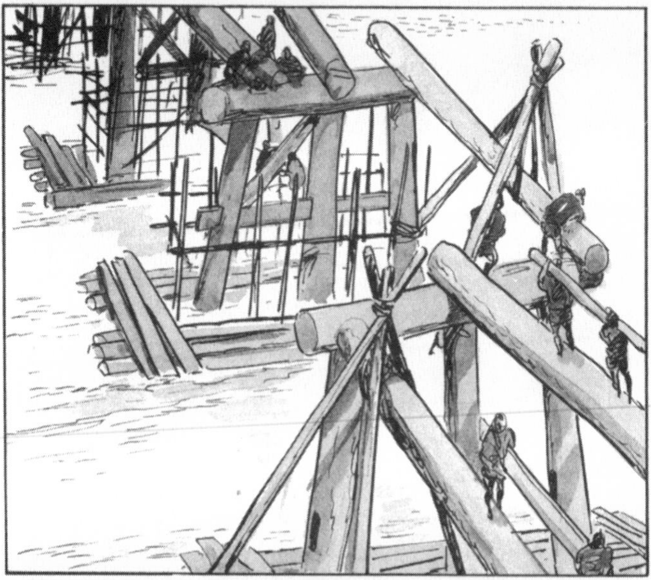

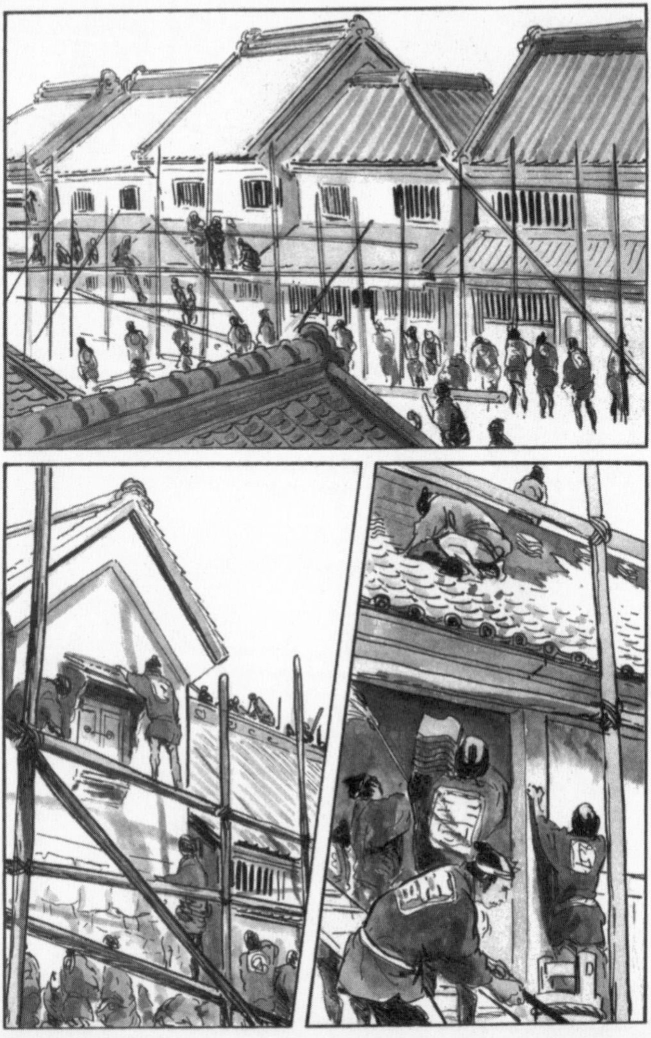

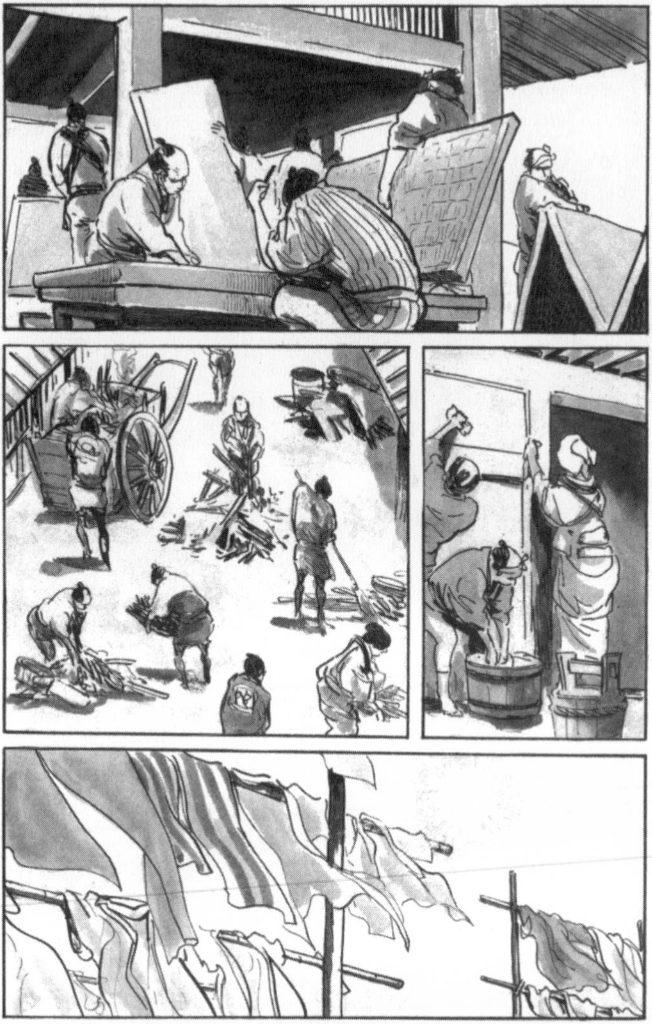

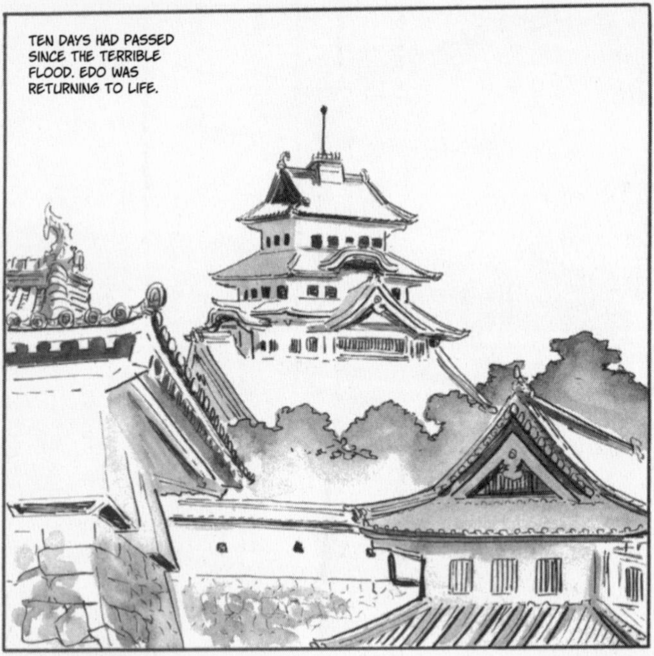
TEN DAYS HAD PASSED SINCE THE TERRIBLE FLOOD. EDO WAS RETURNING TO LIFE.
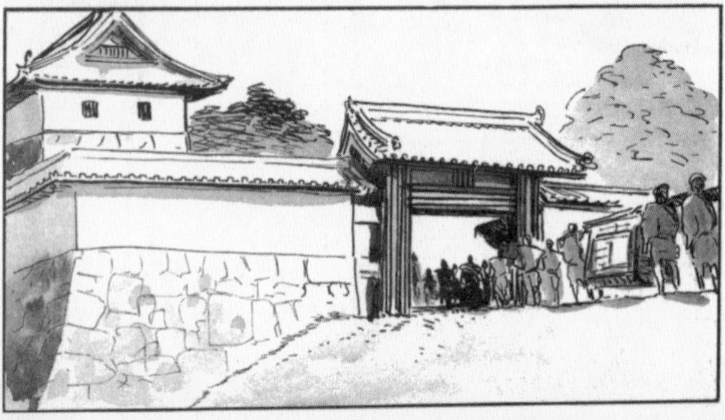

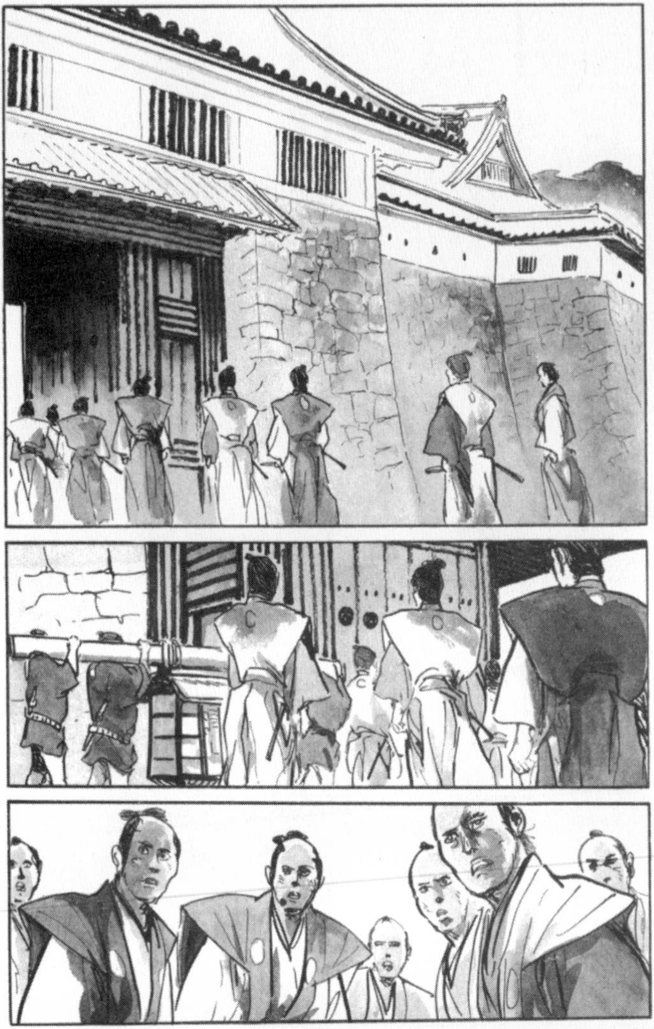

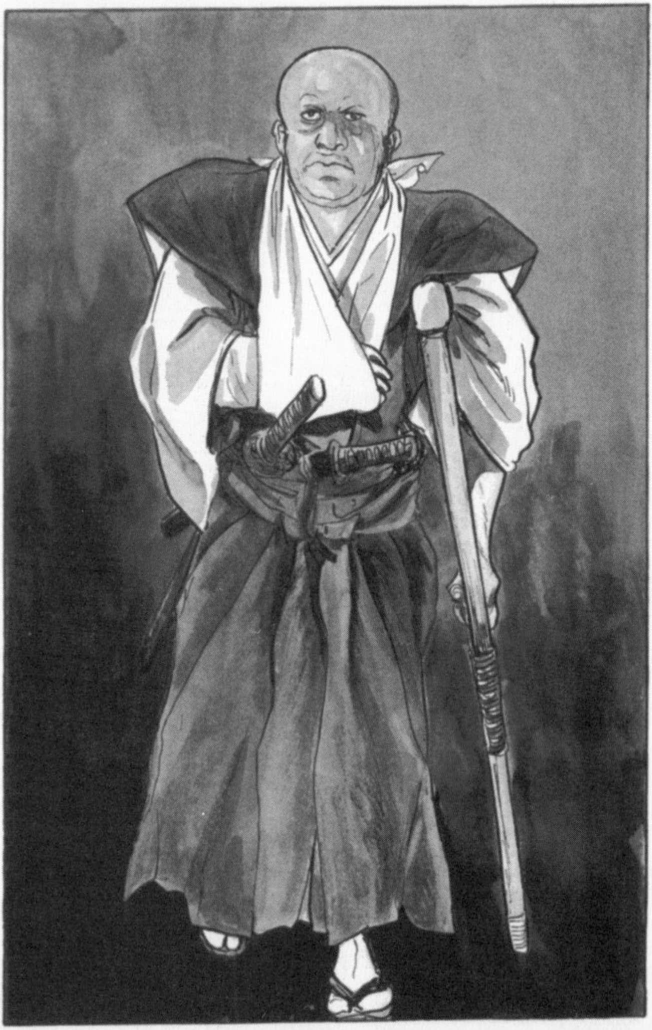

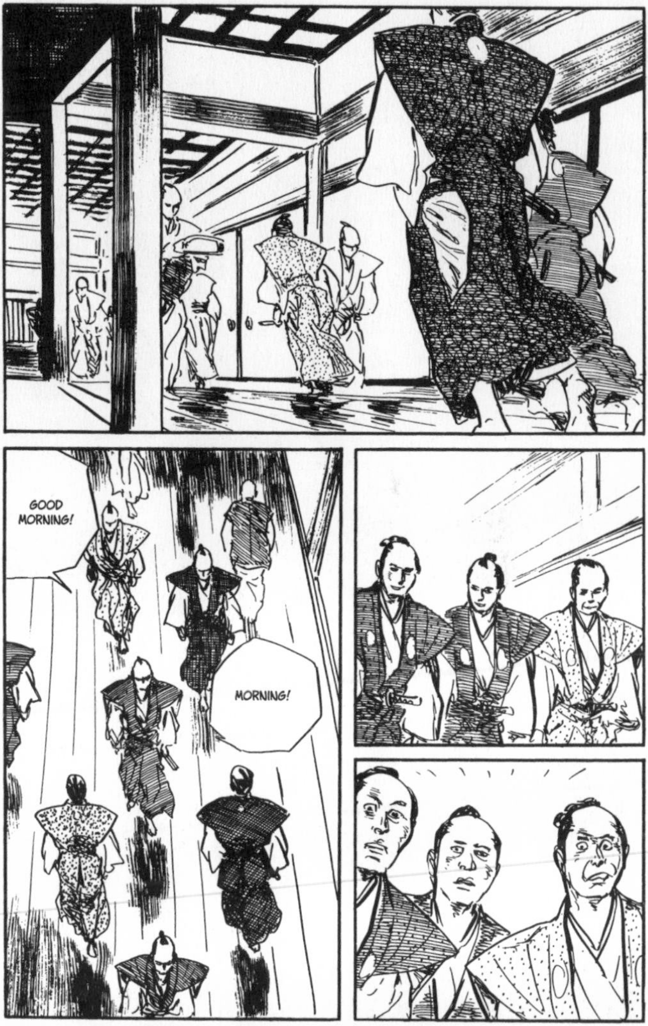
GOOD MORNING!
MORNING!

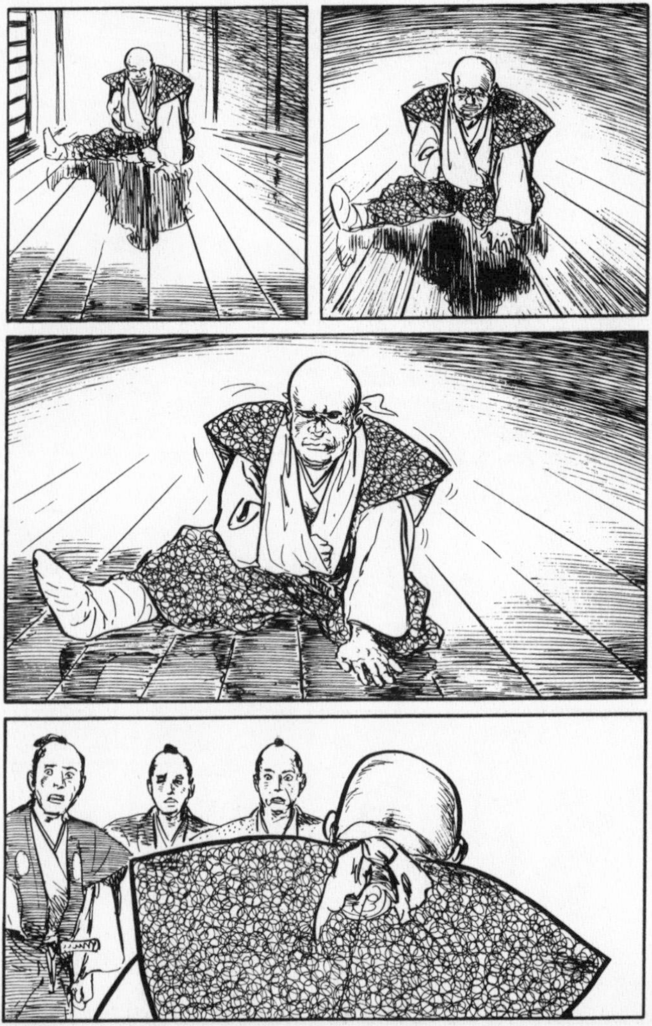

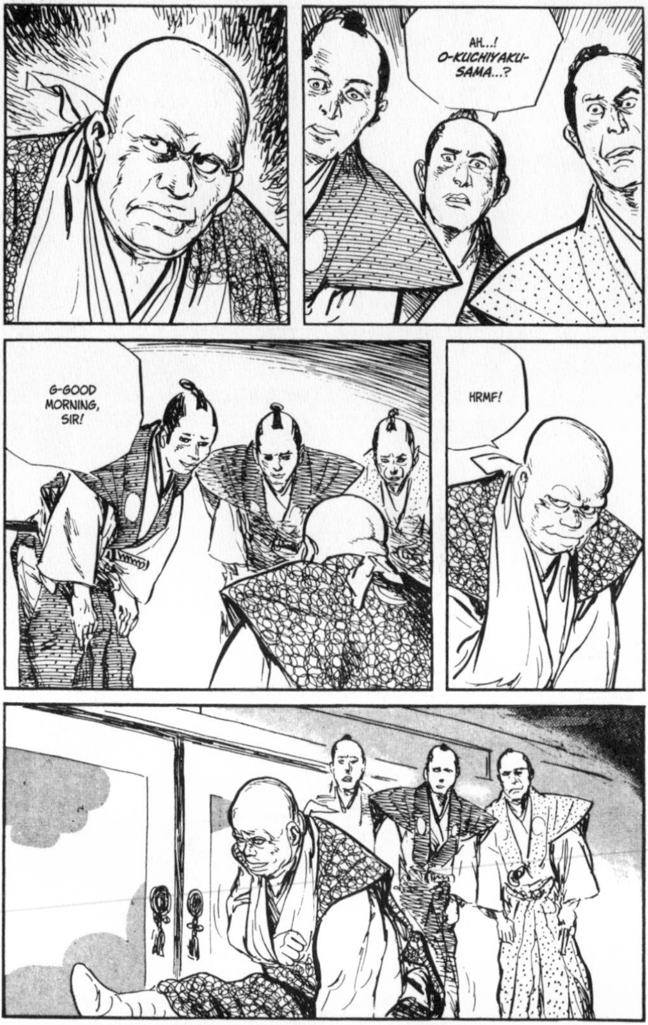
AH...!
O-KUCHIYAKU-
SAMA...?
G-GOOD
MORNING,
SIR!
HRMF!

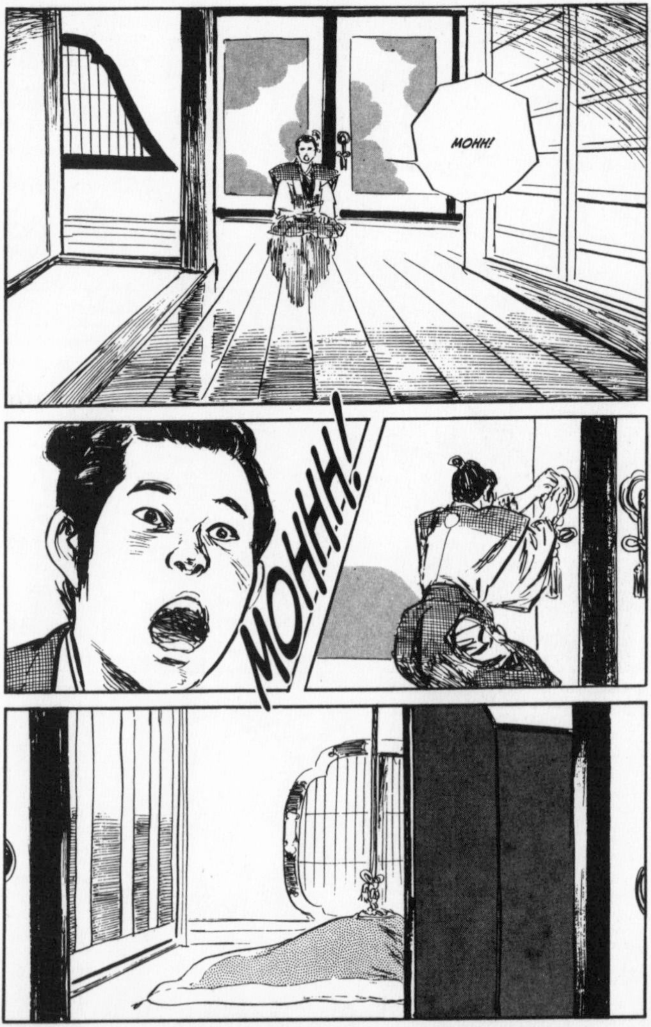
MOHH!
MOHH.H.!

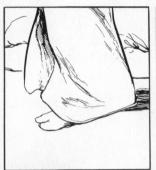

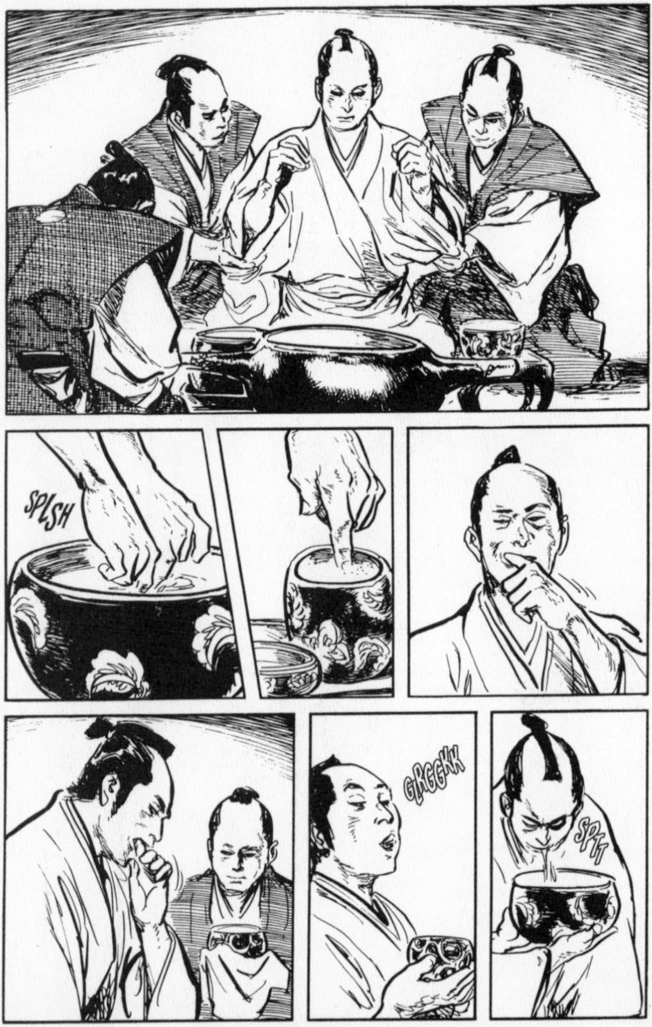
SPLSH
GLRGGKK
SPTT

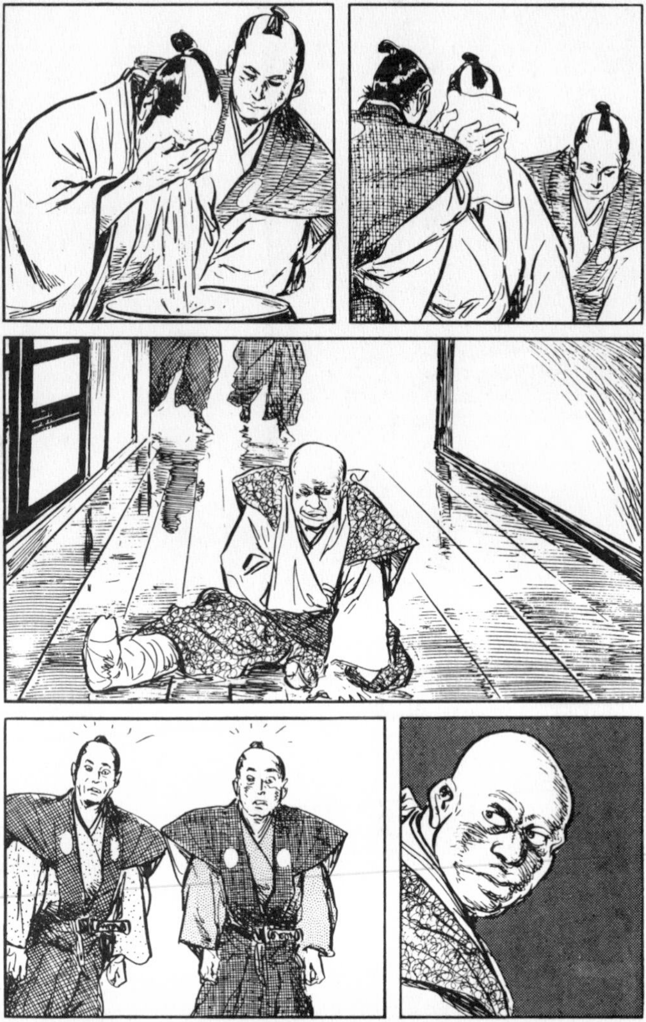

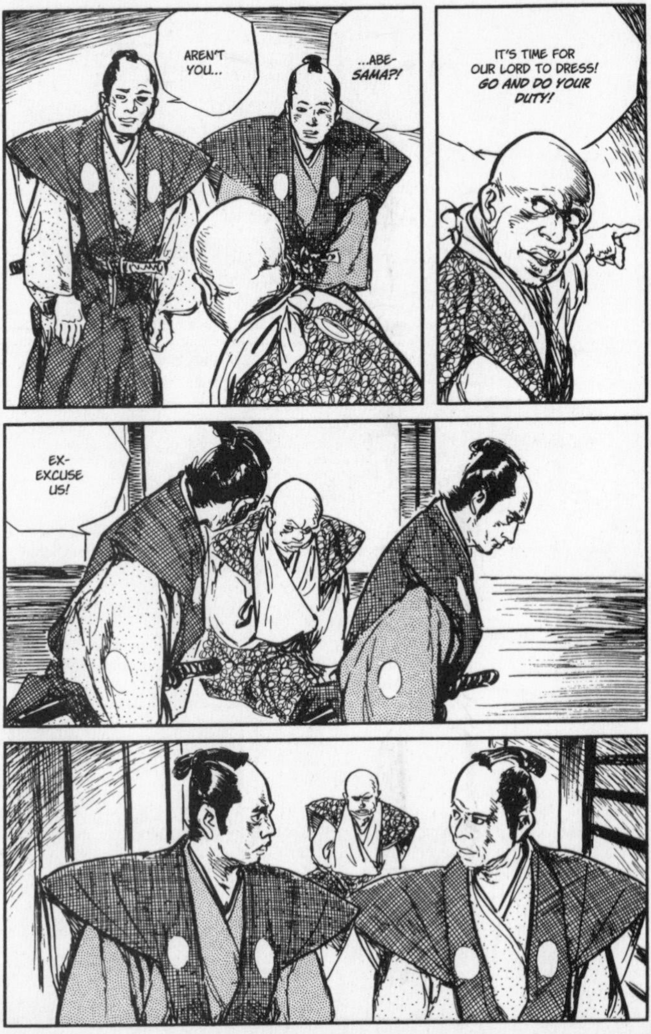
AREN'T YOU...
...ABE-SAMA?!
IT'S TIME FOR OUR LORD TO DRESS! GO AND DO YOUR DUTY!
EX-EXCUSE US!

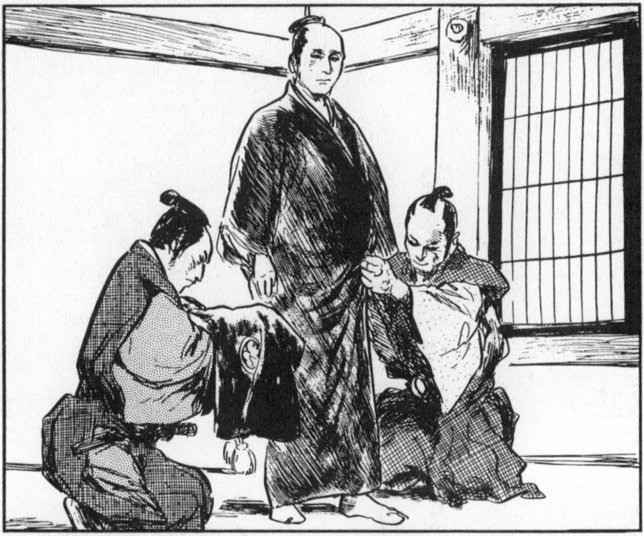

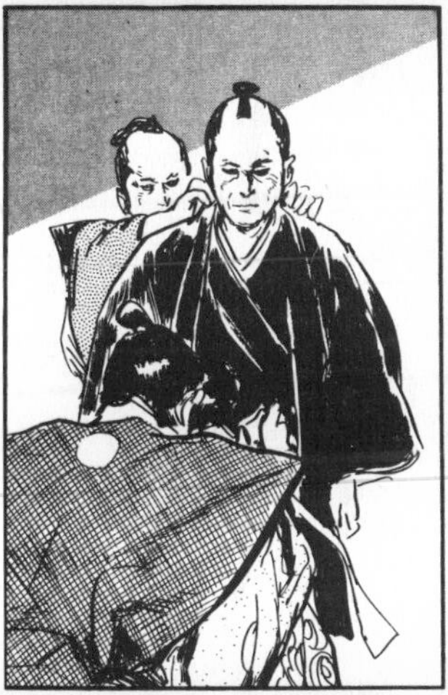

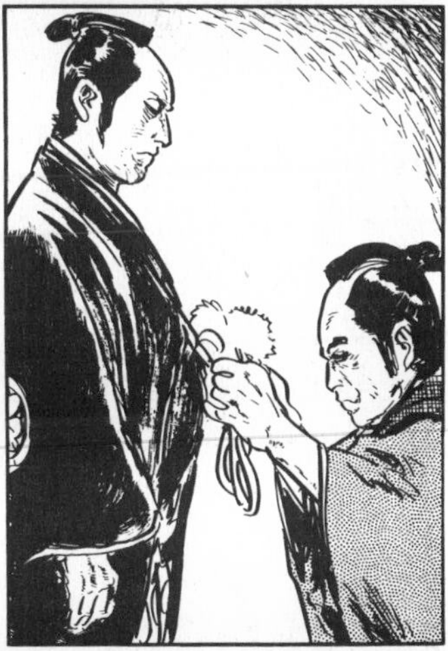

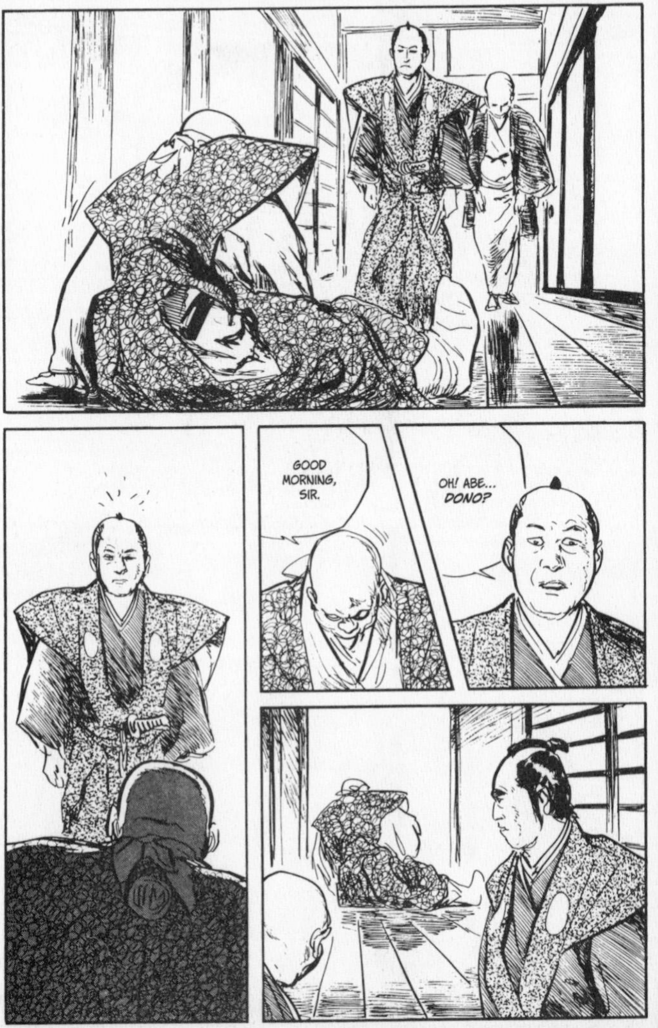
GOOD MORNING, SIR.
OH! ABE... DONO?

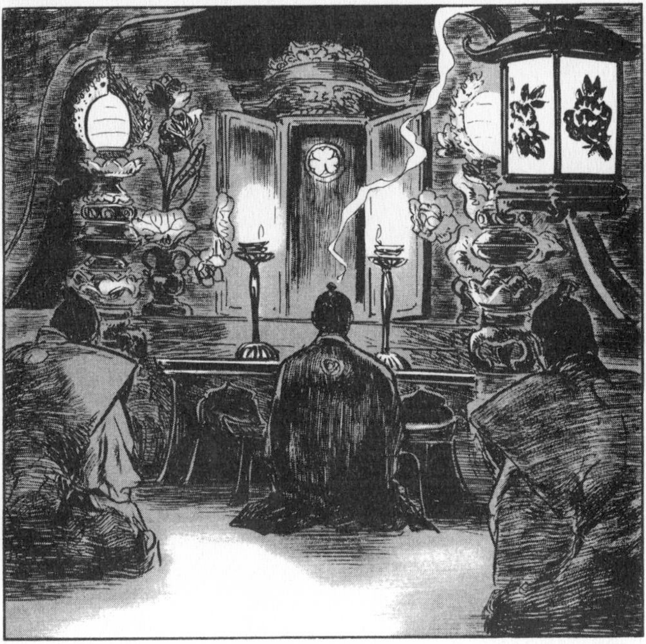

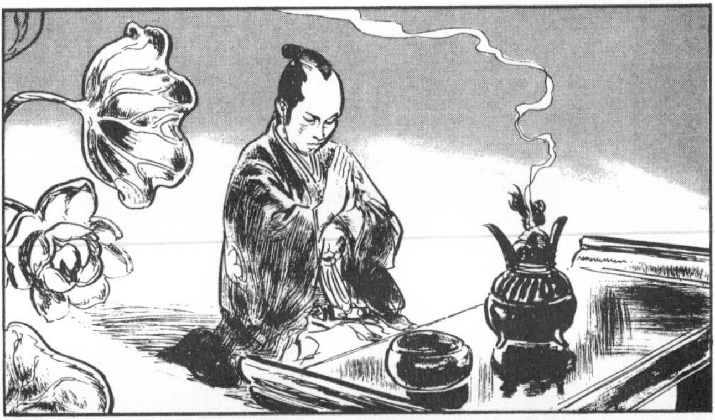

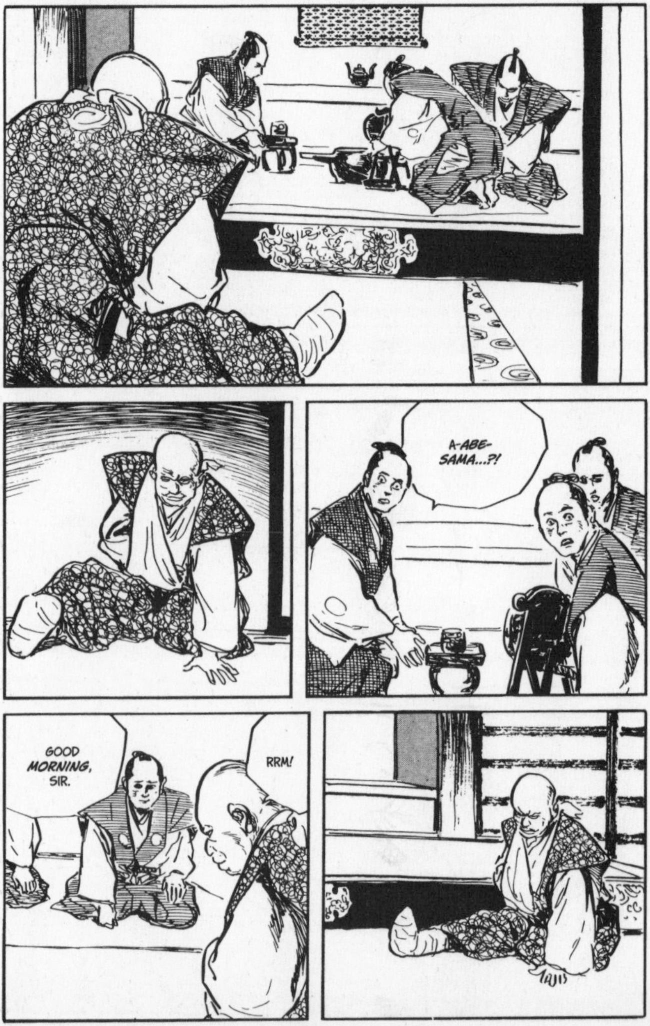
A-ABE-
SAMA...?!
GOOD
MORNING,
SIR.
RRM!

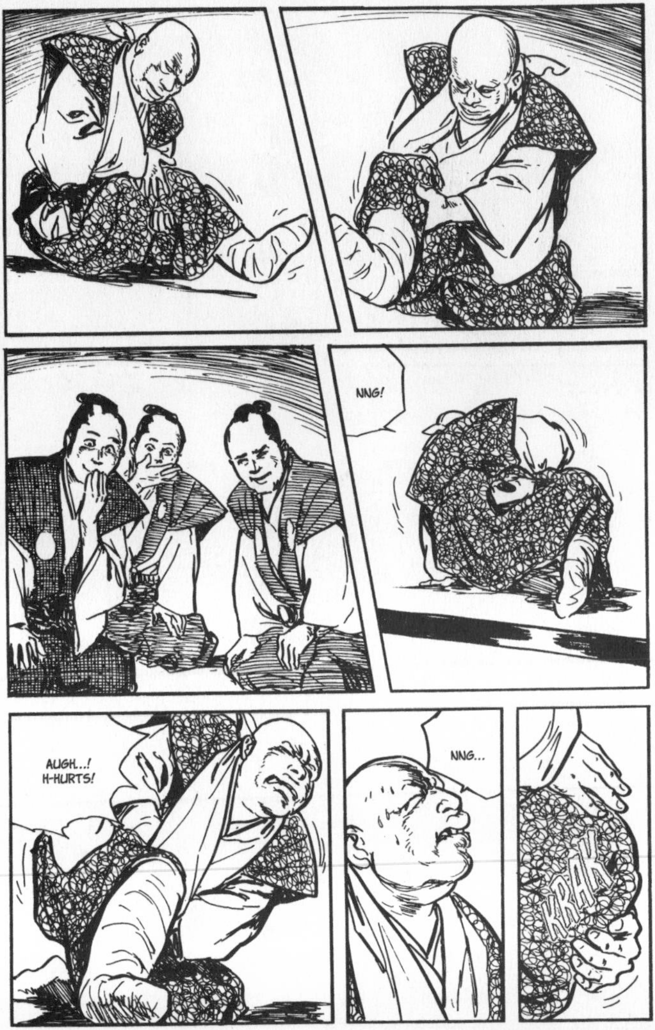
NNG!
AUGH...!
H-HURTS!
NNG...
KRAK

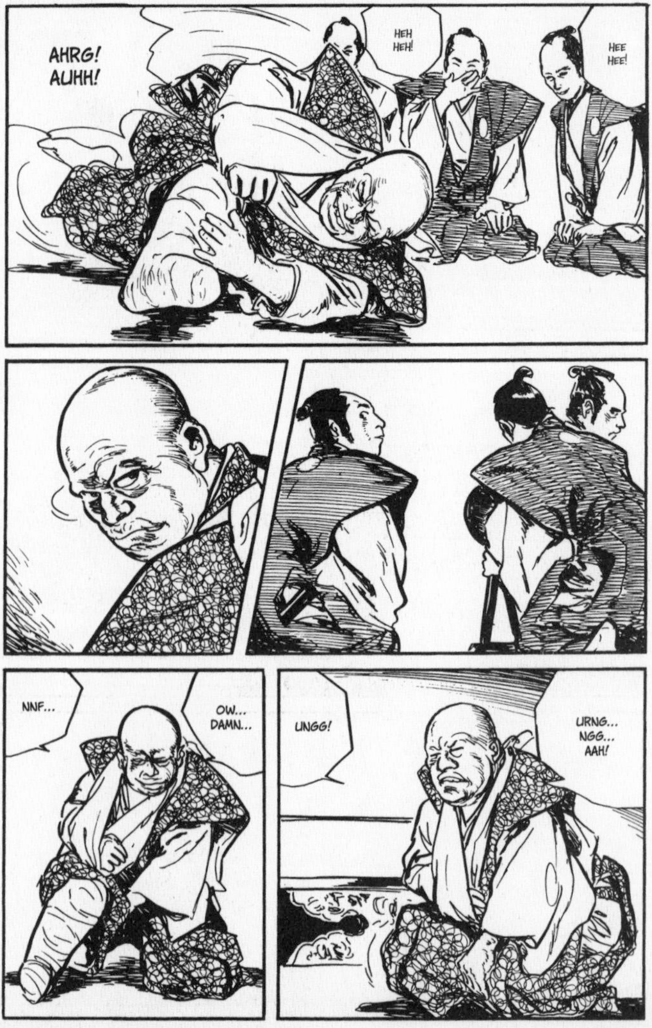
AHRG!
AUHH!
HEH
HEH!
HEE
HEE!
NNF...
OW...
DAMN...
UNGG!
URNG...
NGG...
AAH!

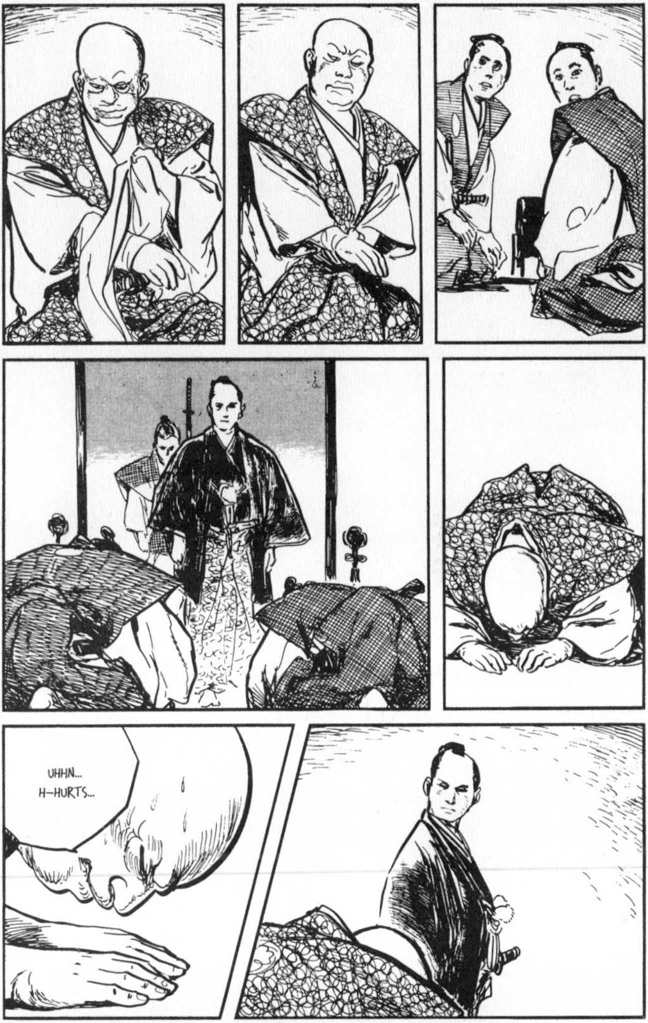
UHHN... H-HURTS...

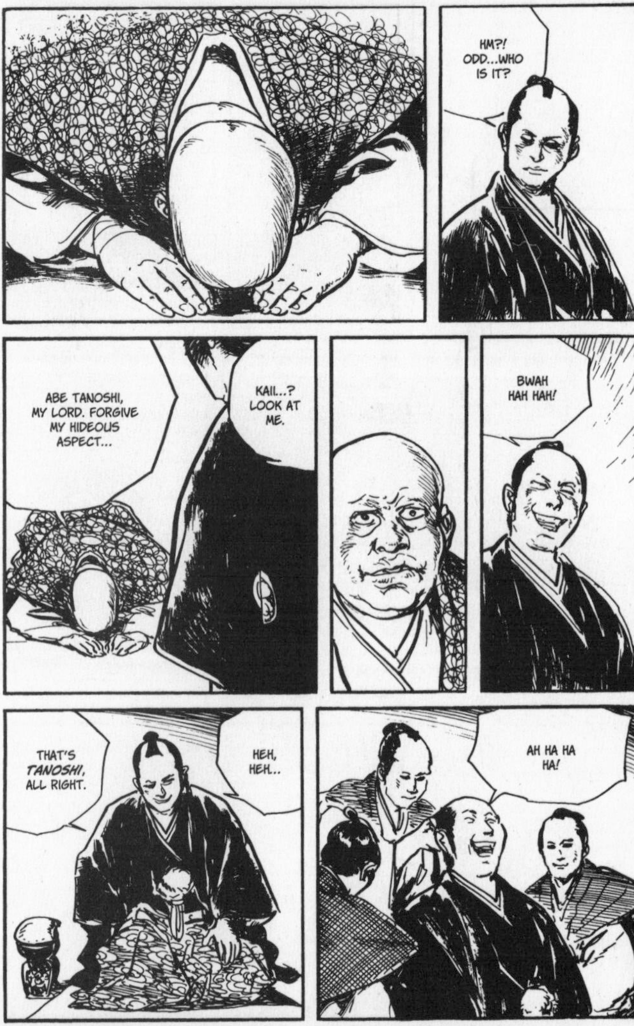
HM?! ODD...WHO IS IT?
ABE TANOSHI, MY LORD. FORGIVE MY HIDEOUS ASPECT...
KAIL..? LOOK AT ME.
BWAH HAH HAH!
THAT'S *TANOSHI,* ALL RIGHT.
HEH, HEH...
AH HA HA HA!

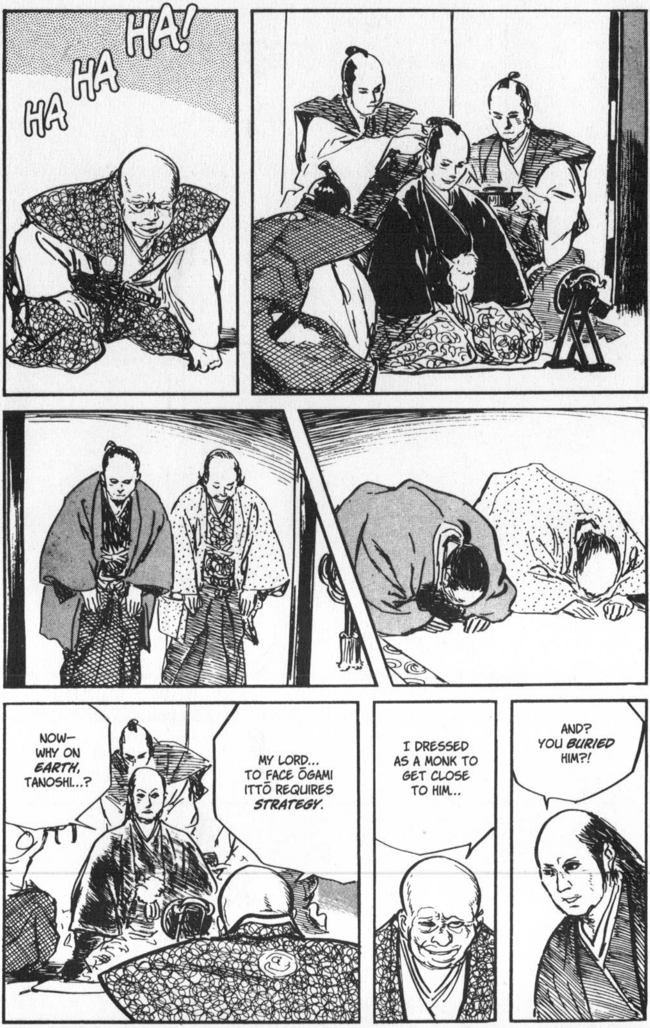
HA HA HA!
NOW— WHY ON EARTH, TANOSHI...?
MY LORD... TO FACE ŌGAMI ITTŌ REQUIRES STRATEGY.
I DRESSED AS A MONK TO GET CLOSE TO HIM...
AND? YOU BURIED HIM?!

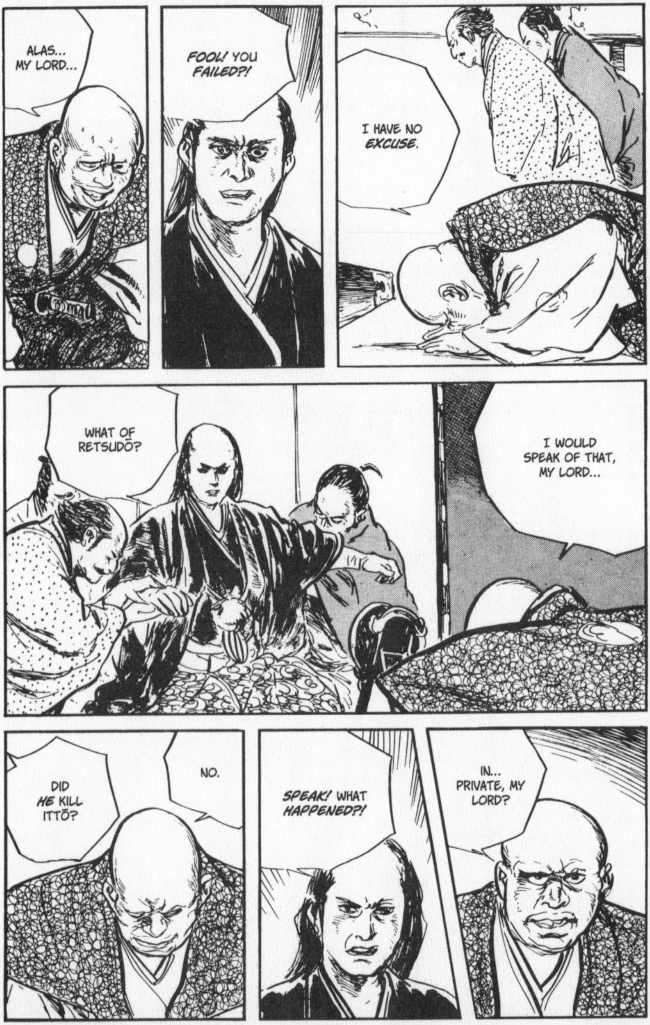
ALAS... MY LORD...
FOOL! YOU FAILED?!
I HAVE NO EXCUSE.
WHAT OF RETSUDŌ?
I WOULD SPEAK OF THAT, MY LORD...
DID HE KILL ITTŌ?
NO.
SPEAK! WHAT HAPPENED?!
IN... PRIVATE, MY LORD?

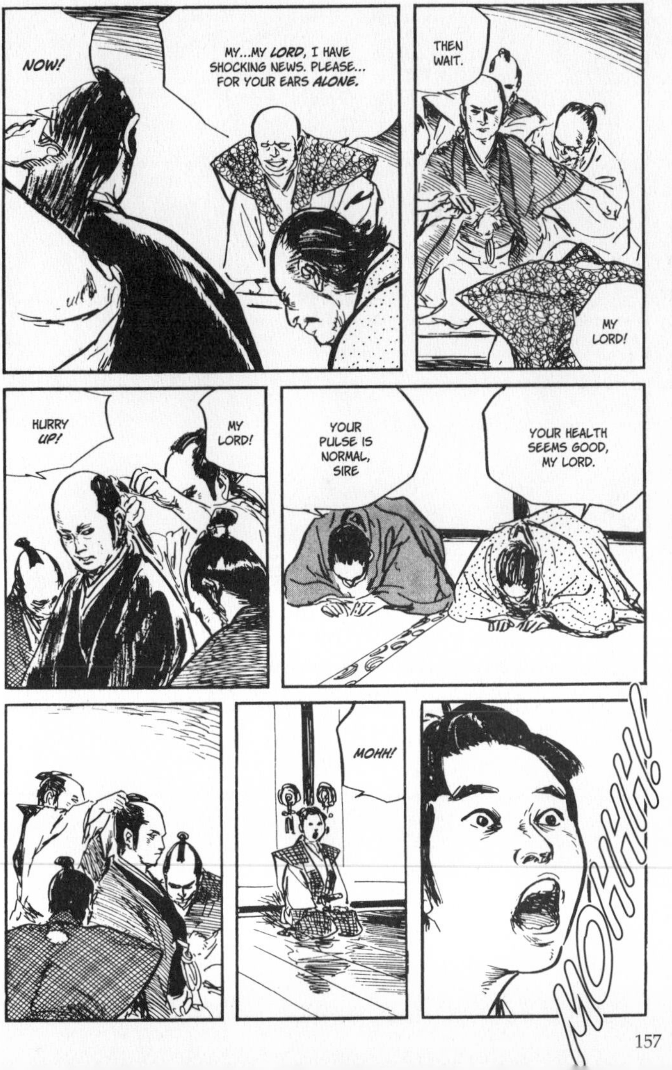
NOW!
MY...MY *LORD*, I HAVE SHOCKING NEWS. PLEASE... FOR YOUR EARS *ALONE.*
THEN WAIT.
MY LORD!
HURRY *UP!*
MY LORD!
YOUR PULSE IS NORMAL, SIRE
YOUR HEALTH SEEMS GOOD, MY LORD.
MOHH!
MOHHH!!

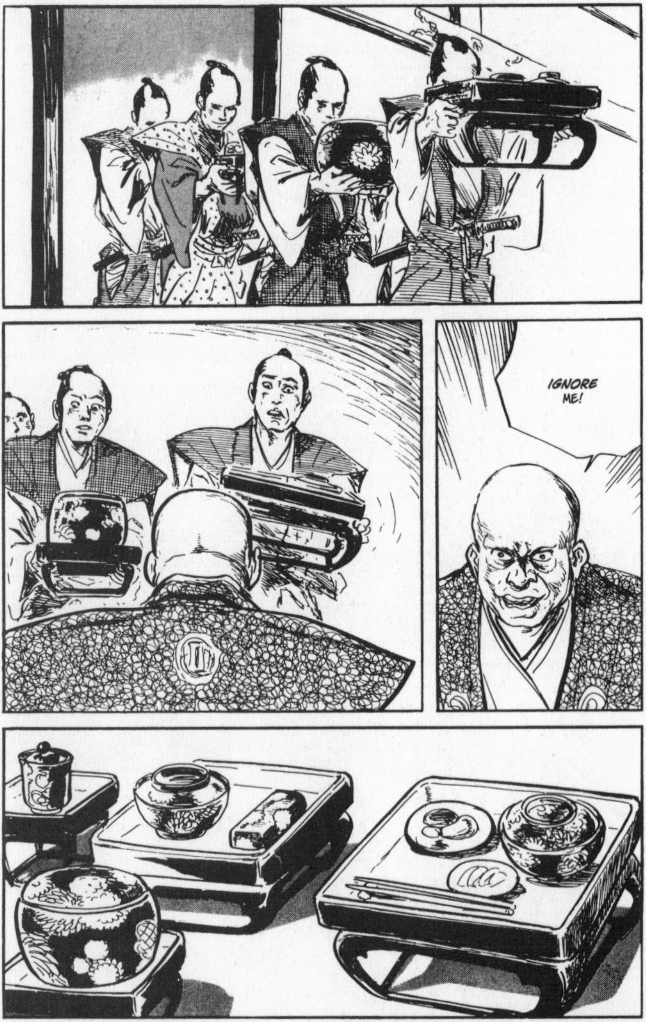
IGNORE
ME!

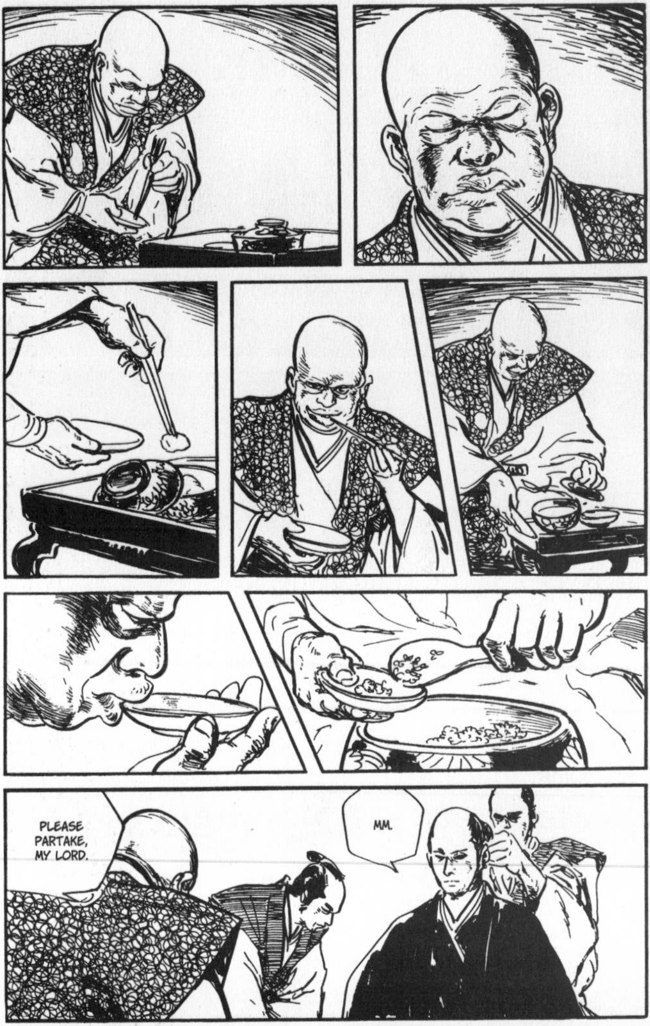
PLEASE PARTAKE, MY LORD.
MM.

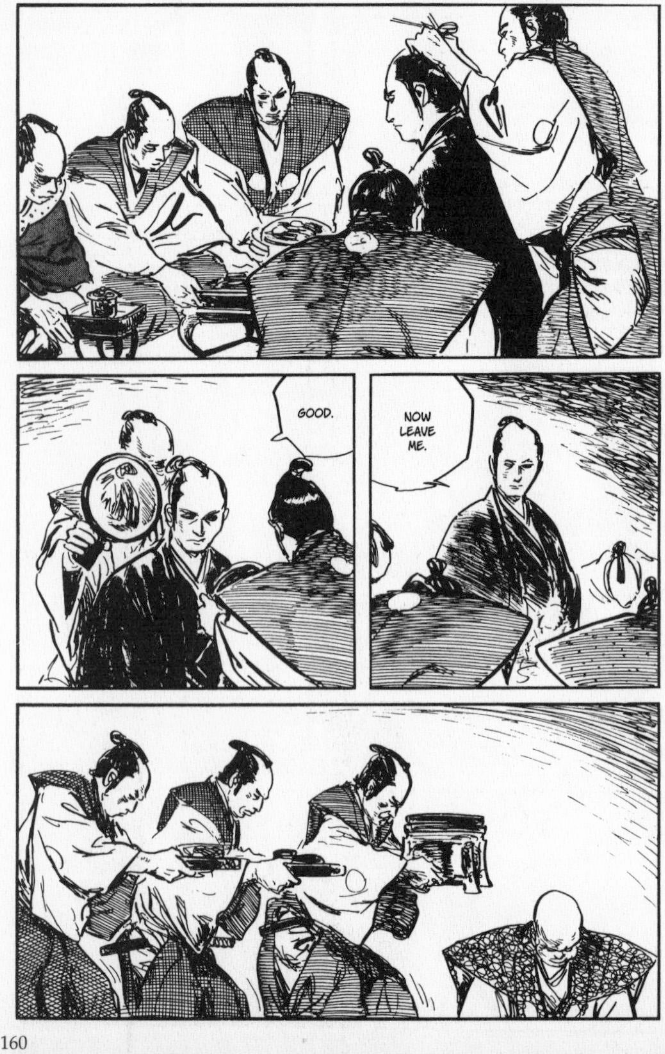
GOOD.
NOW LEAVE ME.

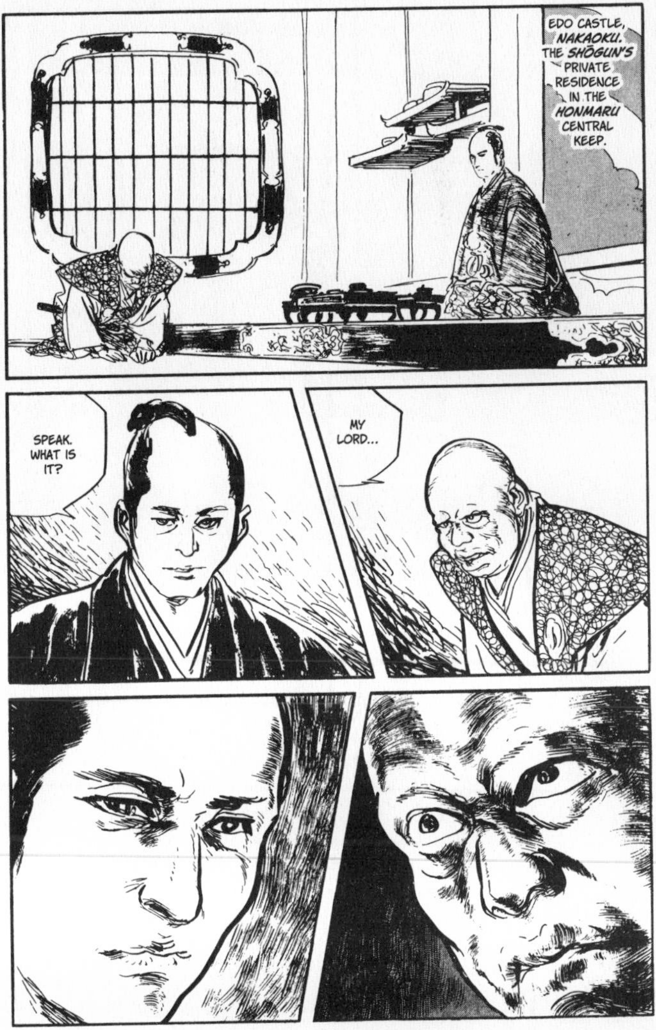
EDO CASTLE, NAKAOKU. THE SHŌGUN'S PRIVATE RESIDENCE IN THE HONMARU CENTRAL KEEP.
SPEAK. WHAT IS IT?
MY LORD...

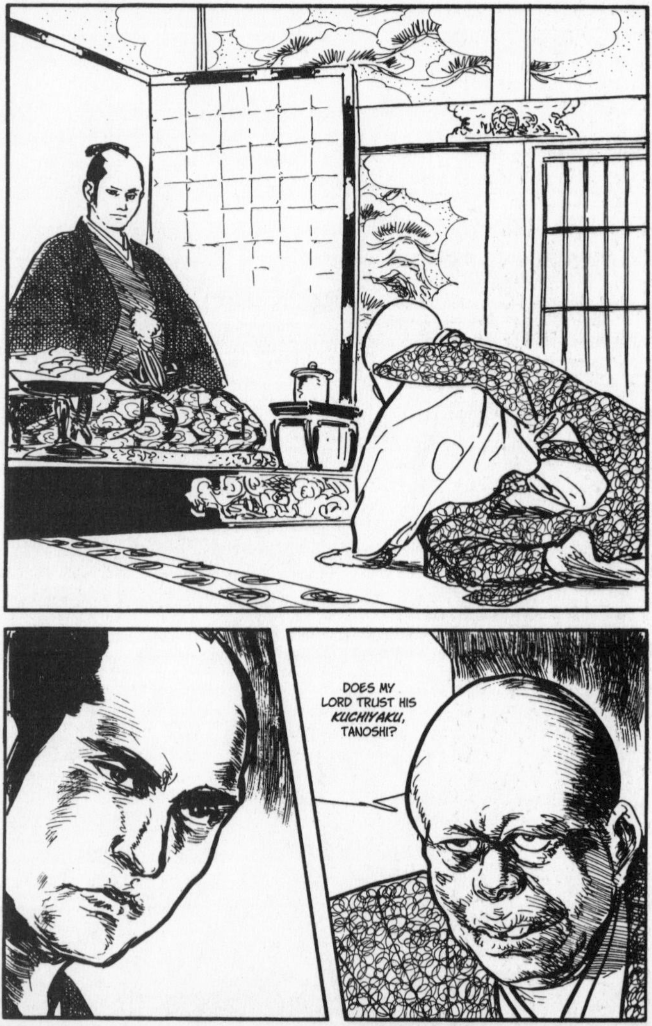
DOES MY LORD TRUST HIS *KUCHIYAKU*, TANOSHI?

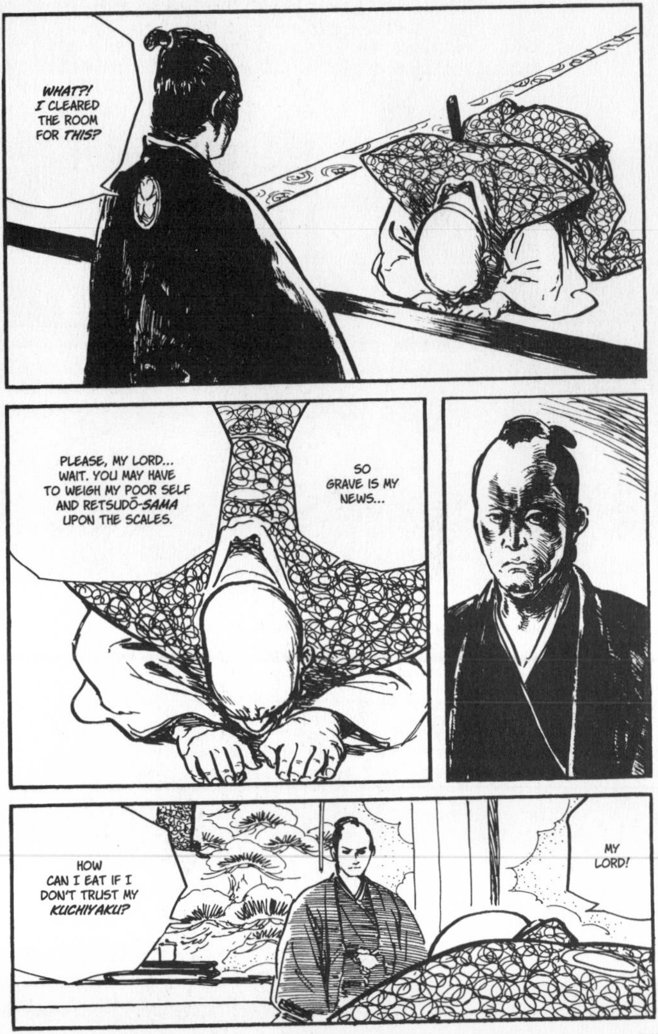
WHAT?! I CLEARED THE ROOM FOR THIS?
PLEASE, MY LORD... WAIT. YOU MAY HAVE TO WEIGH MY POOR SELF AND RETSUDŌ-SAMA UPON THE SCALES.
SO GRAVE IS MY NEWS...
HOW CAN I EAT IF I DON'T TRUST MY KUCHIYAKU?
MY LORD!

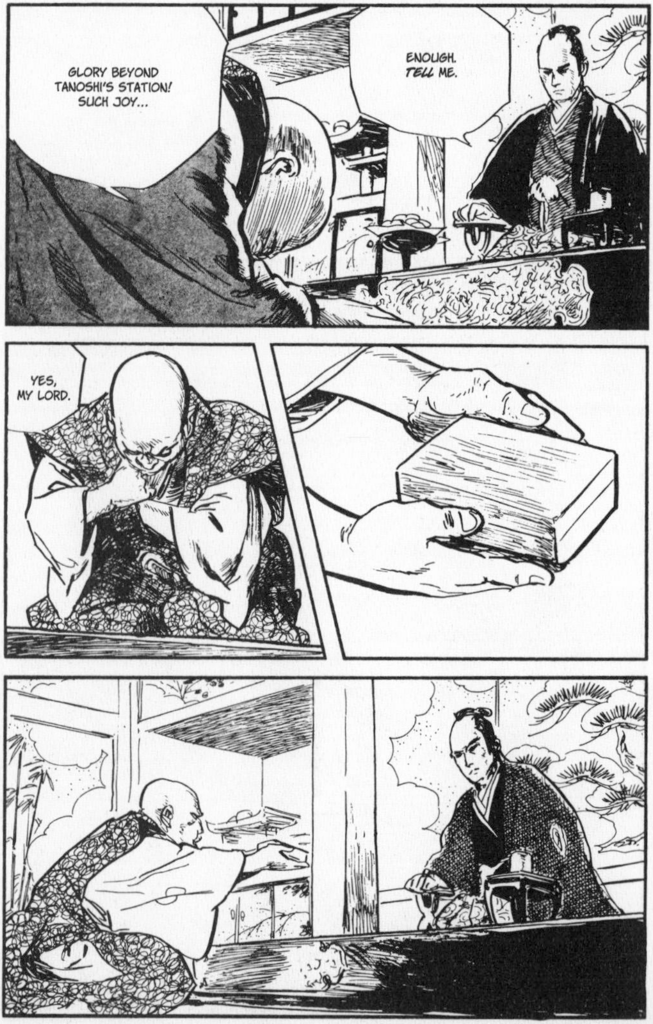
GLORY BEYOND TANOSHI'S STATION! SUCH JOY...
ENOUGH. *TELL* ME.
YES, MY LORD.

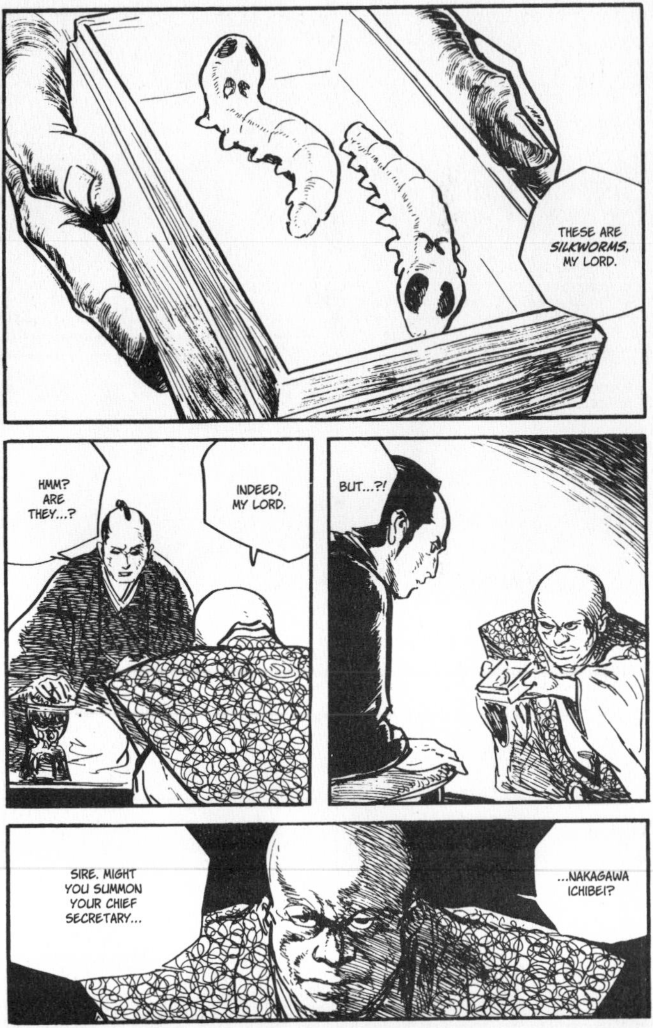
THESE ARE SILKWORMS, MY LORD.
HMM? ARE THEY...?
INDEED, MY LORD.
BUT...?!
SIRE. MIGHT YOU SUMMON YOUR CHIEF SECRETARY...
...NAKAGAWA ICHIBEI?

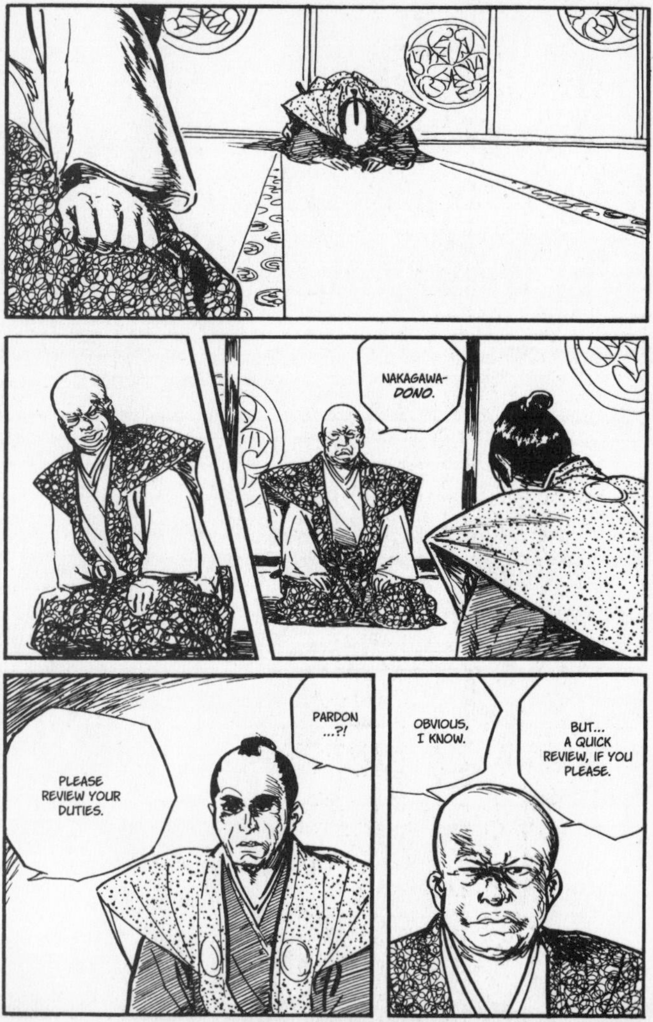
NAKAGAWA-DONO.
PLEASE REVIEW YOUR DUTIES.
PARDON ...?!
OBVIOUS, I KNOW.
BUT... A QUICK REVIEW, IF YOU PLEASE.

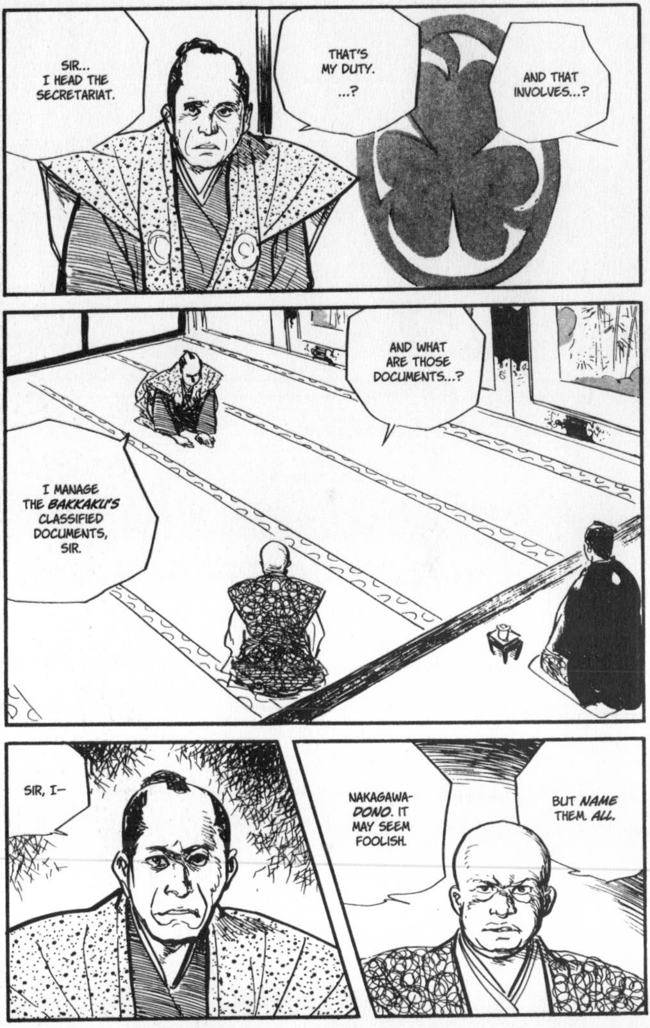
SIR... I HEAD THE SECRETARIAT.
THAT'S MY DUTY. ...?
AND THAT INVOLVES...?
AND WHAT ARE THOSE DOCUMENTS...?
I MANAGE THE *BAKKAKU'S* CLASSIFIED DOCUMENTS, SIR.
SIR, I—
NAKAGAWA-*DONO*. IT MAY SEEM FOOLISH.
BUT *NAME* THEM. *ALL*.

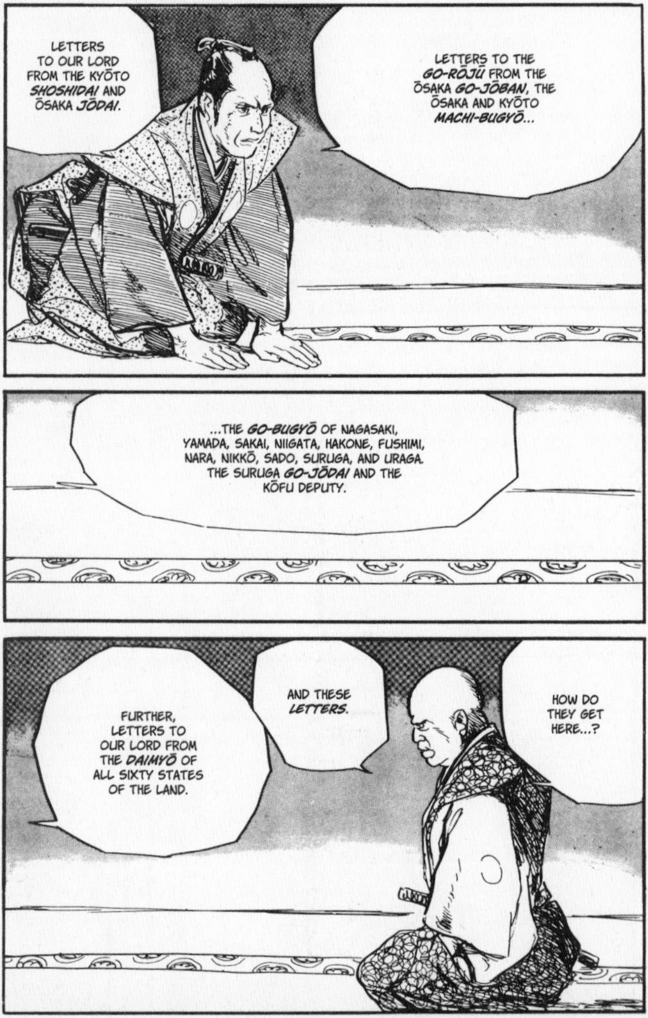
LETTERS TO OUR LORD FROM THE KYŌTO *SHOSHIDAI* AND ŌSAKA *JŌDAI*.
LETTERS TO THE *GO-RŌJŪ* FROM THE ŌSAKA *GO-JŌBAN*, THE ŌSAKA AND KYŌTO *MACHI-BUGYŌ*...
...THE *GO-BUGYŌ* OF NAGASAKI, YAMADA, SAKAI, NIIGATA, HAKONE, FUSHIMI, NARA, NIKKŌ, SADO, SURUGA, AND URAGA. THE SURUGA *GO-JŌDAI* AND THE KŌFU DEPUTY.
FURTHER, LETTERS TO OUR LORD FROM THE *DAIMYŌ* OF ALL SIXTY STATES OF THE LAND.
AND THESE *LETTERS*.
HOW DO THEY GET HERE...?

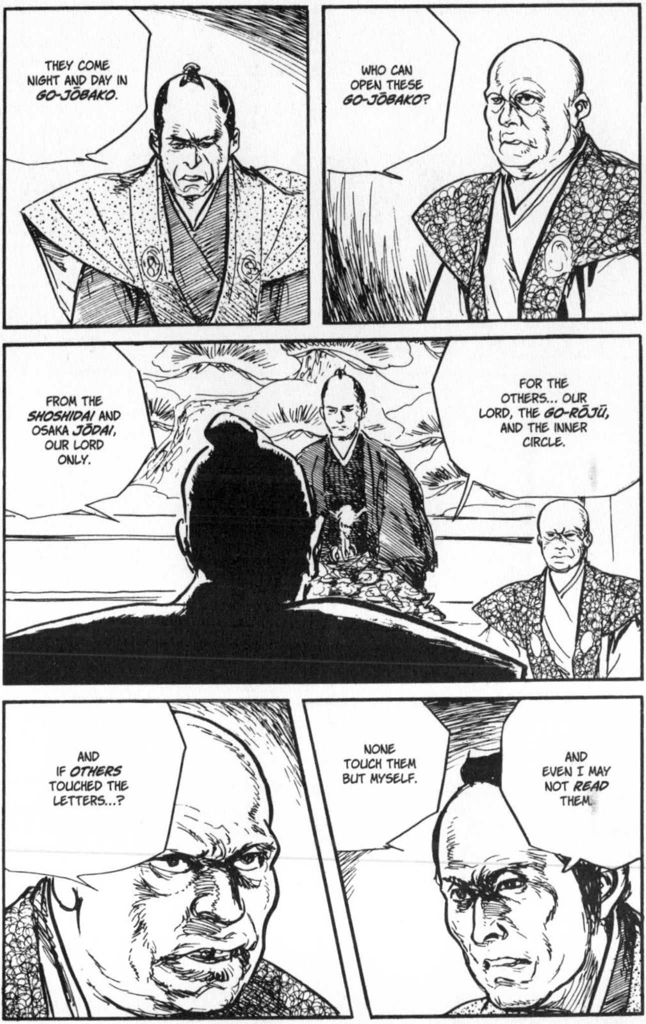
THEY COME NIGHT AND DAY IN *GO-JŌBAKO*.
WHO CAN OPEN THESE *GO-JŌBAKO*?
FROM THE *SHOSHIDAI* AND OSAKA *JŌDAI*, OUR LORD ONLY.
FOR THE OTHERS... OUR LORD, THE *GO-RŌJŪ*, AND THE INNER CIRCLE.
AND IF *OTHERS* TOUCHED THE LETTERS...?
NONE TOUCH THEM BUT MYSELF.
AND EVEN I MAY NOT *READ* THEM.

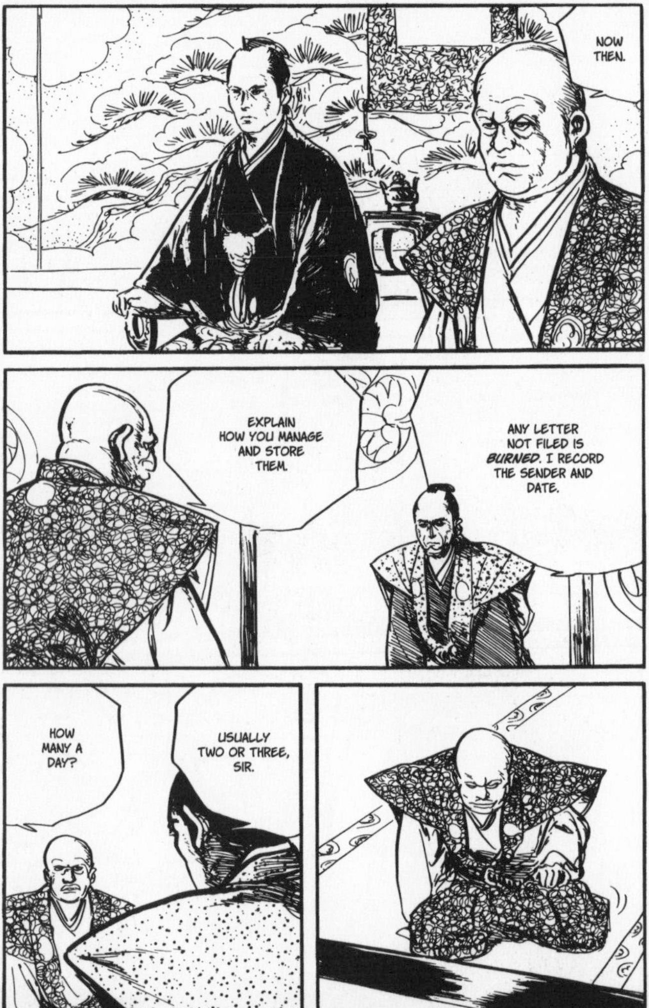
NOW THEN.
EXPLAIN HOW YOU MANAGE AND STORE THEM.
ANY LETTER NOT FILED IS *BURNED*. I RECORD THE SENDER AND DATE.
HOW MANY A DAY?
USUALLY TWO OR THREE, SIR.

FORGIVE ME.

DID MY LORD READ YESTERDAY'S LETTERS?

I DID.

I HUMBLY ASK THAT ONE BE BROUGHT.

NAKAGAWA. THE OSAKA *JŌDAI'S* LETTER.

MY LORD.

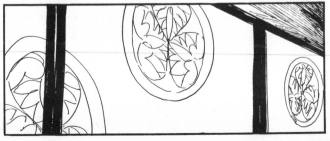

171

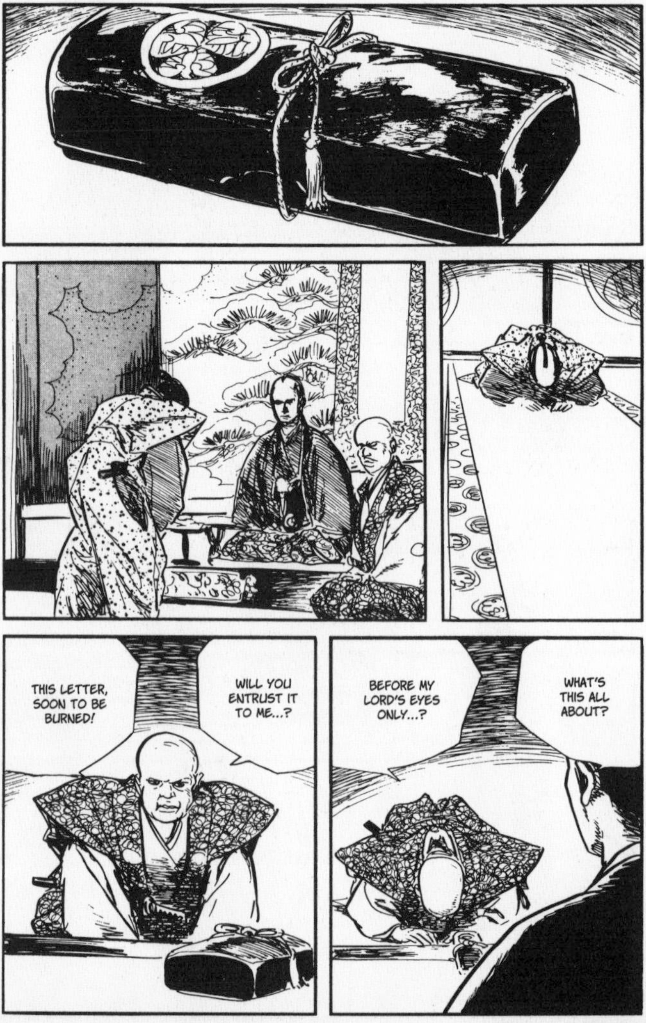
THIS LETTER, SOON TO BE BURNED!
WILL YOU ENTRUST IT TO ME...?
BEFORE MY LORD'S EYES ONLY...?
WHAT'S THIS ALL ABOUT?

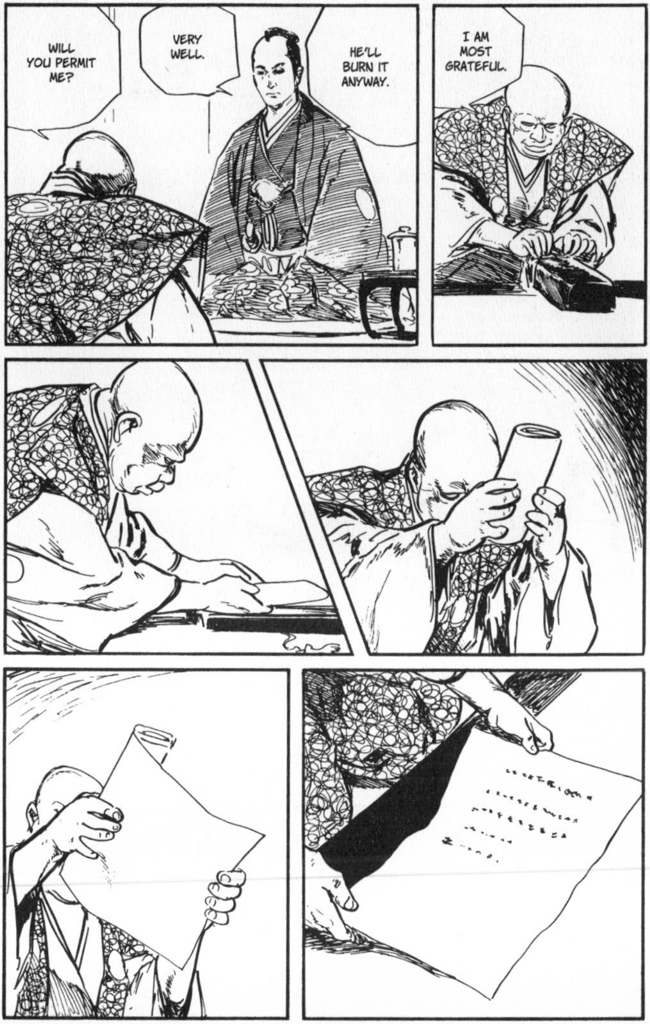
WILL YOU PERMIT ME?
VERY WELL.
HE'LL BURN IT ANYWAY.
I AM MOST GRATEFUL.

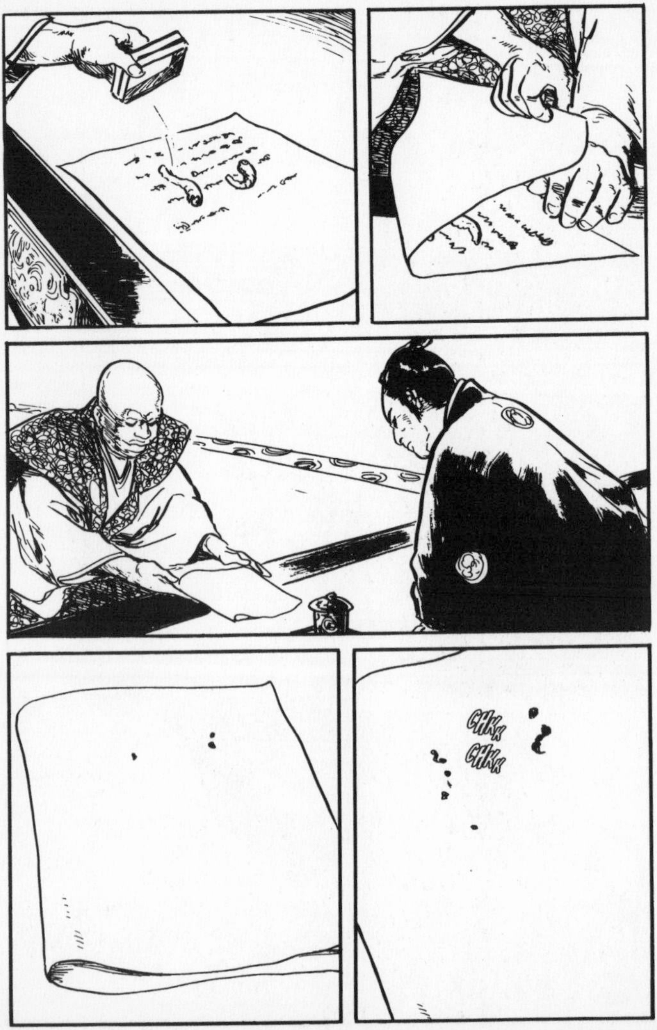
CHKK
CHKK

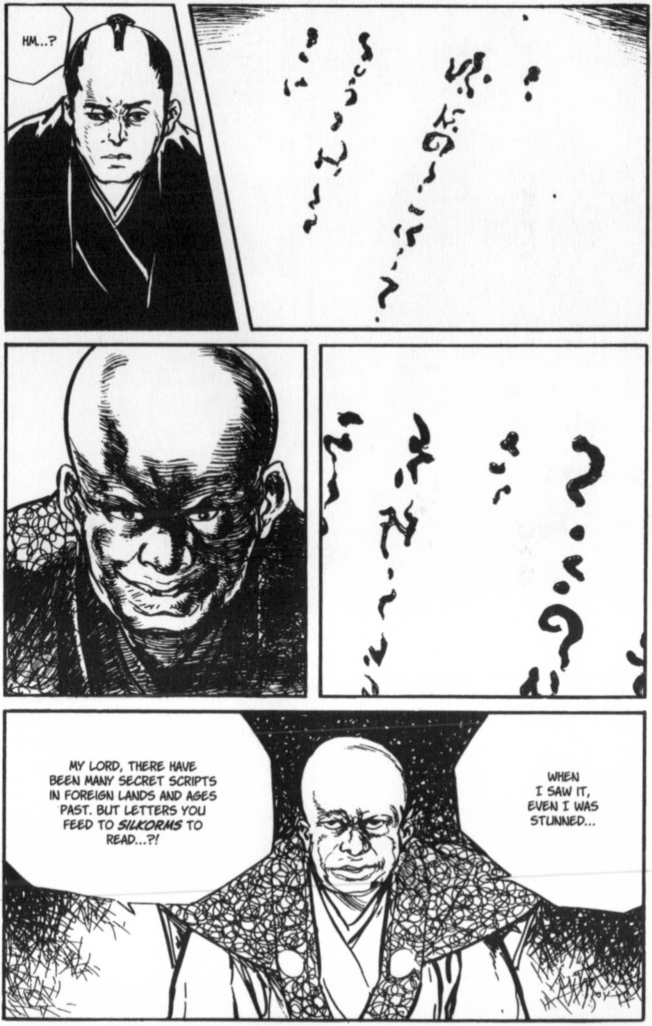

HM...?
MY LORD, THERE HAVE BEEN MANY SECRET SCRIPTS IN FOREIGN LANDS AND AGES PAST. BUT LETTERS YOU FEED TO *SILKORMS* TO READ...?!
WHEN I SAW IT, EVEN I WAS STUNNED...

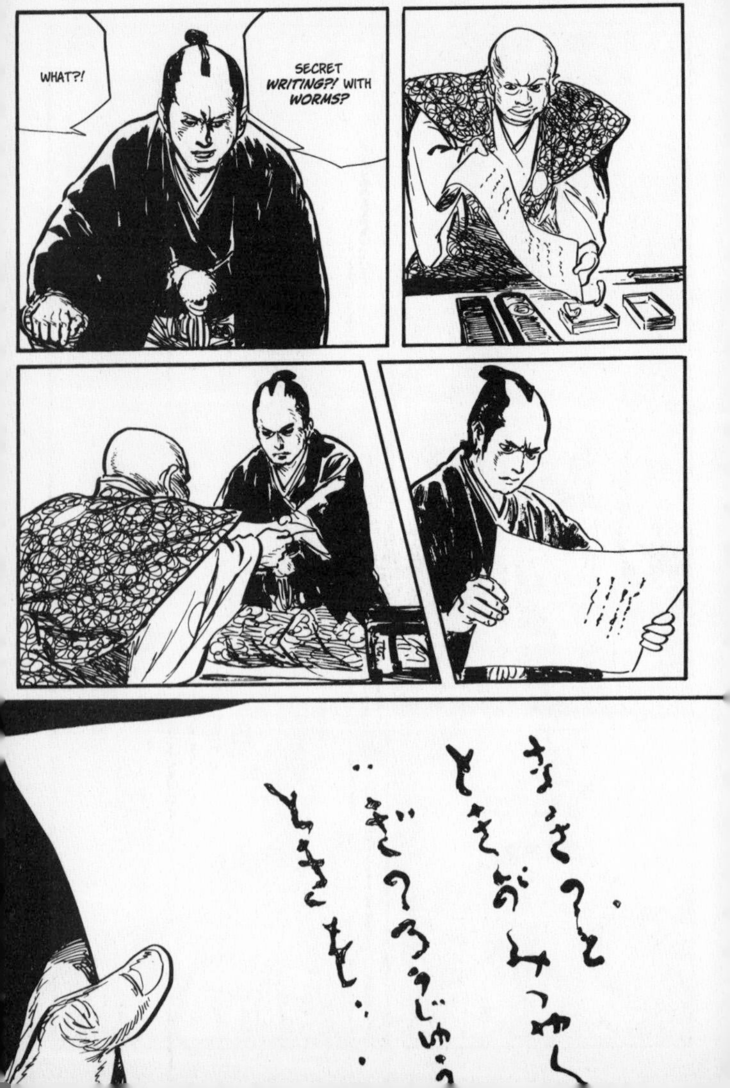
WHAT?!
SECRET WRITING?! WITH WORMS?

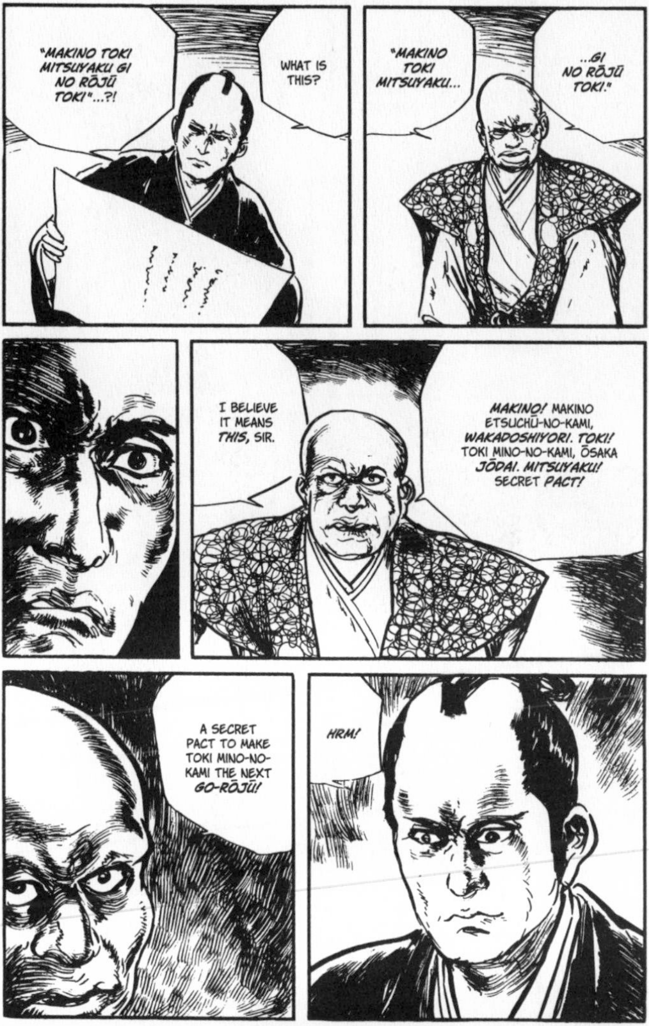
"MAKINO TOKI MITSUYAKU GI NO RŌJŪ TOKI"...?!
WHAT IS THIS?
"MAKINO TOKI MITSUYAKU...
...GI NO RŌJŪ TOKI."
I BELIEVE IT MEANS THIS, SIR.
MAKINO! MAKINO ETSUCHŪ-NO-KAMI, WAKADOSHIYORI. TOKI! TOKI MINO-NO-KAMI, ŌSAKA JŌDAI. MITSUYAKU! SECRET PACT!
A SECRET PACT TO MAKE TOKI MINO-NO-KAMI THE NEXT GO-RŌJŪ!
HRM!

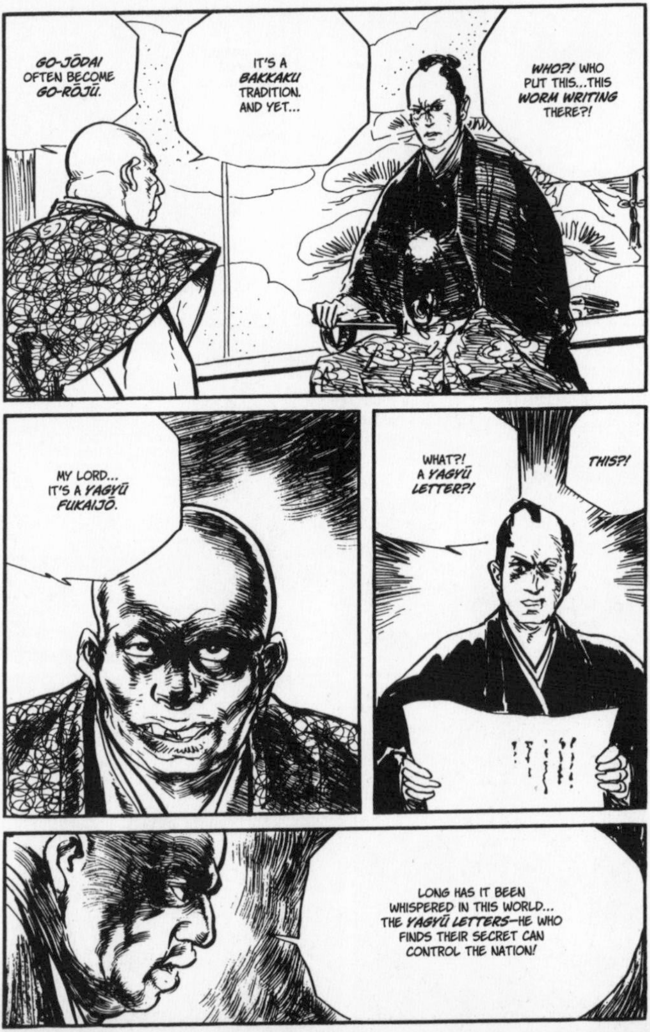
GO-JŌDAI OFTEN BECOME GO-RŌJŪ.
IT'S A BAKKAKU TRADITION. AND YET...
WHO?! WHO PUT THIS...THIS WORM WRITING THERE?!
MY LORD... IT'S A YAGYŪ FUKAIJŌ.
WHAT?! A YAGYŪ LETTER?!
THIS?!
LONG HAS IT BEEN WHISPERED IN THIS WORLD... THE YAGYŪ LETTERS—HE WHO FINDS THEIR SECRET CAN CONTROL THE NATION!

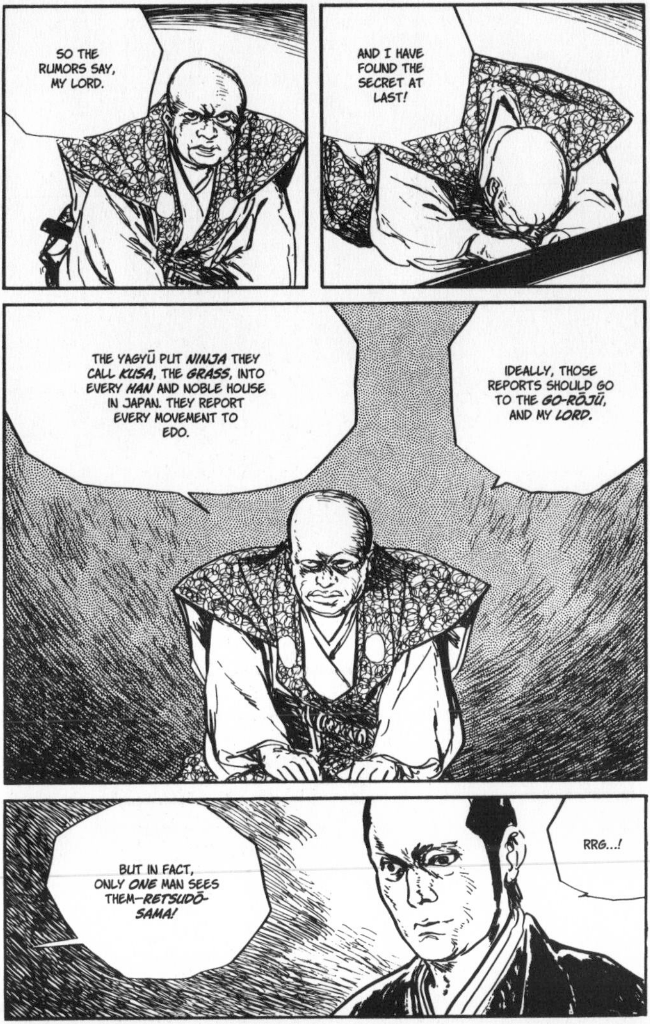
SO THE RUMORS SAY, MY LORD.
AND I HAVE FOUND THE SECRET AT LAST!
THE YAGYŪ PUT *NINJA* THEY CALL *KUSA*, THE *GRASS*, INTO EVERY *HAN* AND NOBLE HOUSE IN JAPAN. THEY REPORT EVERY MOVEMENT TO EDO.
IDEALLY, THOSE REPORTS SHOULD GO TO THE *GO-RŌJŪ*, AND MY *LORD*.
BUT IN FACT, ONLY *ONE* MAN SEES THEM—*RETSUDŌ-SAMA!*
RRG...!

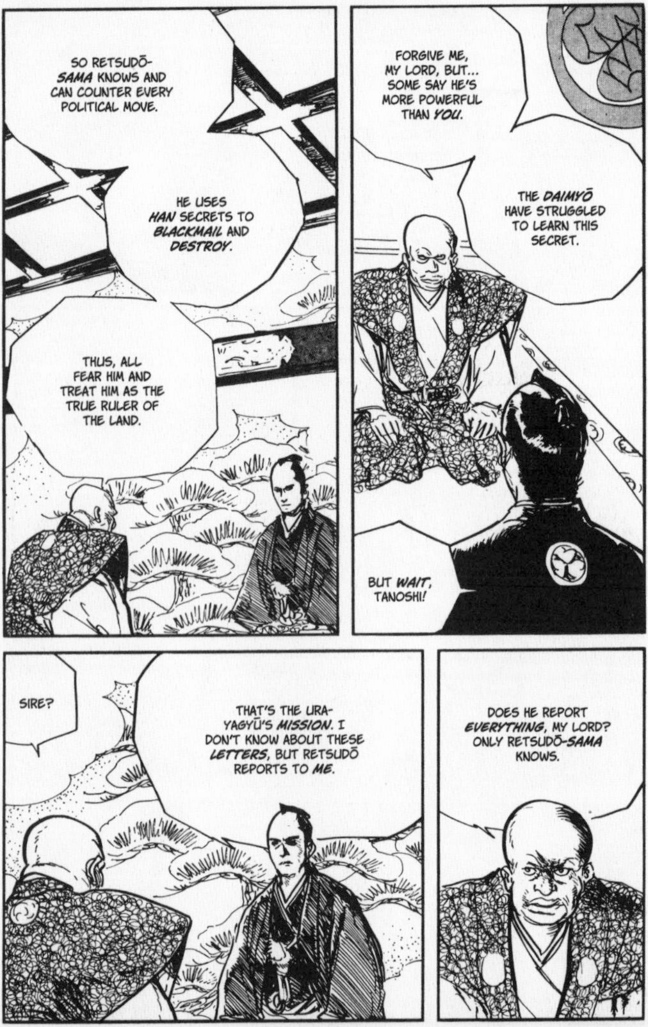
SO RETSUDŌ-*SAMA* KNOWS AND CAN COUNTER EVERY POLITICAL MOVE.
HE USES *HAN* SECRETS TO *BLACKMAIL* AND *DESTROY*.
THUS, ALL FEAR HIM AND TREAT HIM AS THE TRUE RULER OF THE LAND.
FORGIVE ME, MY LORD, BUT... SOME SAY HE'S MORE POWERFUL THAN *YOU*.
THE *DAIMYŌ* HAVE STRUGGLED TO LEARN THIS SECRET.
BUT *WAIT*, TANOSHI!
SIRE?
THAT'S THE URA-YAGYŪ'S *MISSION*. I DON'T KNOW ABOUT THESE *LETTERS*, BUT RETSUDŌ REPORTS TO *ME*.
DOES HE REPORT *EVERYTHING*, MY LORD? ONLY RETSUDŌ-*SAMA* KNOWS.

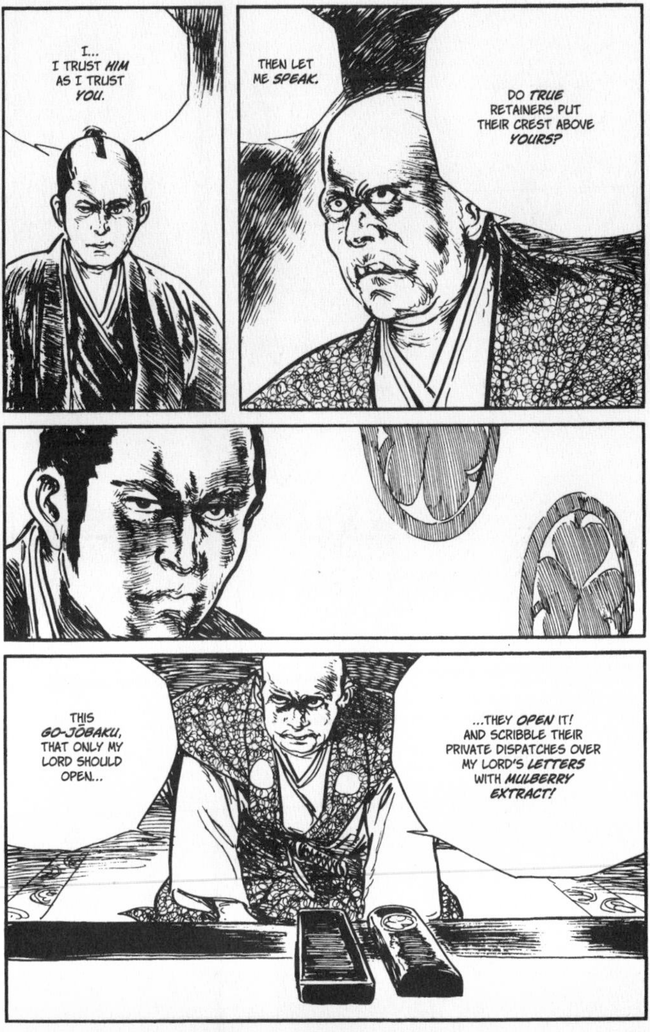
I... I TRUST *HIM* AS I TRUST *YOU.*
THEN LET ME *SPEAK.*
DO *TRUE* RETAINERS PUT THEIR CREST ABOVE *YOURS?*
THIS *GO-JŌBAKU,* THAT ONLY MY LORD SHOULD OPEN...
...THEY *OPEN* IT! AND SCRIBBLE THEIR PRIVATE DISPATCHES OVER MY LORD'S *LETTERS* WITH *MULBERRY EXTRACT!*

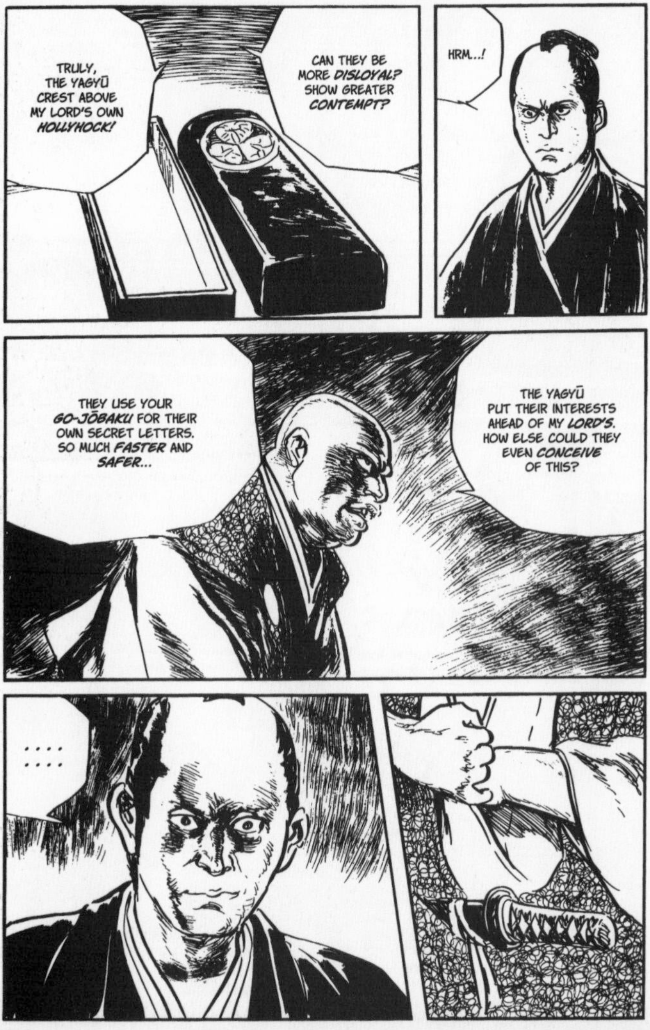
TRULY, THE YAGYŪ CREST ABOVE MY LORD'S OWN *HOLLYHOCK!*
CAN THEY BE MORE *DISLOYAL?* SHOW GREATER *CONTEMPT?*
HRM...!
THEY USE YOUR *GO-JŌBAKU* FOR THEIR OWN SECRET LETTERS. SO MUCH *FASTER* AND *SAFER...*
THE YAGYŪ PUT THEIR INTERESTS AHEAD OF MY *LORD'S.* HOW ELSE COULD THEY EVEN *CONCEIVE* OF THIS?
....
....

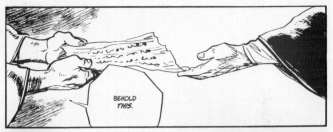

BEHOLD *THIS.*

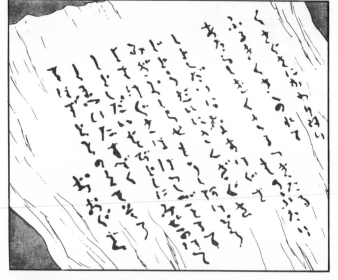

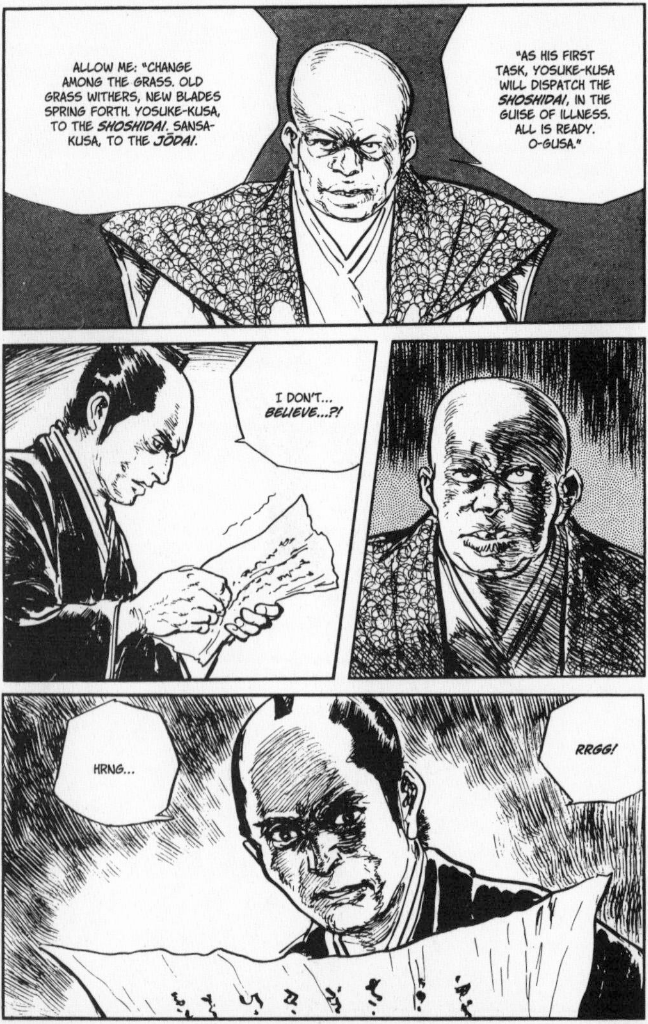
ALLOW ME: "CHANGE AMONG THE GRASS. OLD GRASS WITHERS, NEW BLADES SPRING FORTH. YOSUKE-KUSA, TO THE *SHOSHIDAI*. SANSA-KUSA, TO THE *JŌDAI*.
"AS HIS FIRST TASK, YOSUKE-KUSA WILL DISPATCH THE *SHOSHIDAI*, IN THE GUISE OF ILLNESS. ALL IS READY. O-GUSA."
I DON'T... *BELIEVE*...?!
HRNG...
*RRGG!*

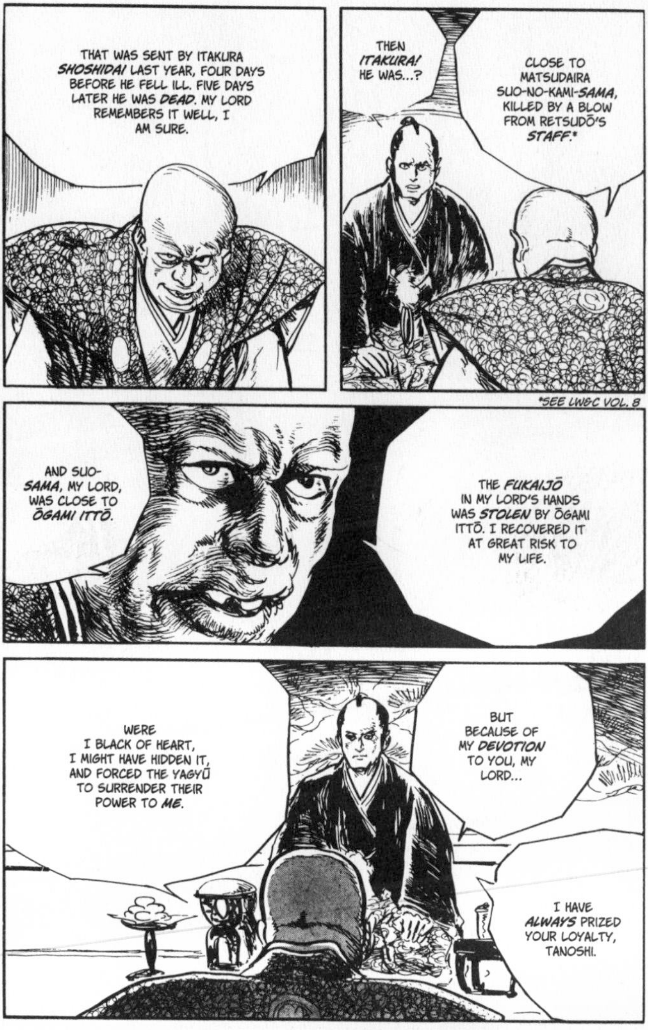
THAT WAS SENT BY ITAKURA SHOSHIDAI LAST YEAR, FOUR DAYS BEFORE HE FELL ILL. FIVE DAYS LATER HE WAS DEAD. MY LORD REMEMBERS IT WELL, I AM SURE.
THEN ITAKURA! HE WAS...?
CLOSE TO MATSUDAIRA SUO-NO-KAMI-SAMA, KILLED BY A BLOW FROM RETSUDŌ'S STAFF.*
*SEE LW&C VOL. 8
AND SUO-SAMA, MY LORD, WAS CLOSE TO ŌGAMI ITTŌ.
THE FUKAIJŌ IN MY LORD'S HANDS WAS STOLEN BY ŌGAMI ITTŌ. I RECOVERED IT AT GREAT RISK TO MY LIFE.
WERE I BLACK OF HEART, I MIGHT HAVE HIDDEN IT, AND FORCED THE YAGYŪ TO SURRENDER THEIR POWER TO ME.
BUT BECAUSE OF MY DEVOTION TO YOU, MY LORD...
I HAVE ALWAYS PRIZED YOUR LOYALTY, TANOSHI.

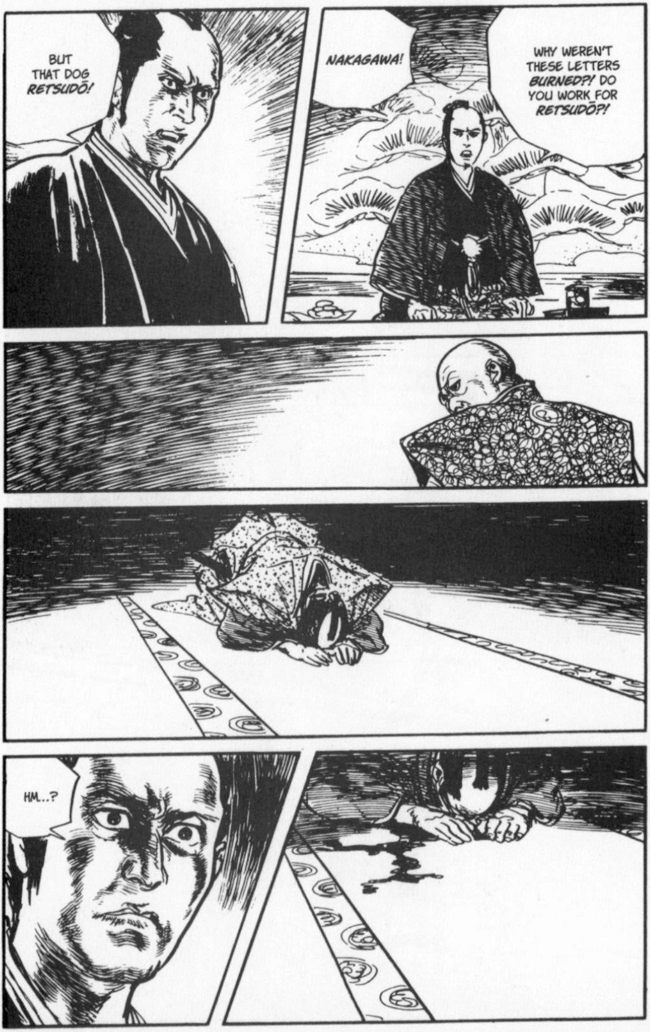
BUT THAT DOG RETSUDŌ!
NAKAGAWA!
WHY WEREN'T THESE LETTERS BURNED?! DO YOU WORK FOR RETSUDŌ?!
HM..?

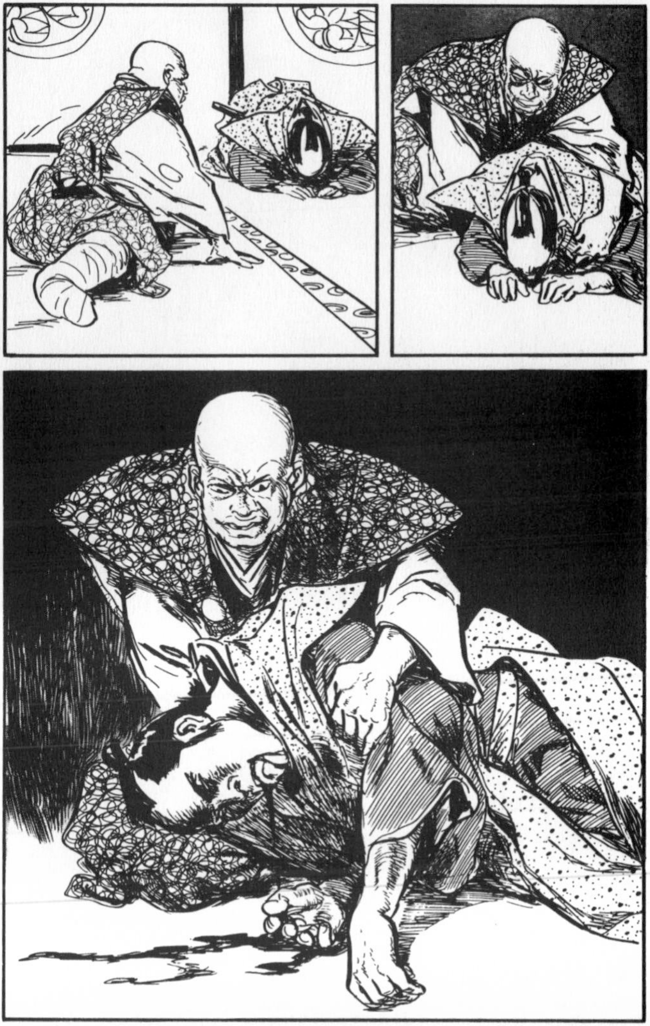

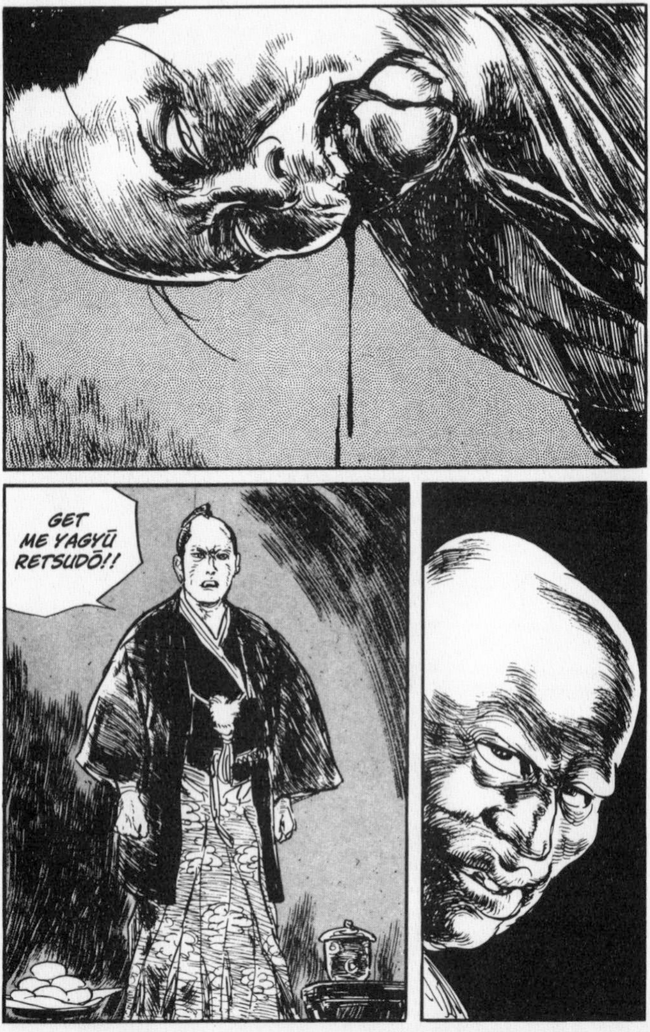
GET ME YAGYŪ RETSUDŌ!!

the hundred and
twentieth

# The Last
# Cherry
# Blossoms

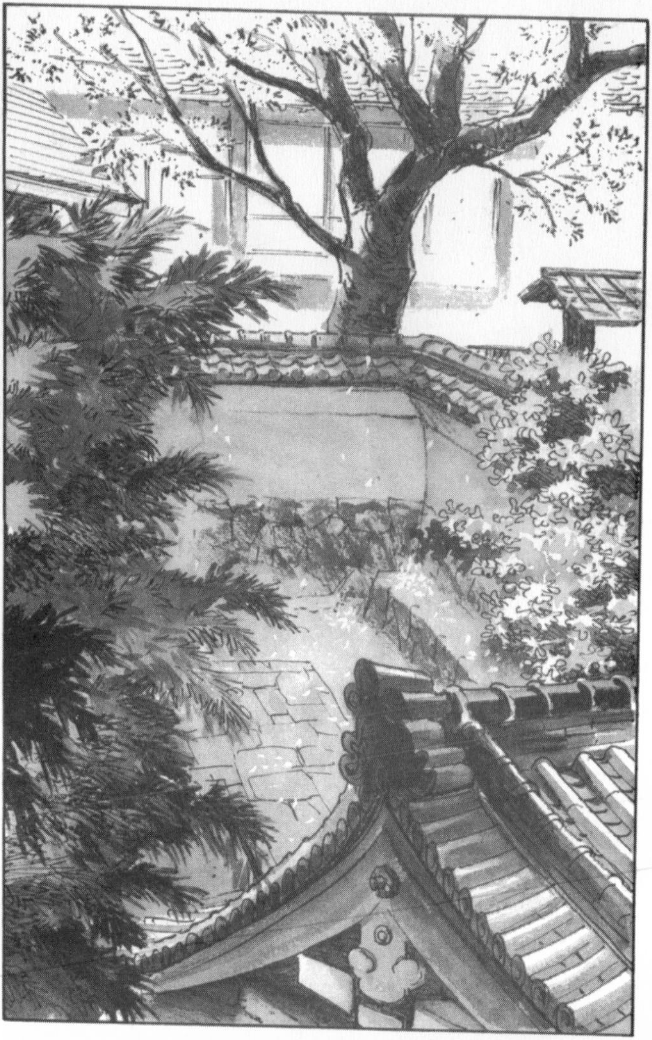

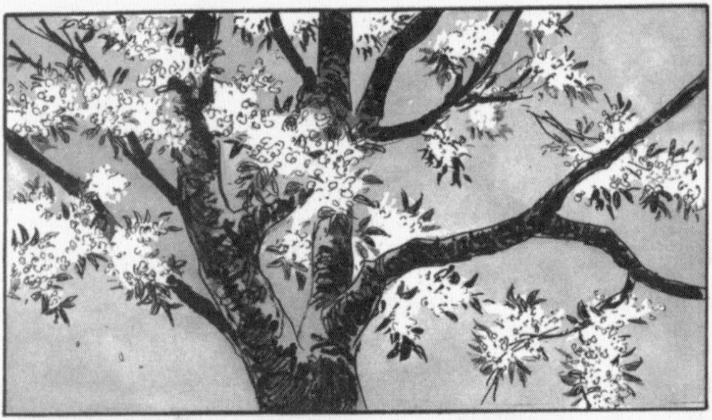
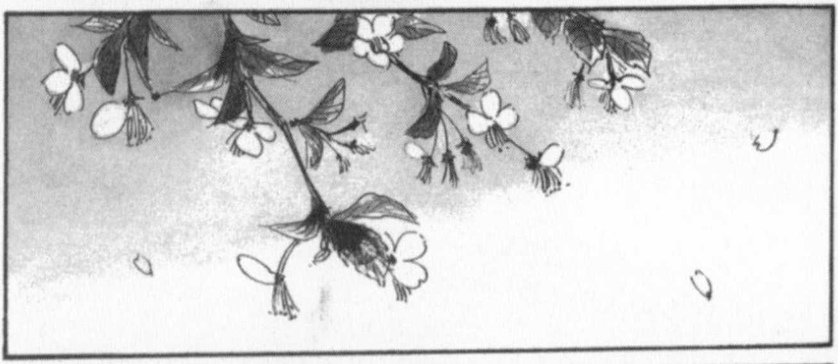
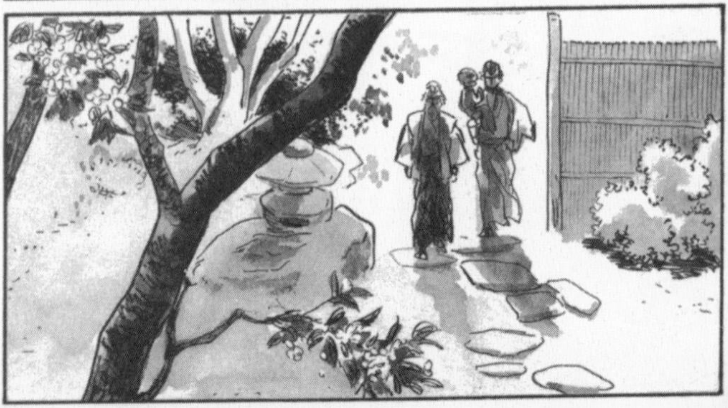

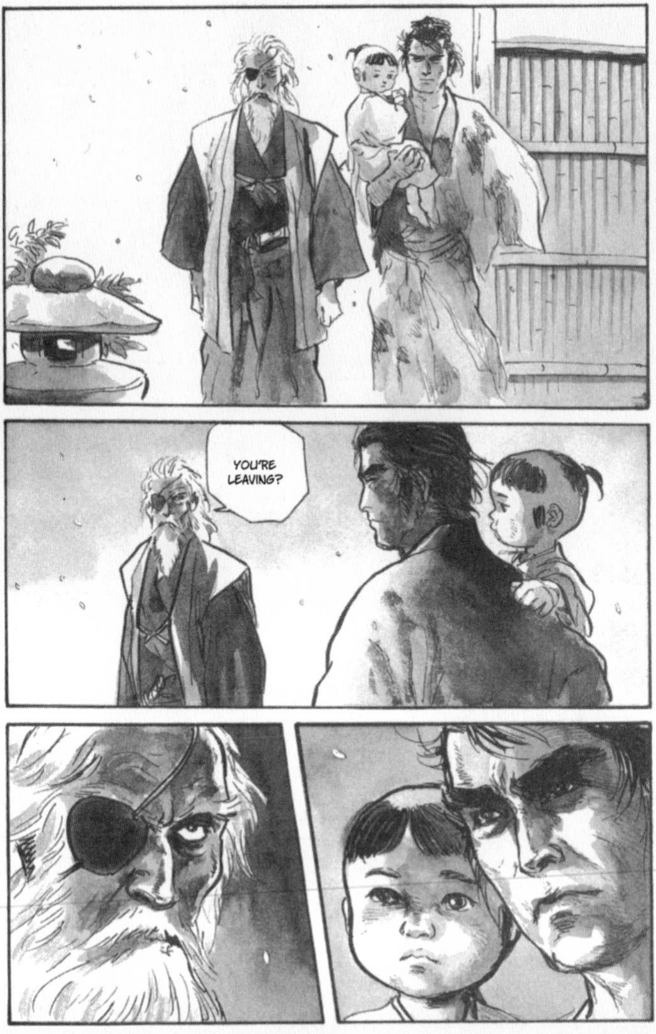
YOU'RE LEAVING?

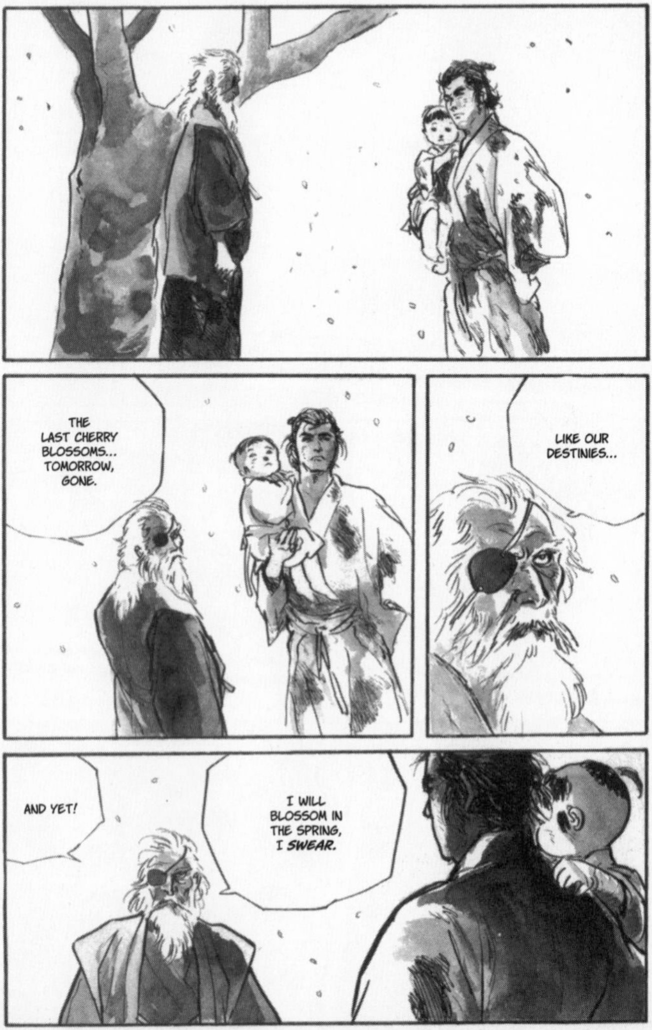

THE LAST CHERRY BLOSSOMS... TOMORROW, GONE.
LIKE OUR DESTINIES...
AND YET!
I WILL BLOSSOM IN THE SPRING, I *SWEAR.*

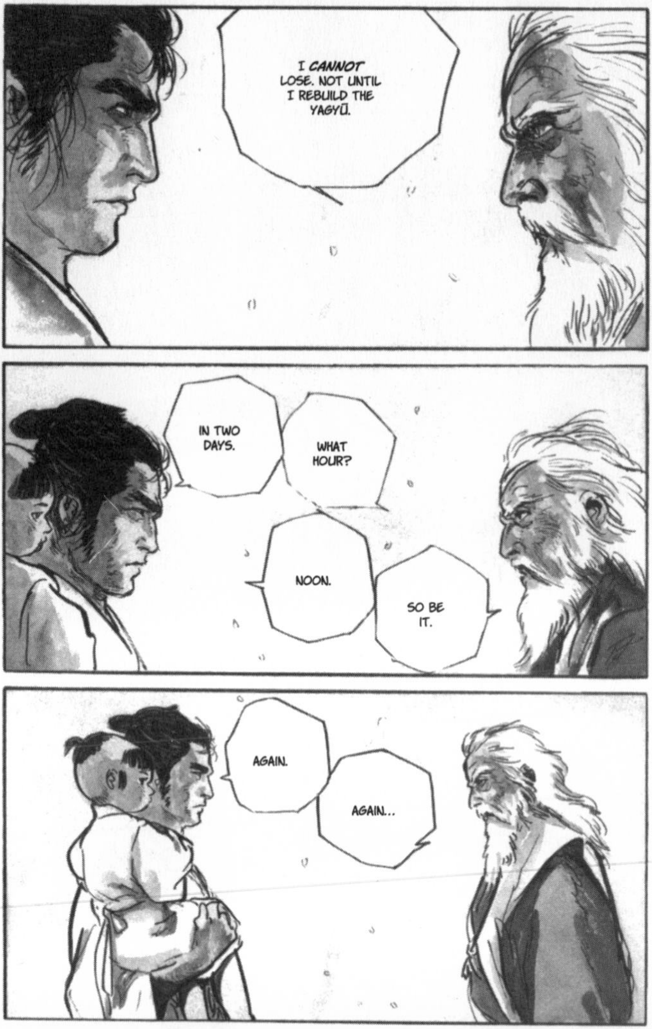
I *CANNOT* LOSE. NOT UNTIL I REBUILD THE YAGYŪ.
IN TWO DAYS.
WHAT HOUR?
NOON.
SO BE IT.
AGAIN.
AGAIN...

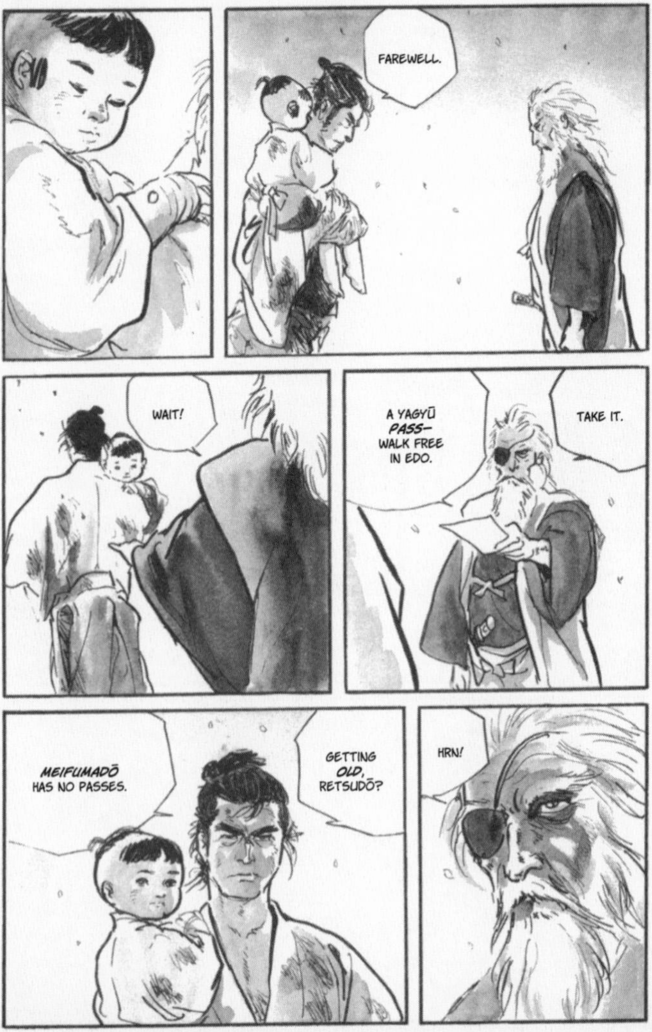
FAREWELL.
WAIT!
A YAGYŪ PASS— WALK FREE IN EDO.
TAKE IT.
MEIFUMADŌ HAS NO PASSES.
GETTING OLD, RETSUDŌ?
HRN!

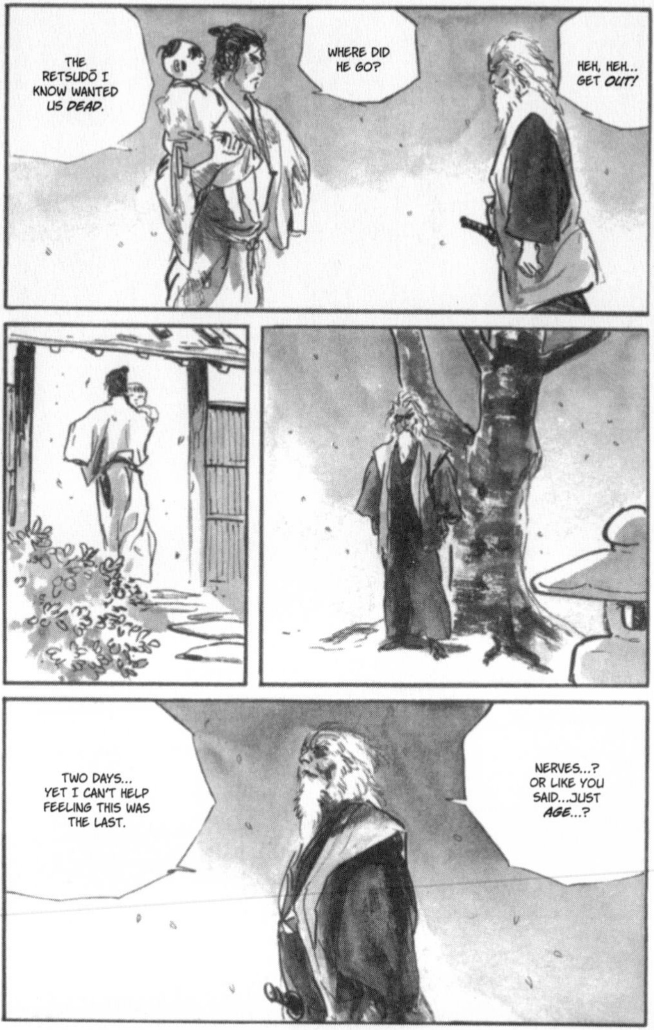
THE RETSUDŌ I KNOW WANTED US DEAD.
WHERE DID HE GO?
HEH, HEH... GET OUT!
TWO DAYS... YET I CAN'T HELP FEELING THIS WAS THE LAST.
NERVES...? OR LIKE YOU SAID...JUST AGE...?

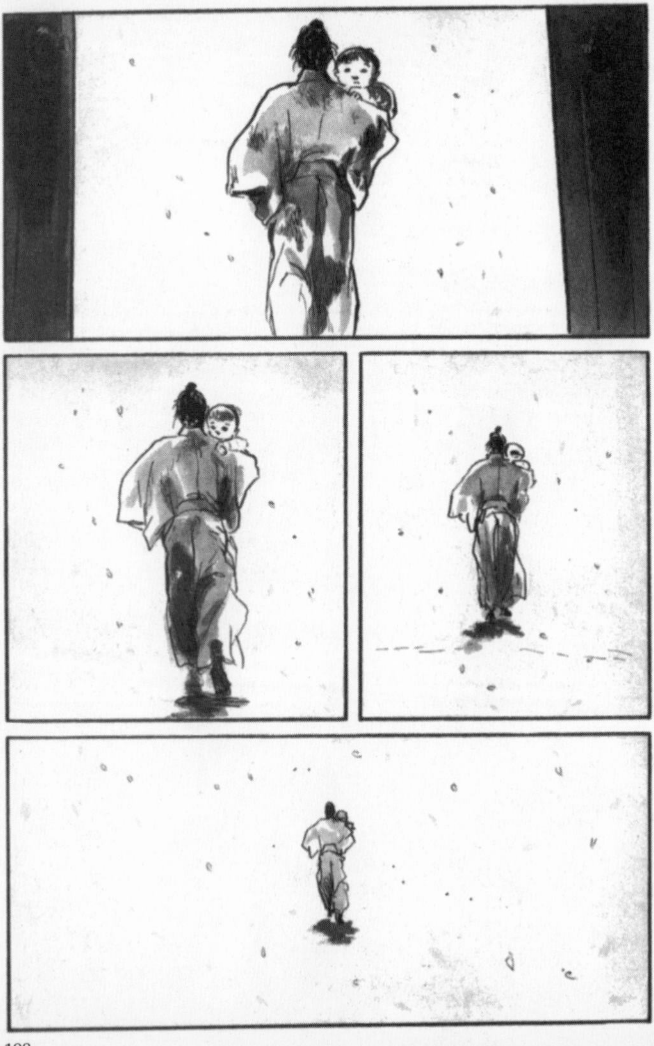

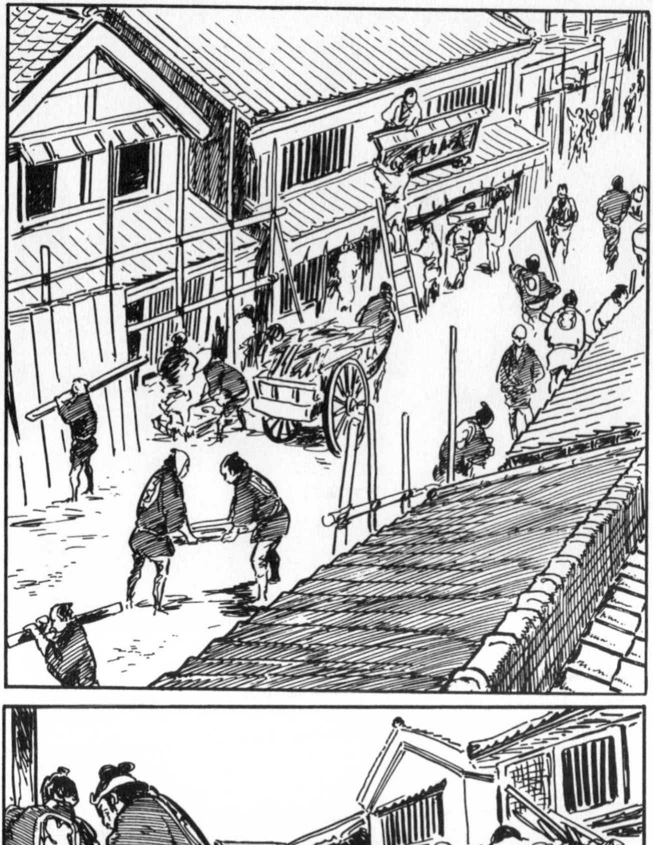

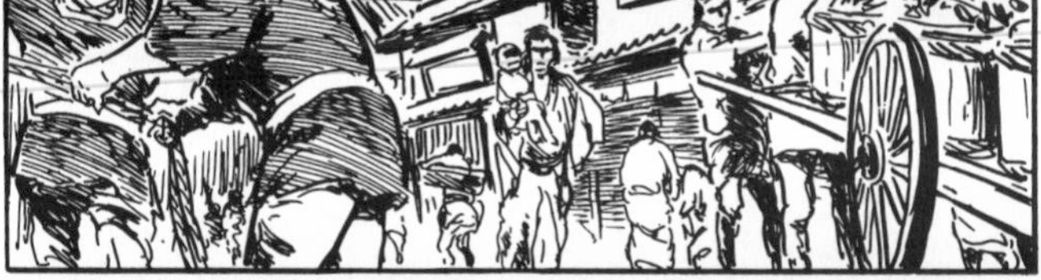

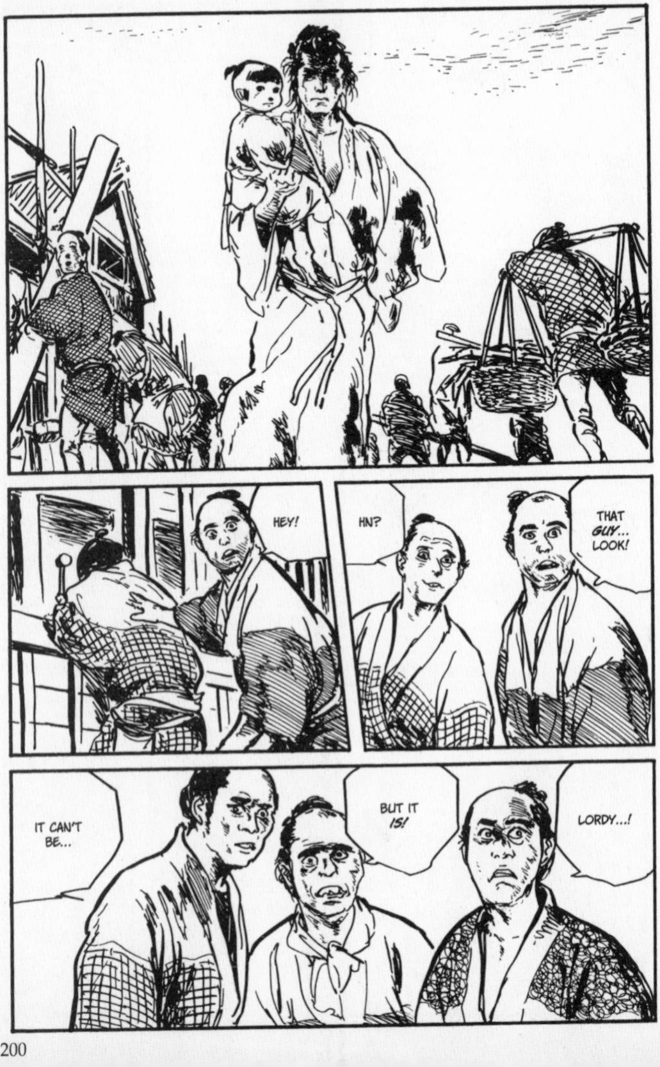
HEY!
HN?
THAT *GUY*... LOOK!
IT CAN'T BE...
BUT IT *IS!*
LORDY...!

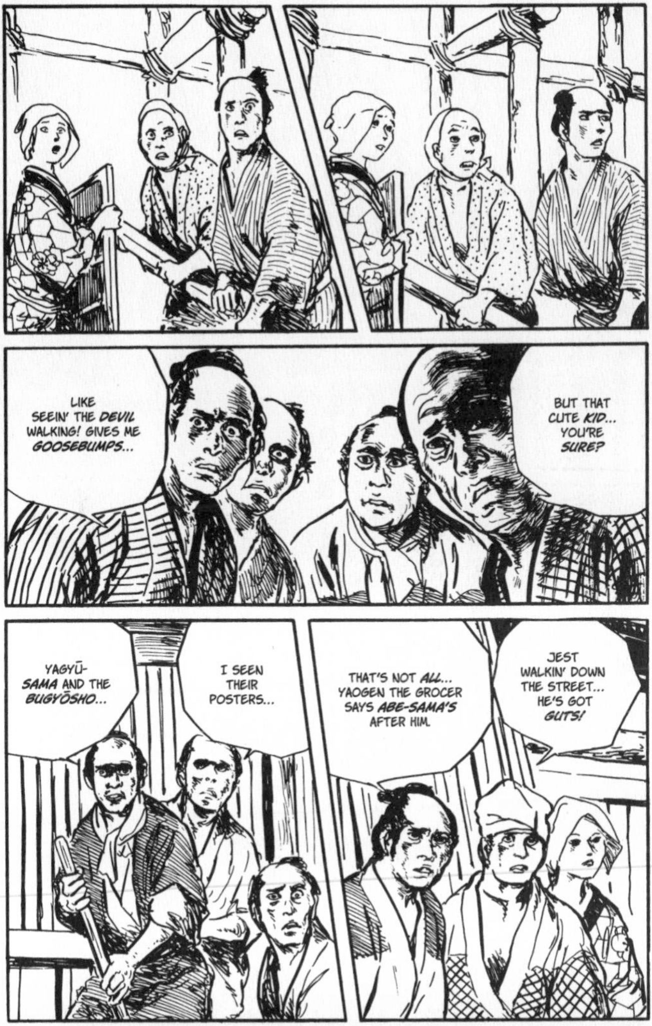
LIKE SEEIN' THE *DEVIL* WALKING! GIVES ME *GOOSEBUMPS*...
BUT THAT CUTE *KID*... YOU'RE *SURE?*
YAGYŪ-*SAMA* AND THE *BUGYŌSHO*...
I SEEN THEIR POSTERS...
THAT'S NOT *ALL*... YAOGEN THE GROCER SAYS *ABE-SAMA'S* AFTER HIM.
JEST WALKIN' DOWN THE STREET... HE'S GOT *GUTS!*

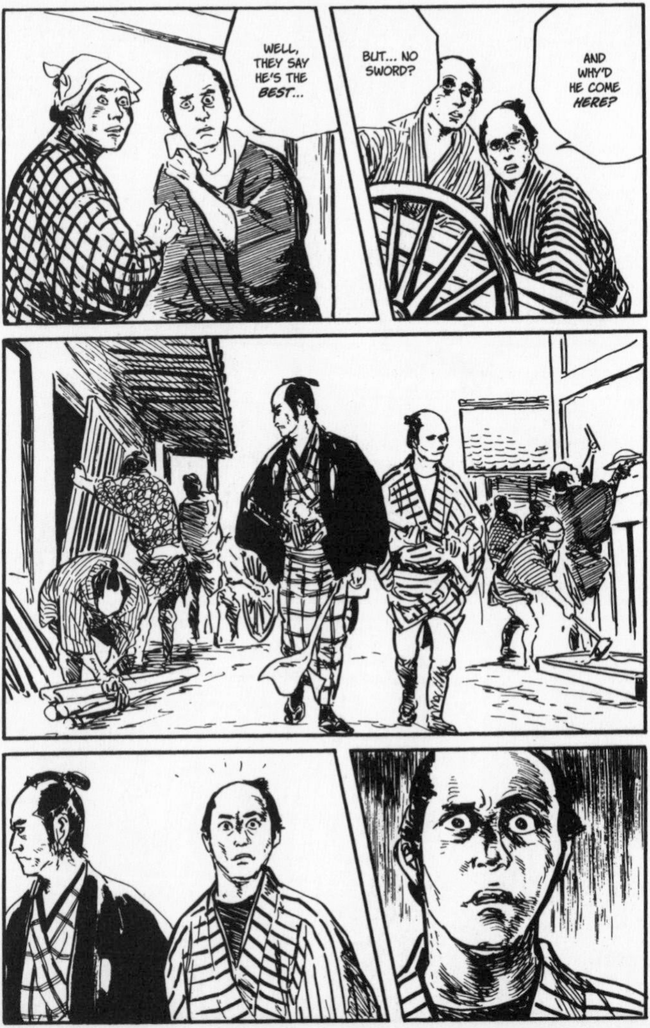
WELL, THEY SAY HE'S THE BEST...
BUT... NO SWORD?
AND WHY'D HE COME HERE?

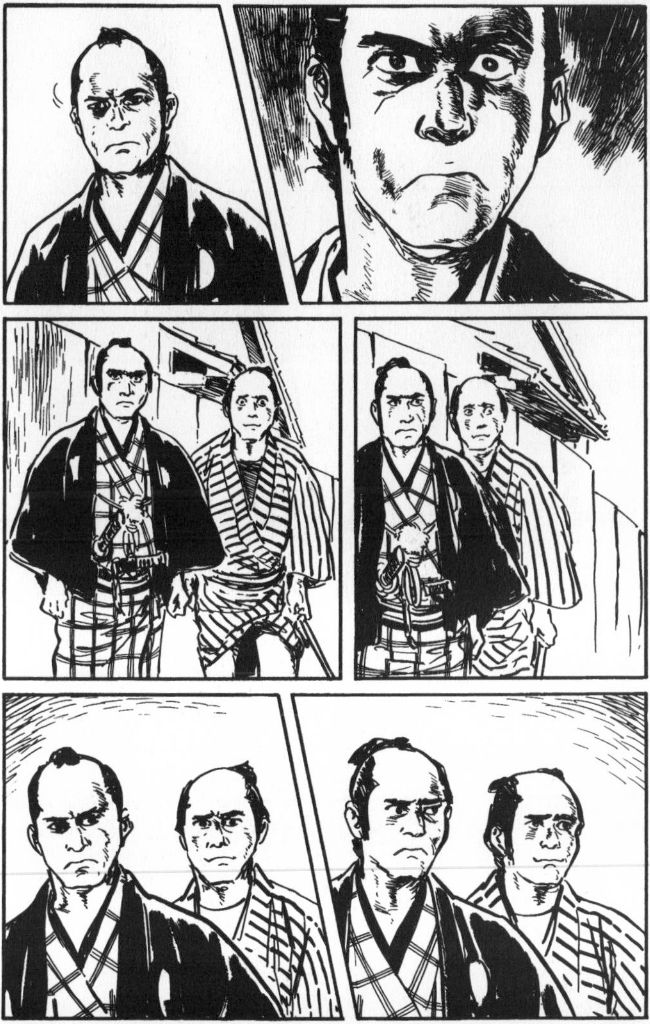

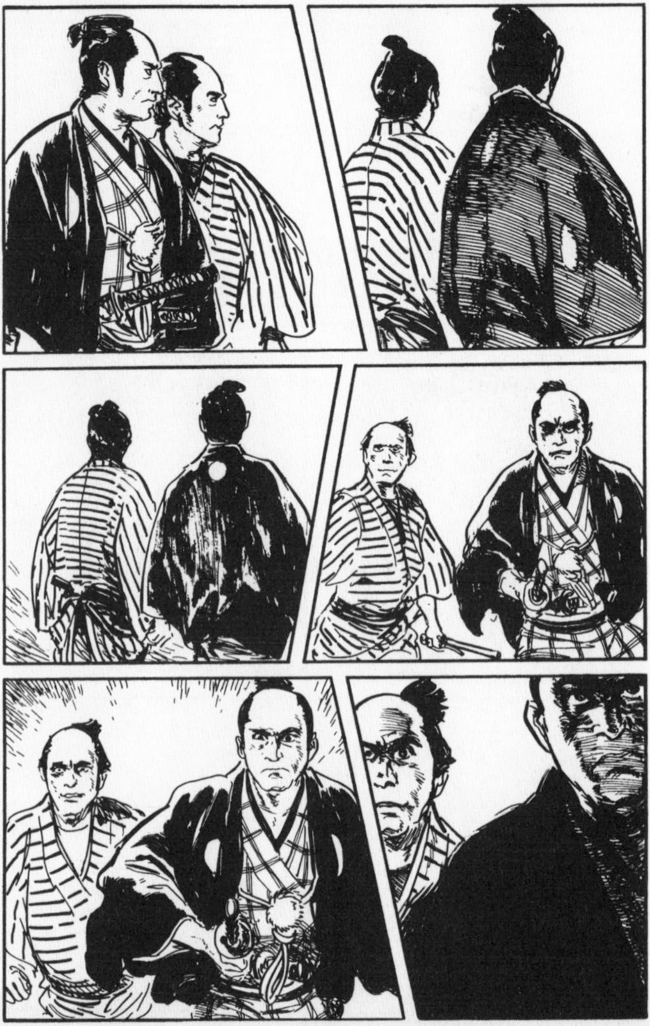

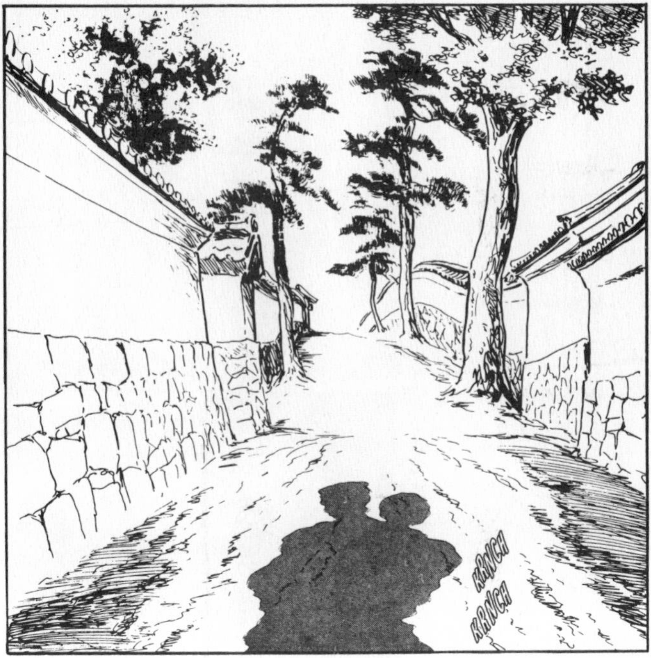
KRNCH
KRNCH

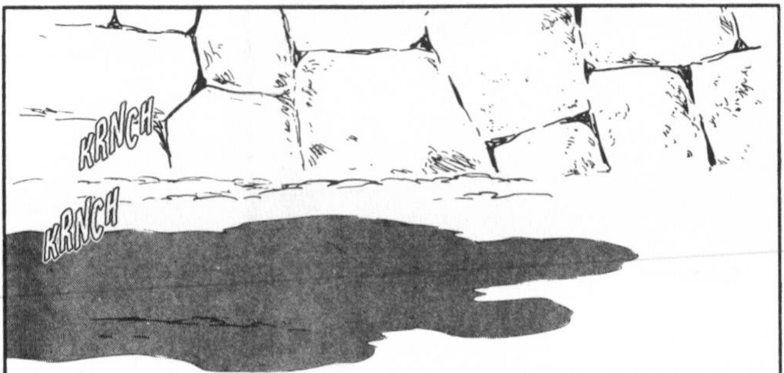
KRNCH
KRNCH

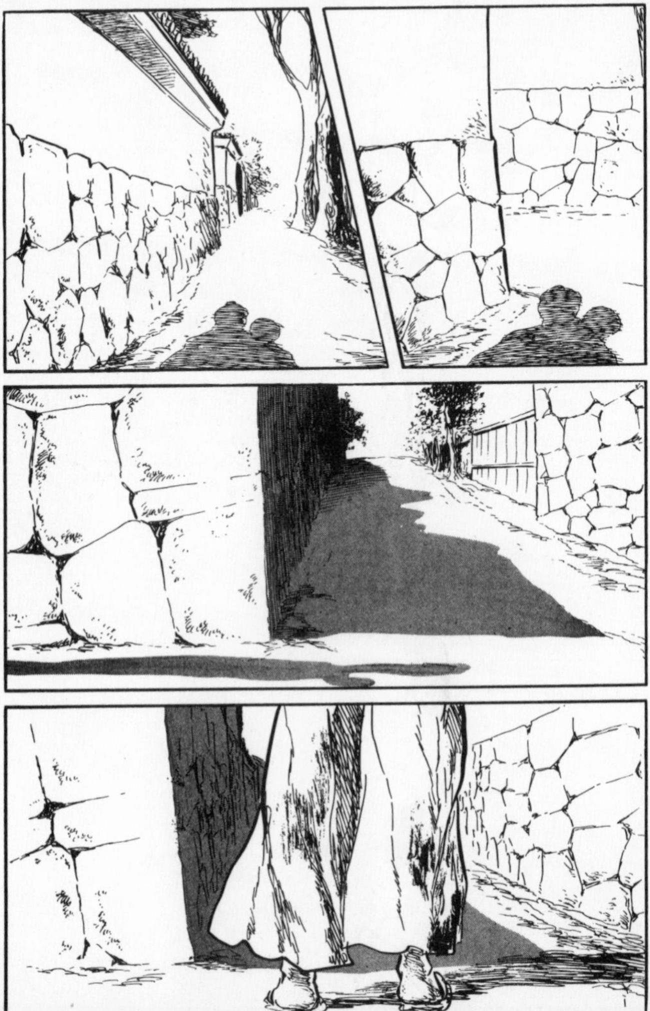

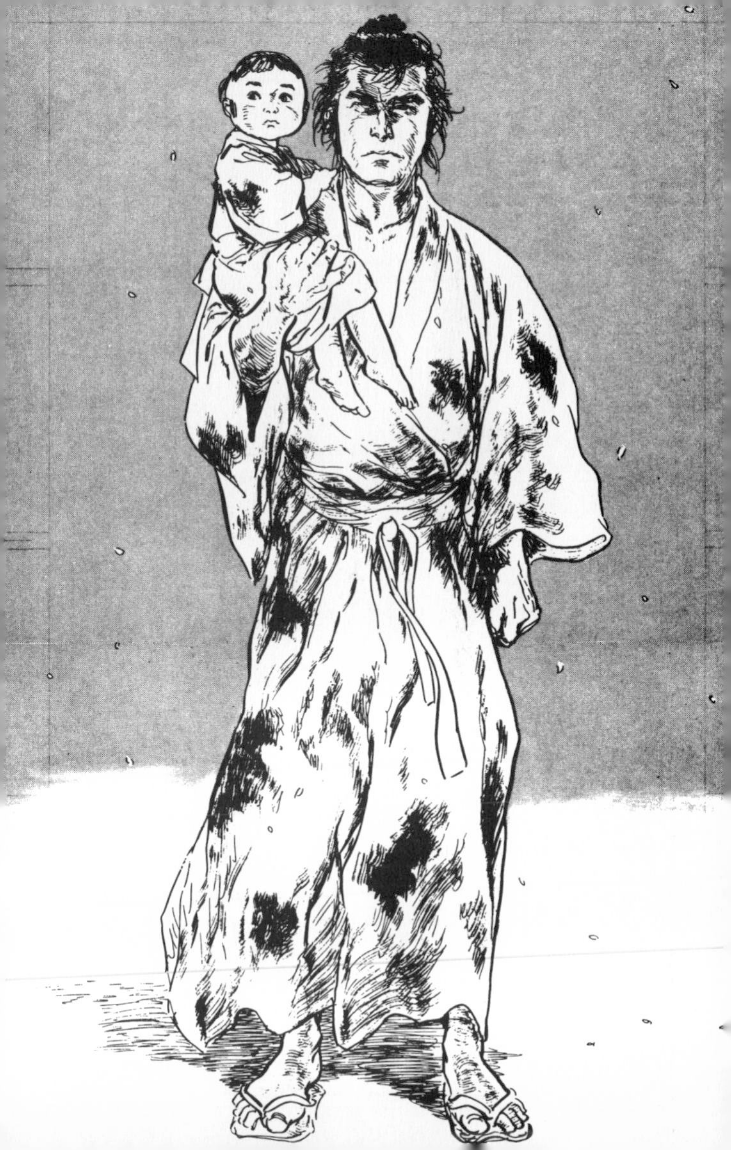

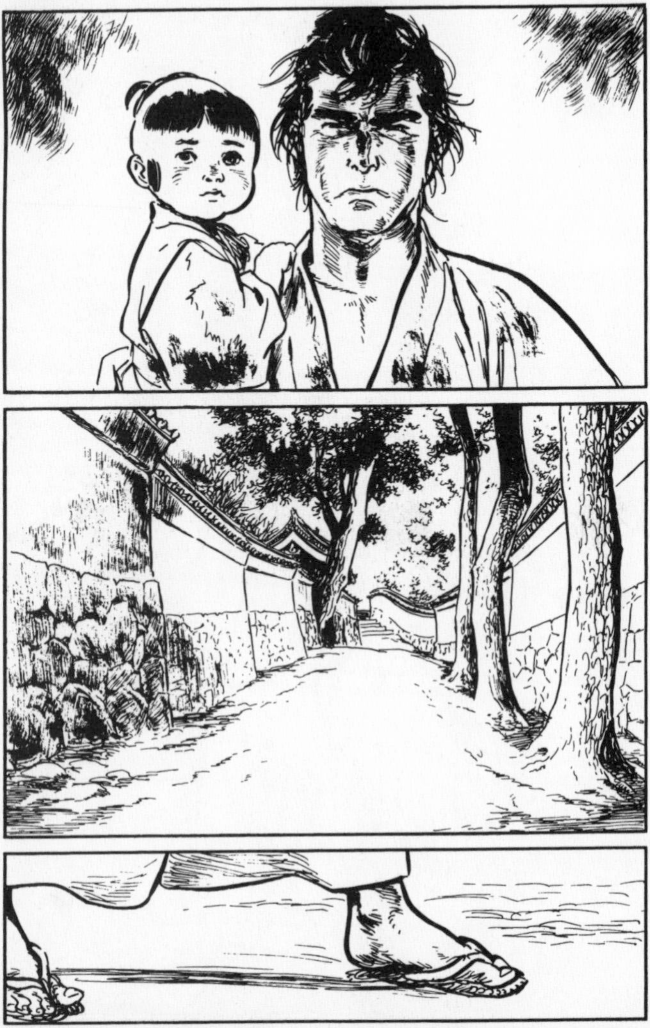

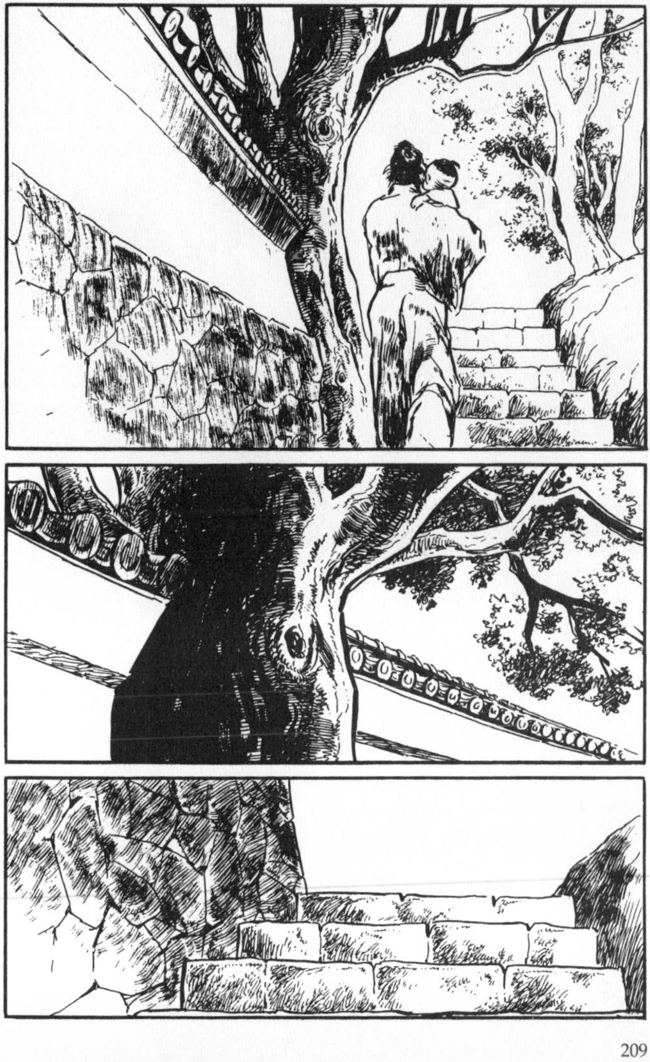

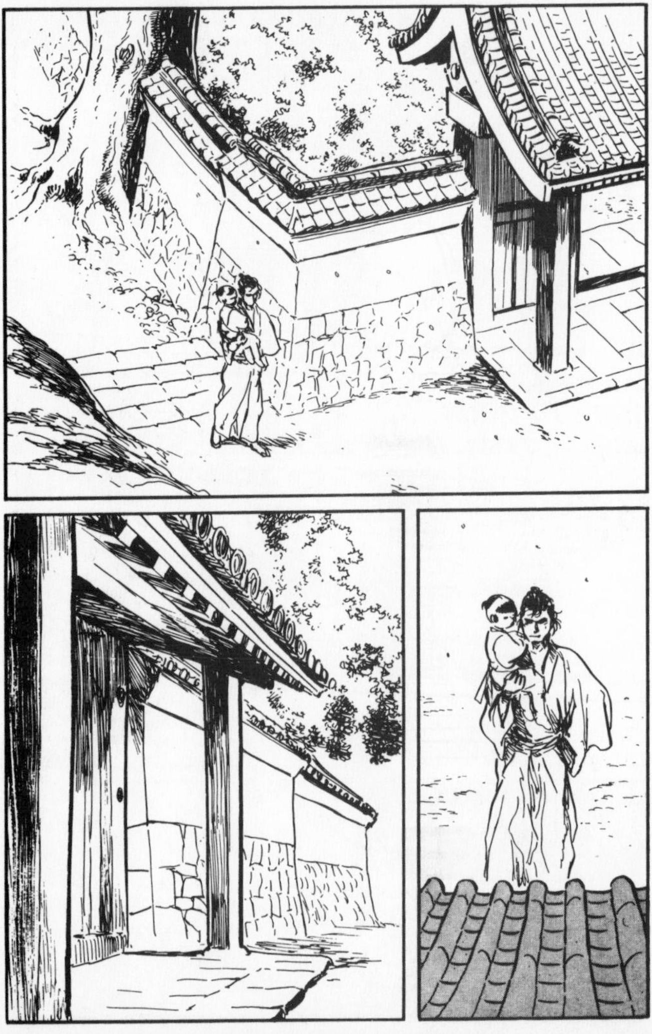

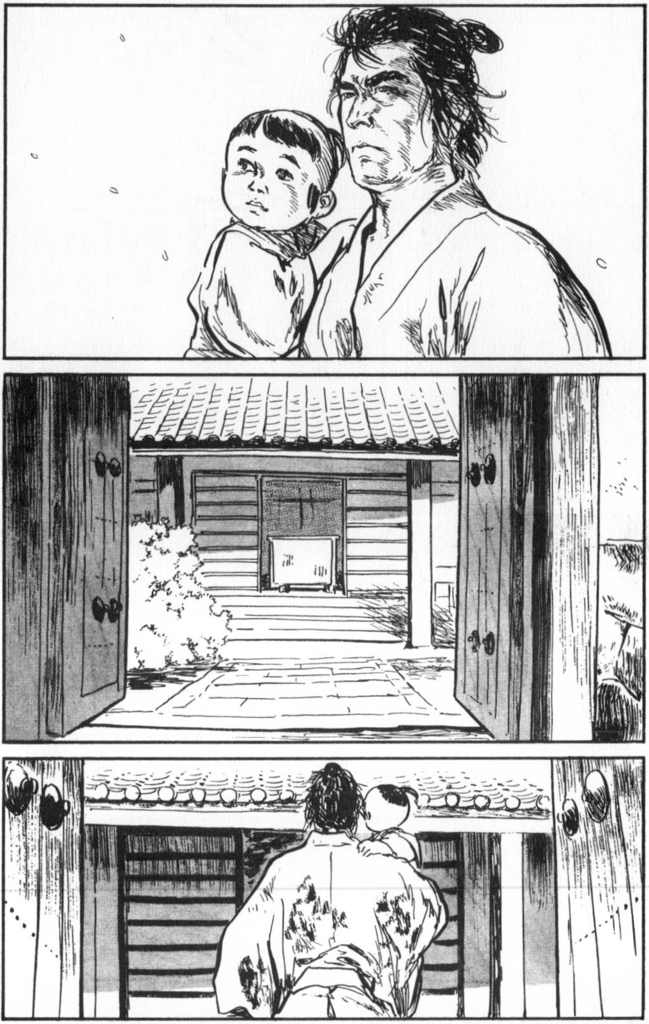

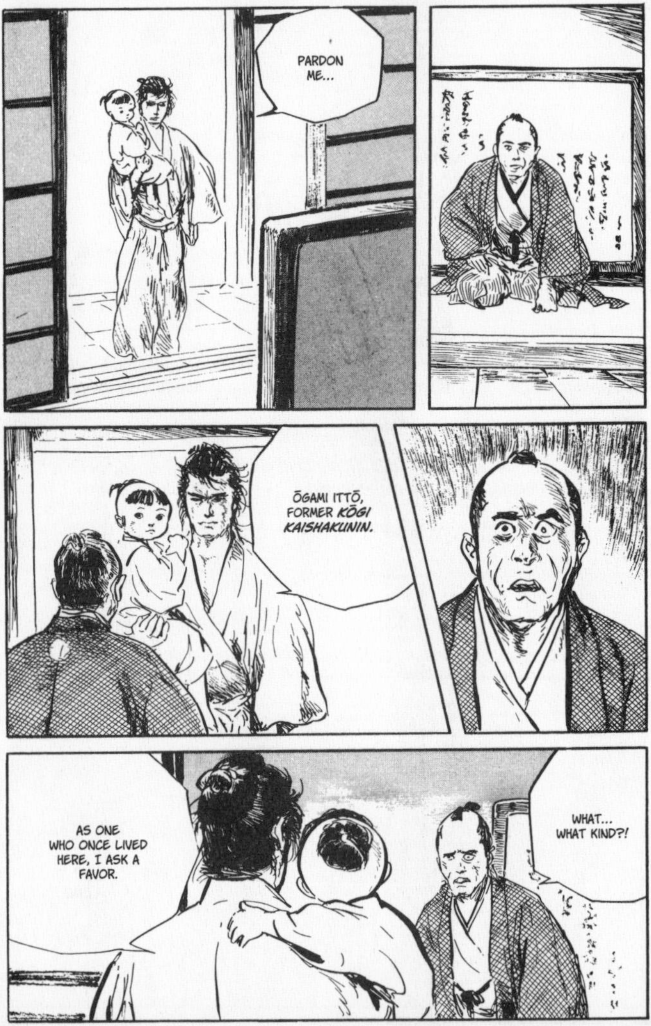
PARDON ME...
ŌGAMI ITTŌ, FORMER *KŌGI KAISHAKUNIN.*
AS ONE WHO ONCE LIVED HERE, I ASK A FAVOR.
WHAT... WHAT KIND?!

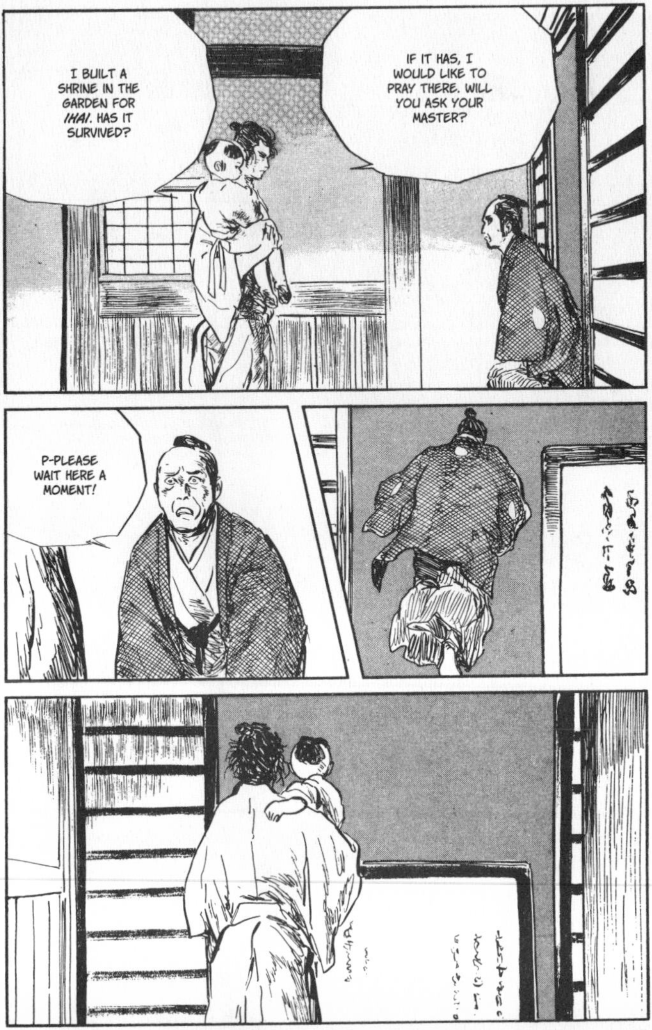
I BUILT A SHRINE IN THE GARDEN FOR *IHAI*. HAS IT SURVIVED?
IF IT HAS, I WOULD LIKE TO PRAY THERE. WILL YOU ASK YOUR MASTER?
P-PLEASE WAIT HERE A MOMENT!

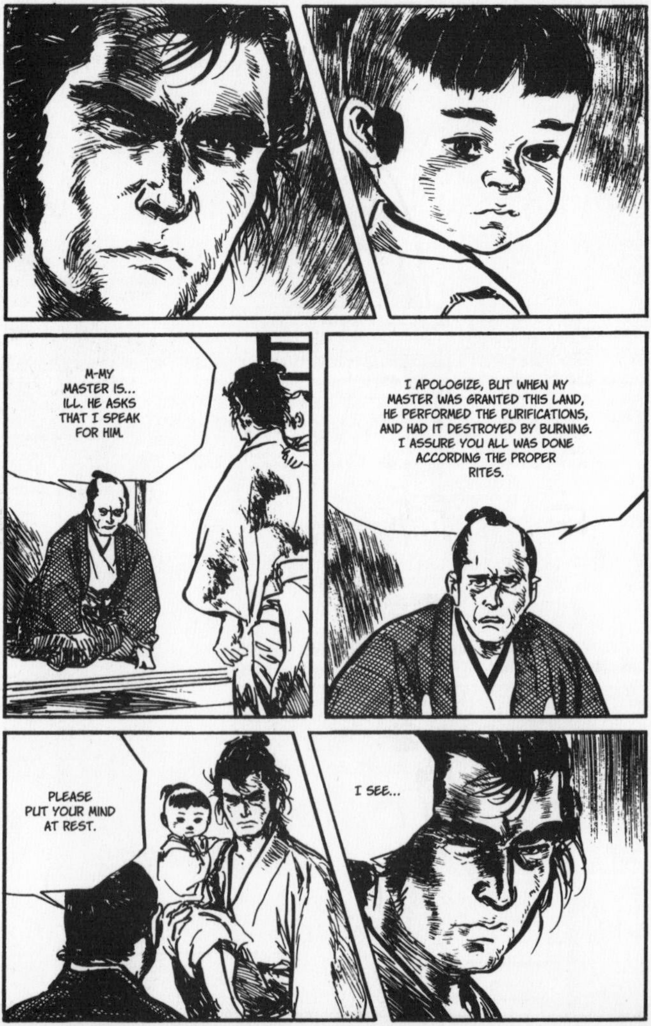
M-MY MASTER IS... ILL. HE ASKS THAT I SPEAK FOR HIM.
I APOLOGIZE, BUT WHEN MY MASTER WAS GRANTED THIS LAND, HE PERFORMED THE PURIFICATIONS, AND HAD IT DESTROYED BY BURNING. I ASSURE YOU ALL WAS DONE ACCORDING THE PROPER RITES.
PLEASE PUT YOUR MIND AT REST.
I SEE...

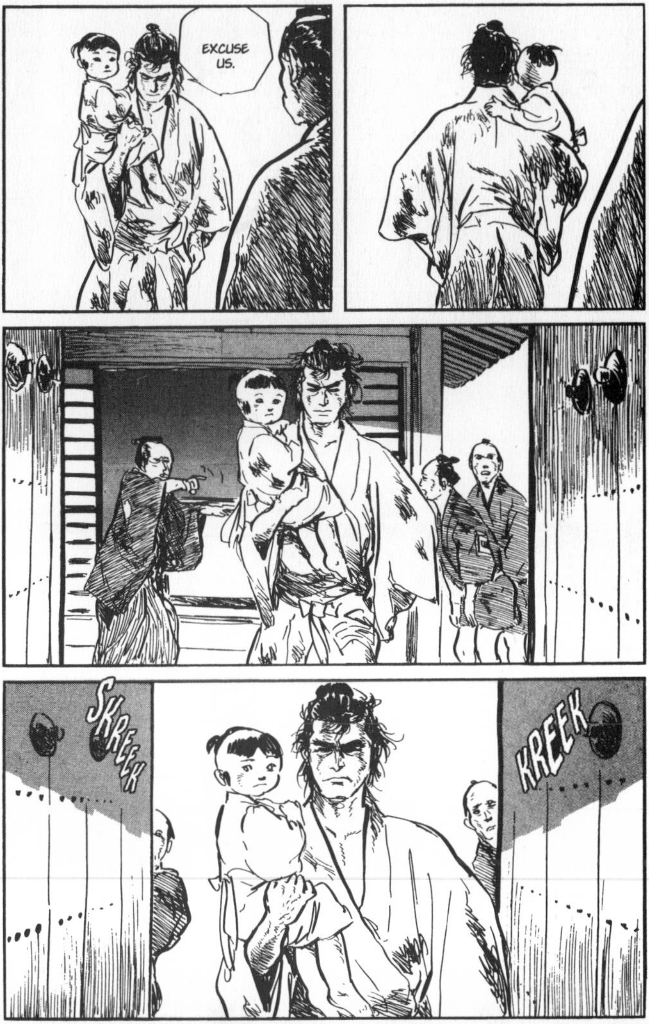
EXCUSE US.
SKREEK
KREEK

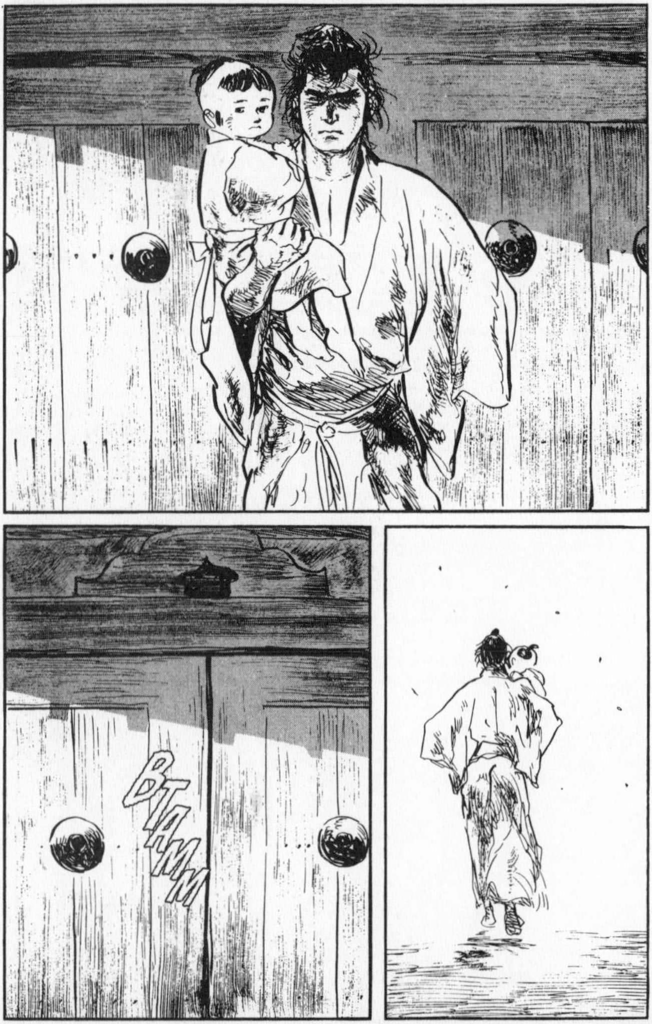
BTAMM

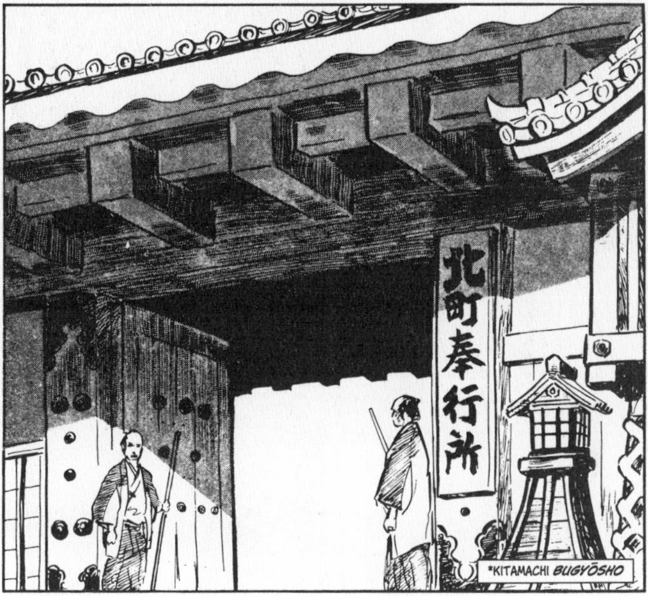
北町奉行所
*KITAMACHI *BUGYŌSHO*
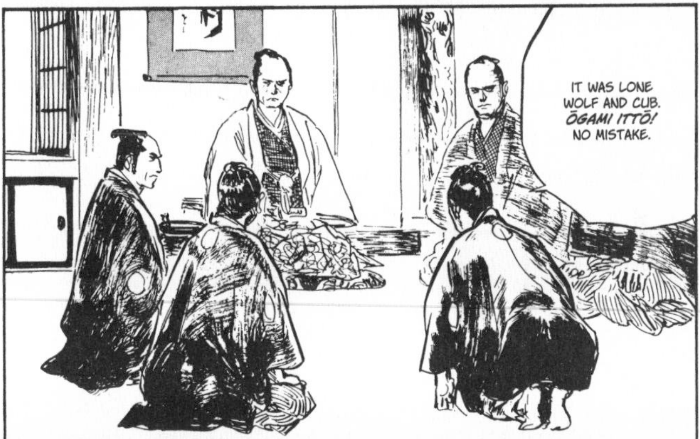
IT WAS LONE WOLF AND CUB. *ŌGAMI ITTŌ!* NO MISTAKE.

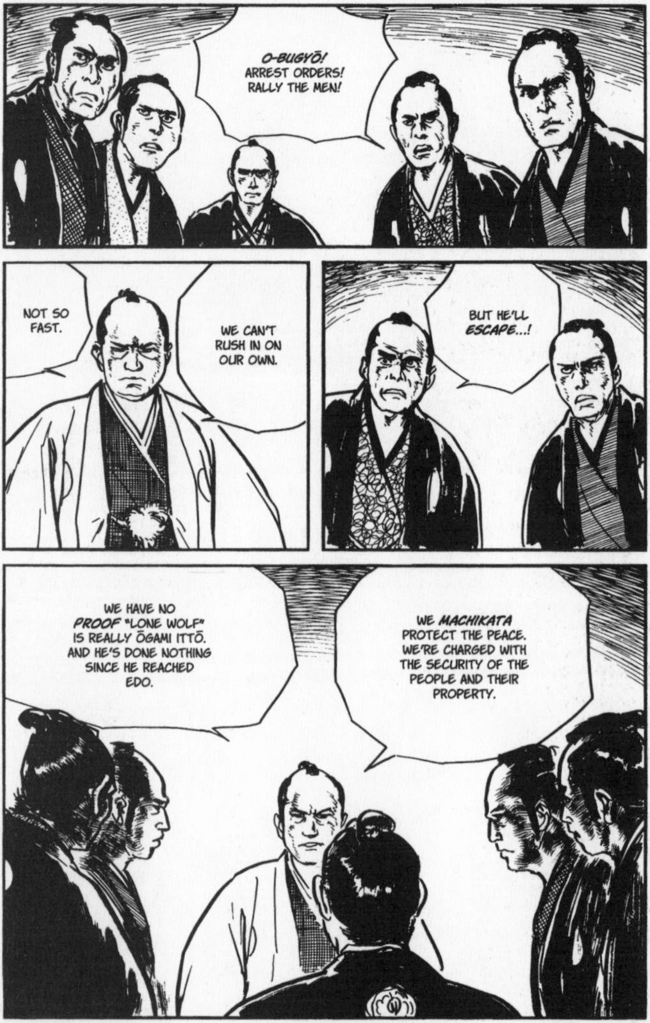
O-BUGYŌ! ARREST ORDERS! RALLY THE MEN!
NOT SO FAST.
WE CAN'T RUSH IN ON OUR OWN.
BUT HE'LL ESCAPE...!
WE HAVE NO PROOF "LONE WOLF" IS REALLY ŌGAMI ITTŌ. AND HE'S DONE NOTHING SINCE HE REACHED EDO.
WE MACHIKATA PROTECT THE PEACE. WE'RE CHARGED WITH THE SECURITY OF THE PEOPLE AND THEIR PROPERTY.

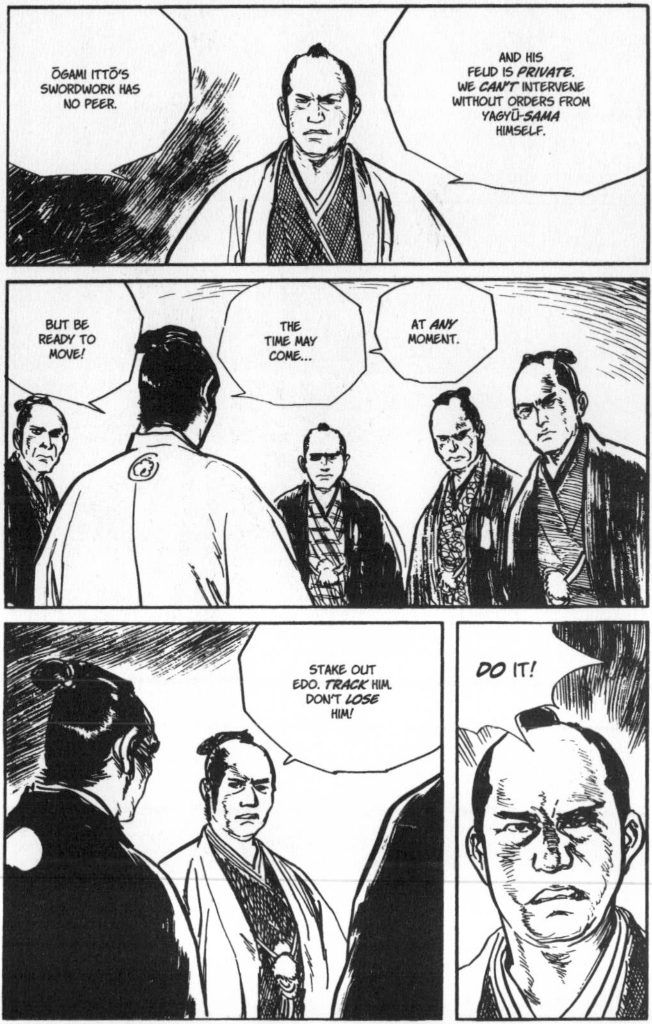
ŌGAMI ITTŌ'S SWORDWORK HAS NO PEER.
AND HIS FEUD IS *PRIVATE*. WE *CAN'T* INTERVENE WITHOUT ORDERS FROM YAGYŪ-*SAMA* HIMSELF.
BUT BE READY TO MOVE!
THE TIME MAY COME...
AT *ANY* MOMENT.
STAKE OUT EDO. *TRACK* HIM. DON'T *LOSE* HIM!
*DO* IT!

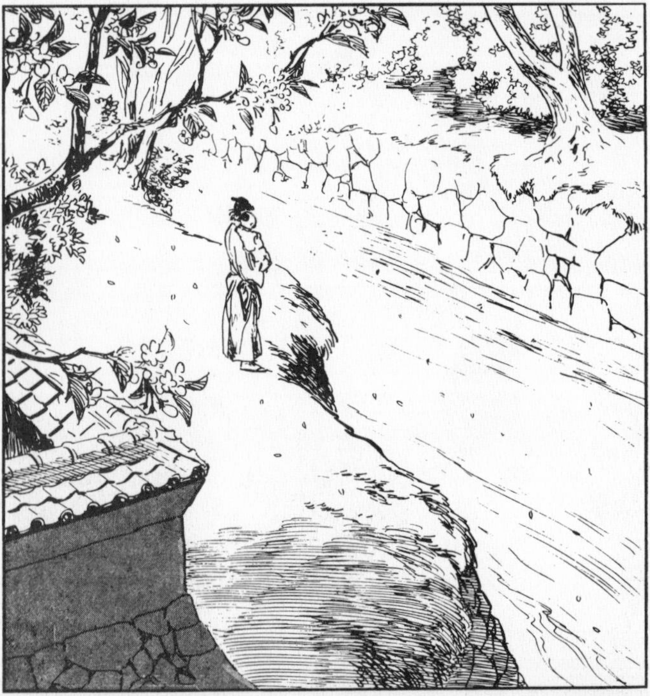

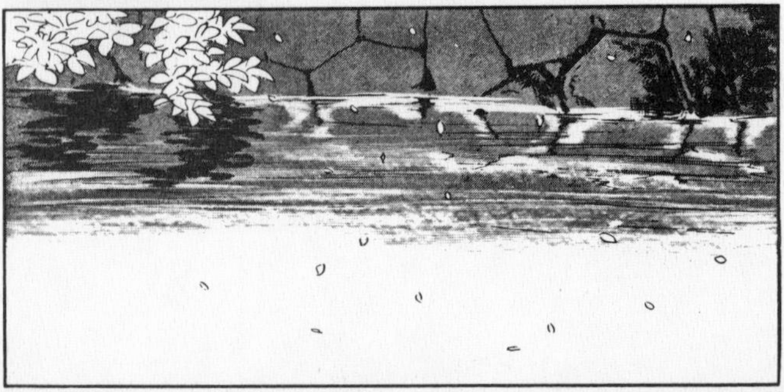

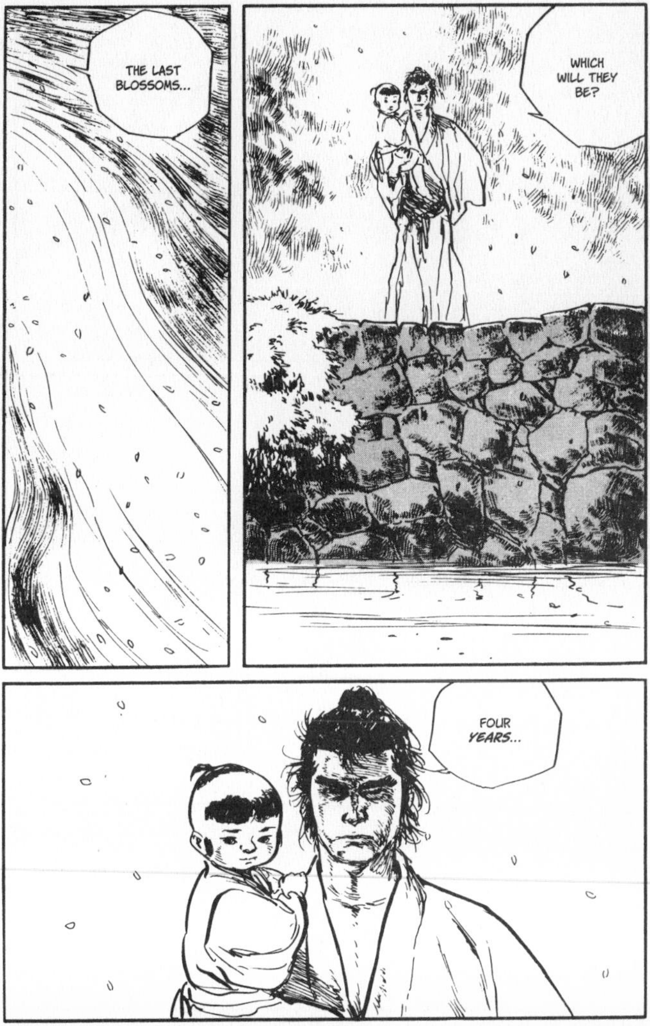
THE LAST BLOSSOMS...
WHICH WILL THEY BE?
FOUR *YEARS*...

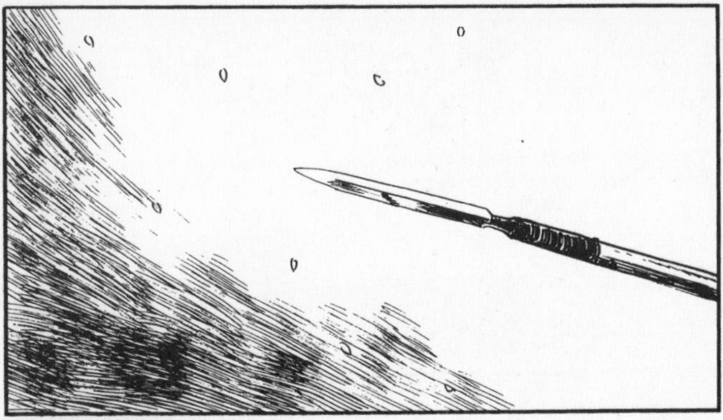
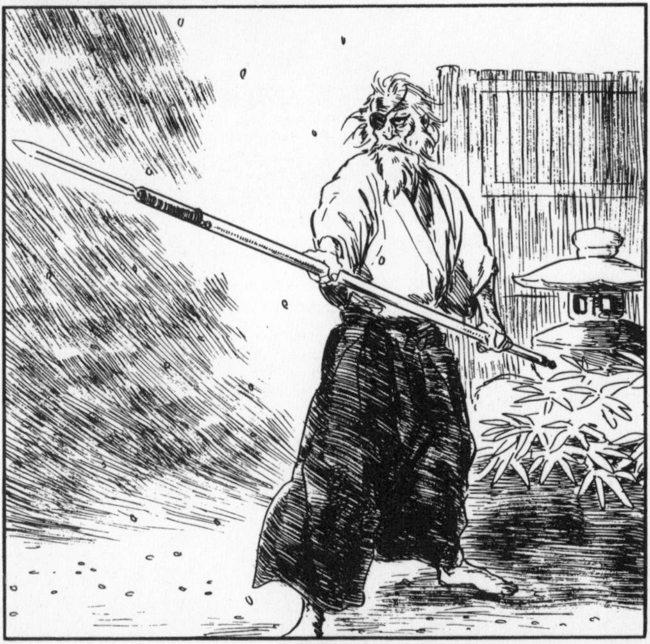

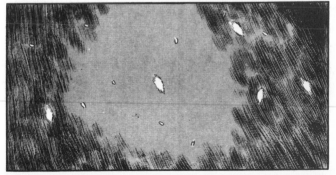

223

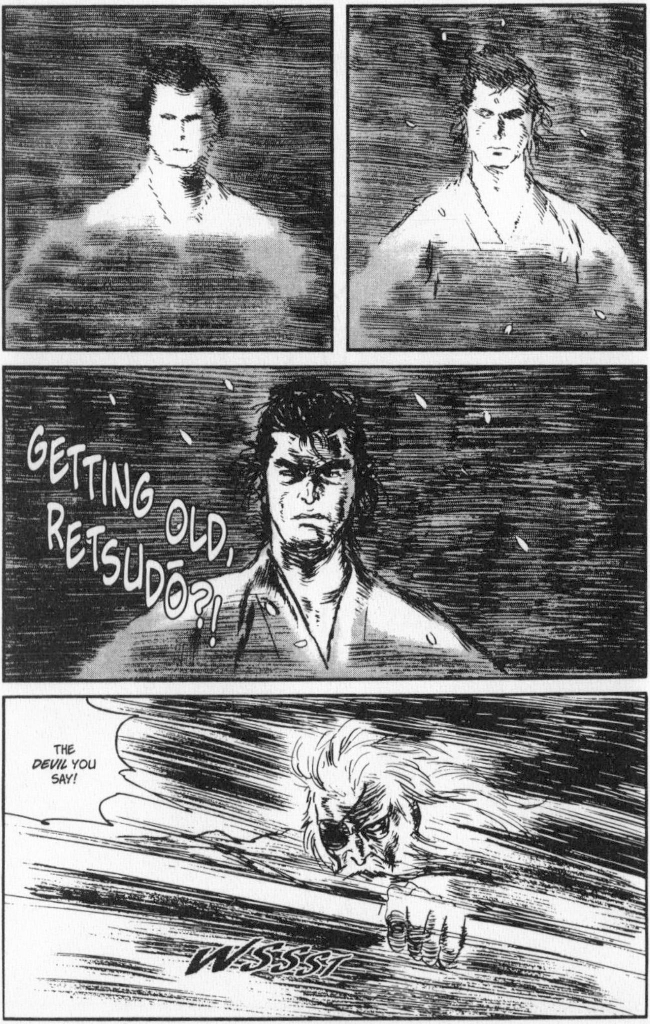
GETTING OLD, RETSUDŌ?!
THE DEVIL YOU SAY!
WSSSST

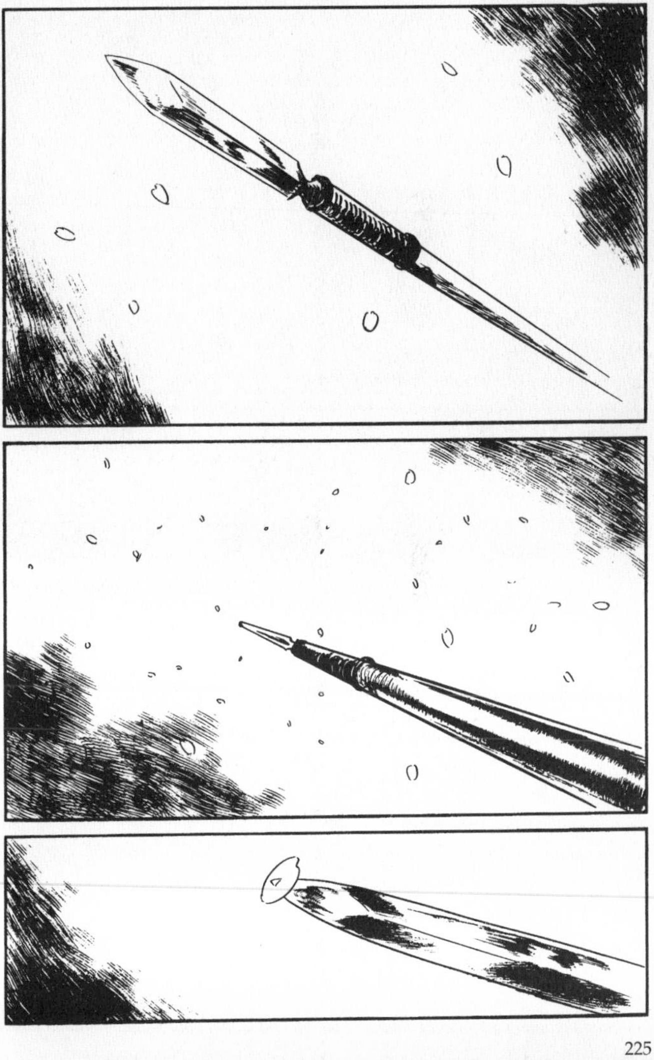

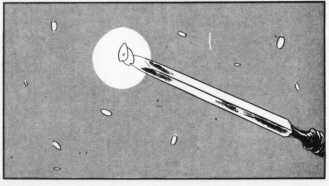

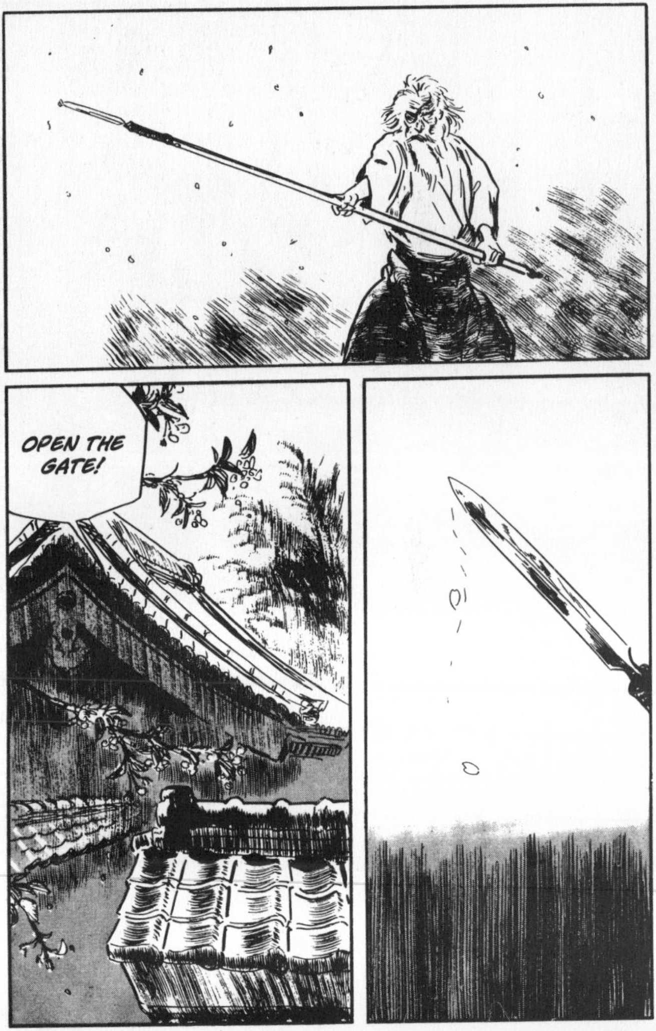
OPEN THE GATE!

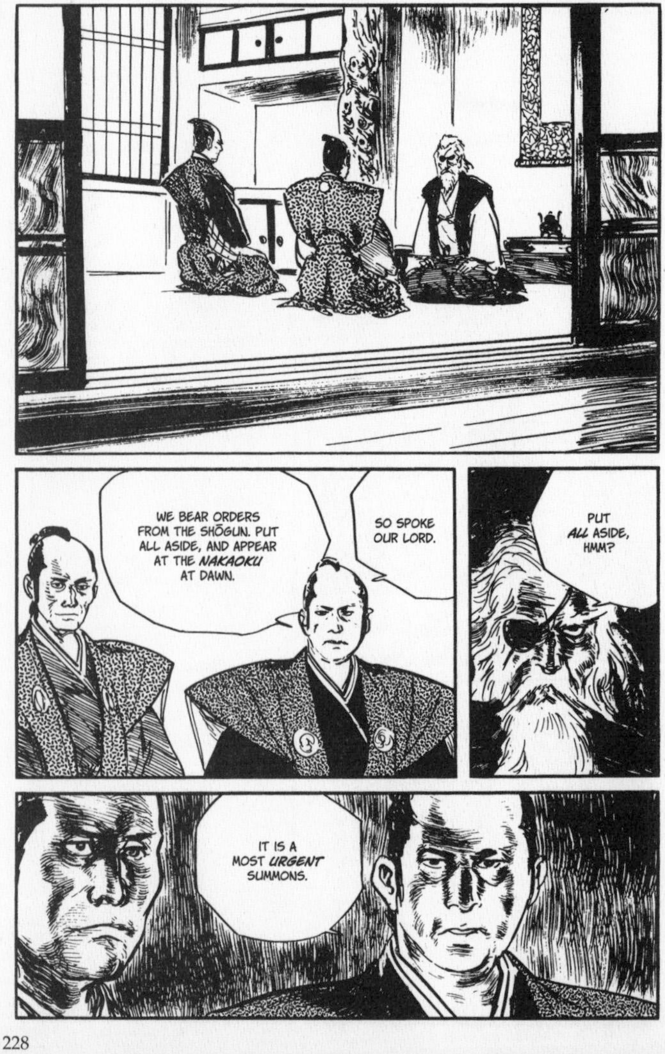
WE BEAR ORDERS FROM THE SHŌGUN. PUT ALL ASIDE, AND APPEAR AT THE *NAKAOKU* AT DAWN.
SO SPOKE OUR LORD.
PUT *ALL* ASIDE, HMM?
IT IS A MOST *URGENT* SUMMONS.

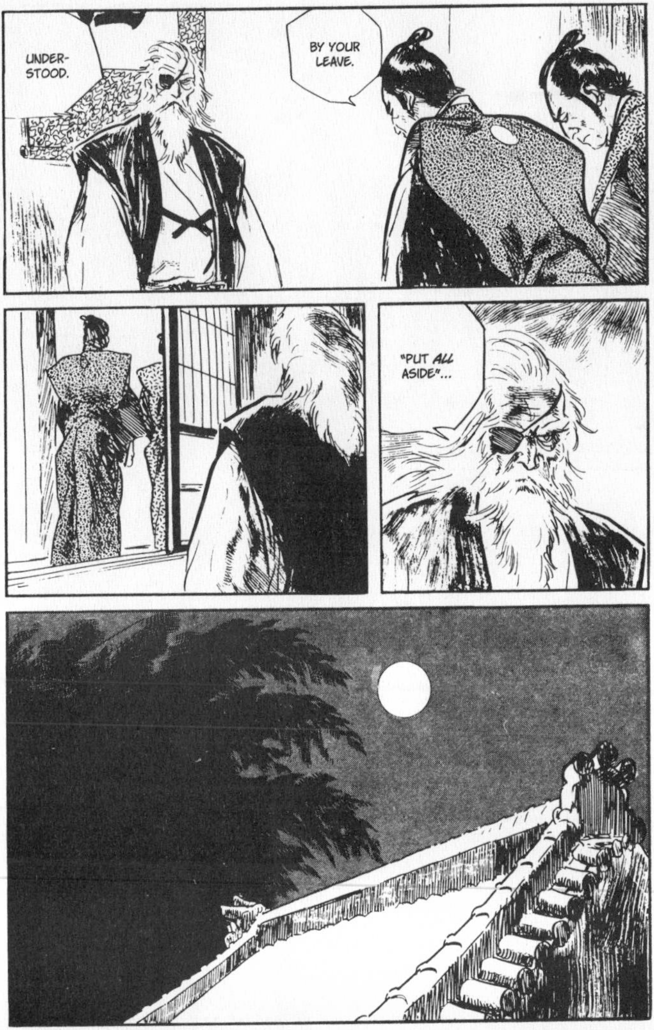
UNDER-STOOD.
BY YOUR LEAVE.
"PUT ALL ASIDE"...

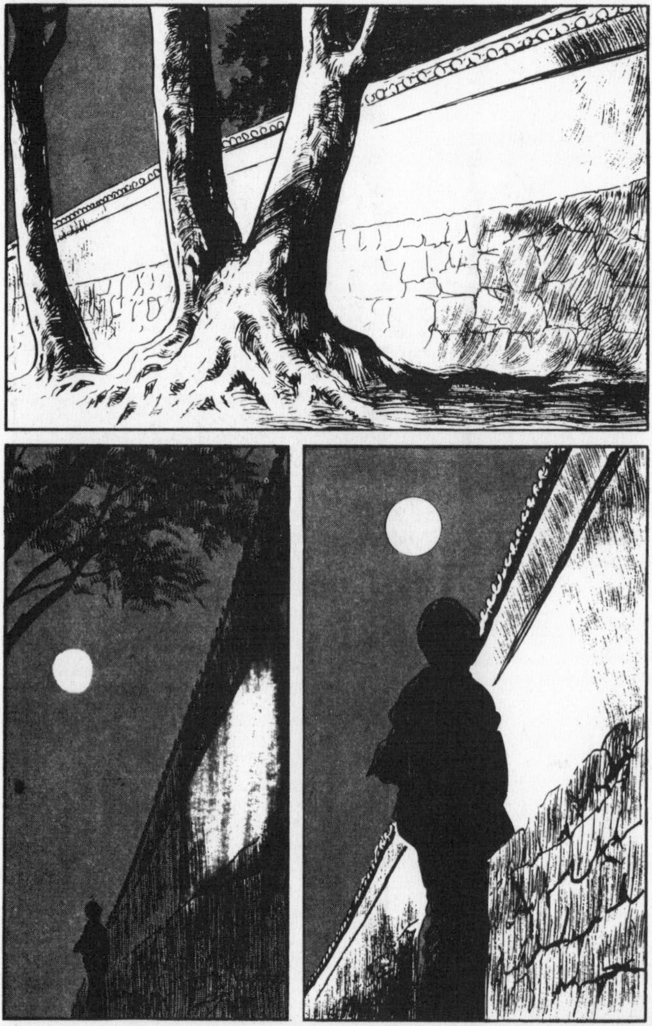

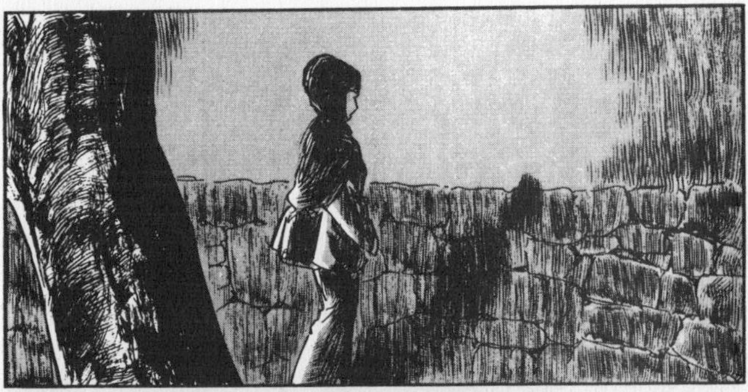

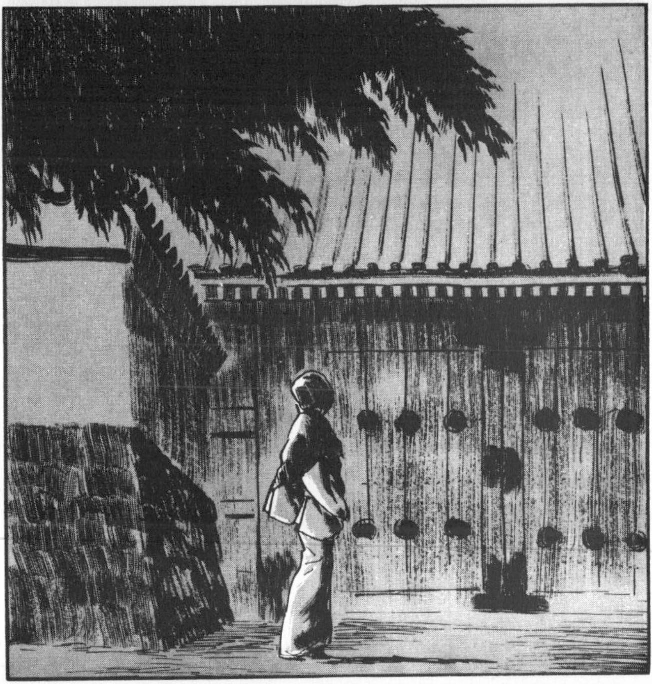

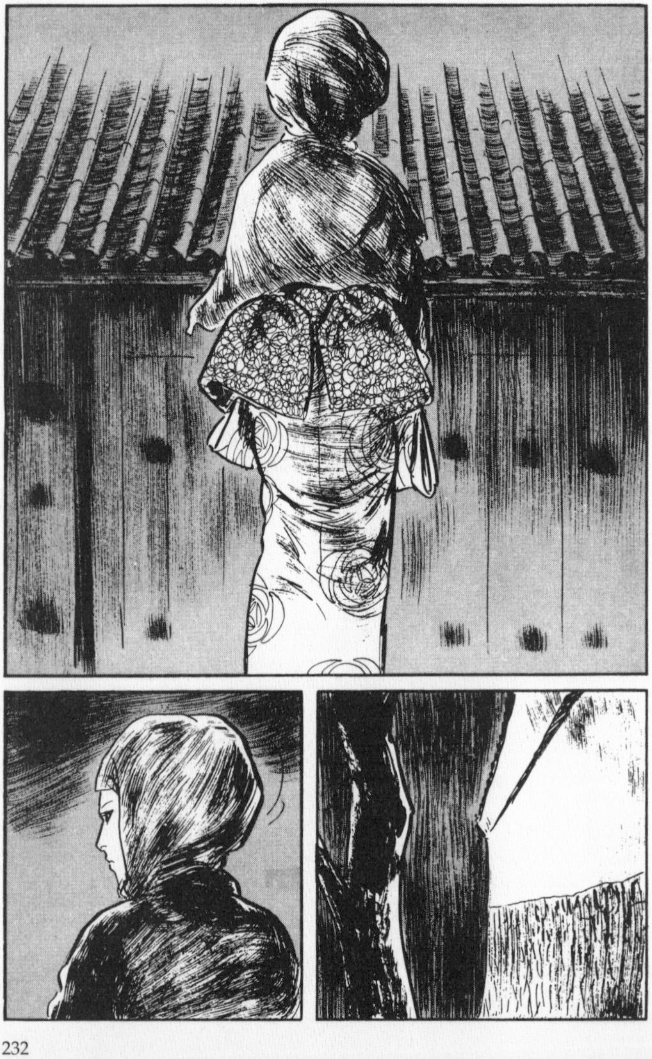

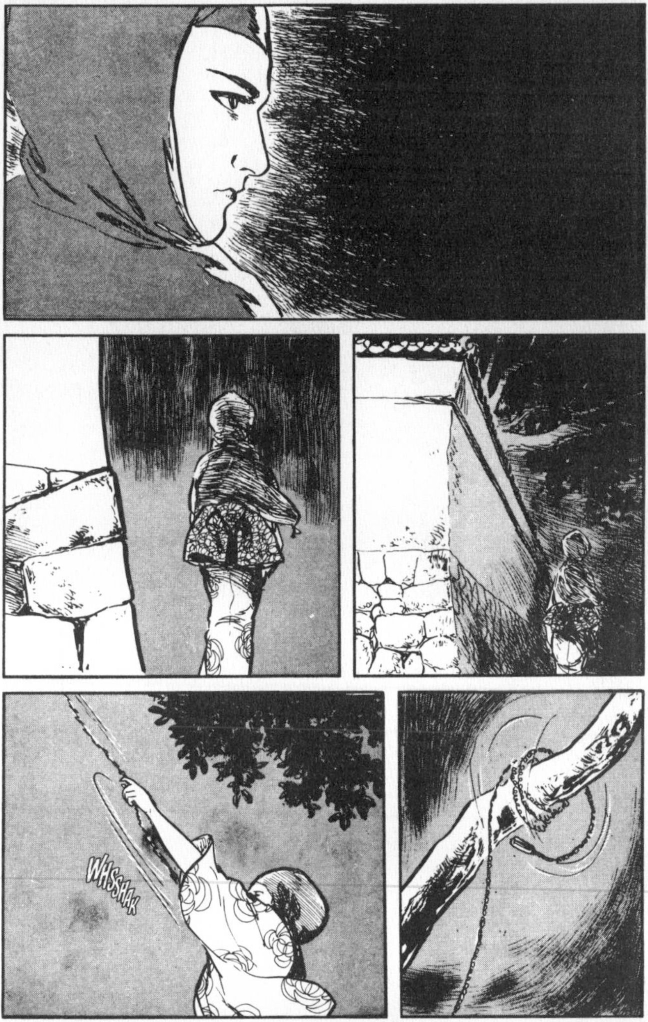
WHSSHAK

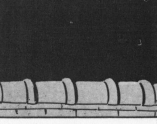

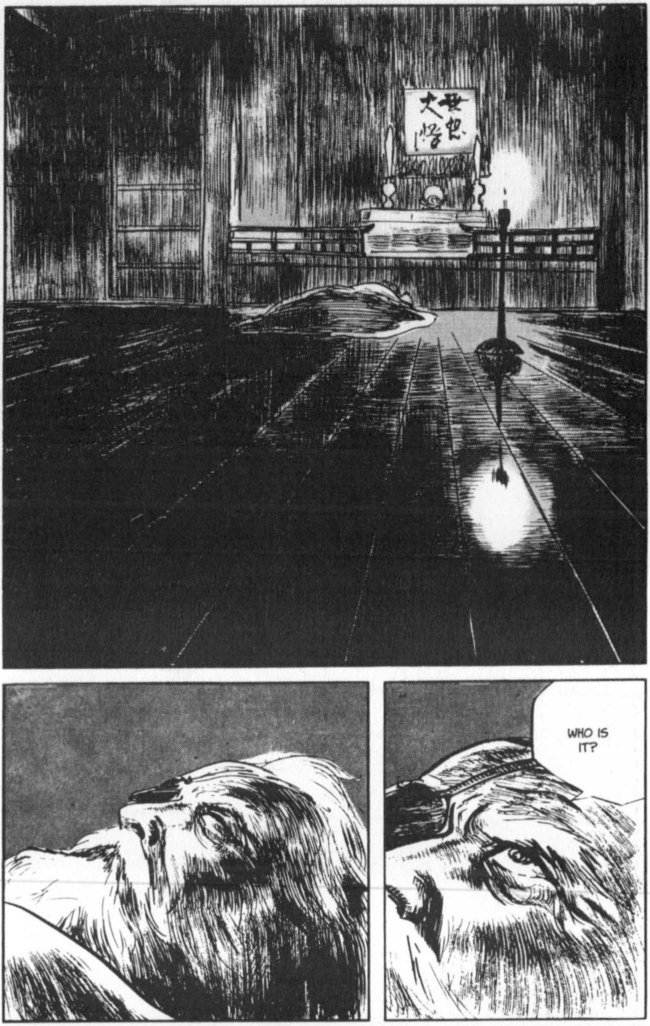
WHO IS IT?

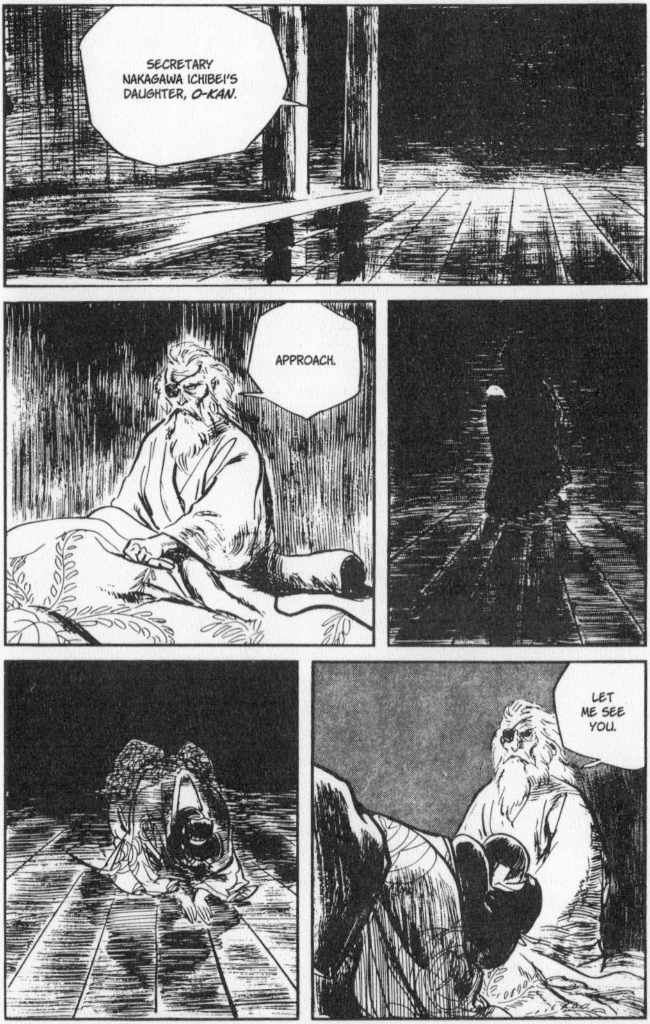
SECRETARY NAKAGAWA ICHIBEI'S DAUGHTER, *O-KAN*.
APPROACH.
LET ME SEE YOU.

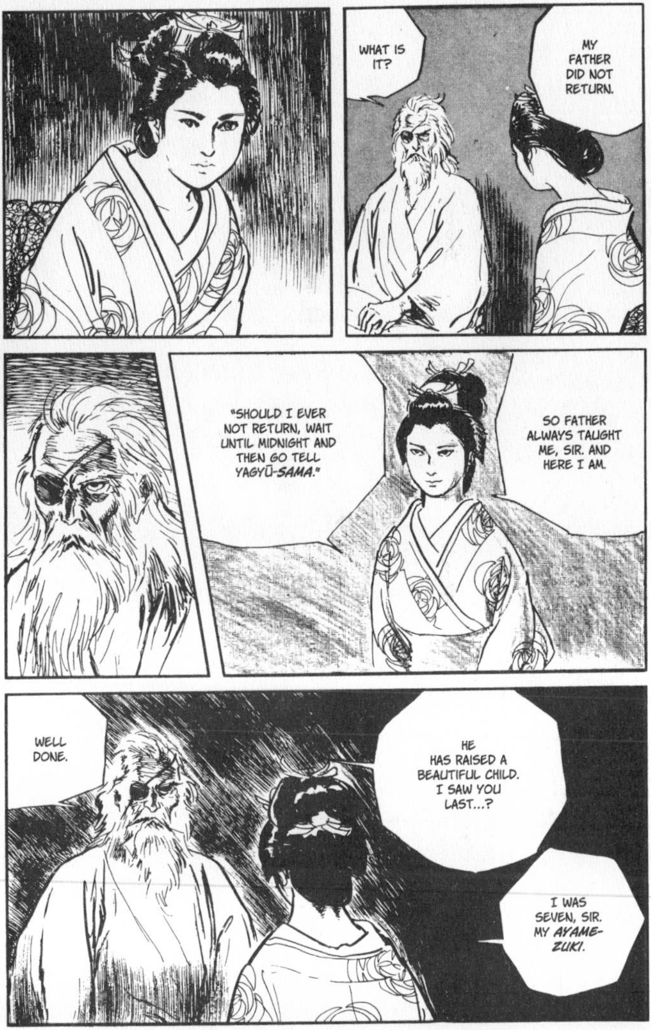
WHAT IS IT?
MY FATHER DID NOT RETURN.
"SHOULD I EVER NOT RETURN, WAIT UNTIL MIDNIGHT AND THEN GO TELL YAGYŪ-*SAMA.*"
SO FATHER ALWAYS TAUGHT ME, SIR. AND HERE I AM.
WELL DONE.
HE HAS RAISED A BEAUTIFUL CHILD. I SAW YOU LAST...?
I WAS SEVEN, SIR. MY *AYAME-ZUKI*.

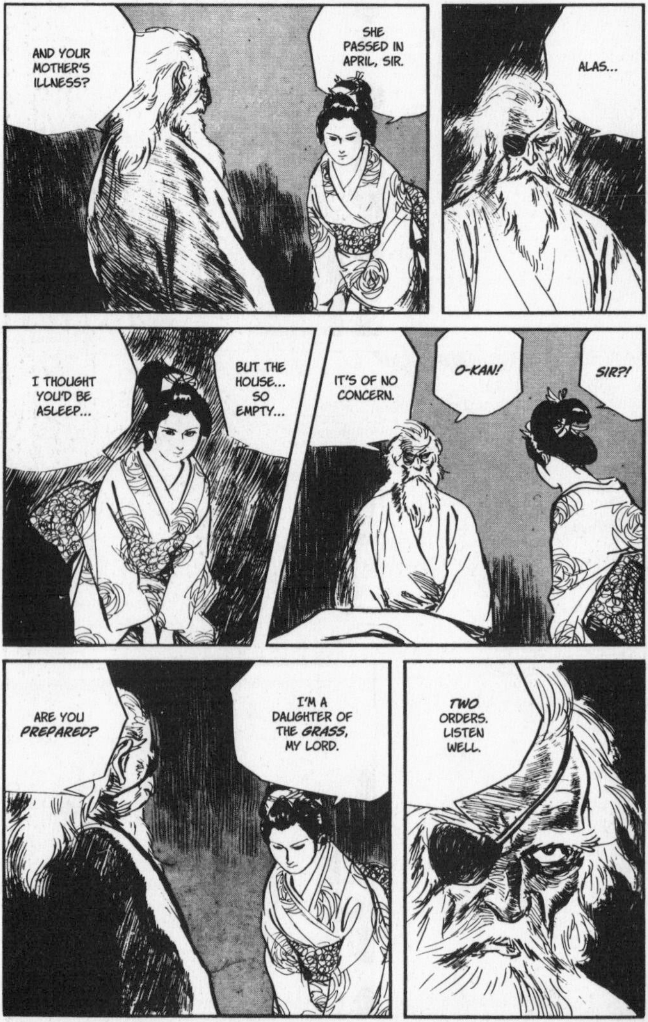
AND YOUR MOTHER'S ILLNESS?
SHE PASSED IN APRIL, SIR.
ALAS...
I THOUGHT YOU'D BE ASLEEP...
BUT THE HOUSE... SO EMPTY...
IT'S OF NO CONCERN.
O-KAN!
SIR?!
ARE YOU *PREPARED?*
I'M A DAUGHTER OF THE *GRASS,* MY LORD.
*TWO* ORDERS. LISTEN WELL.

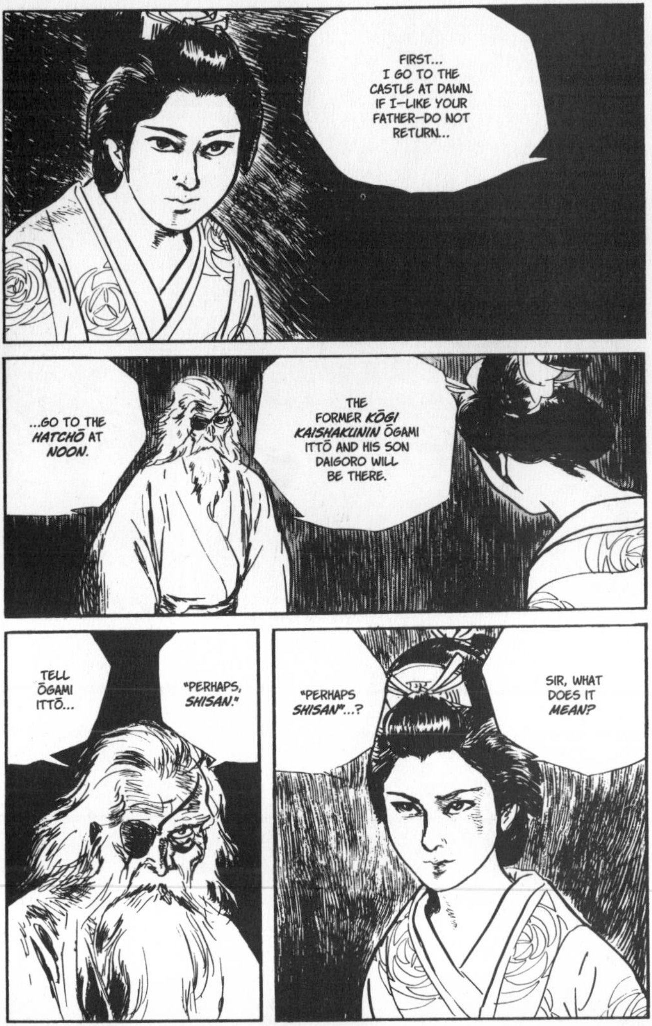

FIRST... I GO TO THE CASTLE AT DAWN. IF I—LIKE YOUR FATHER—DO NOT RETURN...
...GO TO THE *HATCHŌ* AT *NOON.*
THE FORMER *KŌGI KAISHAKUNIN* ŌGAMI ITTŌ AND HIS SON DAIGORO WILL BE THERE.
TELL ŌGAMI ITTŌ...
"PERHAPS, *SHISAN.*"
"PERHAPS *SHISAN*"...?
SIR, WHAT DOES IT *MEAN?*

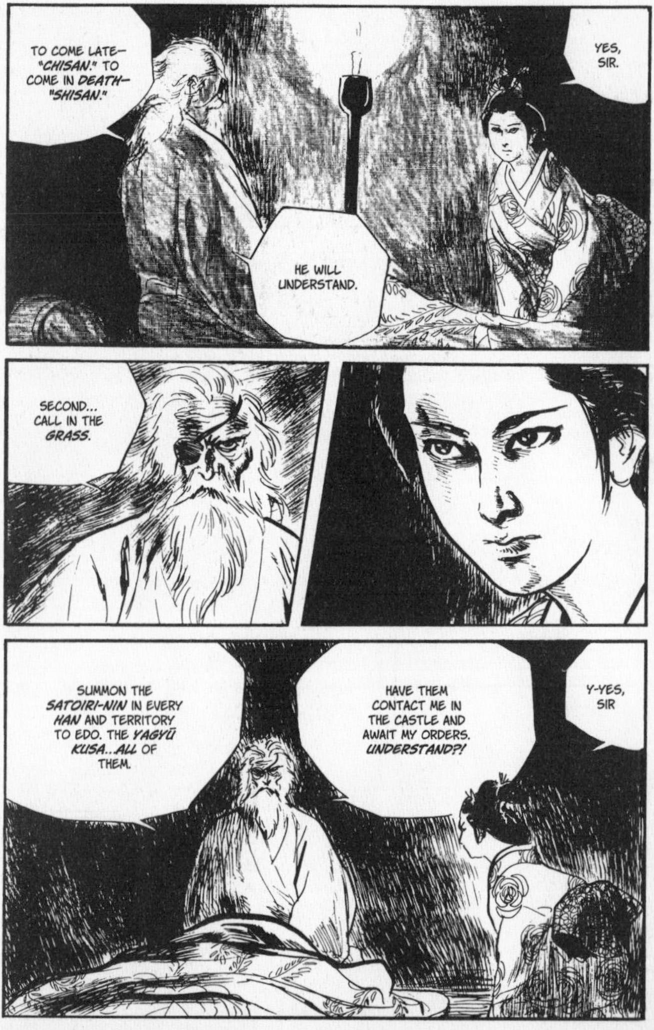

TO COME LATE— "CHISAN." TO COME IN DEATH— "SHISAN."
YES, SIR.
HE WILL UNDERSTAND.
SECOND... CALL IN THE GRASS.
SUMMON THE SATOIRI-NIN IN EVERY HAN AND TERRITORY TO EDO. THE YAGYŪ KUSA...ALL OF THEM.
HAVE THEM CONTACT ME IN THE CASTLE AND AWAIT MY ORDERS. UNDERSTAND?!
Y-YES, SIR

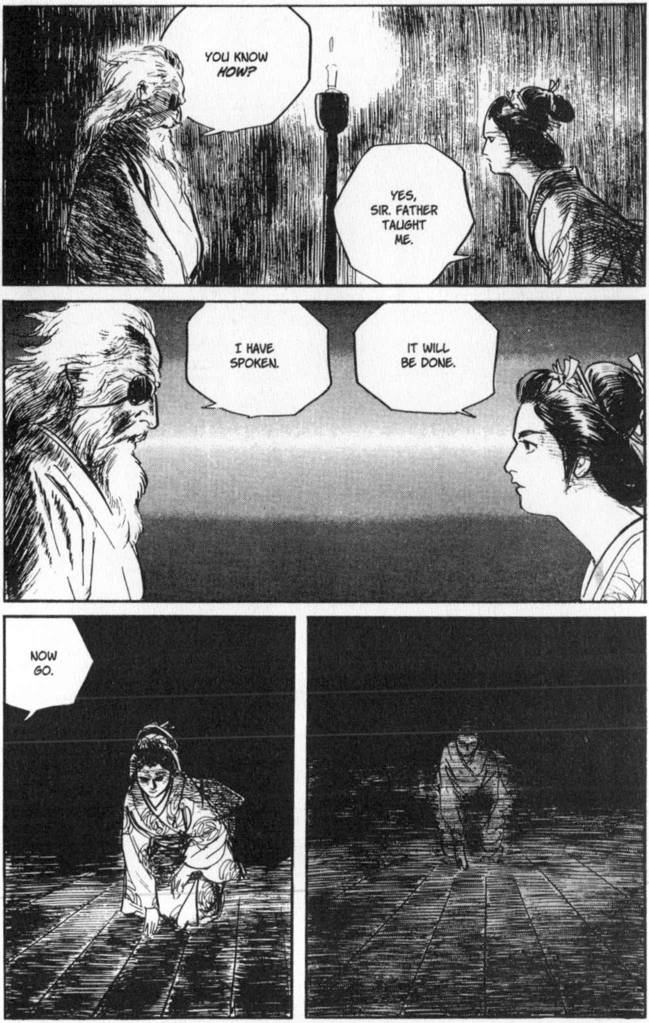
YOU KNOW *HOW?*
YES, SIR. FATHER TAUGHT ME.
I HAVE SPOKEN.
IT WILL BE DONE.
NOW GO.

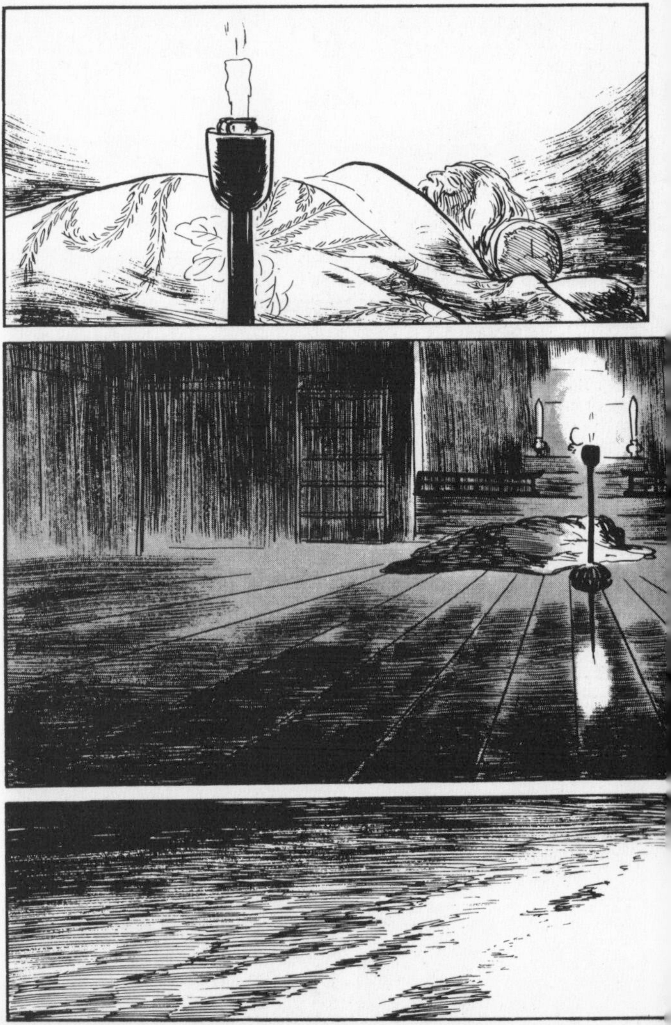

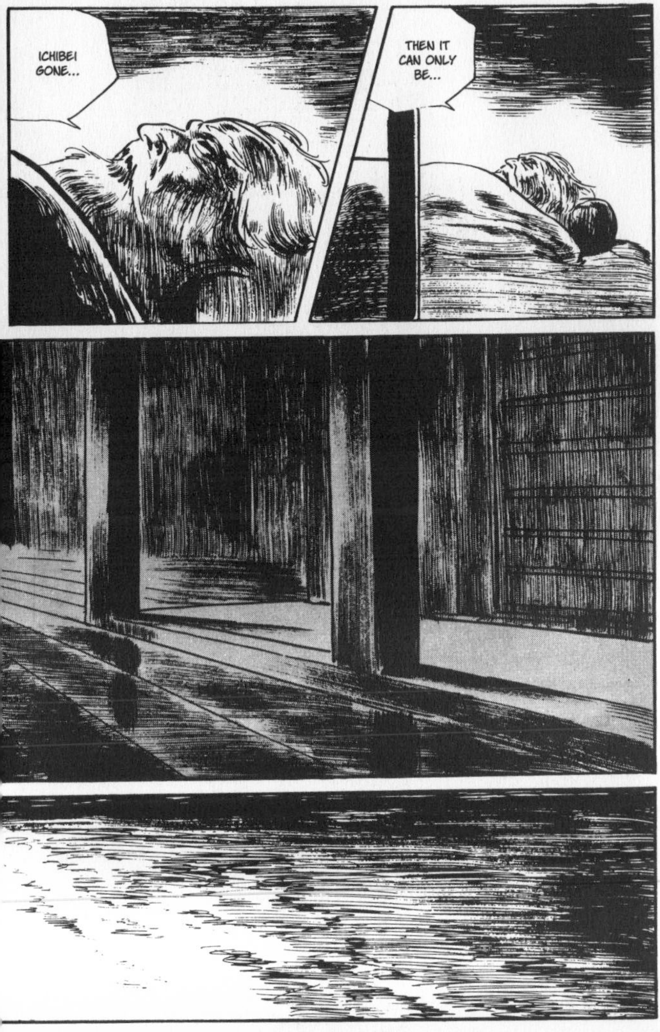
ICHIBEI GONE...
THEN IT CAN ONLY BE...

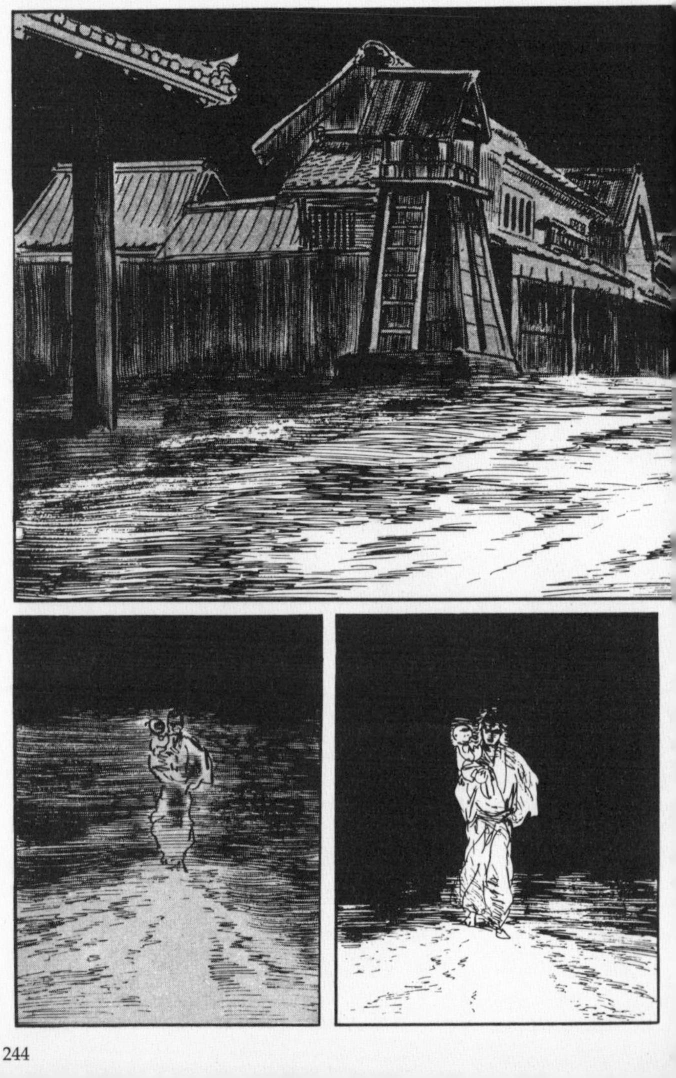

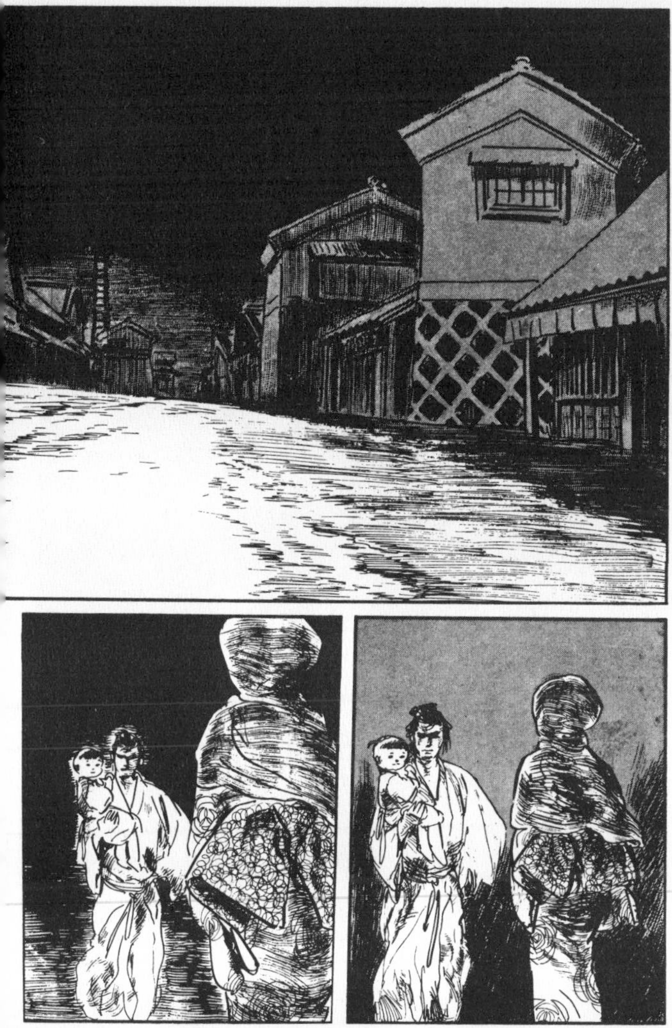

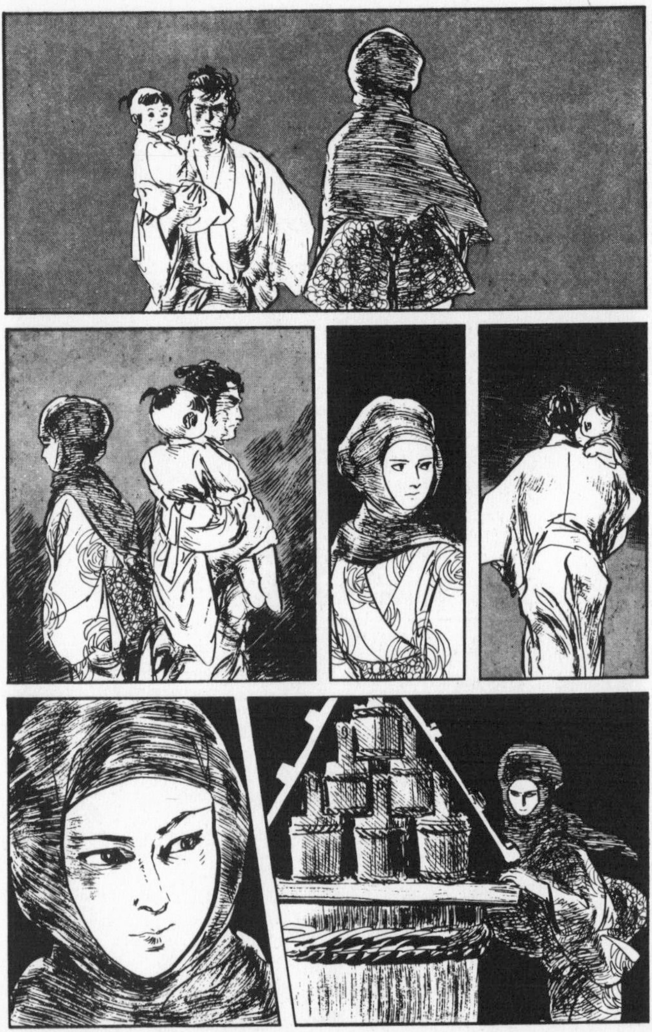

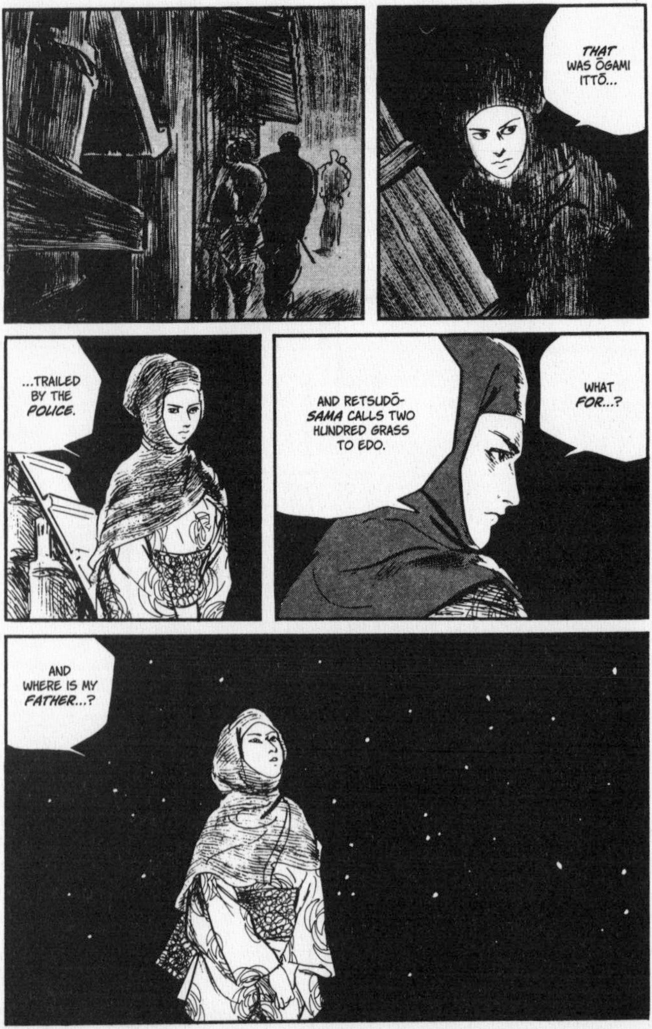
THAT WAS ŌGAMI ITTŌ...
...TRAILED BY THE POLICE.
AND RETSUDŌ-SAMA CALLS TWO HUNDRED GRASS TO EDO.
WHAT FOR...?
AND WHERE IS MY FATHER...?

the hundred and twenty-first

# Stone Upon Stone

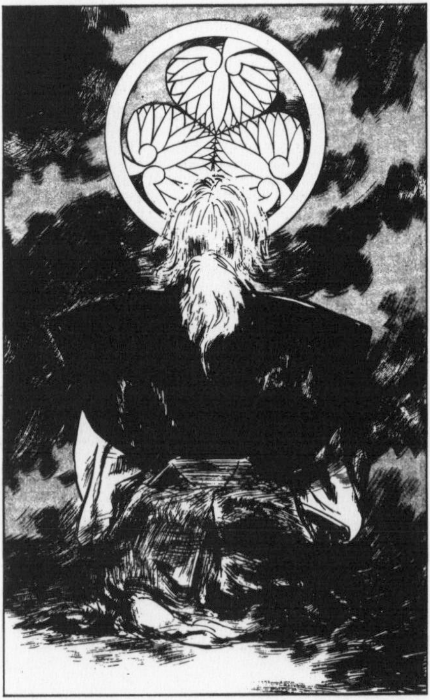

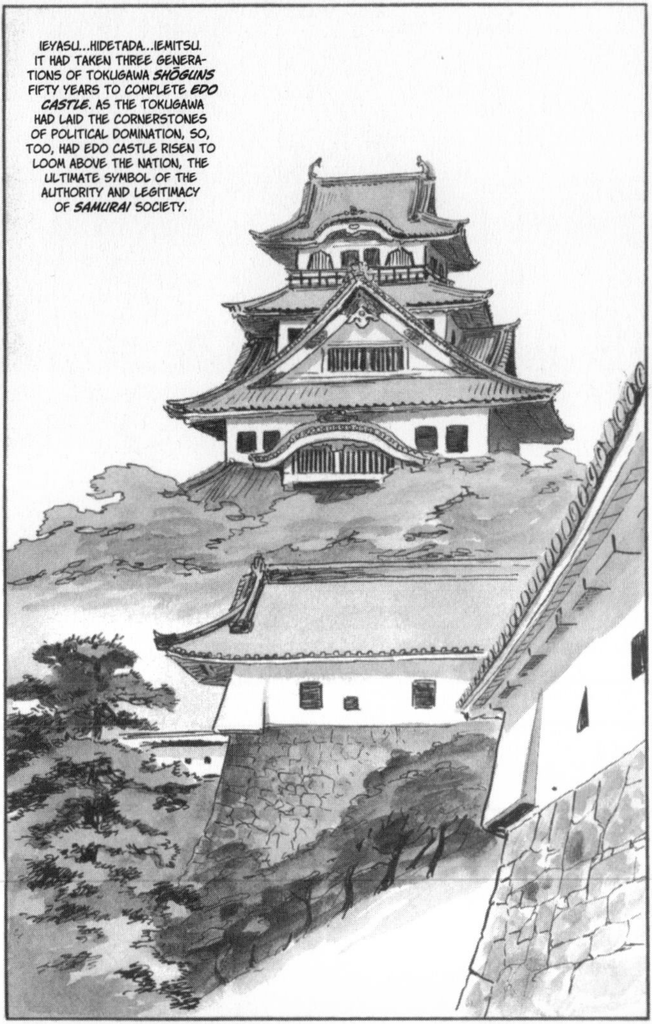
IEYASU...HIDETADA...IEMITSU. IT HAD TAKEN THREE GENERATIONS OF TOKUGAWA SHŌGUNS FIFTY YEARS TO COMPLETE EDO CASTLE. AS THE TOKUGAWA HAD LAID THE CORNERSTONES OF POLITICAL DOMINATION, SO, TOO, HAD EDO CASTLE RISEN TO LOOM ABOVE THE NATION, THE ULTIMATE SYMBOL OF THE AUTHORITY AND LEGITIMACY OF SAMURAI SOCIETY.

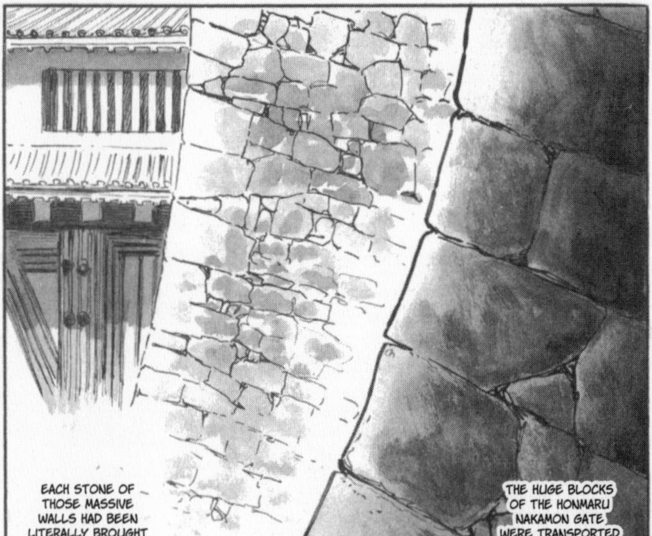
EACH STONE OF THOSE MASSIVE WALLS HAD BEEN LITERALLY BROUGHT TO EDO AND RAISED INTO PLACE BY THE *DAIMYŌ* OF THE SIXTY STATES OF JAPAN.
THE HUGE BLOCKS OF THE HONMARU NAKAMON GATE WERE TRANSPORTED FROM HIGO BY KATŌ KIYOMASA.

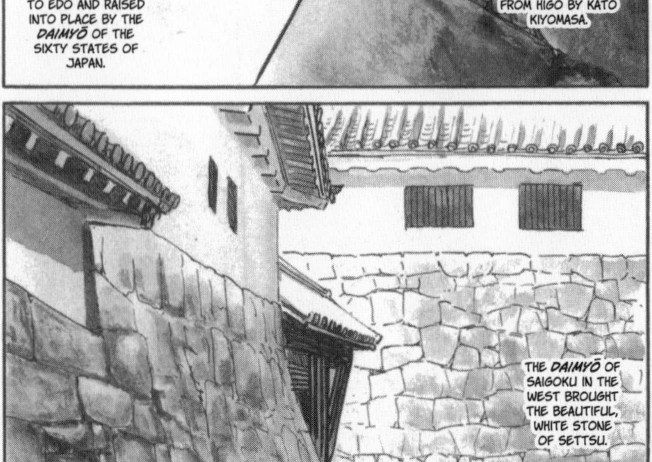
THE *DAIMYŌ* OF SAIGOKU IN THE WEST BROUGHT THE BEAUTIFUL, WHITE STONE OF SETTSU.

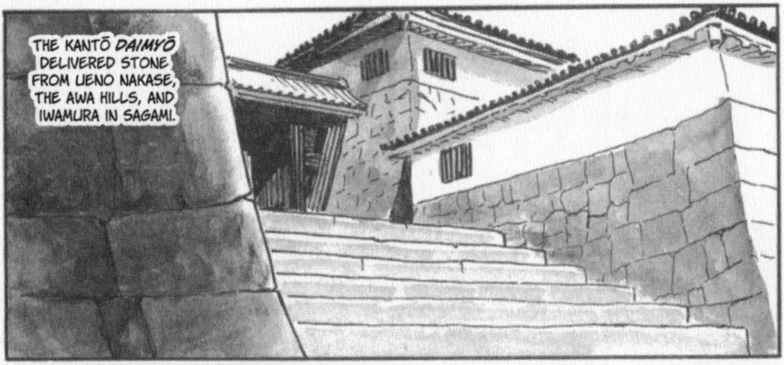
THE KANTŌ *DAIMYŌ* DELIVERED STONE FROM UENO NAKASE, THE AWA HILLS, AND IWAMURA IN SAGAMI.

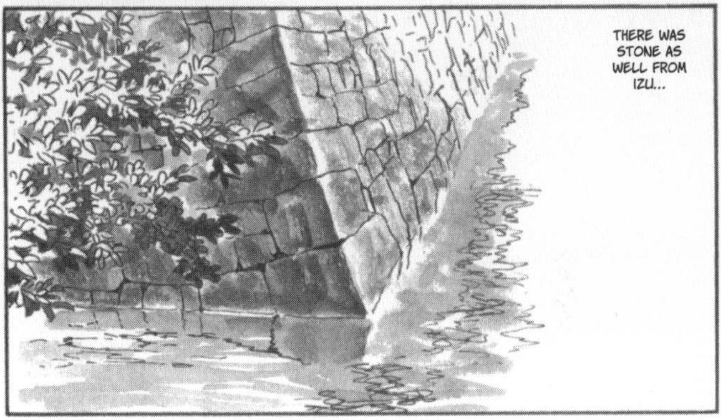
THERE WAS STONE AS WELL FROM IZU...

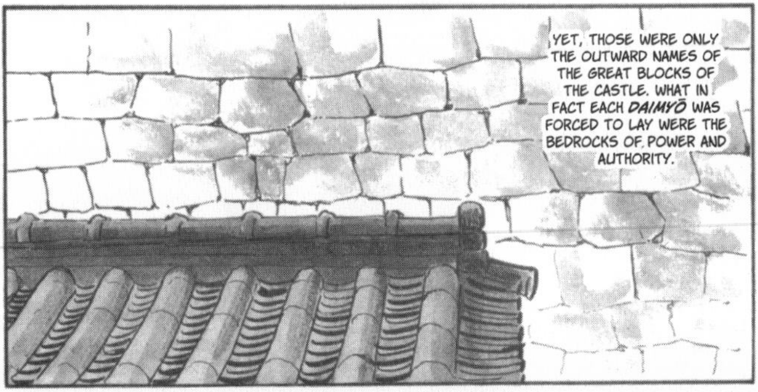
YET, THOSE WERE ONLY THE OUTWARD NAMES OF THE GREAT BLOCKS OF THE CASTLE. WHAT IN FACT EACH *DAIMYŌ* WAS FORCED TO LAY WERE THE BEDROCKS OF POWER AND AUTHORITY.

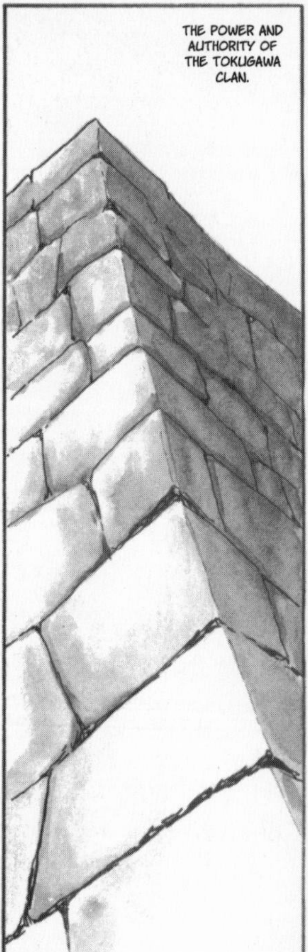
THE POWER AND AUTHORITY OF THE TOKUGAWA CLAN.

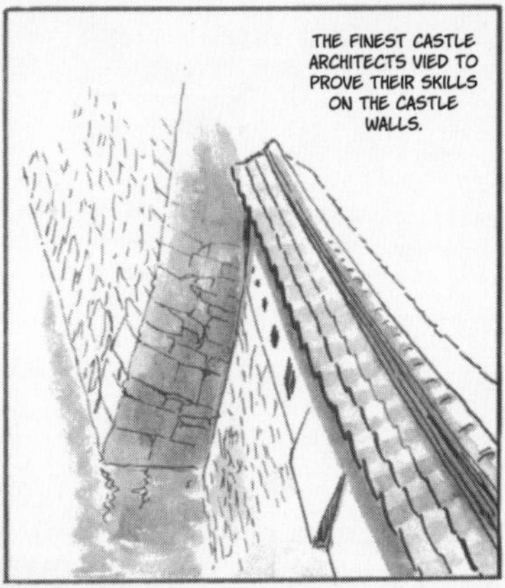
THE FINEST CASTLE ARCHITECTS VIED TO PROVE THEIR SKILLS ON THE CASTLE WALLS.

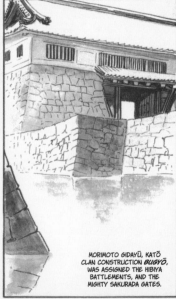

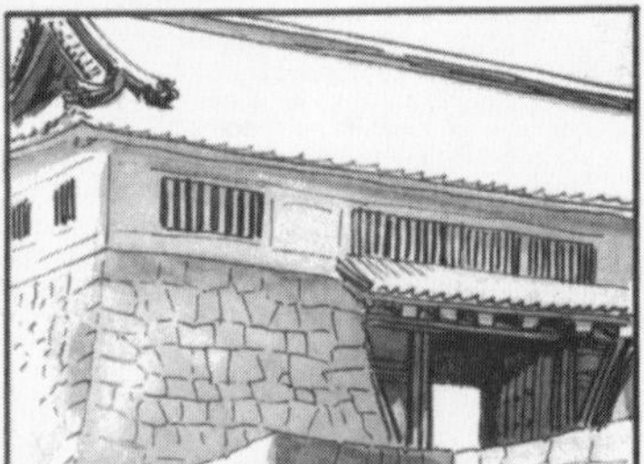
MORIMOTO GIDAYŪ, KATŌ CLAN CONSTRUCTION *BUGYŌ*, WAS ASSIGNED THE HIBIYA BATTLEMENTS, AND THE MIGHTY SAKURADA GATES.

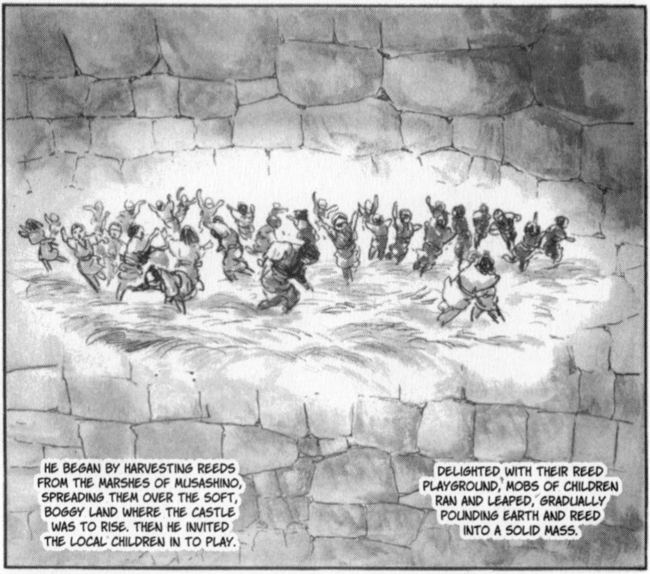
HE BEGAN BY HARVESTING REEDS FROM THE MARSHES OF MUSASHINO, SPREADING THEM OVER THE SOFT, BOGGY LAND WHERE THE CASTLE WAS TO RISE. THEN HE INVITED THE LOCAL CHILDREN IN TO PLAY.
DELIGHTED WITH THEIR REED PLAYGROUND, MOBS OF CHILDREN RAN AND LEAPED, GRADUALLY POUNDING EARTH AND REED INTO A SOLID MASS.
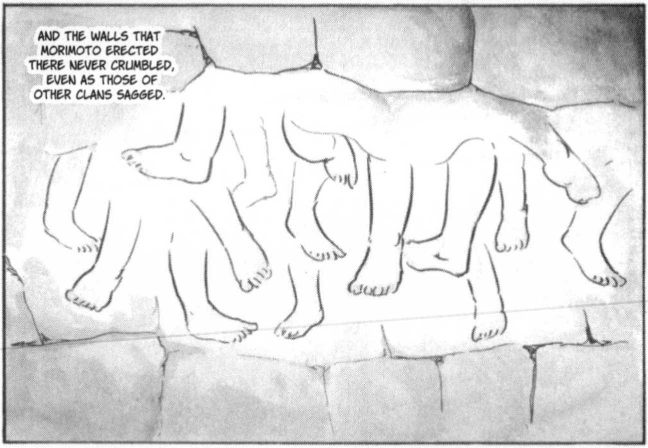
AND THE WALLS THAT MORIMOTO ERECTED THERE NEVER CRUMBLED, EVEN AS THOSE OF OTHER CLANS SAGGED.

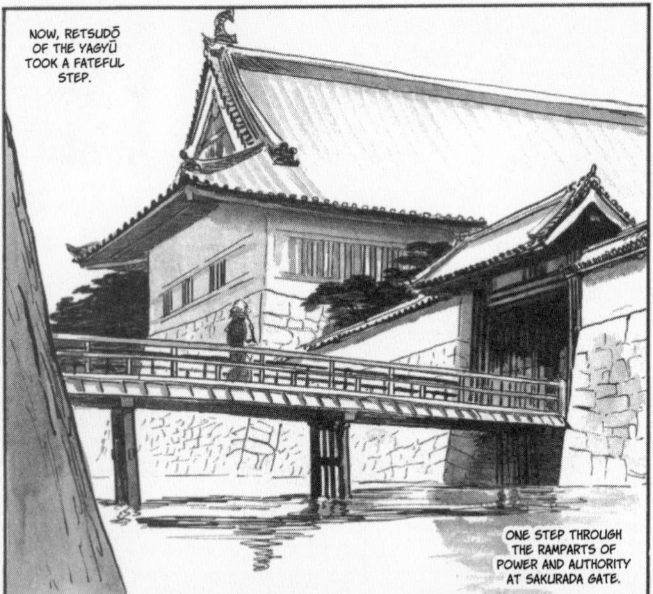
NOW, RETSUDŌ OF THE YAGYŪ TOOK A FATEFUL STEP.
ONE STEP THROUGH THE RAMPARTS OF POWER AND AUTHORITY AT SAKURADA GATE.
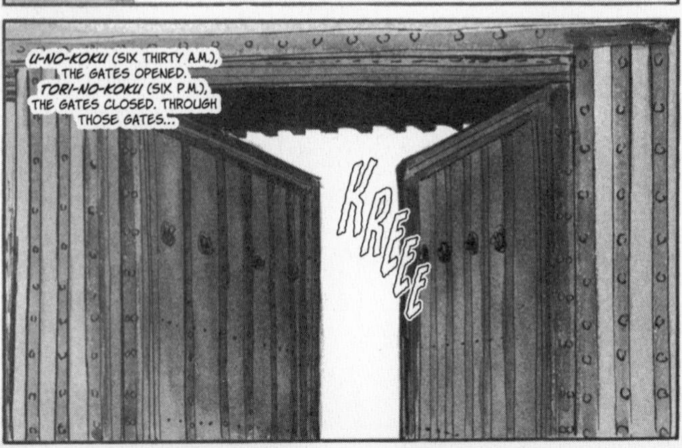
*U-NO-KOKU* (SIX THIRTY A.M.), THE GATES OPENED. *TORI-NO-KOKU* (SIX P.M.), THE GATES CLOSED. THROUGH THOSE GATES...
KREEE

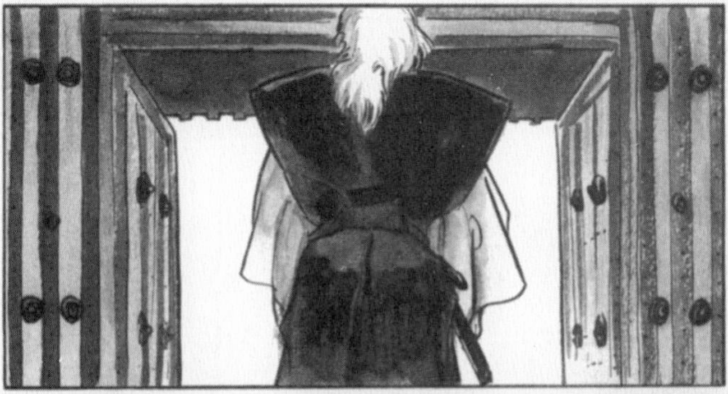
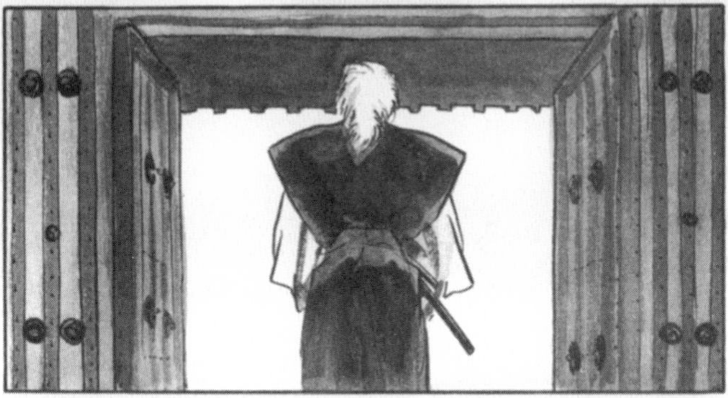
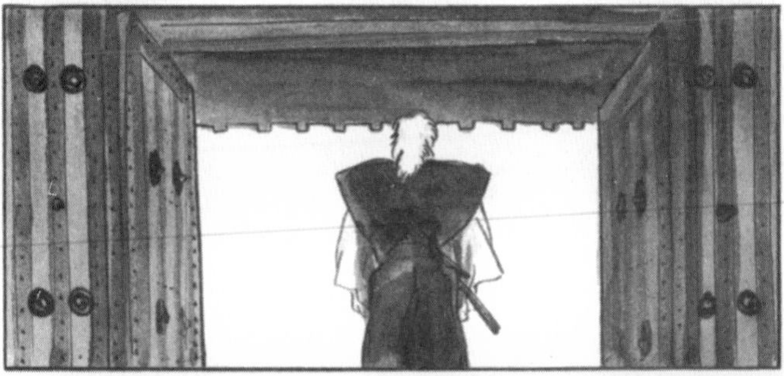

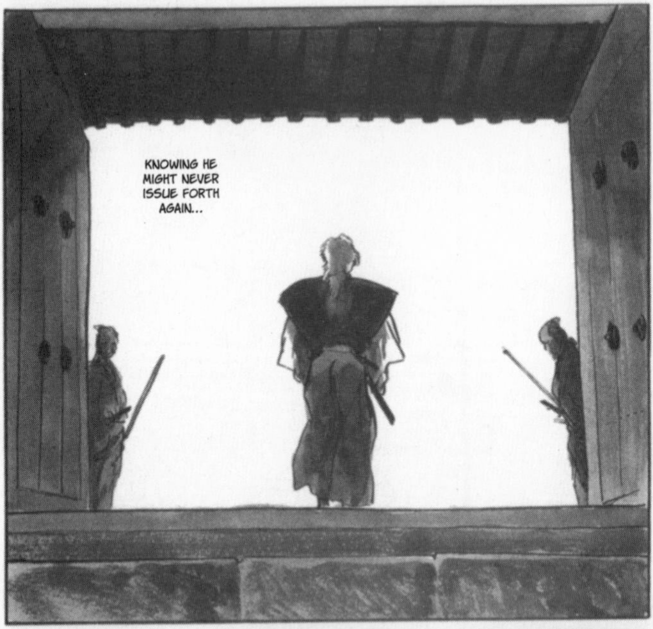
KNOWING HE MIGHT NEVER ISSUE FORTH AGAIN...
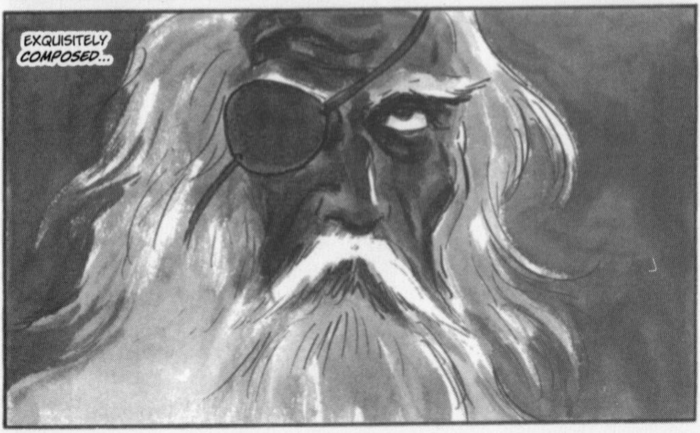
EXQUISITELY COMPOSED...

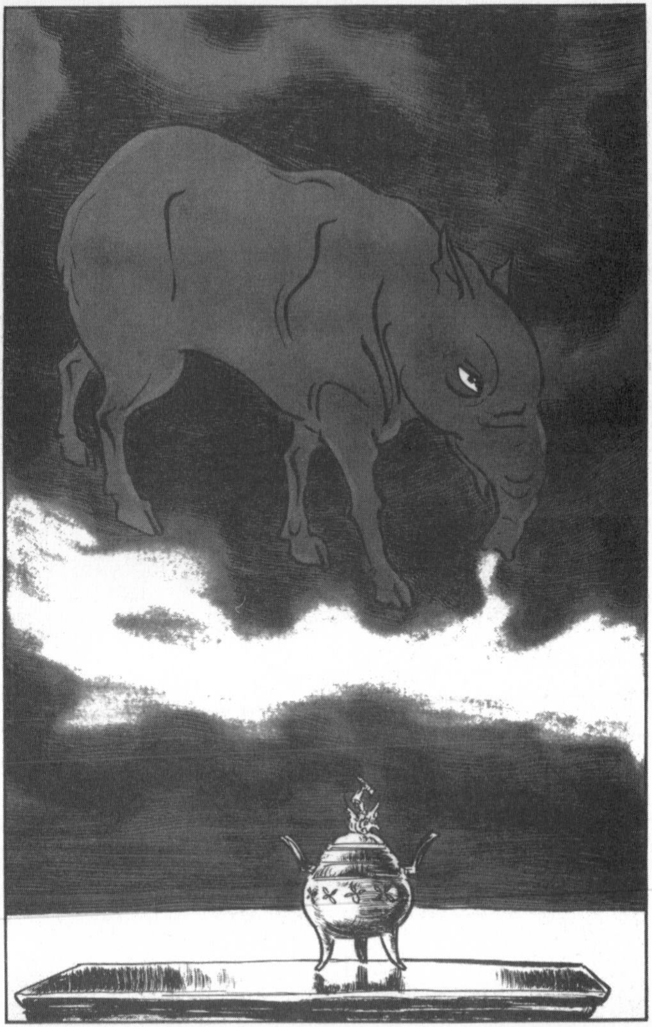

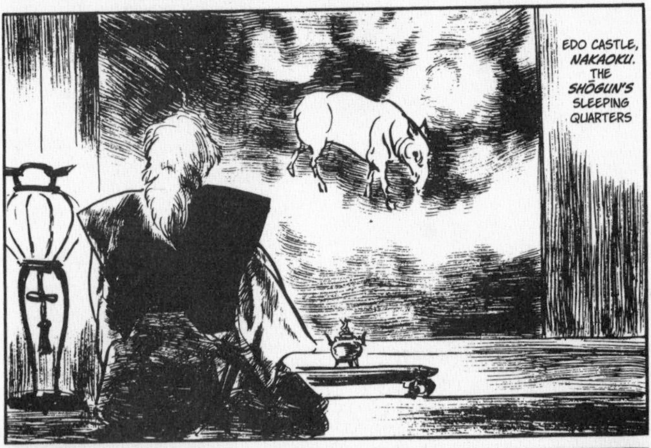
EDO CASTLE, NAKAOKU. THE SHŌGUN'S SLEEPING QUARTERS

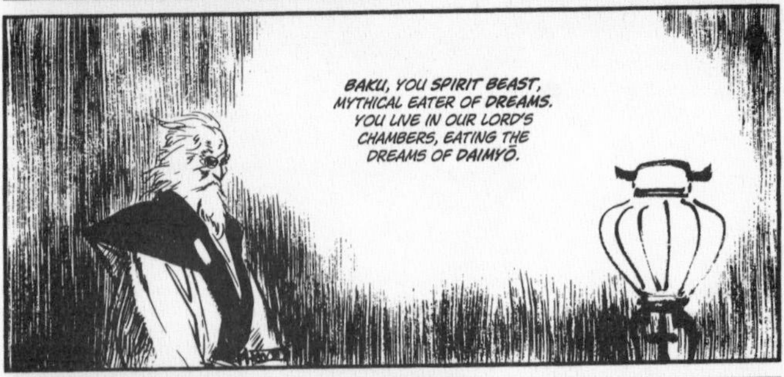
BAKU, YOU SPIRIT BEAST, MYTHICAL EATER OF DREAMS. YOU LIVE IN OUR LORD'S CHAMBERS, EATING THE DREAMS OF DAIMYŌ.

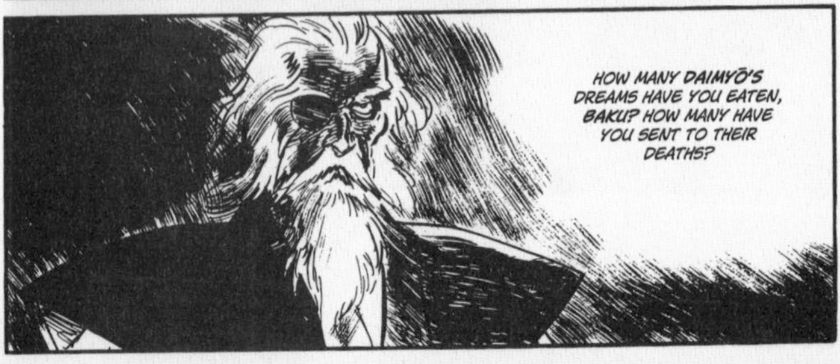
HOW MANY DAIMYŌ'S DREAMS HAVE YOU EATEN, BAKU? HOW MANY HAVE YOU SENT TO THEIR DEATHS?

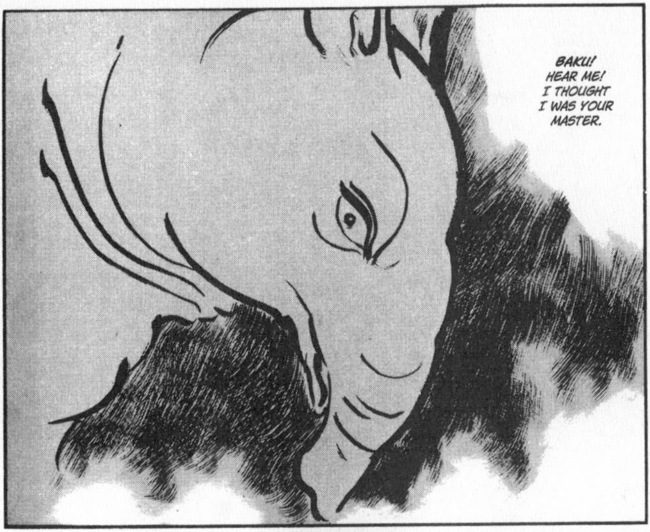
BAKU! HEAR ME! I THOUGHT I WAS YOUR MASTER.

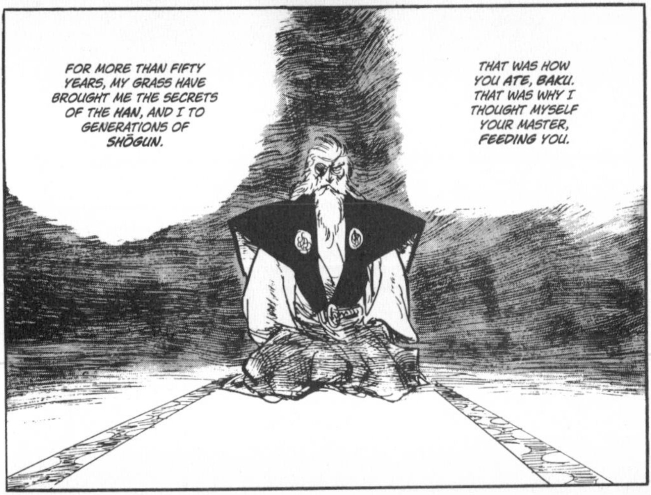
FOR MORE THAN FIFTY YEARS, MY GRASS HAVE BROUGHT ME THE SECRETS OF THE HAN, AND I TO GENERATIONS OF SHŌGUN.
THAT WAS HOW YOU ATE, BAKU. THAT WAS WHY I THOUGHT MYSELF YOUR MASTER, FEEDING YOU.

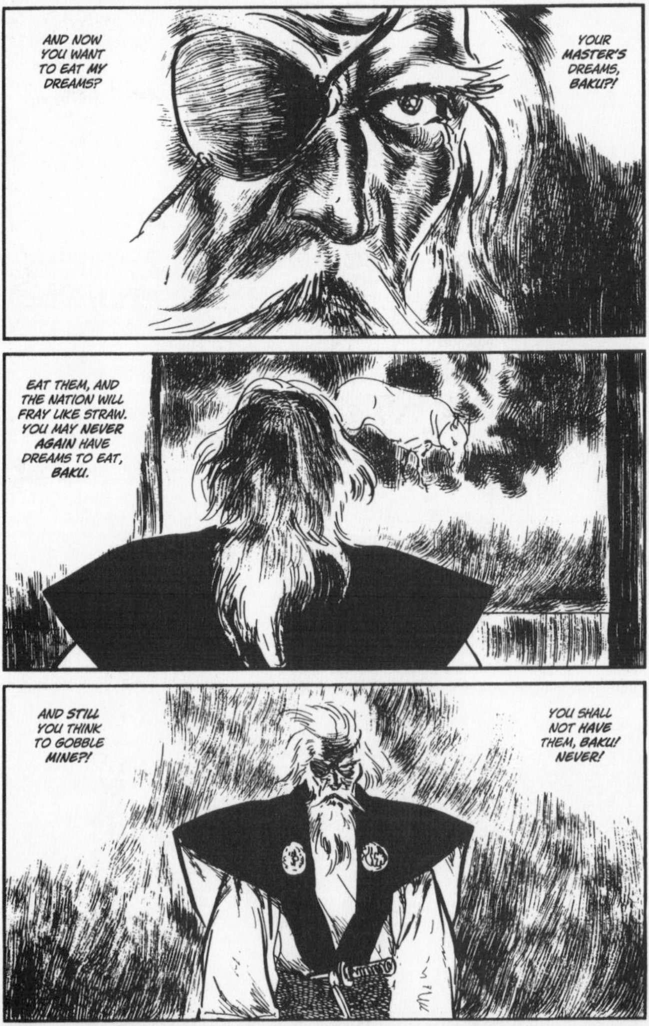
AND NOW YOU WANT TO EAT MY DREAMS?
YOUR MASTER'S DREAMS, BAKU?!
EAT THEM, AND THE NATION WILL FRAY LIKE STRAW. YOU MAY NEVER AGAIN HAVE DREAMS TO EAT, BAKU.
AND STILL YOU THINK TO GOBBLE MINE?!
YOU SHALL NOT HAVE THEM, BAKU! NEVER!

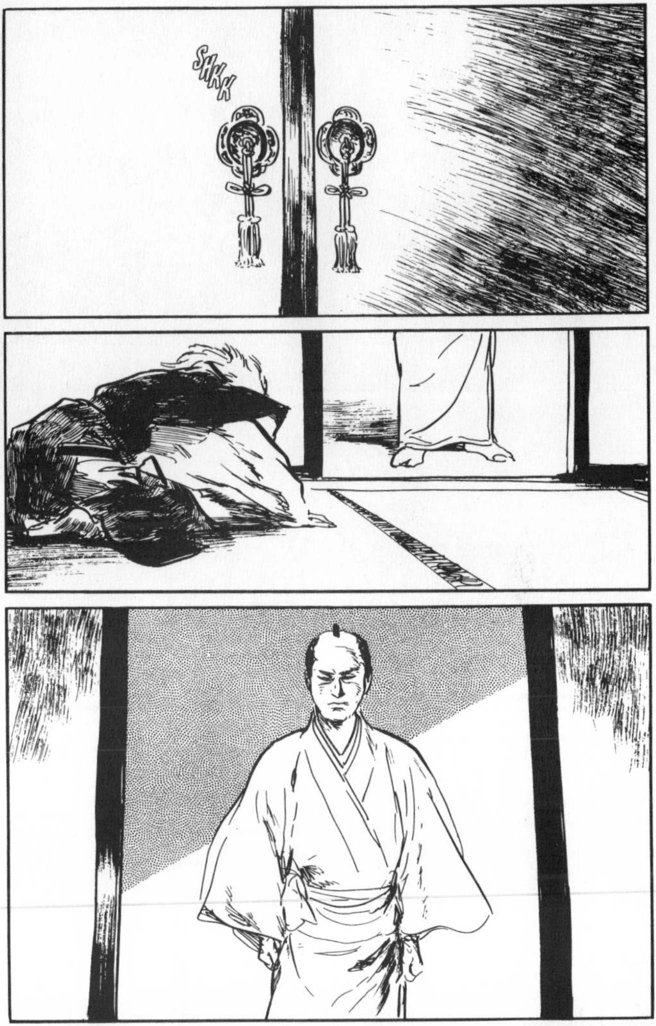
SHKK

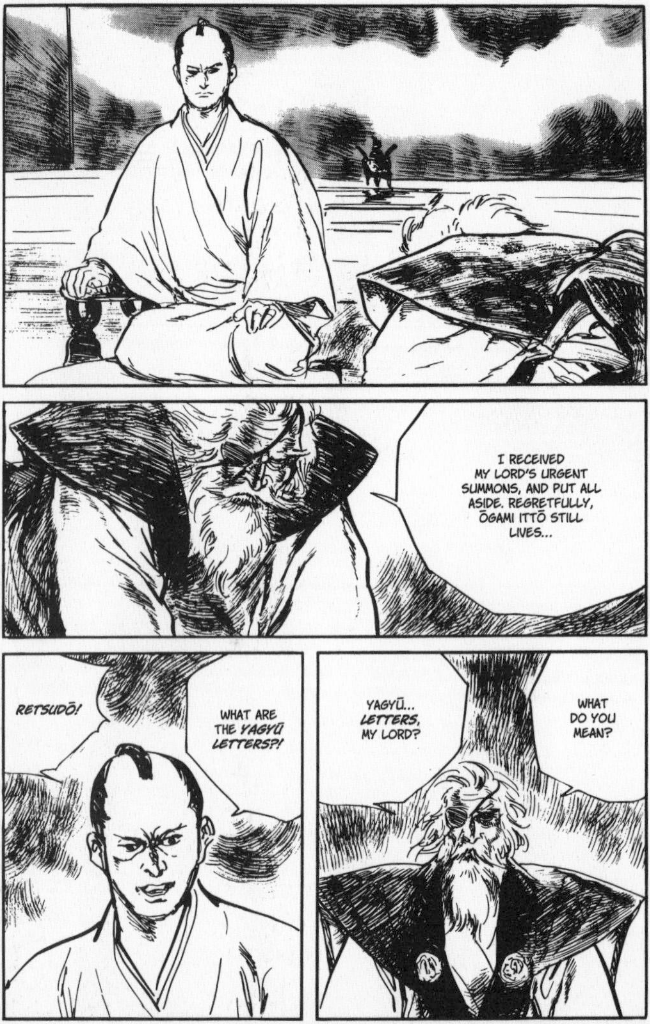
I RECEIVED MY LORD'S URGENT SUMMONS, AND PUT ALL ASIDE. REGRETFULLY, ŌGAMI ITTŌ STILL LIVES...
RETSUDŌ!
WHAT ARE THE *YAGYŪ LETTERS?!*
YAGYŪ... *LETTERS,* MY LORD?
WHAT DO YOU MEAN?

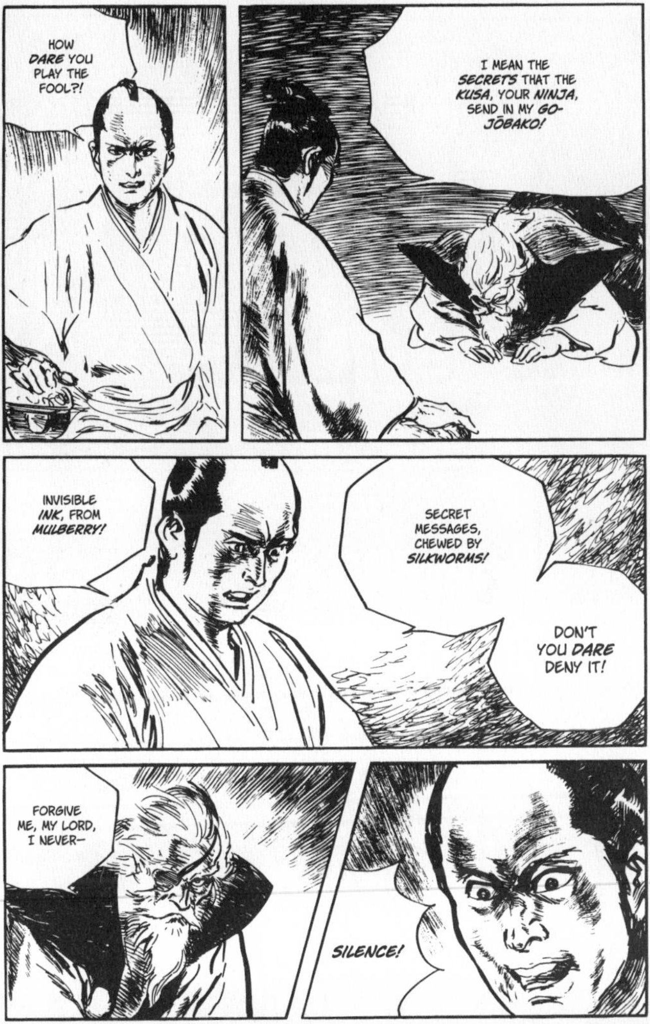
HOW DARE YOU PLAY THE FOOL?!
I MEAN THE SECRETS THAT THE KUSA, YOUR NINJA, SEND IN MY GO-JŌBAKO!
INVISIBLE INK, FROM MULBERRY!
SECRET MESSAGES, CHEWED BY SILKWORMS!
DON'T YOU DARE DENY IT!
FORGIVE ME, MY LORD, I NEVER–
SILENCE!

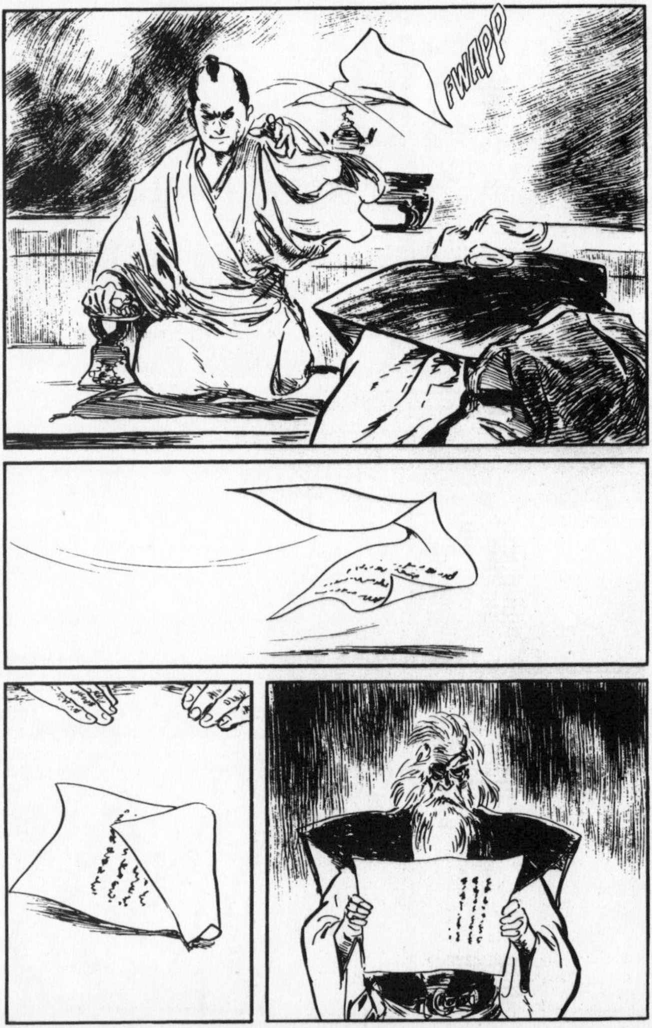
FWAPP

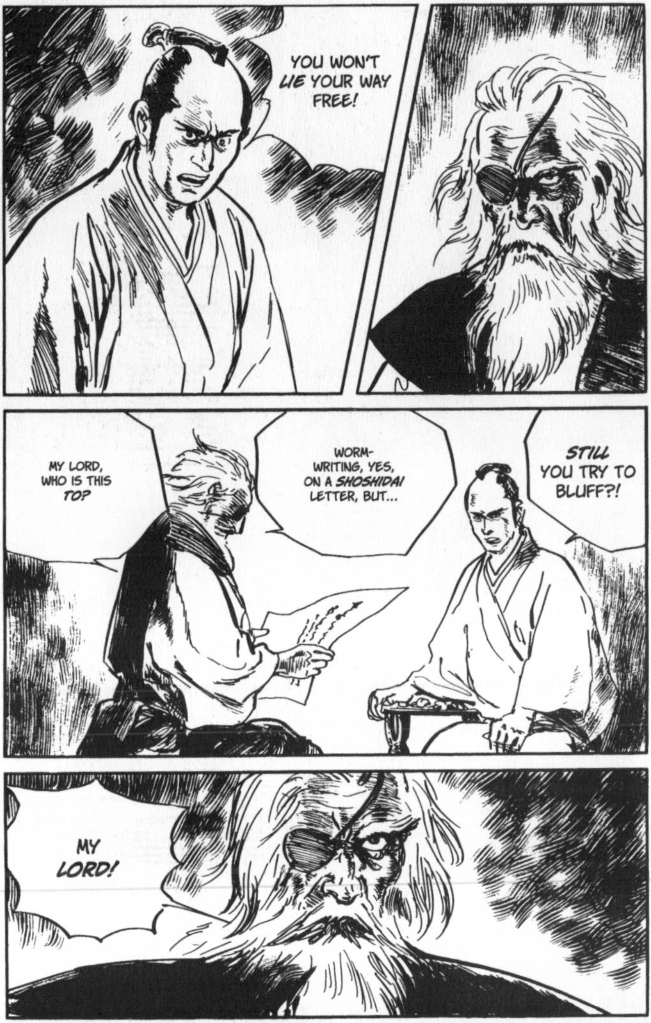
YOU WON'T LIE YOUR WAY FREE!
MY LORD, WHO IS THIS TO?
WORM-WRITING, YES, ON A SHOSHIDAI LETTER, BUT...
STILL YOU TRY TO BLUFF?!
MY LORD!

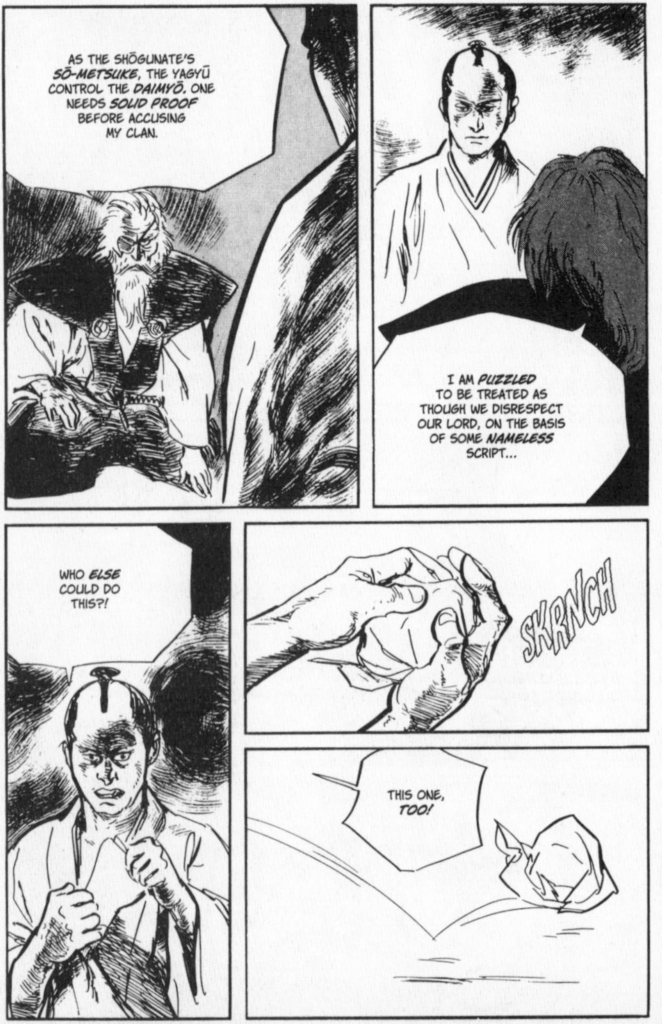
AS THE SHŌGUNATE'S SŌ-METSUKE, THE YAGYŪ CONTROL THE DAIMYŌ. ONE NEEDS SOLID PROOF BEFORE ACCUSING MY CLAN.
I AM PUZZLED TO BE TREATED AS THOUGH WE DISRESPECT OUR LORD, ON THE BASIS OF SOME NAMELESS SCRIPT...
WHO ELSE COULD DO THIS?!
SKRNCH
THIS ONE, TOO!

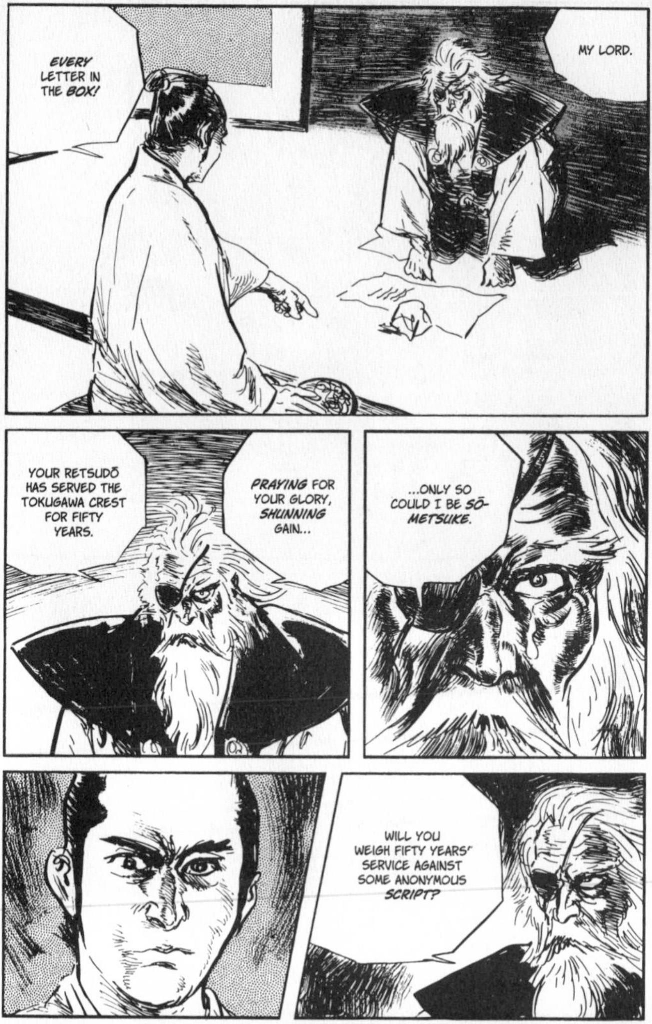
EVERY LETTER IN THE BOX!
MY LORD.
YOUR RETSUDŌ HAS SERVED THE TOKUGAWA CREST FOR FIFTY YEARS.
PRAYING FOR YOUR GLORY, SHUNNING GAIN...
...ONLY SO COULD I BE SŌ-METSUKE.
WILL YOU WEIGH FIFTY YEARS' SERVICE AGAINST SOME ANONYMOUS SCRIPT?

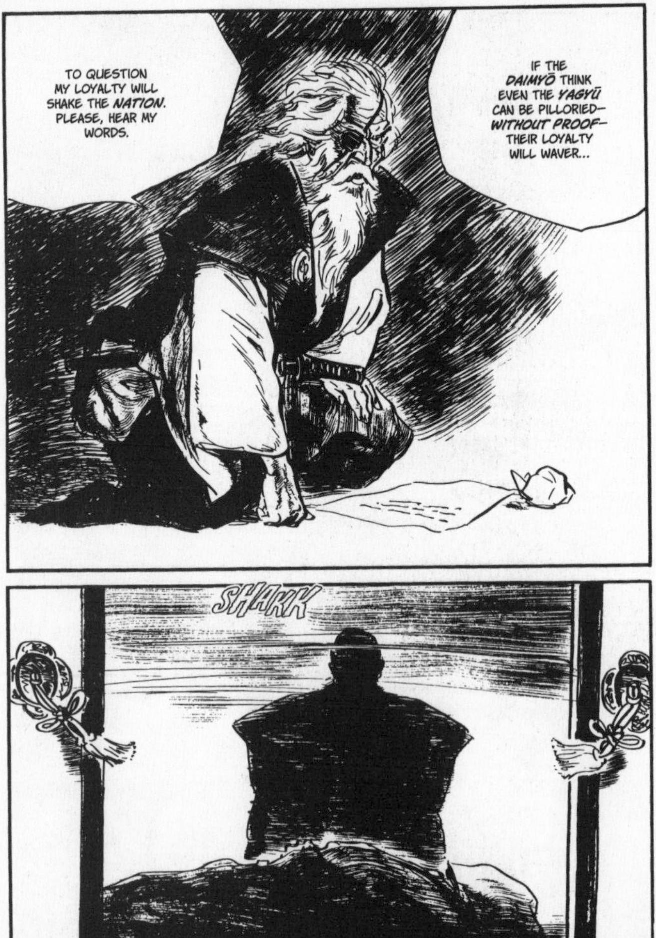
TO QUESTION MY LOYALTY WILL SHAKE THE *NATION*. PLEASE, HEAR MY WORDS.
IF THE *DAIMYŌ* THINK EVEN THE *YAGYŪ* CAN BE PILLORIED— *WITHOUT PROOF*— THEIR LOYALTY WILL WAVER...
SHAKK

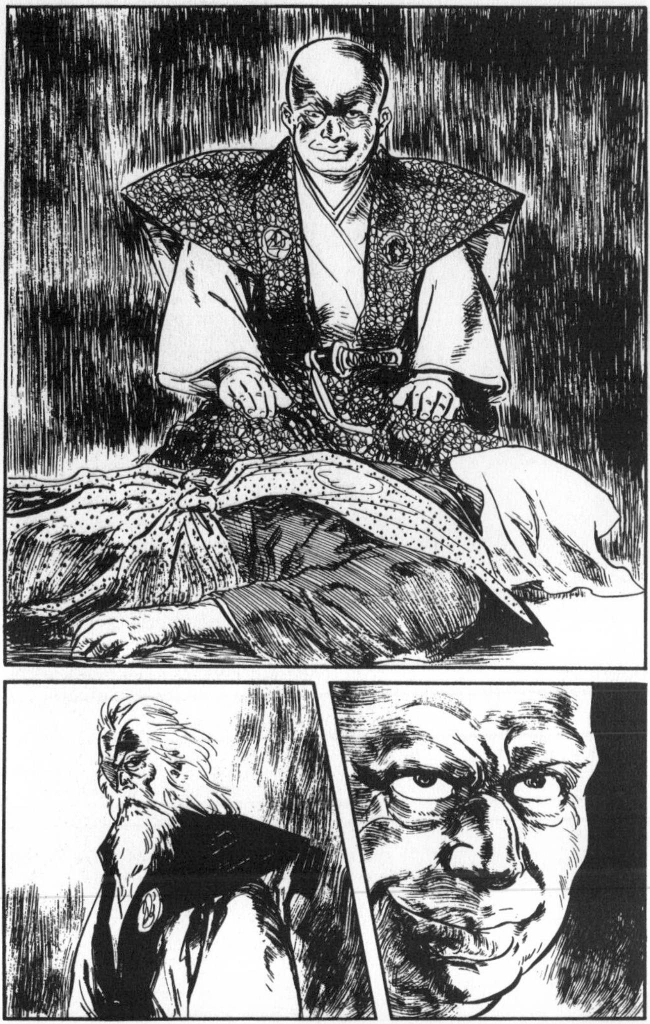

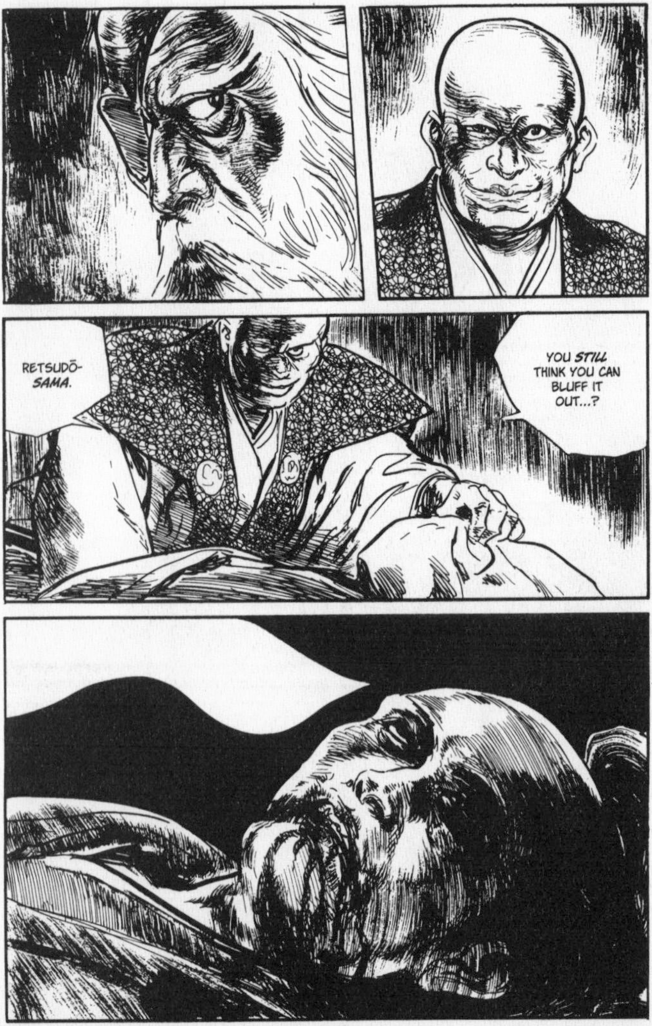
RETSUDŌ-SAMA.
YOU STILL THINK YOU CAN BLUFF IT OUT...?

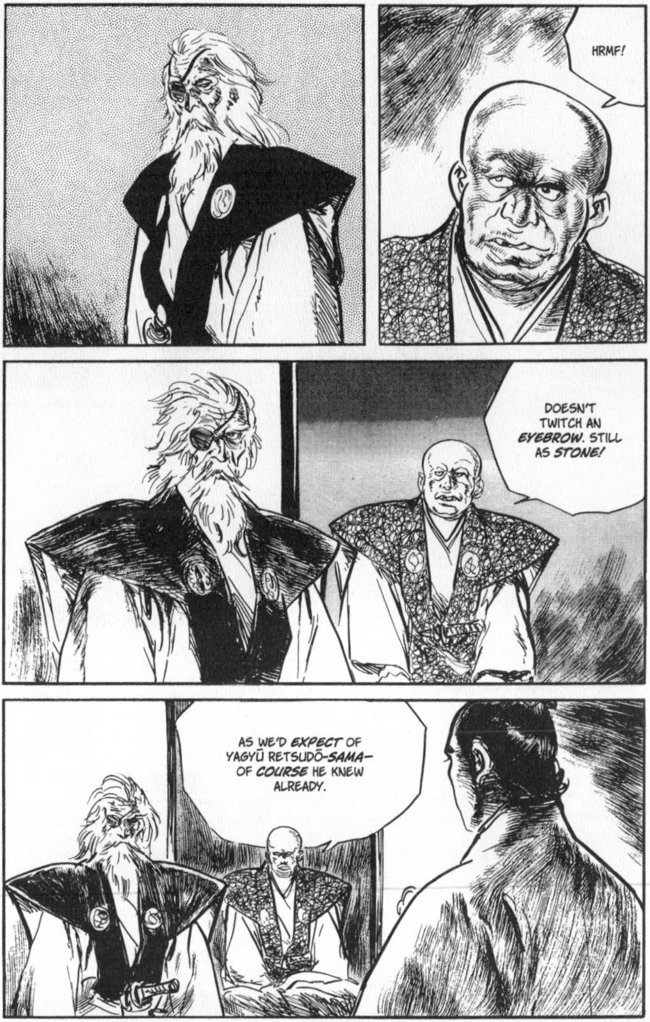
HRMF!
DOESN'T TWITCH AN EYEBROW. STILL AS STONE!
AS WE'D EXPECT OF YAGYŪ RETSUDŌ-SAMA— OF COURSE HE KNEW ALREADY.

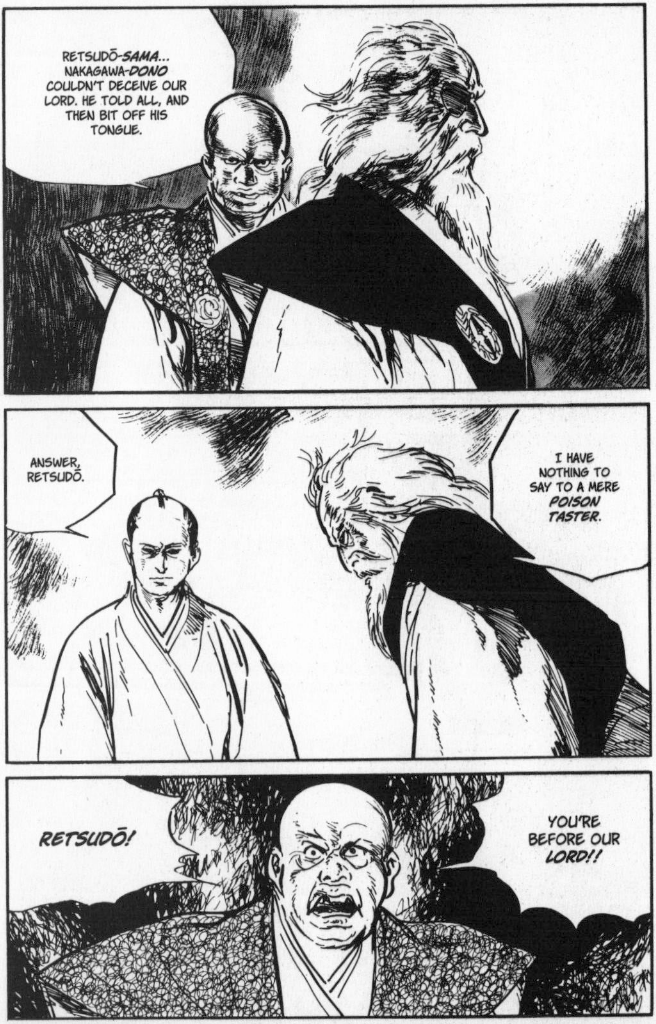
RETSUDŌ-*SAMA*... NAKAGAWA-*DONO* COULDN'T DECEIVE OUR LORD. HE TOLD ALL, AND THEN BIT OFF HIS TONGUE.
ANSWER, RETSUDŌ.
I HAVE NOTHING TO SAY TO A MERE *POISON TASTER*.
*RETSUDŌ!*
YOU'RE BEFORE OUR *LORD!!*

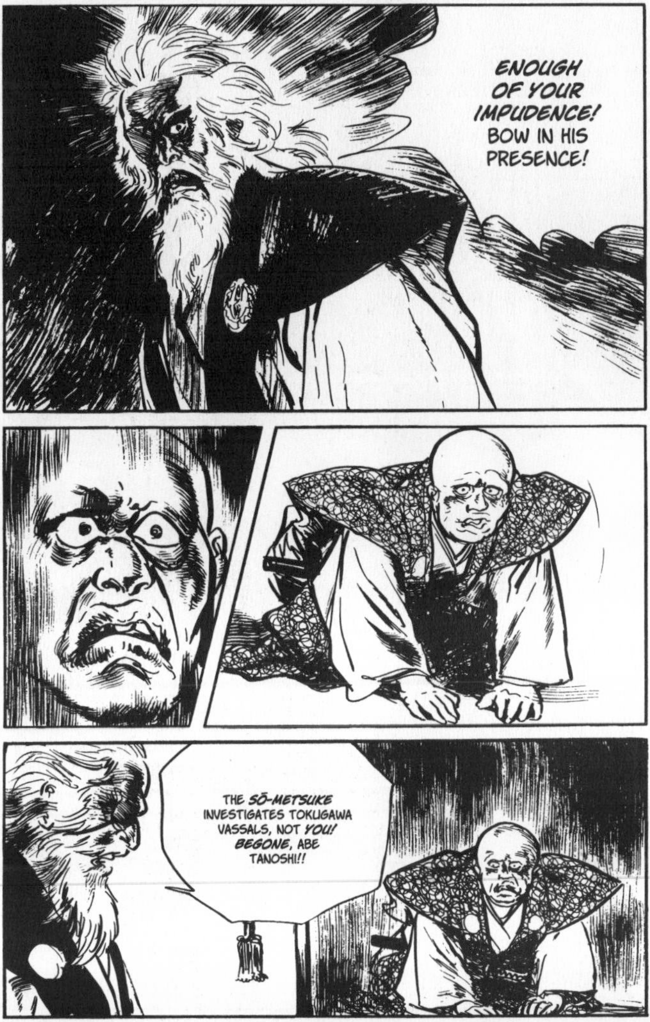

ENOUGH OF YOUR IMPUDENCE! BOW IN HIS PRESENCE!
THE SŌ-METSUKE INVESTIGATES TOKUGAWA VASSALS, NOT YOU! BEGONE, ABE TANOSHI!!

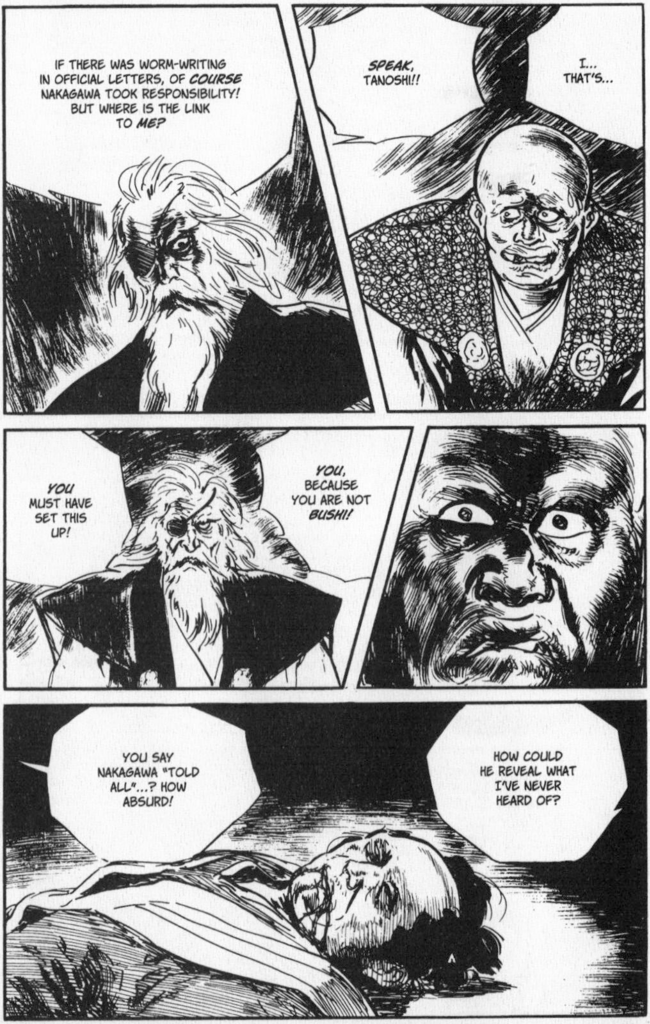
IF THERE WAS WORM-WRITING IN OFFICIAL LETTERS, OF *COURSE* NAKAGAWA TOOK RESPONSIBILITY! BUT WHERE IS THE LINK TO *ME?*
*SPEAK,* TANOSHI!!
I... THAT'S...
*YOU* MUST HAVE SET THIS UP!
*YOU,* BECAUSE YOU ARE NOT *BUSHI!*
YOU SAY NAKAGAWA "TOLD ALL"...? HOW ABSURD!
HOW COULD HE REVEAL WHAT I'VE NEVER HEARD OF?

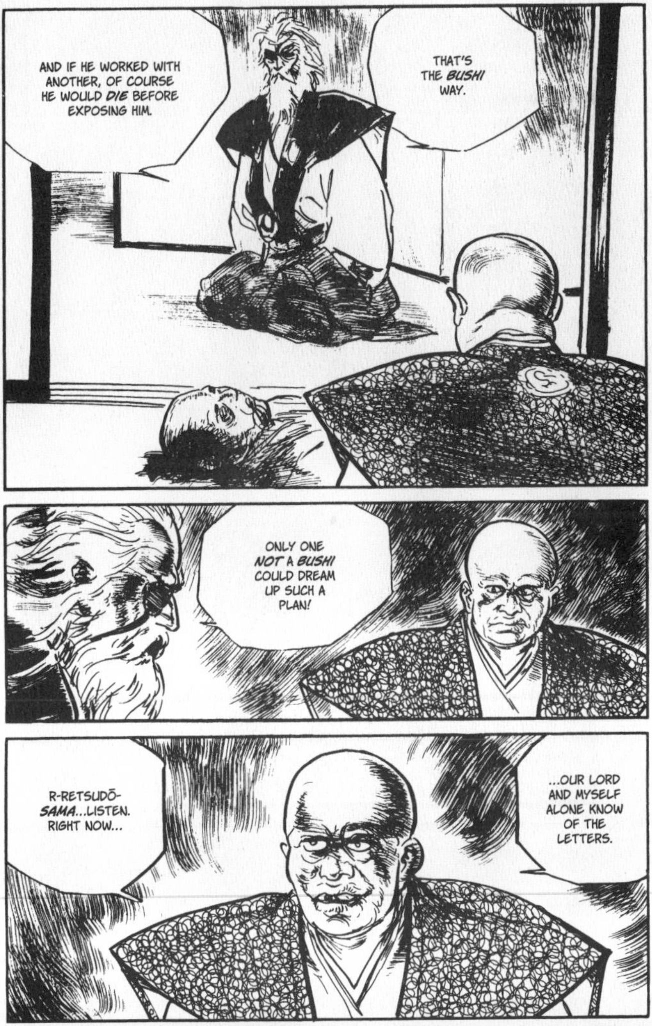
AND IF HE WORKED WITH ANOTHER, OF COURSE HE WOULD *DIE* BEFORE EXPOSING HIM.
THAT'S THE *BUSHI* WAY.
ONLY ONE *NOT* A *BUSHI* COULD DREAM UP SUCH A PLAN!
R-RETSUDŌ-*SAMA*...LISTEN. RIGHT NOW...
...OUR LORD AND MYSELF ALONE KNOW OF THE LETTERS.

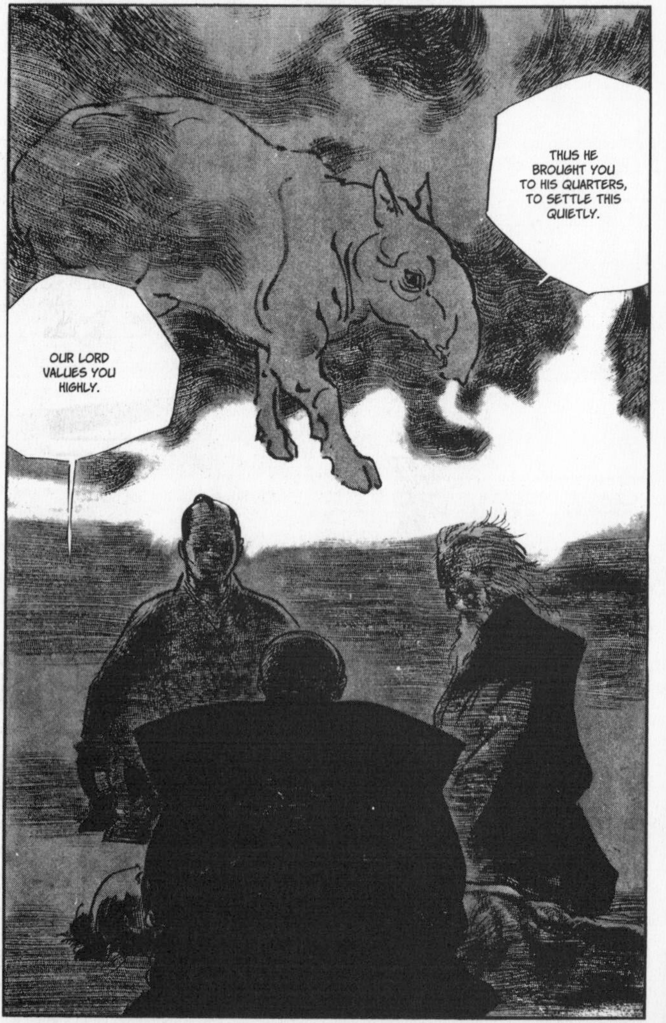
OUR LORD VALUES YOU HIGHLY.
THUS HE BROUGHT YOU TO HIS QUARTERS, TO SETTLE THIS QUIETLY.

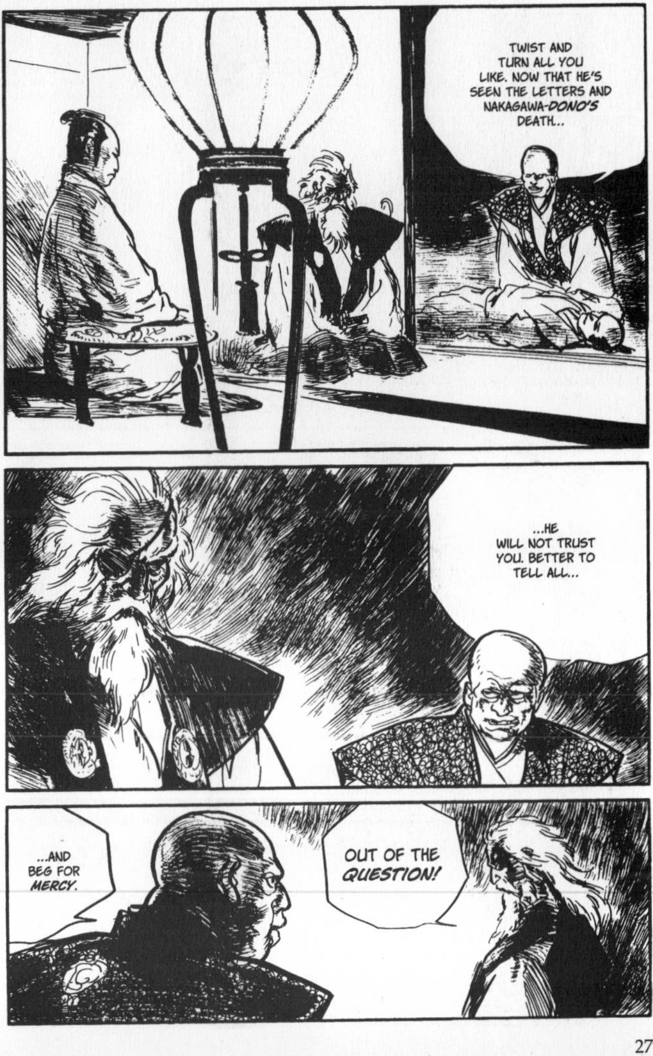
TWIST AND TURN ALL YOU LIKE. NOW THAT HE'S SEEN THE LETTERS AND NAKAGAWA-*DONO'S* DEATH...
...HE WILL NOT TRUST YOU. BETTER TO TELL ALL...
...AND BEG FOR *MERCY.*
OUT OF THE *QUESTION!*

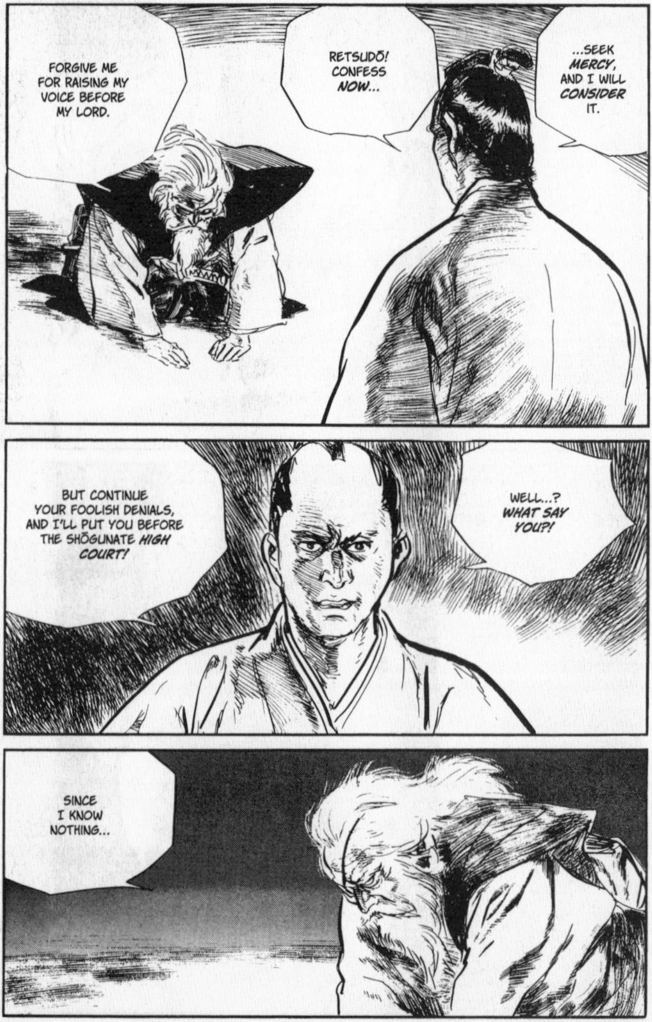
FORGIVE ME FOR RAISING MY VOICE BEFORE MY LORD.
RETSUDŌ! CONFESS *NOW*...
...SEEK *MERCY*, AND I WILL *CONSIDER* IT.
BUT CONTINUE YOUR FOOLISH DENIALS, AND I'LL PUT YOU BEFORE THE SHŌGUNATE *HIGH COURT!*
WELL...? *WHAT SAY YOU?!*
SINCE I KNOW NOTHING...

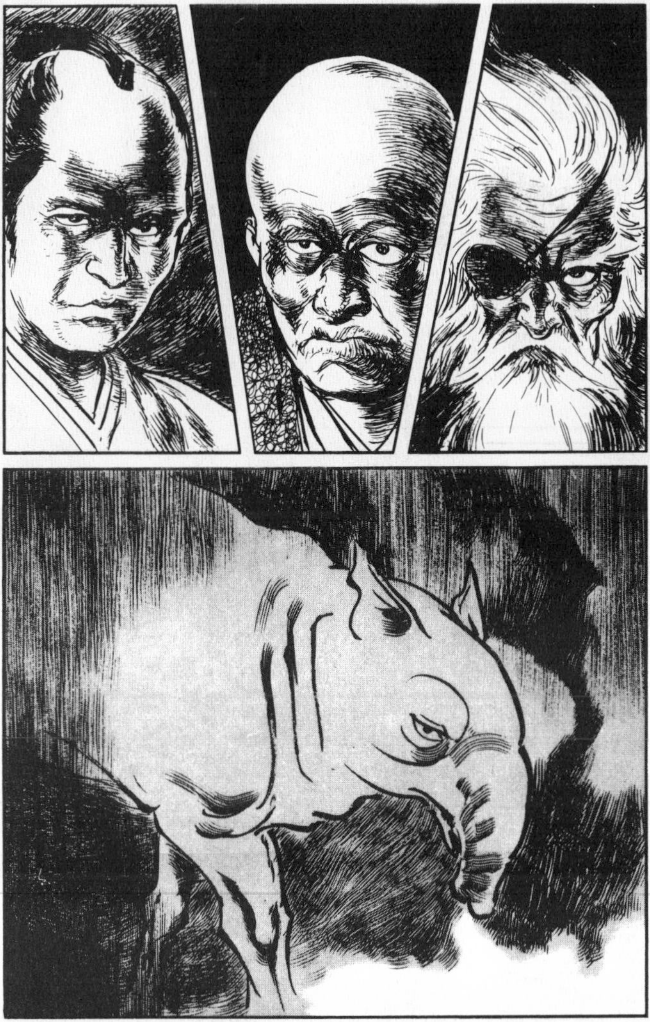

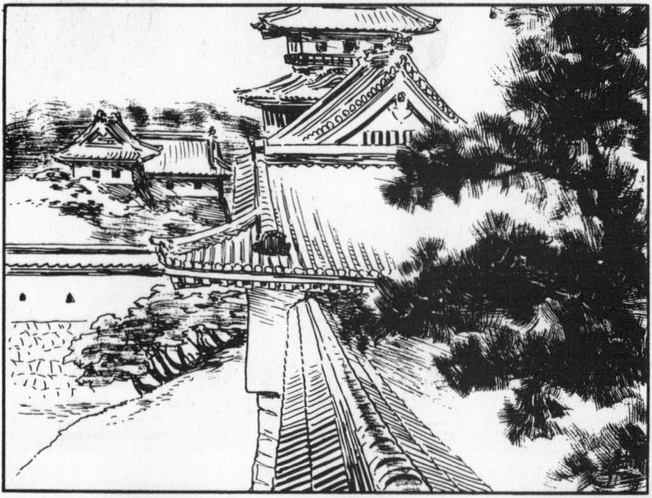

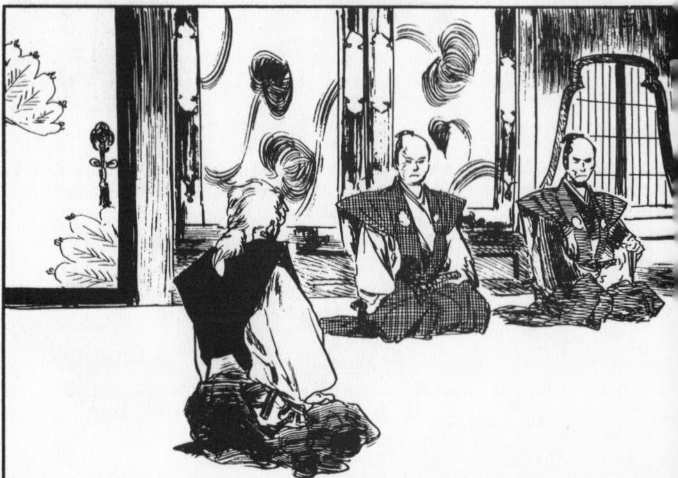

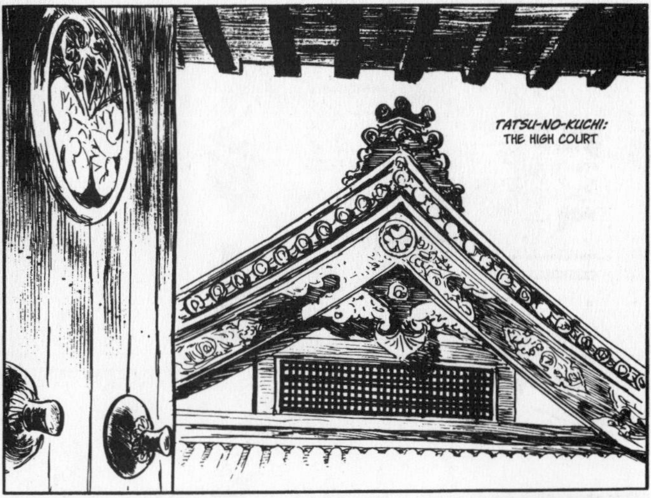
TATSU-NO-KUCHI:
THE HIGH COURT

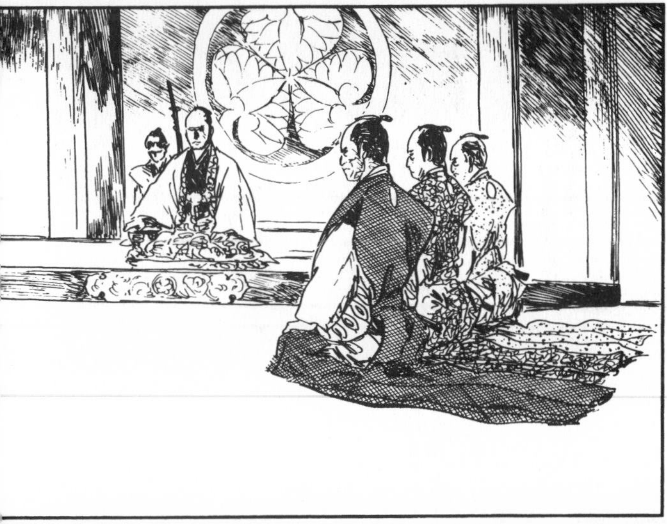

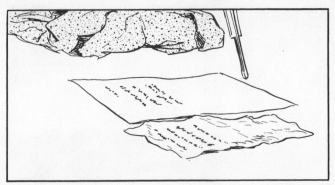

YAGYŪ-
DONO!

THOUGH
FACED WITH
UNDENIABLE
PROOF...

...YOU *STILL* INSIST
YOU KNOW
*NOTHING?*

ONLY BECAUSE I SPEAK THE TRUTH.

THEN, LET ME ASK YOU...

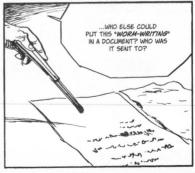

...WHO ELSE COULD PUT THIS *WORM-WRITING* IN A DOCUMENT? WHO WAS IT SENT TO?

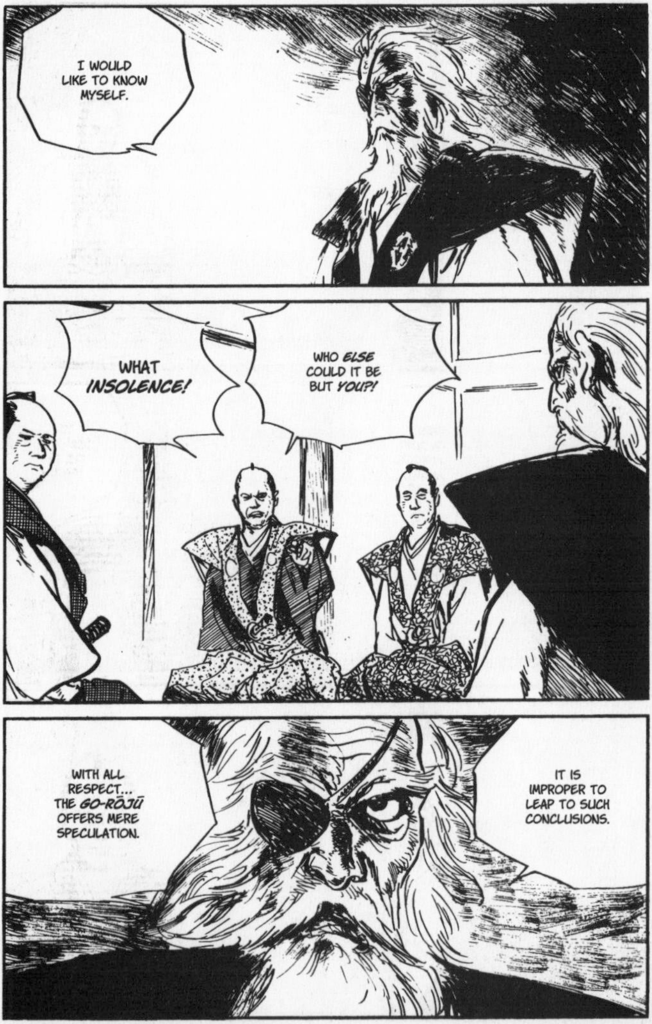
I WOULD LIKE TO KNOW MYSELF.
WHAT *INSOLENCE!*
WHO *ELSE* COULD IT BE BUT *YOU?!*
WITH ALL RESPECT... THE *GO-RŌJŪ* OFFERS MERE SPECULATION.
IT IS IMPROPER TO LEAP TO SUCH CONCLUSIONS.

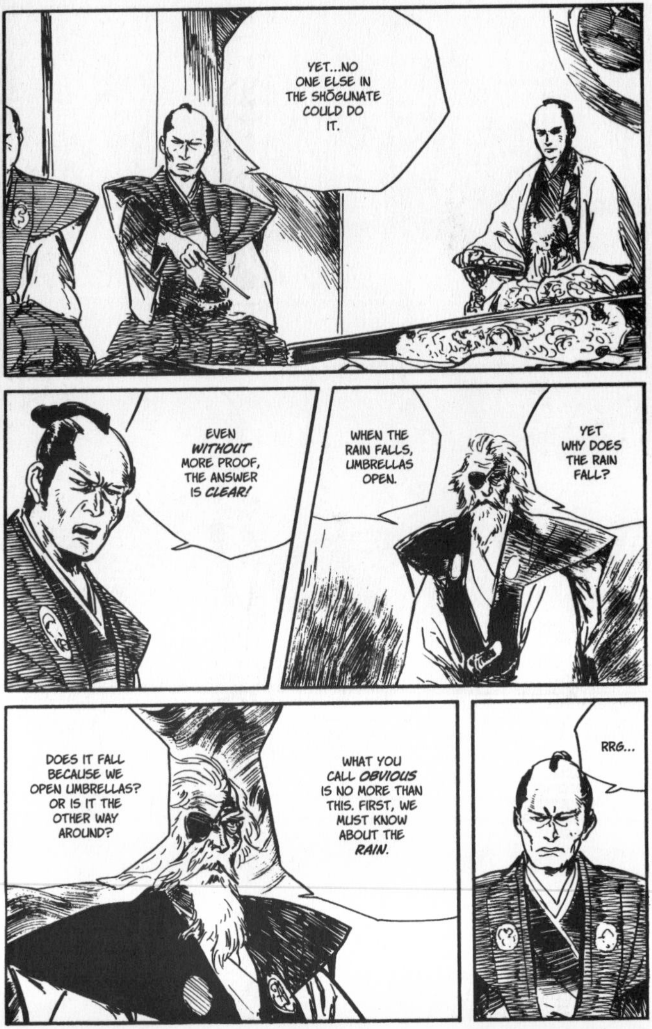
YET...NO ONE ELSE IN THE SHŌGUNATE COULD DO IT.
EVEN WITHOUT MORE PROOF, THE ANSWER IS CLEAR!
WHEN THE RAIN FALLS, UMBRELLAS OPEN.
YET WHY DOES THE RAIN FALL?
DOES IT FALL BECAUSE WE OPEN UMBRELLAS? OR IS IT THE OTHER WAY AROUND?
WHAT YOU CALL OBVIOUS IS NO MORE THAN THIS. FIRST, WE MUST KNOW ABOUT THE RAIN.
RRG...

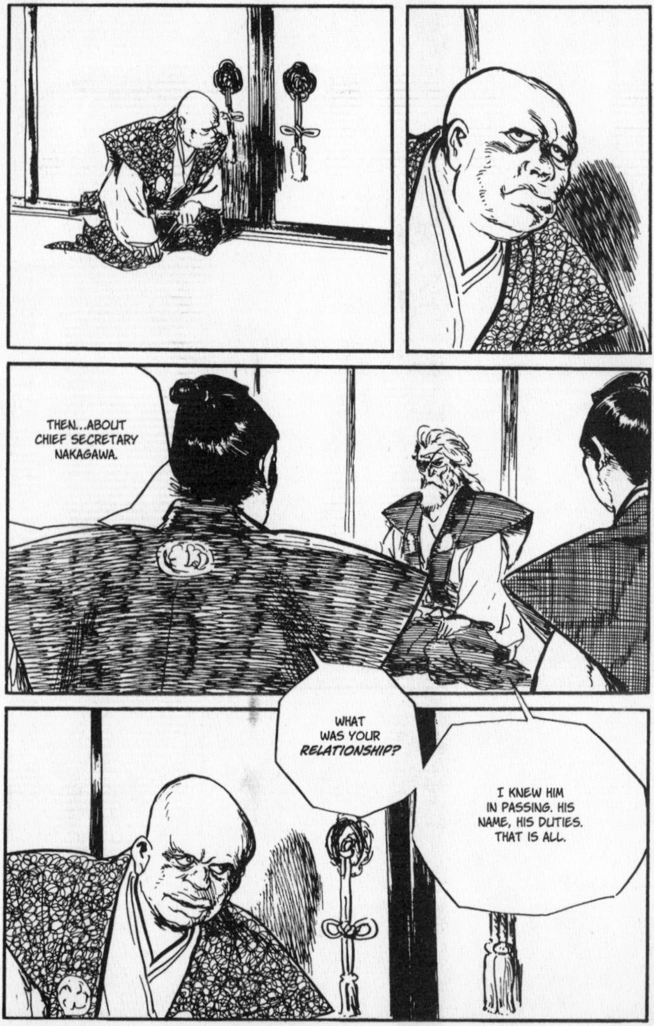
THEN...ABOUT CHIEF SECRETARY NAKAGAWA.
WHAT WAS YOUR *RELATIONSHIP?*
I KNEW HIM IN PASSING. HIS NAME, HIS DUTIES. THAT IS ALL.

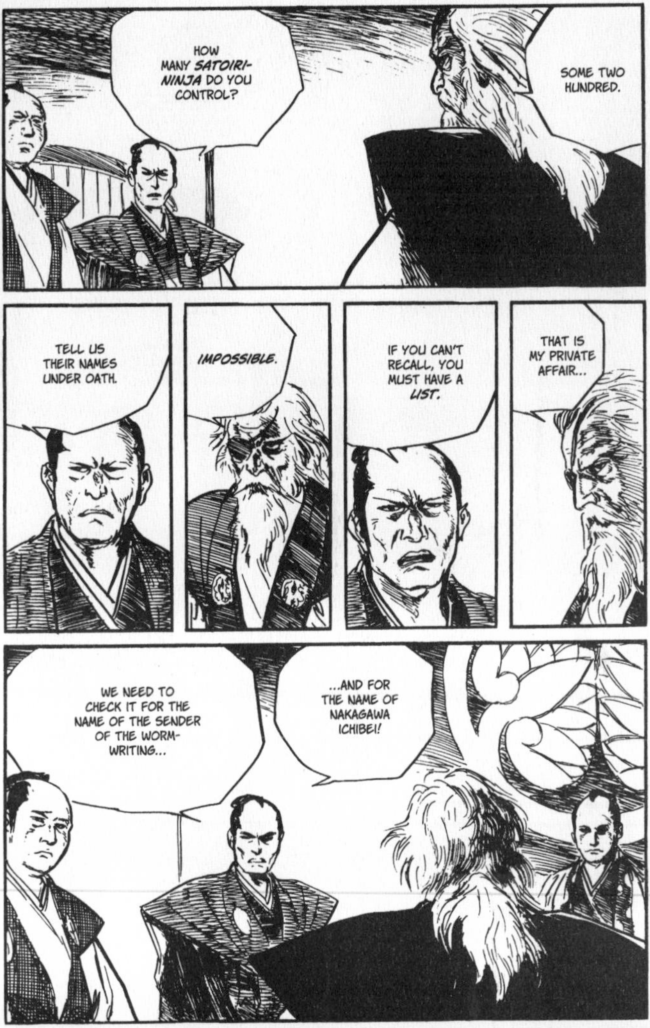
HOW MANY SATOIRI-NINJA DO YOU CONTROL?
SOME TWO HUNDRED.
TELL US THEIR NAMES UNDER OATH.
IMPOSSIBLE.
IF YOU CAN'T RECALL, YOU MUST HAVE A LIST.
THAT IS MY PRIVATE AFFAIR...
WE NEED TO CHECK IT FOR THE NAME OF THE SENDER OF THE WORM-WRITING...
...AND FOR THE NAME OF NAKAGAWA ICHIBEI!

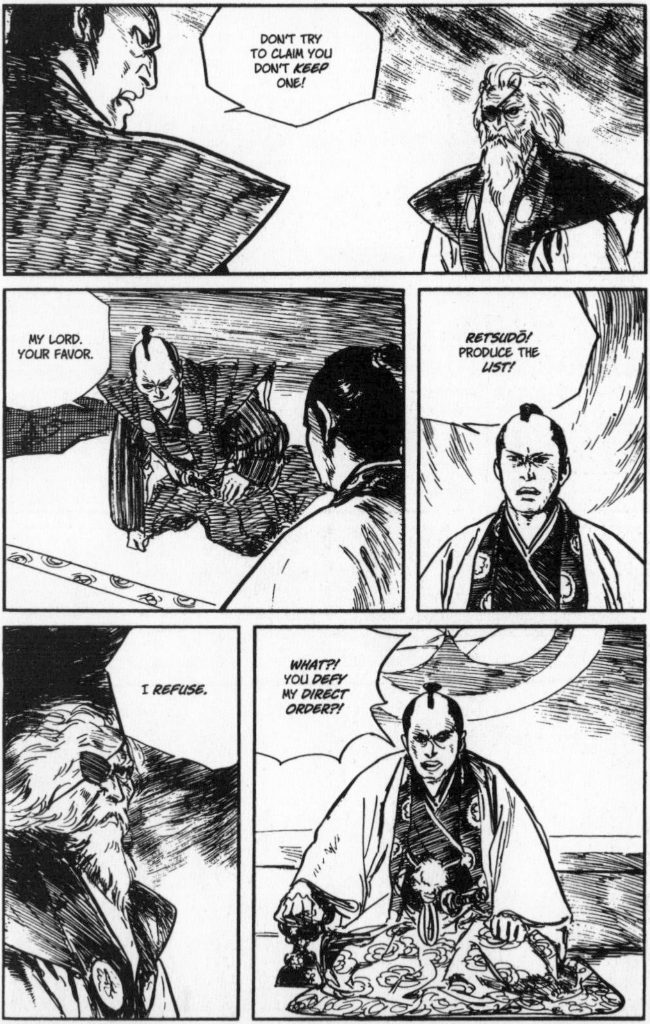
DON'T TRY TO CLAIM YOU DON'T *KEEP* ONE!
MY LORD. YOUR FAVOR.
*RETSUDŌ!* PRODUCE THE *LIST!*
I *REFUSE.*
*WHAT?!* YOU *DEFY* MY *DIRECT ORDER?!*

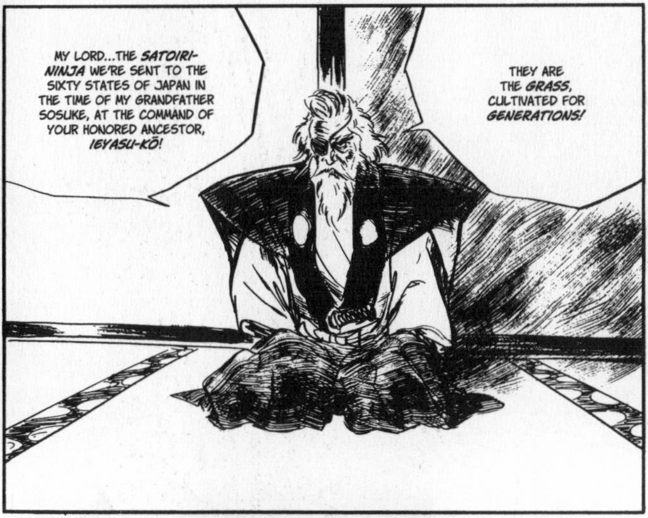
MY LORD...THE SATOIRI-NINJA WE'RE SENT TO THE SIXTY STATES OF JAPAN IN THE TIME OF MY GRANDFATHER SOSUKE, AT THE COMMAND OF YOUR HONORED ANCESTOR, IEYASU-KŌ!
THEY ARE THE GRASS, CULTIVATED FOR GENERATIONS!

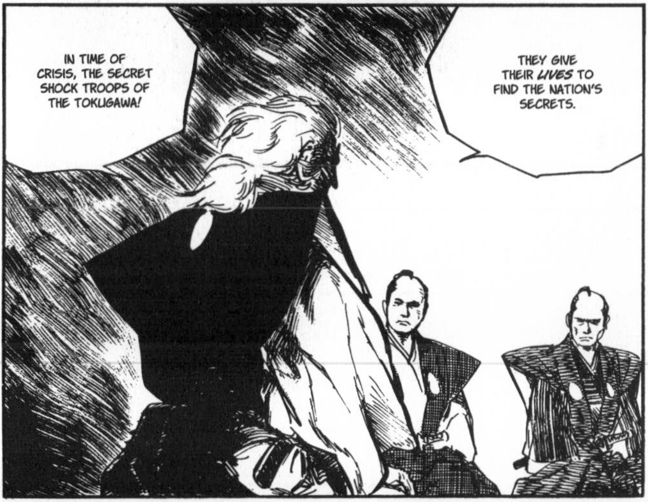
IN TIME OF CRISIS, THE SECRET SHOCK TROOPS OF THE TOKUGAWA!
THEY GIVE THEIR LIVES TO FIND THE NATION'S SECRETS.

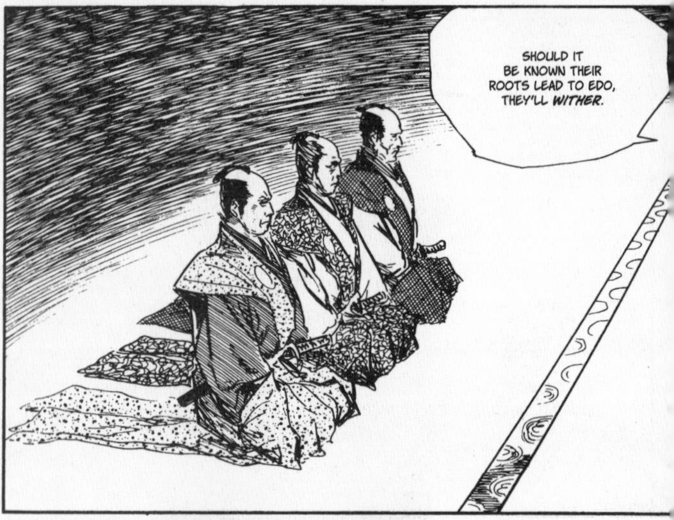
SHOULD IT BE KNOWN THEIR ROOTS LEAD TO EDO, THEY'LL *WITHER*.

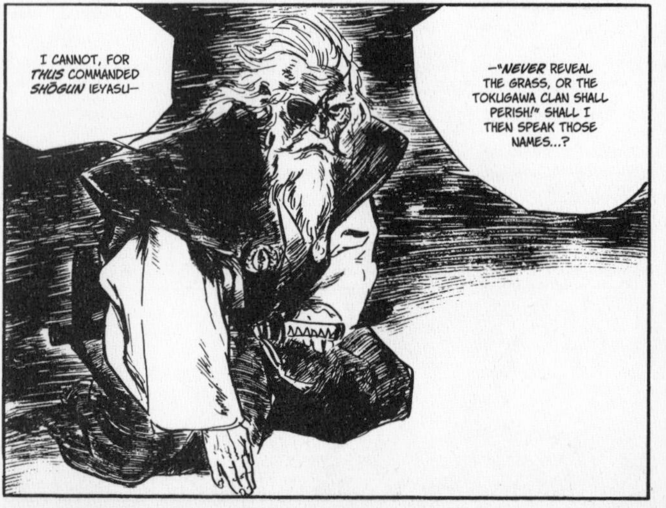
I CANNOT, FOR *THUS* COMMANDED *SHŌGUN* IEYASU—
—"*NEVER* REVEAL THE GRASS, OR THE TOKUGAWA CLAN SHALL PERISH!" SHALL I THEN SPEAK THOSE NAMES...?

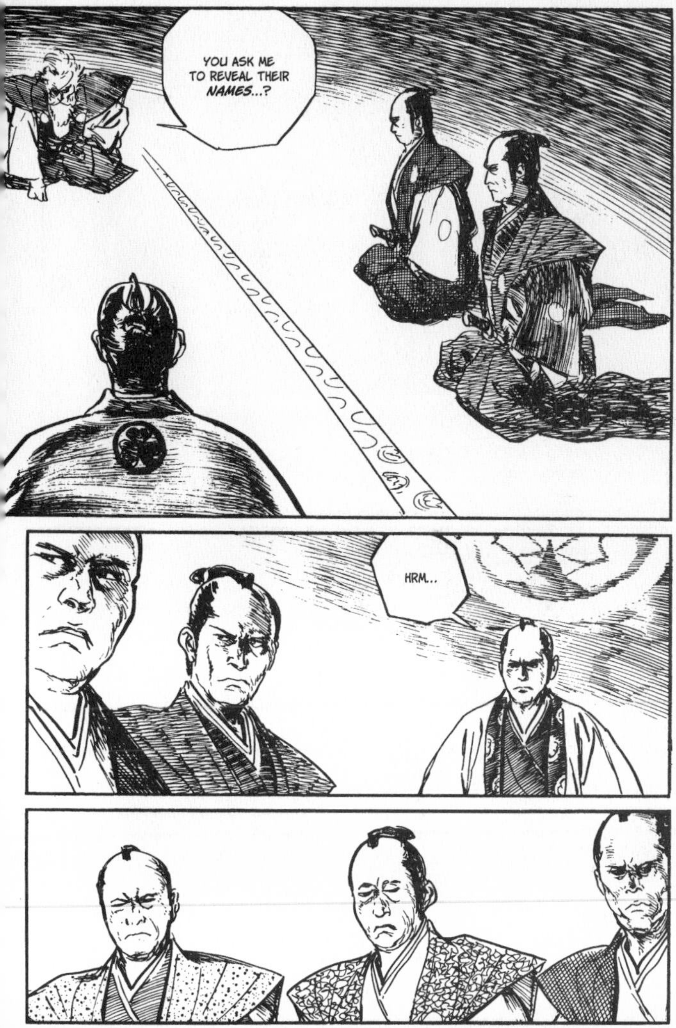
YOU ASK ME TO REVEAL THEIR NAMES...?
HRM...

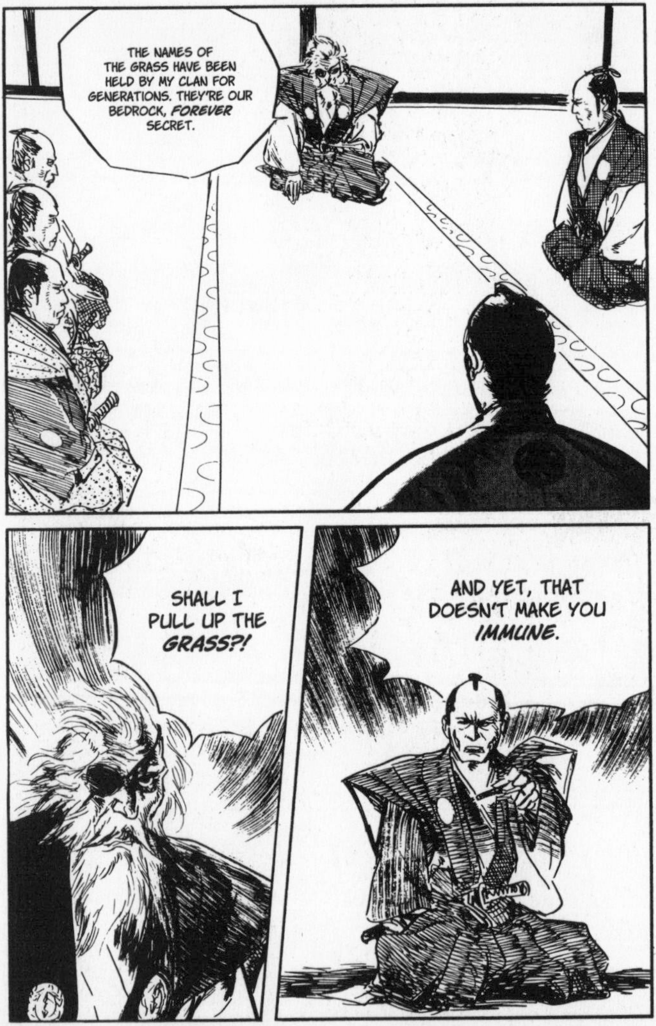
THE NAMES OF THE GRASS HAVE BEEN HELD BY MY CLAN FOR GENERATIONS. THEY'RE OUR BEDROCK, *FOREVER* SECRET.
SHALL I PULL UP THE *GRASS?!*
AND YET, THAT DOESN'T MAKE YOU *IMMUNE*.

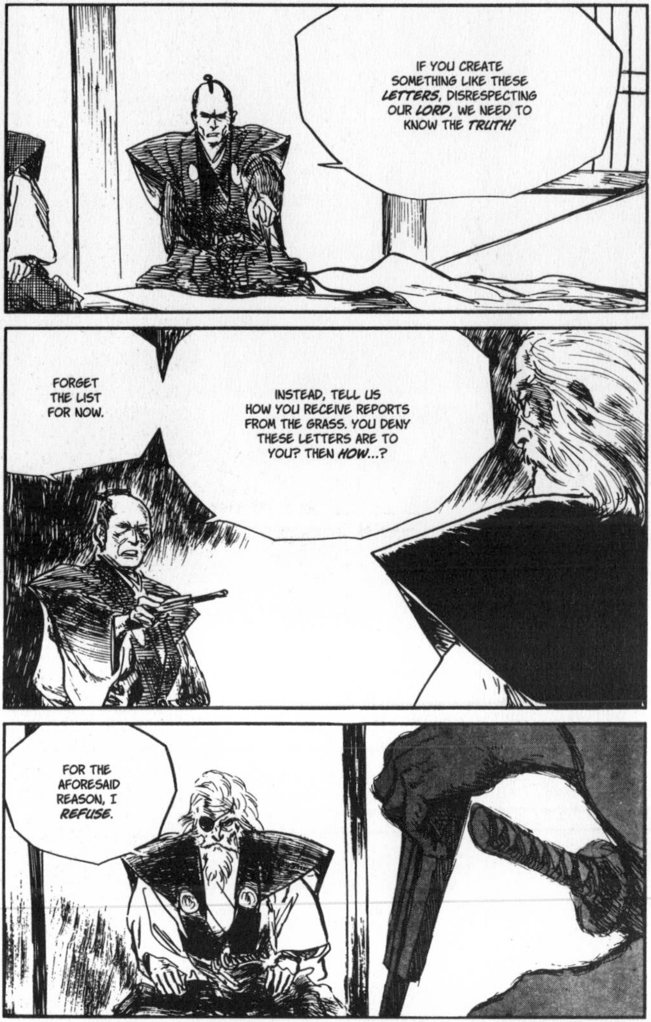
IF YOU CREATE SOMETHING LIKE THESE *LETTERS*, DISRESPECTING OUR *LORD*, WE NEED TO KNOW THE *TRUTH!*
FORGET THE LIST FOR NOW.
INSTEAD, TELL US HOW YOU RECEIVE REPORTS FROM THE GRASS. YOU DENY THESE LETTERS ARE TO YOU? THEN *HOW*...?
FOR THE AFORESAID REASON, I *REFUSE*.

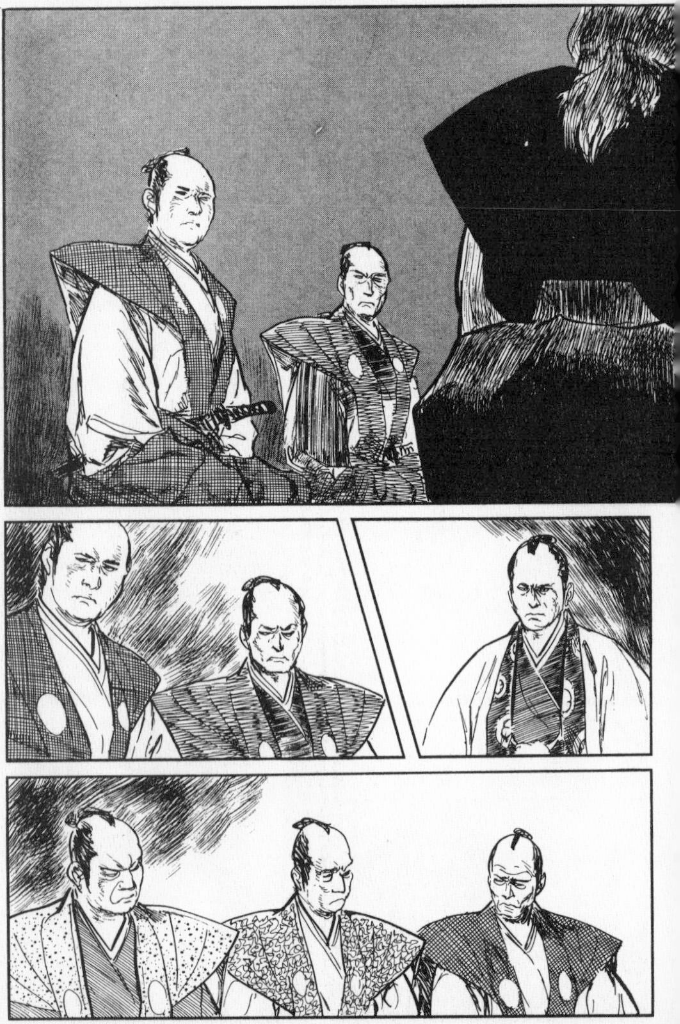

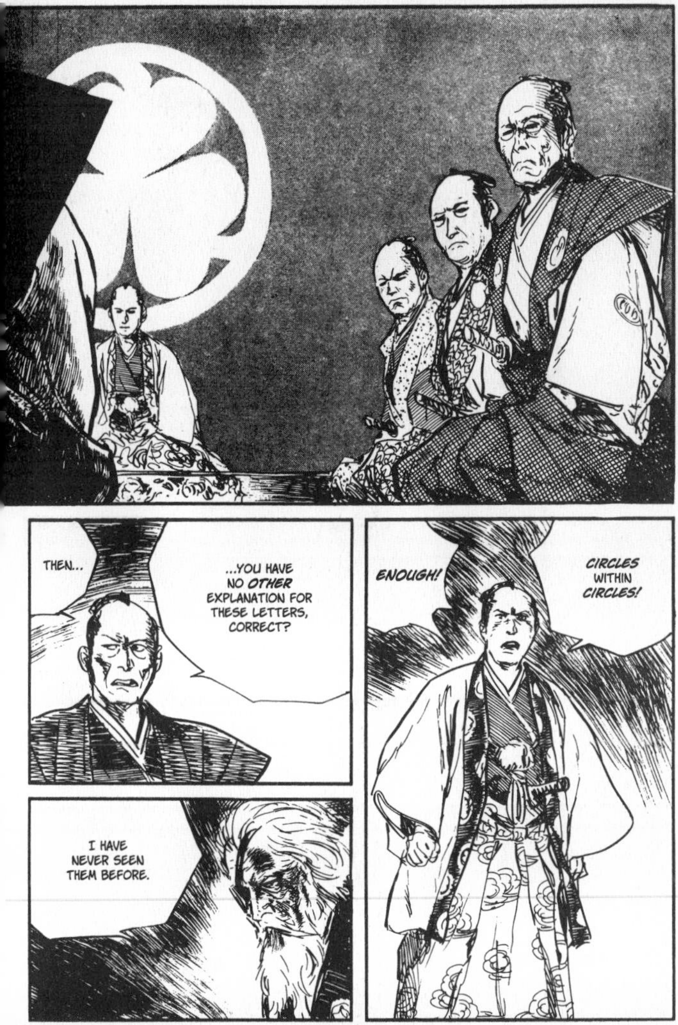
THEN...
...YOU HAVE NO *OTHER* EXPLANATION FOR THESE LETTERS, CORRECT?
I HAVE NEVER SEEN THEM BEFORE.
*ENOUGH!*
*CIRCLES* WITHIN *CIRCLES!*

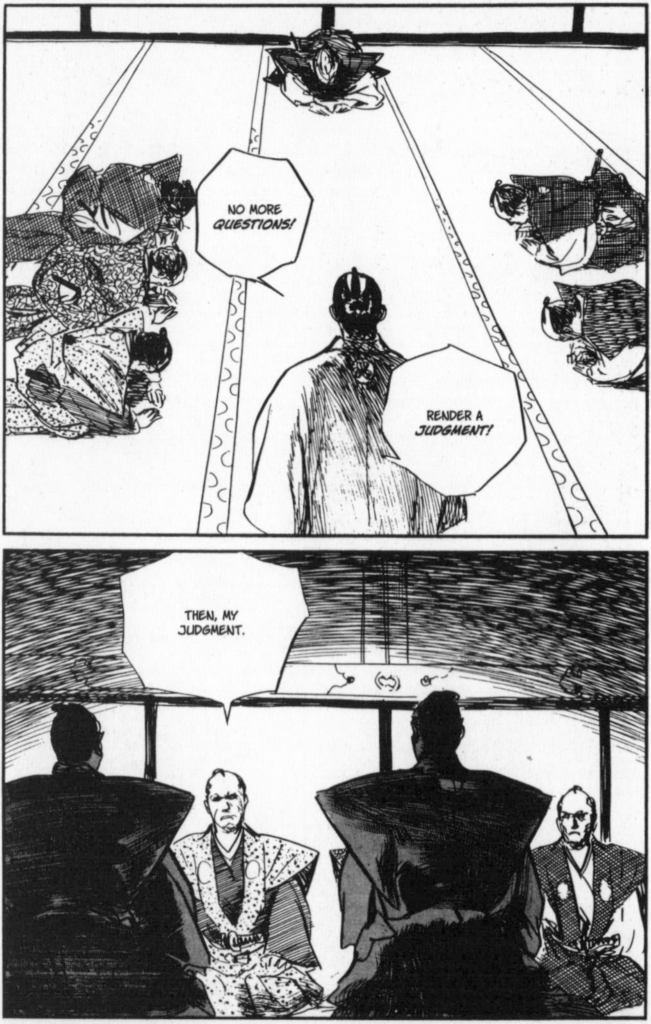
NO MORE QUESTIONS!
RENDER A JUDGMENT!
THEN, MY JUDGMENT.

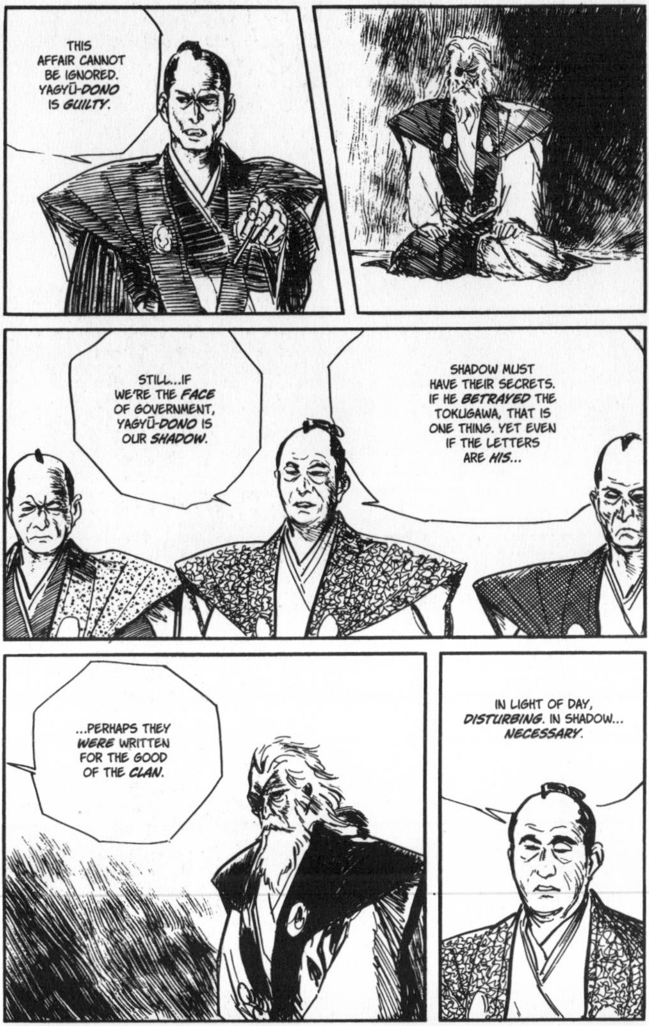
THIS AFFAIR CANNOT BE IGNORED. YAGYŪ-DONO IS GUILTY.
STILL...IF WE'RE THE FACE OF GOVERNMENT, YAGYŪ-DONO IS OUR SHADOW.
SHADOW MUST HAVE THEIR SECRETS. IF HE BETRAYED THE TOKUGAWA, THAT IS ONE THING. YET EVEN IF THE LETTERS ARE HIS...
...PERHAPS THEY WERE WRITTEN FOR THE GOOD OF THE CLAN.
IN LIGHT OF DAY, DISTURBING. IN SHADOW... NECESSARY.

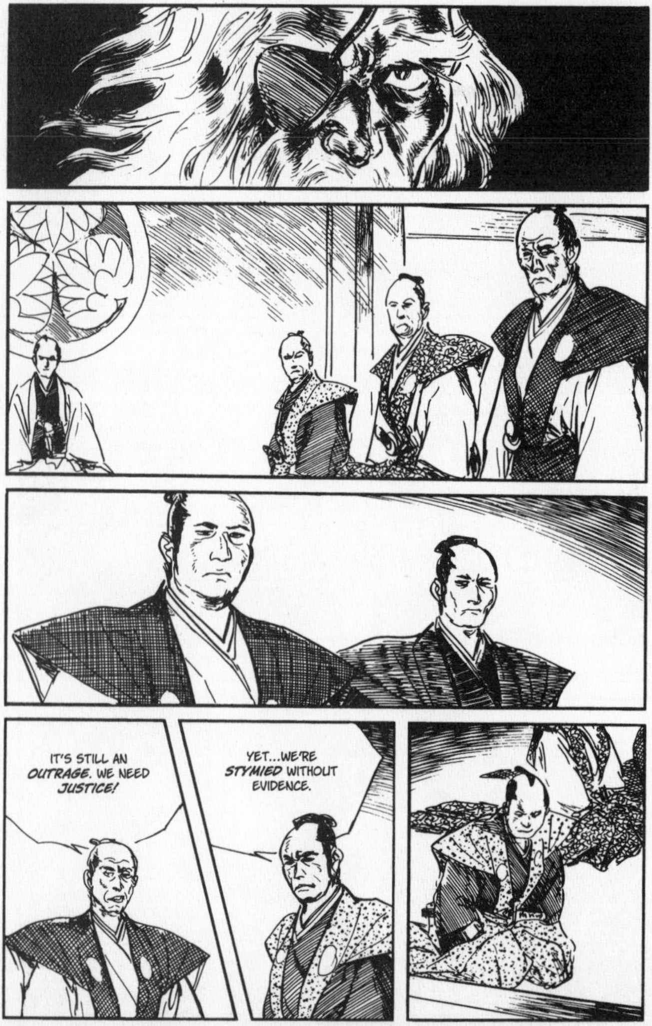
IT'S STILL AN OUTRAGE. WE NEED JUSTICE!
YET...WE'RE STYMIED WITHOUT EVIDENCE.

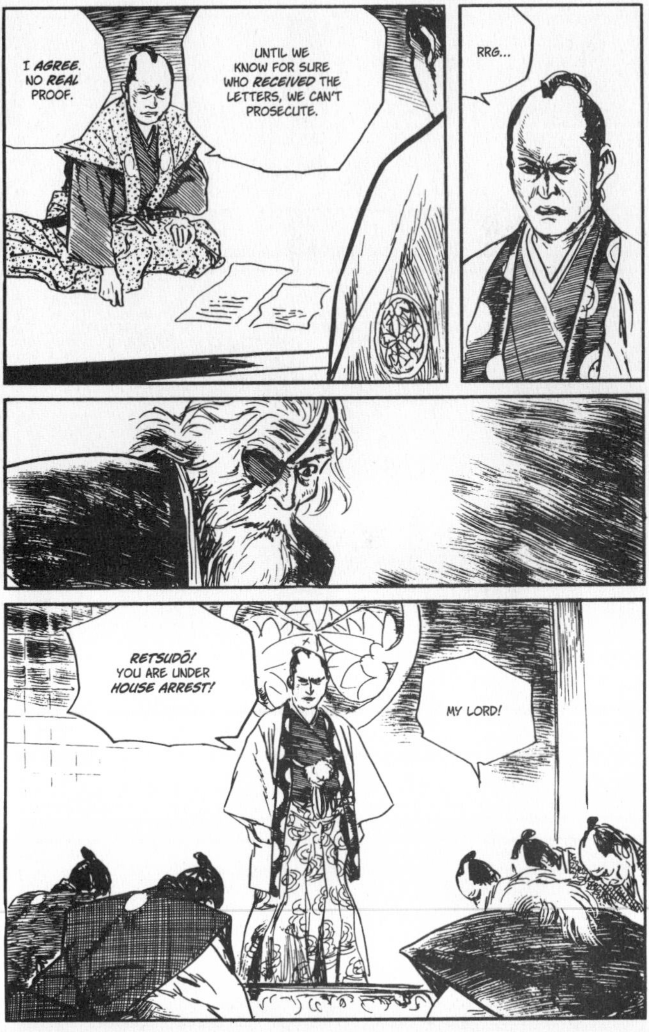
I AGREE. NO REAL PROOF.
UNTIL WE KNOW FOR SURE WHO RECEIVED THE LETTERS, WE CAN'T PROSECUTE.
RRG...
RETSUDŌ! YOU ARE UNDER HOUSE ARREST!
MY LORD!

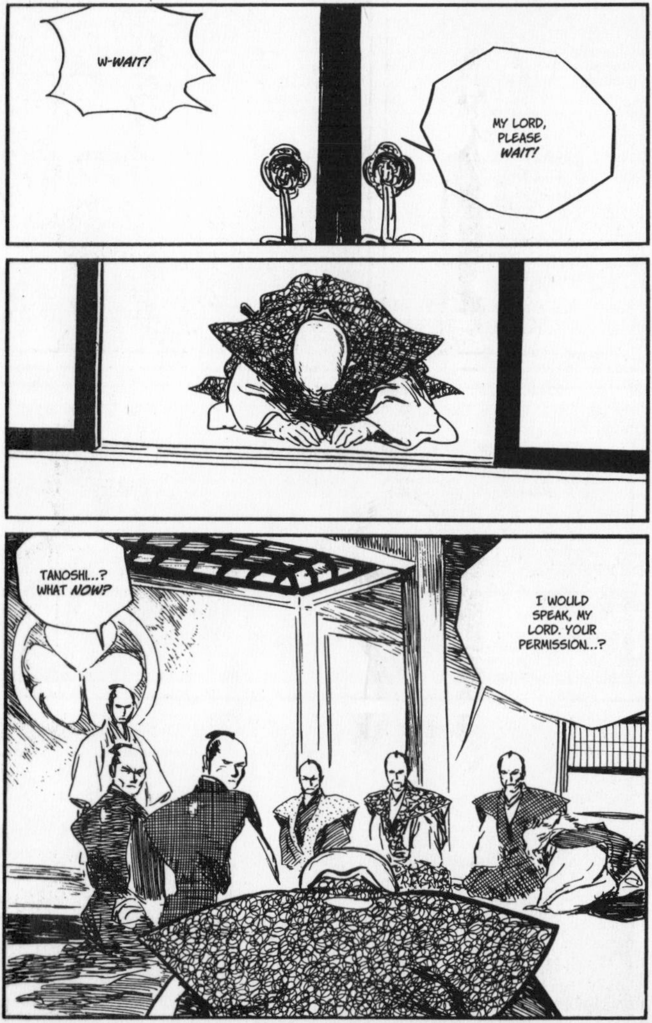
W-WAIT!
MY LORD, PLEASE WAIT!
TANOSHI...? WHAT NOW?
I WOULD SPEAK, MY LORD. YOUR PERMISSION...?

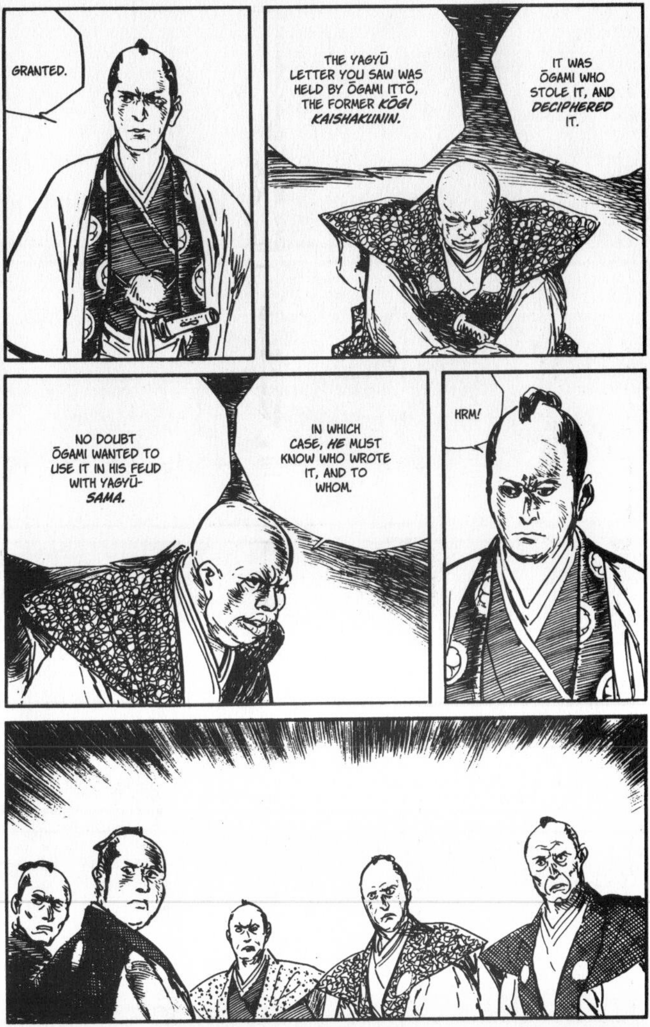
GRANTED.
THE YAGYŪ LETTER YOU SAW WAS HELD BY ŌGAMI ITTŌ, THE FORMER *KŌGI KAISHAKUNIN.*
IT WAS ŌGAMI WHO STOLE IT, AND *DECIPHERED* IT.
NO DOUBT ŌGAMI WANTED TO USE IT IN HIS FEUD WITH YAGYŪ-*SAMA.*
IN WHICH CASE, *HE* MUST KNOW WHO WROTE IT, AND TO WHOM.
HRM!

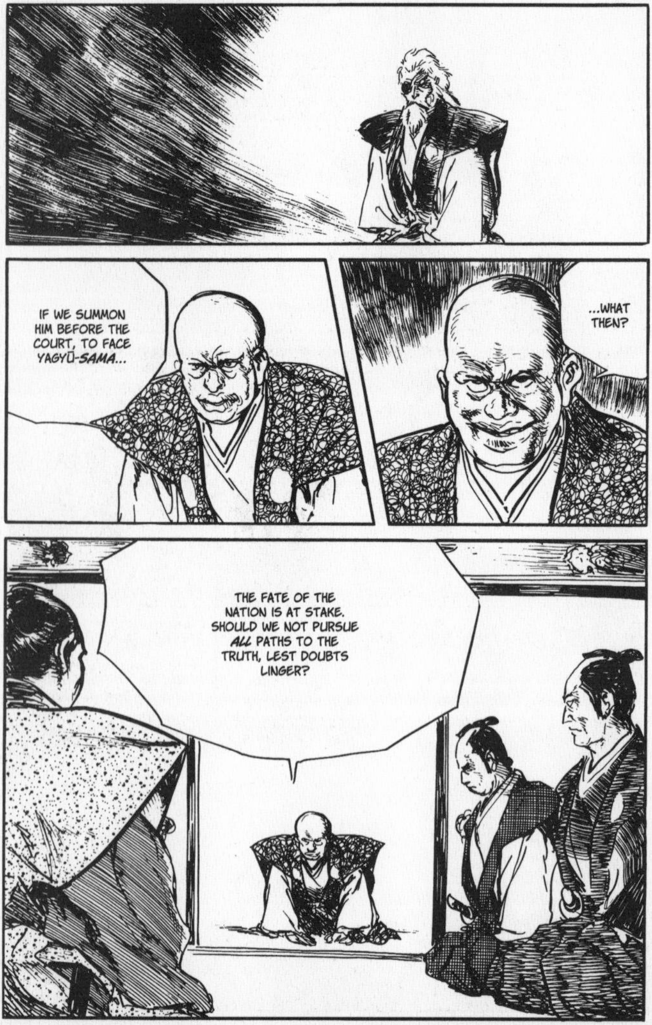
IF WE SUMMON HIM BEFORE THE COURT, TO FACE YAGYŪ-*SAMA*...
...WHAT THEN?
THE FATE OF THE NATION IS AT STAKE. SHOULD WE NOT PURSUE *ALL* PATHS TO THE TRUTH, LEST DOUBTS LINGER?

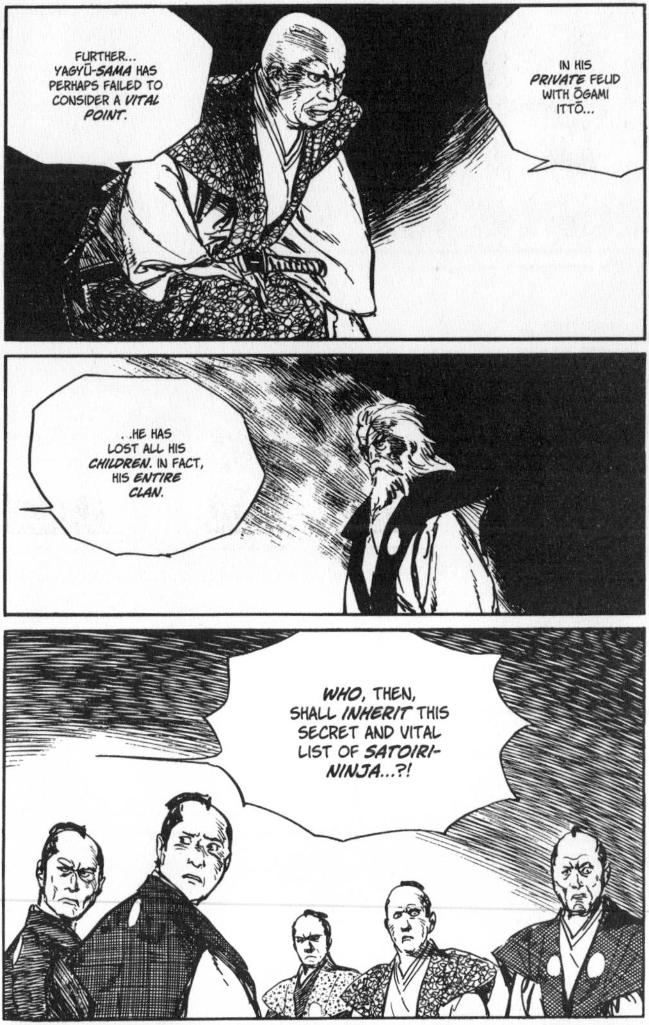
FURTHER... YAGYŪ-SAMA HAS PERHAPS FAILED TO CONSIDER A VITAL POINT.
IN HIS PRIVATE FEUD WITH ŌGAMI ITTŌ...
..HE HAS LOST ALL HIS CHILDREN. IN FACT, HIS ENTIRE CLAN.
WHO, THEN, SHALL INHERIT THIS SECRET AND VITAL LIST OF SATOIRI-NINJA...?!

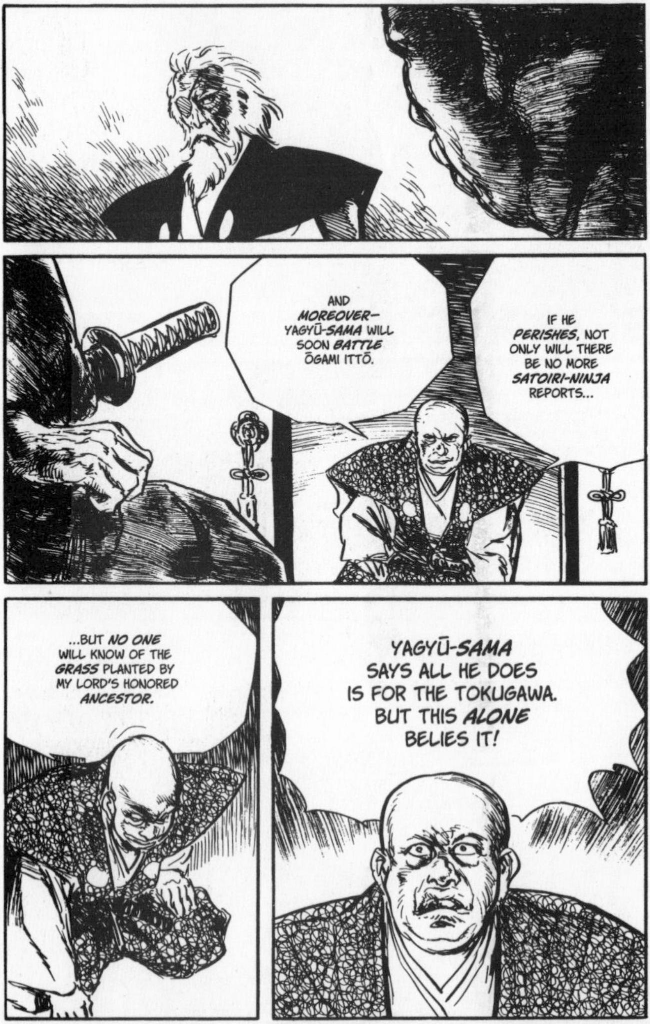
AND *MOREOVER*— YAGYŪ-*SAMA* WILL SOON *BATTLE* ŌGAMI ITTŌ.
IF HE *PERISHES*, NOT ONLY WILL THERE BE NO MORE *SATOIRI-NINJA* REPORTS...
...BUT *NO ONE* WILL KNOW OF THE *GRASS* PLANTED BY MY LORD'S HONORED *ANCESTOR*.
YAGYŪ-*SAMA* SAYS ALL HE DOES IS FOR THE TOKUGAWA. BUT THIS *ALONE* BELIES IT!

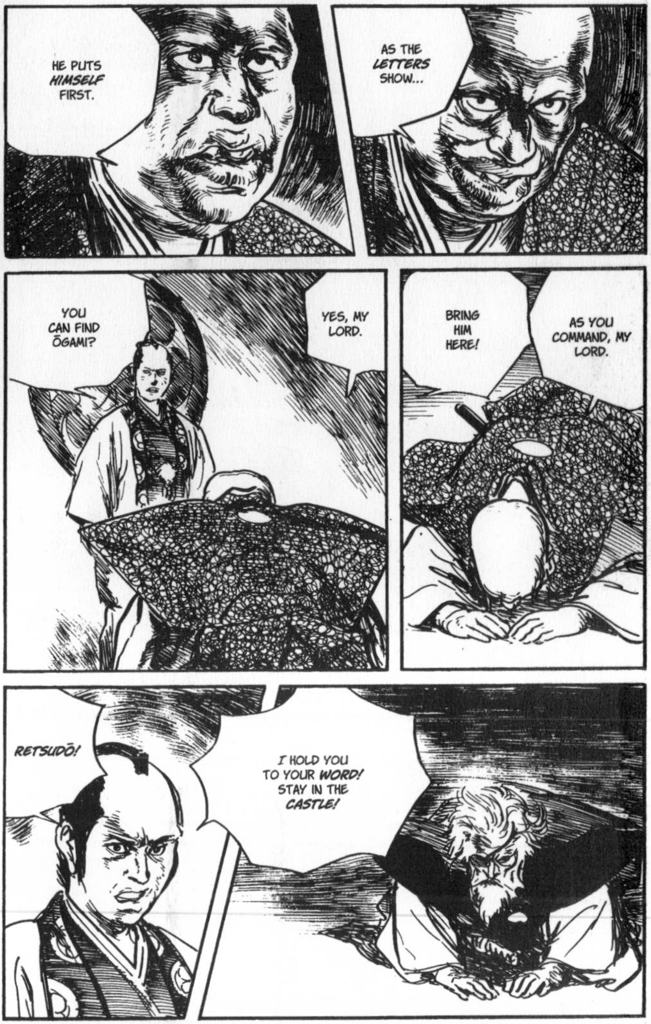
HE PUTS *HIMSELF* FIRST.
AS THE *LETTERS* SHOW...
YOU CAN FIND ŌGAMI?
YES, MY LORD.
BRING HIM HERE!
AS YOU COMMAND, MY LORD.
*RETSUDŌ!*
*I* HOLD YOU TO YOUR *WORD!* STAY IN THE *CASTLE!*

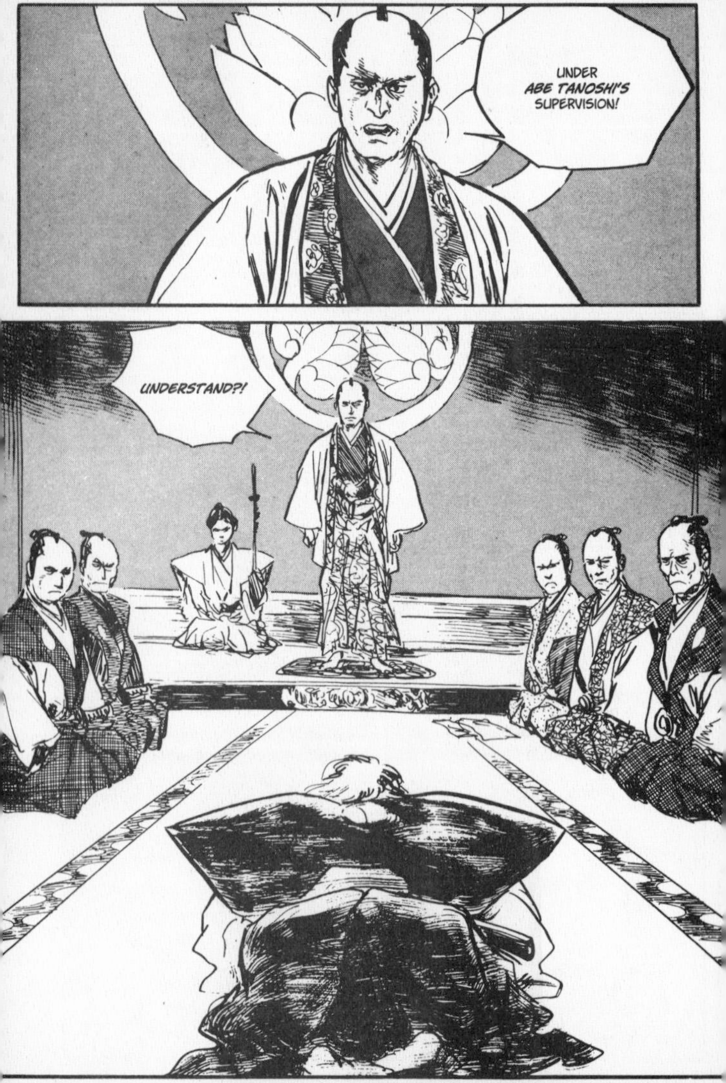
UNDER ABE TANOSHI'S SUPERVISION!
UNDERSTAND?!

*LONE WOLF AND CUB VOLUME TWENTY FOUR: THE END*
*TO BE CONTINUED*

# GLOSSARY

**ayame-zuki**
A coming-of-age celebration.

**bakkaku**
The government. The shōgun, his councilors, and his senior officials.

**bushi**
A samurai. A member of the warrior class.

**bushidō**
The way of the warrior. Also known as *shidō*.

**daimyō**
A feudal lord.

**Edo**
Edo was a castle town, that rose up around the moats and ramparts of Edo castle, the stronghold of the Tokugawa clan. The central core of the city, administered by the *machi-bugyō* city commissioner, who reported directly to the shōgun's senior councilors, and was demarcated on official maps by a black line, the *kurobiki*, and was called the *go-funai*.

**enishi**
A fateful, chance connection between two people.

**gojō-bako**
A lacquered, waterproof box used to carry official correspondence between the shōgunate in Edo and its regional officials.

**go-rōjū**
Inner circle of councilors directly advising the shōgun (*"go"* is used as an honorific term).

**Goetsu Dōshū**
Chinese fable in which two bitter enemies ride in the same boat to reach the other bank of a river.

**han**
A feudal domain.

**honorifics**
Japan is a class and status society, and proper forms of address are critical. Common markers of respect are the prefixes *o* and *go*, and a wide range of suffixes. Some of the suffixes you will encounter in *Lone Wolf and Cub*:
*chan* – for children, young women, and close friends
*dono* – archaic; used for higher-ranked or highly respected figures
*san* – the most common, used among equals or near-equals
*sama* – used for superiors
*sensei* – used for teachers, masters, respected entertainers, and politicians.

**ihai**
A Buddhist mortuary tablet. The death name of the deceased, given after they die, is written on the tablet, which is kept at the family temple.

**jōdai**
Castle warden. The ranking *han* official in charge of a *daimyō's* castle and *han* when the *daimyō* was in Edo. Often the *jōdai* was also the senior elder, or *karō* of the *han*.

**kōgi kaishakunin**
The shōgun's own second, who performed executions ordered by the shōgun.

**kuchiyaku**
Kuchiyaku were the tasters for the shōgun family. They were called *kuchiyaku*, or "official mouths," because they checked for poison with their own tongues.

**machi-bugyō**
The Edo city commissioner, combining the post of mayor and chief of police. A post held in monthly rotation by two senior Tokugawa vassals, in charge of administration, maintaining the peace, and enforcing the law in Edo. Their rule extended only to commoners; samurai in Edo were controlled by their own *daimyō* and his officers. The *machi-bugyō* had an administrative staff and a small force of armed policemen at his disposal.

**machikata**
Town policemen.

**meifumadō**
The Buddhist Hell. The way of demons and damnation.

**mohhh!**
This is a palace convention, signaling the shōgun's next activity.

**rōnin**
A masterless samurai. Literally, "one adrift on the waves." Members of the samurai caste who have lost their masters through the dissolution of *han*, expulsion for misbehavior, or other reasons. Prohibited from working as farmers or merchants under the strict Confucian caste system imposed by the Tokugawa shōgunate, many impoverished *rōnin* became "hired guns" for whom the code of the samurai was nothing but empty words.

**sankin kōtai**
The Tokugawa required that all *daimyō* spend every other year in Edo, with family members remaining behind when they returned to their *han*. This practice increased Edo's control over the *daimyō*, both political and fiscal, since the cost of maintaining two separate households and traveling to and from the capital placed a huge strain on *han* finances.

**shidō**
Bushidō. The way of the warrior.

**shoshidai**
The *shoshidai* was the shōgun's emissary to the imperial court in Kyoto.

**sō-metsuke**
Chief inspector. The supreme law-enforcement officer of the shōgunate.